Riding the Waves

The Price for Fame and Fortune

A sequel to A River Moves Forward

Selena Haskins

RIDING THE WAVES

Published by:
Calidream Publishing
P.O. Box 4201
Capitol Heights, MD 20791
Publisher, Selena Haskins

Editor:
Michelle Browne, Magpie Editing Services

Cover Designer:
Adrienne Thompson, Pink Cashmere Publishing

Book Designer:
Karen Perkins, LionheART Publishing House

For book signings or speaking engagements, please contact media@calidreampub.com. Bulk orders: sales@calidreampub.com

ACKNOWLEDGEMENT

I thank my Heavenly Father Jehovah God and my savior Jesus Christ for blessing me with the gift to write. There were many adversities I faced while trying to write this book, and I thought I would never finish, but thank God for giving me the patience, endurance, and support from friends and family during difficult trials. I thank my husband, Ken for his emotional support, and contributing his amazing talents to my website, book events, and also sharing his business tips. My beloved son, who continues to amaze me with each milestone he achieves. He *is* the brightest crayon in the box! Shout-out to my "Hoorah" Corner- Tish, Toni, Stevie, Tony, Trina, Mika, Nadine, Seedie, Yvette, Maurice, Dominique, Mike, Tangie, Henry and Veria, Edwina, Belinda and Glenda, and Virgil. The list keeps growing. If I forgot your name, blame my memory and not my heart.

A very special thanks to my new editor—Michelle Patricia Browne, whose honesty helps me continue to grow as a writer.

Thank you Karen Perkins for providing an extra pair of eyes to review my manuscript.

Special thanks to my sister writers of JBU (Just Between Us) - Janice G. Ross, Tina "TM" Brown, Adrienne Thompson, Nicole Dunlap, and Tamika Christy. You all have been very supportive and encouraging to me. It's been a pleasure in knowing each one of you. (*Just Between Us- Inspiring Stories by Women*) is FREE at online bookstores! Download your copy today!

Many thanks to the following radio stations: Cyrus Webb, *Conversations Live* in Memphis, Anthony D. Collins and the B. Fly Show from *Vibrations Radio* in Chicago. Tammy Jones *That's Entertainment Radio* in New York, and Janice G. Ross—*Cultural Cocktails* in Delaware. You guys gave me the platform to discuss my books and I really appreciate your support.

Shout-out to my hometown the DMV! Many thanks to Chicago, Philly, Canada and the UK for embracing me.

Last but not least, I thank YOU the reader for spending your hard-earned money to buy this book. I hope you enjoy it!

I dedicate this book to my mother, Celestine A. Freeman, whose strength I've always admired. She motivates me to keep going even when I feel like giving up. She reminds me to be thankful, see the good in others and myself, and never stop believing. Every time I hear Patti LaBelle's song, *You are My Friend*, I think of my mother, because she's always been a friend to me.

CONTENTS

Part One

CHAPTER ONE
IT GETS BETTER WITH TIME

They say there is an art to making love, and Connie felt that couldn't have been truer of Dean. This morning, she craved him like chocolate. Her long legs clamped around his waistline as her hands stroked the tightness of his back. The thunder outside her window couldn't muffle the moans. The rain drummed heavily against their luxury home in Highland Park, Chicago, making their bedroom windows look like blurred glass. With each stroke of genius, Connie was convinced Dean was the Picasso of love making. As the thunder roared, the bed squeaked with a calculated rhythm as Connie's love came down in gentle waves. Dean kissed her as she lay in the fold of his arm, feeling pleased that her every desire had been satisfied.

Dean held the intoxicating stare of her dreamy green eyes, and his lips curved in a proud grin. They both felt thankful to have uninterrupted moments like this. Gone were the days of trying to make love quietly when the children were home. The freedom made them feel glad the children were all grown up, now with lives of their own. Tracey and Devin were still in California, and Dean Jr. had decided to stay in New York after graduating from NYU. Nothing or no one else was around to spoil this moment.

Dean's eyes shifted from Connie to the window. "It's pouring cats and dogs out there," he said softly. They lay snuggled in each other's arms. "So much for going for my morning jog. It doesn't sound like the rain will end anytime soon."

"Makes you miss California, doesn't it?"

"No way!" He shook his head, laughed lightly. He knew there was no place like sweet home Chicago. He still remembered how relieved he was when Connie retired from BigStar Records as Vice President back in 2004. Afterwards, they made the decision to return to Chicago to be near their families, especially Dean's elderly parents who needed care.

"You may not miss California, but I do, especially on days like this," Connie stated. "I'll take the sunshine any day."

"Don't get any ideas." Dean raised an eyebrow and a few wrinkles formed in his forehead.

"What do you mean, don't get any ideas?"

"I heard you talking to that real estate agent yesterday. I know it was him, because you left his card next to the phone," Dean replied. "We're not moving back to California, Connie."

"You think you know everything, don't you Mr. Wilson?"

"I know *you, Mrs.* Wilson." He playfully pinched her thigh under the covers.

"Well, F.Y.I., the real estate agent was calling to confirm that he received the Deed from us for my father's property in South Carolina."

"The property finally sold, huh?"

Connie nodded her head and slid back against the pillows. "Yes…it's official now." She sighed, as Dean shifted his weight closer to her, and put his arm around her.

"I'm sorry for assuming the wrong thing."

"That's okay, I'm just glad it's over with," Connie replied. "I haven't seen that many papers since the days I used to have artists sign their record deals. I'm just glad that me, Willie and Margaret agreed to split the four million dollars. Margaret was sweet about everything. She's going to take her share and move back to her hometown in Alabama, and Willie is going to invest some of his money into his computer consulting firm. I'll put a portion of mine into the Freedom for Frieda Foundation, make repairs on your parents' house, and put the rest away for our children and grandchildren."

"Sounds like you have it all planned out," Dean thought.

"I'd give all the money back to see my father one more time, and tell him I love him."

"Papa Scott was a good man. I miss him too," Dean kissed the side of her cheek. "I'm glad he went peacefully in his sleep, and didn't have to suffer."

Connie looked up into Dean's dark, piercing eyes and smiled. She never questioned why she still loved him after all these years.

"My father said he always knew we would get married."

"Really?"

"He said it was the way you looked at me. It's the same stare that you're giving me now."

"I guess I was one of the lucky ones," he kissed the bridge of her nose then her forehead.

The loud ringing of the phone broke the quietness in the room. Dean stretched his long arm across the bed to grab it off the nightstand.

"…Oh sure, Anna, we'll be done shortly. You can just leave it in the microwave for now. Thank you."

"I take it breakfast is ready?"

"Yep, and I'm starving. I'm glad this is Anna's week to be here helping out," Dean stepped out of bed one leg at a time. He rose slowly from the extra-king size bed and headed into the bathroom. Connie followed behind him.

In the shower, she lathered the washcloth heavily with soap and washed him down. Though he had just turned sixty-five, Dean still worked out every day and took his vitamins. If he didn't have grey hair, he could easily be mistaken for a man in his early fifties, Connie thought to herself as she cleaned his muscular chest and soaped down his package. He tilted his head down so she could shampoo his hair. Connie loved Dean's dusted white-grey hair against his chocolate coated skin. He complained about getting old and wanted to dye it, but Connie insisted it made him look handsomely mature. When it was his turn to care for her body, Connie turned her back to him. She always felt self-conscious about her body image whenever they showered together. At fifty-eight (soon-to-be-fifty-nine), she was past menopause, and her body was simply slowing down. No matter how much she took long walks with Dean or worked out, the love handles and the breasts would be with her for the rest of her life. Dean didn't complain one bit.

A half hour later, Connie and Dean were sitting at the island in their kitchen, eating breakfast while wearing *his* and *her* blue robes that their grandchildren had bought them last year for their anniversary.

"This is just really sad reading about all of these young folks killing each other," Connie shook her head in dismay as she read the local news in the *Chicago Tribune* newspaper. "Peaches and I have done everything we could to try to help the young ones in the inner city through our foundation."

"What's that?" Dean set the sports section aside.

"There's been another gang shooting, and a child was killed." Connie shook her head, and set the paper down next to her plate. "It's just sad. Now another mother has lost her child."

"Well, you and Peaches have done all you could do. I mean, you built two recreation centers, a learning center, bowling alley, and a skating rink," Dean reminded her. "It's like that old saying. You can bring a donkey to a well, but you can't make him drink."

"Things are worse now than it was back in the 70's and 80's," Connie recalled.

"Now here we are, thirty-something years later, right back in the same boat. That's why I don't read or listen to the news as much."

"Can't blame you, Dean, but we need to get with Peaches to find out what else we can do to help."

"Well, you can't save the world, baby. The bigwigs in Washington are doing all they can to put in laws for gun control, but the prevention starts with us. We got a lot of underground sells of guns and weapons coming in, from only God knows where, and they're being sold in back alleys like lollipops. Until *we* get sick and tired, and start helping the police solve these murders, it's going to keep happening."

"Excuse me, Mrs. Wilson, your mail has arrived," Anna interrupted, and handed Connie a few letters and a package.

"Thank you, Anna, but you didn't have to go out in that rain. It could have waited," Connie said, opening the letters first.

"It's no problem, Mrs. Wilson. Do you guys need anything else? I actually need to run out to the grocery store anyway."

"Anna, why don't you hold off for today. It's raining cats and dogs outside. No need in you getting all wet," Dean stated. "You're already drenched from grabbing the mail."

"Are you sure?"

"We're sure Anna," Connie insisted. "Make yourself a hot cup of tea or something and take it easy today. Relax."

"Maybe you're right. I will go tomorrow," Anna thought about it. "If you need anything just call me in my room."

"Sure thing," Dean added.

Connie continued to read through her mail.

"Finally, my check is here," Connie read the amount. "Remember I was a guest judge last season on Who's Got Talent," Connie smiled. From time-to-time, she still participated in Hollywood shows or events.

Last year, she was a co-host at the *Grammy Awards*.

"I guess that means more purses and shoes. We'll have to build another closet for you," Dean joked.

"Wrong again Mr. Wilson. I'm going to give this to our grandchildren who are graduating next year."

Dean twisted his lips. "Mm hmm, sure."

Connie then eyed the square-shaped box with the famous happy face logo on the side. "I bet I know what this is."

Dean folded his arms and watched as Connie opened it.

"*Riding the Waves: The Price of Fame and Fortune*, by Tracey G. Michaels," Connie read.

"Oh boy, she went through with it anyway, I see." Dean slowly got up from the stool and collected their empty plates.

"Yep, the one we asked her not to write during our family meeting last year," Connie flipped through the book to see how many pages it was.

"Well, I'm going to work out in the gym downstairs, since it's still raining outside. If you decide to read that, I don't want to hear you complaining," Dean warned.

"I won't complain. If I do, I know how to call Tracey and vent to her myself." Connie grabbed Tracey's book off the counter and retreated to the bedroom so she could start reading it.

> "...and to my beloved mother: I love you with all of my heart! I am truly grateful for everything you have done for me—past and present. I know I may not have always shown that I appreciate it, but I do. You are a beautiful woman inside and out. You have the most caring and genuine spirit than anyone on this planet! I thank you for being my mother, my friend, and my rock. To Daddy, I love you and thank you for being so very patient with me. You are truly my hero! To my brothers, Devin and Dean, I love you guys. Thanks for protecting me and always looking out for me!
> Love Always,
> Tracey

"Oh boy," Connie sighed, putting on her reading glasses. She flipped through the pages. "Here we go..."

CHAPTER TWO
TRACEY'S BOOK

So, Mom and Dean got married in March 1986 in our hometown Chicago, and what a beautiful wedding it was! I'm not saying that because Cat Morris is my famous mother, but she *was* a very beautiful bride. Stevie Wonder sang "Ribbon in the Sky", and there wasn't a dry eye in the room. She and Dean honeymooned in the Cayman Islands. Nine months later, my brother Devin was born on December 12th. I admit I became a little jealous of Devin because he got so much attention. When we graced the covers of *Ebony* and *Essence*, reporters seemed to highlight Devin and the fact that Mom had given birth at thirty-two. After the wedding, we retreated back to our home in Bel-Air, California. I did my best to accept our new life as one big happy family, but I wanted to make a name for myself.

[*You sure did,* Connie thought to herself as she read Tracey's book.]

I wanted to be on the covers of magazines by myself, like my mother. I wanted my own star on the Hollywood Walk of Fame, like my mother had earned before she retired. I wanted to sign autographs and become a big star with my acting career, and I was willing to do anything to get it.

See, I was born in Chicago, and then Mom and I moved to New York where she started working at WHKY, a new radio station in the heart of New York City. Initially, my mother told me we were moving solely because of her new job, but later I would learn the truth when Aunt Peaches got out of jail. Aunt Peaches told me that Mom accepted the job in New York because their father Mason had threatened to kill my mother by setting fires to our home and her place of business, *CMP* (Connie Morris Promotions). So anyway, Mom came to New York and turned it up! She was already famous from working at WCHI radio station in Chicago, but she became even more famous in New York. Mr. Yancy, Mom's boss, gave her the *Sunnyside Up Morning Show.* From that day forward, I remember seeing my mother's face on the billboards, the side of busses, taxi-cabs, and in the glittering lights of Times Square. My mother was the first African-American woman to have a lucrative contract in radio.

My father, Vernon "Jet" Michaels, was a star running-back for the Buffalo Bills at that time, and he was well-known in his career too. So, I had two famous parents who both handled their celebrity and parenting differently. With Jet, he wanted me to have the best of everything, mostly for bragging rights if you ask me. So I became the girl version of Ricky Schroeder from *Silver Spoons*.

My bedroom at Jet's mansion in Buffalo, New York was the size of the penthouse living room that Mom and I were living in on Park Avenue. I had a Jacuzzi bathtub, floor model color TV, a limousine picking me up and taking me places, and all the toys and clothes that a kid could ever want. No one told me "no", including Jet's girlfriend Sabrina.

[*He spoiled you rotten.* Connie flipped the page and continued to read.]

On the other hand, my mother set boundaries with me. I had to get good grades in school, perform chores, and pretty much *earn* my toys and other things I wanted. At the private school I attended, the kids all wanted to be my friend because of my famous parents. They either wanted to be on the radio because of my mother or get football tickets or NFL memorabilia from my dad. I loved the admiration. The only thing I didn't like about private school was wearing those ugly blue and white uniforms, and when we would get teased by public school kids who wanted to kick the crap out of us.

By the time I reached the sixth grade, I was the most popular girl in school, but I really had nothing in common with the other kids besides having rich parents, and mine were the only parents who had the fame to go along with the riches. That's when Keyshia King came into my life. We call her "Kay-Kay." She was tall, with coconut brown skin, full-lips, high cheekbones, and brown eyes. Kay-Kay was an ugly duckling to some because of her exotic looks. Being the tallest one in the class, with bony legs, arched cheek bones, and talking in her native Nigerian accent made her awkward amongst us New Yorkers. But Kay-Kay grew into a beautiful swan princess if you ask me. I liked Kay-Kay right away. Not because I felt sorry for her for getting teased by the other kids, but I admired her strong spirit. She never said anything when she was teased, but when one kid threw his apple at her during lunch; she beat him up so bad that he had to get stitches. She was expelled of course, but only for one day. Her parents, who were lawyers, got her back into the school. I'm not sure what their persuasive argument was, but Kay-Kay returned to school and sat right next to me in class. She was surprised when I started talking to her, and I would share my lunch. Before long, Kay-Kay and I became best friends, and all hell broke loose in school. Kay-Kay turned me into a rebel without a cause. I started getting into trouble for cursing out the teachers, beating up other girls who looked at me wrong, and disobeying other school rules. I went from being a popular, respectful girl to a class bully. [*And I spanked your behind for it too!* Connie recalled].

Kay-Kay and I learned early how to use our privileged upbringing to do whatever we wanted. Don't get me wrong, there were fun times at school, and we weren't always fighting or getting into trouble. We helped with school bake sales, science fairs, tutored the younger kids, and during our last year, we participated in the school talent show. We decided to perform Salt n' Pepa's "My Mike Sounds Nice". I was Salt and Kay-Kay was Pepa. I'm sure my mother has the videotape somewhere in her house, if it still plays. To this day, Kay-Kay and I are still BFFs. She can come over my house and stink up the bathroom with no problem and I can do the same with her. That's how close we are.

When we moved to California, Kay-Kay and I cried like Ceely and Nettie did in *The Color Purple*. We would write letters to each other but it wasn't the same. About a year later in 1987, as irony would have it, Kay-Kay and her family moved to Bel-Air, California too. We both attended another private school together, called The Carter Academy.

This academy was a junior and high school combined, except if you were in junior high, your classes were on the left-side of the building, and high school was on the right. It felt so good to have my best friend back. I found out they moved to California because Kay-Kay's parents started their own law firm, the Law Offices of King & King where they specialized in entertainment law. They made a killing!

[*Yes, they did earn a lot of high profile clients. Only the elite could afford them, and sometimes they were in over their heads, like "forgetting" to pay Uncle Sam their taxes. I believe they went to court for tax issues. Fortunately for them, they worked out a deal and managed to avoid jail time.* Connie remembered].

Despite moving to the West Coast, Mom and Jet agreed that I would still visit him in Buffalo. It was really Sabrina who urged my father to try to be in my life more. Otherwise, I don't think my father would have reached out. Anyway, Jet sent his private plane to pick me up from LAX airport and fly me out to Buffalo every other holiday, birthday, and summer. In case you're wondering why I call him by his nickname "Jet", it's because I don't want you to confuse him when I mention Dean my stepfather. My stepfather really deserves to be called "Dad", but we will get to those reasons why later.

Moving right along, my visits with Jet were fun for a while. Publicly, I was Jet's most prized possession. We did commercials together, photo shoots, and in his interviews he bragged about how well I was doing in school. After he and Sabrina got married, everyone thought we were the perfect family. Jet earned more endorsements and public favor by appearing to be family-oriented, but little did they know that my father was rarely ever home. I spent more time with Sabrina and my friends than I did with him. I couldn't even tell you what his favorite color was or what he liked to eat. The most I ever saw of my father was on the football field. When he was home, he was busy watching films with his coaches or shooting pool with his friends. At night, he went out partying, and would come home drunk. It was like a routine. I often overheard him and Sabrina arguing about him coming home late and smelling like other women's perfume.

[*No wonder they're divorced now. Jet could never be satisfied with just one woman.* Connie recalled the day he cheated on her when they were in high school together.]

My father and I had no real dialogue besides "I want" and "Sure, you can have it." My visits were about material things, not quality time. The only thing I liked about my visits to Buffalo [besides driving to Niagara Falls] was the Buffalo wings, beef sandwiches, and the local festivals they had during the summer. Most of the time, Sabrina and I would fly to New York City because there was more to do. Sometimes my brother Dean Jr. would meet us at Greenwich Village, since he was still at NYU studying computer engineering. I was always glad to see my brother, and I missed Dean so much when he was away at school.

By the time I was sixteen, we had been living in California for at least five years. Jet retired and moved from Buffalo to South Beach, Florida. He always loved Florida ever since he went to Florida University before getting drafted to the NFL. I continued to visit Jet, and fell in love with South Beach too. South Beach and Buffalo had no comparisons. I loved New York, and all the five boroughs, but I couldn't stand Buffalo; there was nothing there for a girl my age to do. Anyway, for my sixteenth birthday, Jet bought me a red Ferrari. I flew from Bel Air to Florida in a private jet with Kay-Kay and the rest of my friends, so I could check out my birthday ride. I didn't want to wait until Jet shipped it out to me. When we got to Florida, we partied hard, South Beach style, to house music. I was fried, and ended up wrecking the brand new Ferrari that Jet bought me. I didn't even have it for a week! Jet bailed me and my friends out of jail, and later that year, he replaced the Ferrari with another one for Christmas. Although months had passed since the drunken driving incident, Mom didn't approve because I had never shown any remorse. She yelled at Jet on the phone.

"You aren't helping Tracey, Jet, she needs discipline. You can't keep buying her things when she doesn't appreciate it!" I would always hear them arguing on the phone until one of them would hang up. Sometimes they argued so much I wondered how in the world they conceived me.

[*Jet had no business buying you another car when you wrecked the first one, but your father was always a show-off. His ego was twice the size of his head. He felt he had money to burn, so he burned it; now he's paying the price for it.* Connie shook her head].

When it came to friends, my parents was never short, but my mother was always careful, especially after getting burned by her high school pals Smokey and May. To this day, Mom calls only a handful of people her true friends, despite knowing hundreds of people in show business. Mom always threw big parties at the house, and many celebrities would come through, especially after she became V.P. at BigStar Records. I've met Quincy Jones, Michael Jackson, Chaka Khan, Teena Marie, Stevie Wonder, and many others. All of them she said were 'friends', but her closest ones weren't even in the business. "Not everyone who smiles in your face is your friend. Despite what you read in the papers about people claiming to be BFFs, behind closed doors, they probably can't stand each other," Mom used to warn me. I learned over the years that Mom was right about friends, and I went through my share of fakes who were only cool with me when I was spending money on them. As I grew and matured, I wised up with the quickness. The word '*No*' made them scatter like roaches. Some guys tried to get with me so they could get to my mother for a record deal, but when I peeped their game, I dumped them. The only person who stuck around through hell and high waters was Kay-Kay. We always *clicked*. We had more in common than I did with my other friends and not just having rich parents; but we loved doing the same things. Also like me, Kay-Kay had two brothers, and she knew what it was like to be the only girl. I had my brothers Dean Jr. and Devin, and Kay-Kay had an older brother, Kwame, and a younger brother, Noah. Noah is three years younger than us and he used to try to hang out with us. He was like the annoying Steve Urkel from *Family Matters*, and he would always stare at me whenever I came over to their house. Now, the little scrawny Noah with *Hershey* chocolate skin like his sister is the truth! He's a model now, and please believe me, he's *the business!* But we'll get to *Mr. Noah* later.

[*"Oh boy!"* Connie braced herself as she shifted her body to lie on her side while keeping her eyes glued to the book.]

As for my Mom and Dad, they were still lovebirds on into my teens and even now. I remember Dad would call the house from his cellphone, and when I would answer, he would tell me to ask Mom if he could take her out. I thought that was so cute. Sometimes I would find them cuddled up in the theater room, watching a movie together and sharing popcorn. I wanted someone to love me the way my parents loved each other. My search for love grew stronger during my teenage years. I felt lonely whenever Kay-Kay and my friends weren't around. Maybe I just needed attention, but I found it very hard to be alone. I still do.

After a while, I felt Mom and I had outgrown the level of intimacy we shared when I was growing up in New York. She had Dean for the rest of her life now, no more on-again and off-again relationship with him.

Mom had also kicked the bottle; no more drinking. When she wasn't with my dad, she was spending time with my little brother Devin, her girlfriends, or doing charity work. As for me, I was on my own. That's when we started to bump heads. When I look back, I think it's because my mother didn't give me enough time and attention.

[*We bumped heads because you never knew how to share me with other people, and yes, during your teens you were lonely at times because your own behavior didn't make you a pleasant person to be around. It could have been puberty and your changing hormones, but in a lot of ways, my daughter, you are selfish like your father Jet. And how dare you mention my drinking problem! That was a long time ago! Isn't this supposed to be "your" story?* Connie pushed her reading glasses over the bridge of her nose and hesitated to continue at first, but she turned to the next page.]

Mom and I began to clash about everything during my teen years- from the way I dressed, to my curfew, choice of music, and the company I kept. If she said turn right, I went left just to spite her. I think I was subconsciously trying to get her to pay attention to me, but going about it the wrong way. Mom was trying to help me become an independent woman. She tried to teach me how to do a lot of domesticated things like wash my own clothes, sew, and cook. I left that stuff to the maids until Mom decided to have a maid only a few times a week, and that was because she needed help with Devin. I had no choice but to clean my own room and wash my own clothes.

I remember Mom was having a dinner fundraiser on behalf of the Freedom for Frieda Foundation. They were celebrating the move to Chicago, because Aunt Peaches found some real estate there and turned the building into the foundation. Plus she wanted to be near my cousin BJ once he came home from the military. So anyway, instead of hiring a caterer, Mom and Aunt Peaches decided to do all the cooking. Aunt Peaches was even upset that Mom didn't hire caterers. [*She was not upset!*].

Mom was wearing a fly outfit, her hair and makeup was flawless, the whole nine. Yet she was in the kitchen cooking for her guests with an apron tied around her waist. She had decided not to cater the event, claiming she was sick of catered food and wanted soul food, but let's face it, my mother can be cheap!

[*I swear, I am going to remember you saying this when you call asking me for money next time!*]

My mother was so cheap she kept the same Mercedes for two years. No celebrity I knew did that! Anyway, Mom slipped on her apron and was throwing down in the kitchen, right along with Aunt Peaches, who at least had the decency enough not to put on her good clothes while doing it. Mom claimed she didn't want to have to get dressed at the last minute, but guess what? She had to get dressed at the last minute anyway, because she smelled like a mixture of all the food she had cooked. You would have thought it was Thanksgiving. I wanted to compliment her on how good she looked, but I felt enough people did that. Besides, she would just think I wanted something from her. I watched her move throughout the kitchen, dashing from counter to counter, and setting up one dish after another. I could only admire her as I sat at the island on the barstool. I remember wishing that I would still look gorgeous like her when I turned her age.

I have my mother's long hair, but Jet's brown hair color.

[Connie turned the book over to glance at Tracey's author photo. She was wearing an off-the-shoulder blouse that revealed her warm golden skin. Her soft complexion made her hazel eyes stand out. *You still look more like me than Jet, but you have more of his personality, that's for sure.*]

"Don't just sit there watching me and daydreaming, Tracey, start buttering the dinner rolls," Mom had said to me. I couldn't believe she had asked me to do that.

"Mom, you cannot be serious right now. Me? Butter dinner rolls? That's funny." I shook my head in disbelief. "Besides, I just got my nails done."

Mom rolled her eyes to the ceiling. "You're so lazy, Tracey. How do you ever expect to learn how to cook if you don't start doing the simple things now? How will your family eat when you get married?"

"I'll hire a personal chef."

"And, what if you can't afford one?" Aunt Peaches interjected.

"Auntie, are you serious? Of course I'll be able to afford a chef. I'm going to have a chef, maid, a personal assistant, and a limo driver to take me places. You won't see me standing at a hot stove in my best clothes that's for sure!"

"Who do you think you're talking to? Girl, I will scratch your eyeballs out and feed them to my dogs!" Aunt Peaches threatened, pointing at me with the cooking spatula. I knew not to play with Aunt Peaches. I think she developed a bipolar disorder when she was incarcerated.

Anyway, I remember leaving the kitchen because I felt like Mom and Aunt Peaches were ganging up on me. I called Kay-Kay, and we met up at a club on Sunset Boulevard not too far from the *Laugh Factory*. We were only sixteen and way underage, but no bouncer at the door was going to turn down children with rich and famous parents. Besides, we tipped them well. We partied the whole night and I remember asking the DJ to play my favorite song, *"The Power"* by Snap, at least three times. He played every version of that song, and the crowds went wild. I lost my shoes on the dance floor and so did Kay-Kay [who was a much better dancer than I was]. After Snap played, the DJ kept coming with the songs from artists like Soul II Soul, Bell, Bell Biv Devoe, Tony Toni Tone, and CeCe Pineston. We jammed all night long. I remember waking up in my bed the next morning to a set of dark eyes staring back at me. I blinked twice until the face came into clearer vision.

"You must have lost your mind coming in this house drunk like that, and you knew we had company!"

"Dad?" I wiped the sleep from my eyes and slobber from the corners of my mouth.

"Yeah it's me!" he shouted, and I felt my head throb. He was standing over me like a security officer. "What's wrong with you, girl? A young lady is not supposed to act like that. You think it's cool to get drunk and have the cops to follow you home. I had to rush you upstairs to your room before any more guests saw you standing in the doorway drunk!" he shouted. "That's it! I'm taking you to the morgue so you can look at all the dead teenagers who also thought it was cool to get drunk!"

Dad dragged me to the morgue. He muscled me into his BMW, and I still had on my clothes from last night. Seeing those dead bodies made me throw up all the liquor I'd had from the night before. I can still remember what those bodies looked like to this day. Driving under the influence is not a joke! I took my father's message to heart, and I encourage you young ones reading this not to play Russian roulette with your own life by driving drunk. I didn't get into an accident, but I could have been.

Dad took the keys to my Ferrari. I was so pissed off I called Jet, and then he and Dad got into an argument over the phone. I remember overhearing Dad say to Jet, "Man, you don't live here, and this is my house so as long as Tracey is here with us, she's going to abide by our rules. She's not getting her car keys back until I say so!" I thought the arguing would never end, but Dad soon hung up the phone. The two of them never got along, and I think it was mostly because of my mischief that drove a wedge between the two of them.

[*That's part of the reason, but Jet never liked the idea that Dean was taking care of you when he should have been. I think Jet's guilty conscious made him defensive.*]

Mom didn't speak to me for a while, since it was my second DUI. The first DUI was in South Beach when I was celebrating my birthday. The police officer told my mother he would let it slide, but of course that meant greasing his palms. I found out later from Aunt Peaches that Mom paid the officer ten thousand dollars to keep quiet about the whole thing. I should have been grateful, but instead I was mad at Mom for not speaking to me. Whenever Mom stopped talking, you knew she was upset. The evil look she gave you and the non-verbal way she communicated her anger, like slamming doors, brushing by you, and rolling her eyes, made you feel like you stepped in dog's poop on a rainy day. You almost wished she just smacked the hell out of you and got over it.

Eventually, I decided to break the silence. Boldly, I walked into the library room, where Mom was lying comfortable on the leather half-back sofa, reading her Bible.

"Ma," I called.

She looked at me over the brim of her glasses.

"I'm sorry. I got a little twisted or whatever, but it won't happen again."

Mom cocked her head to the side. "You got a *little* twisted? Is that what you just said to me?"

By the tone of her voice, I dared to repeat what I had said. Mom set her Bible on the table before her, and I knew only prayer could save me. She abruptly stood up from the sofa.

"You came in *my* house tore up from the floor up and embarrassed me in front of *my* guests, and that's all you got to say for yourself, Tracey Gina Michaels?"

"Uhm…I…I didn't know I was going to get drunk like that," I started backing away from her, and didn't realize I backed myself into the corner of the room.

Her eyes bucked in shock at my response. "You're only sixteen!"

I dropped my head, mumbled, "I'm sorry, Mom."

Since this was the second time I got drunk, my mother feared I had a drinking problem like she did, so they made me attend some kind of teenage AA program for thirty days. It was so uncool, like totally. Who sends their child to rehab when they don't have a drinking problem?

[*"Parents who love and care, that's who!"* Connie said aloud as she continued reading.]

Everything I did was screened from that point on, and the only time I was allowed out the house was to go on auditions. As a kid, Mom had allowed me to do commercials and school plays, so I was still determined at sixteen that I would become a professional actress. Mom hired an agent for me when I started high school, so I was doing commercials and other small roles, but when I landed the small recurring role on the TV-sitcom *A Different World* in 1990, I was hyped! This was season three, when characters Dwayne Wayne and Whitley Gilbert were flirty with their friendship, so no one was paying *me* much attention, but I was happy to be on TV. Being on the set also gave me a chance to sneak around and do what I wanted to do without being monitored by my parents like I was a kid. By season four, I was cut and replaced with the fast-talking Charmaine, who was part of the new freshman class. I was upset at first, because I naturally talk fast and don't have to pretend to be a speed talker, but looking back, Karen Malina White did a great job.

After losing the TV gig, Kay-Kay told me about a video audition for a rapper by the name of Zeek. Kay-Kay was also going to school on the weekends to earn her hair license. She met Zeek's manager, who came to the hair school to get her hair done. I earned the audition for Zeek's video, and from there, I was cast for several other rappers and singers' videos. I had two things in my favor for starring in videos: I was pretty and I had a body that rocked! People judge video girls, but let me tell you, one video can pay up to five thousand dollars if you hook up with the right artist. In six months, I was driving a brand new Porsche. Eventually, I would buy Kay-Kay a new car too. She was my best friend, and she deserved it for hooking me up with Zeek.

Once I got that first taste of being a video girl, I knew from then on I could use my looks to get whatever I wanted, and believe me I did! Some music artists were weak for pretty girls like me. Some of them would peel off the dough and give me money just because I looked good. When I would run into Zeek at parties, he would get jealous whenever he saw me talking to artists beside him. I boldly asked him one night what his problem was. Kay-Kay tried to stop me from approaching him, because Zeek used to be a bouncer before he became a rapper. He was extremely buff and had an intimidating expression, but when I approached him everything softened.

"I'm just waiting for you to stop messing with these weak dudes and get with a real man," Zeek said, puffing a cigar.

I stared him up and down flirtatiously. "So what's this real man going to do for me?" I stroked his big buff arms and could feel his tight muscles protruding through the sleeves. He pulled out a money clip with nothing but Ben Franks and handed it to me.

"And there's more where that came from if you do right by me. If you don't, you'll wish you had."

Silly me. I saw the money and took it. Zeek was one of the highest ballers in the rap game, with a jail body and gremlin face, but he was rich! Zeek bought me anything I wanted–jewelry, clothes, shoes, purses, and he paid to get my hair, nails, and feet done. I can't say that I couldn't get these things from my parents or even with the money I made from videos, but if I didn't have to spend my own money, why would I? The more money I got, the more I wanted. I was in love with money, and instant gratification was my thing. I was young, vigorous, ambitious, and filled with life. I felt like a boss. I felt like my Mom in a way. I was finally in charge...or so I thought.

[*Child, you'll never be like me. You only wanted to have the good parts of my life. You weren't there during the come up, and if you were, you wouldn't have been able to handle my struggles. You'll never understand why God allowed me to have the success I had, and be the "boss" I am today, as you put it.* Connie shook her head at her daughter's twisted way of thinking.]

I pulled up at The Carter Academy in my Porsche and slowly rolled down the tinted windows and flashed a smile, winked my eye. My friends came running up to the car. I felt like a superstar. We all took pictures hanging around the Porsche, and then we went inside to class. Me and Kay-Kay would ride everywhere in my Porsche. Kay-Kay normally drove a nice little Maximum that her parents gave her. It was cute and everything, but it wasn't a Porsche. We looked more fly in a Porsche than a Maximum on any day. But eventually, I would buy her a sports car, though it wasn't a Porsche. I couldn't have her riding flashier than me. She was my girl and all, but why would I scoot myself in second place? That wasn't going to happen.

In the mist of being a premiere celebrity and earning wealth from starring in videos, I had forgotten about my little Hispanic boyfriend Pedro who became my first love inside the girls' locker room. The whole thing happened on a bet, really. I was the first out of my group of friends to lose it. I gave it to Pedro since he was the cutest guy in school and my friends bet me I couldn't get with him, because Pedro was quiet, and into his studies. He was adopted and had really strict parents who forbade him from dating girls, but I turned him out over a three month period. I'm not proud of it; Pedro was a good guy and I feel bad now just to think about how I treated him. The day he approached me and asked me about the rumors of me and Zeek being together, I bluntly told him it was true, and that it was over between us. He stood at his locker and cried in front of everybody, and I just walked away. I know what you're thinking, and you're right; it was very cold and heartless, but that was my mindset back then.

[*So you lost your precious virginity to a bet? I taught you better than that. You just threw your pearls to swine.*]

Although it was over between me and Pedro, I still had my Todd. Todd was from Baldwin Hills, and headed to college at the end of summer. Todd spent his allowance money on me all the time and would buy me jewelry and nice things. He was so sweet, but I didn't need his money, honestly. I already received an allowance from my parents— three hundred dollars every week that I spent on clothes. Plus Zeek gave me money. With Todd, it wasn't about money. He was already putting moves on my heart. Todd was the guy I would go out to the movies with. Zeek was the guy I hung out with in the studio or went to celebrity events together. Todd wasn't into Hollywood as much. He had a quiet and shy way about him. In fact, we met at church, and our parents were friends. Todd was a good egg, and I liked the fact that he was older than me. Zeek was older than me too, but Todd was so much more mature than the cocky Zeek. Mom seemed to like Todd, but Dad was suspicious and always questioned Todd's motives when he bought me things.

"He must want something back from you in return," Dad would say. I would argue against it. Little did he know it was Zeek who was getting it back from me in return. Todd never expected anything back, nor did he pressure me or bug me about sex the way Zeek did.

[*Now why would you say all of that in this book, Tracey?* Connie thought. She set the book down, and decided she had read enough, at least for today…]

CHAPTER THREE
KAY-KAY

"Tracey, why do you keep calling me?" Kay-Kay answered her cell-phone for the third time. Each time she saw Tracey's name pop up, she wanted to hit the 'ignore' button.

"What part are you on now?" Tracey asked anxiously.

"Tracey you just called me thirty minutes ago, and if you keep calling, I'll never get through it," Kay-Kay protested.

"Okay, just tell me which part you're on."

Kay-Kay heaved a long sigh, flipped the page forward and then backwards, and replied, "I just finished the part where you and Pedro broke up. Now you're dating Todd and Zeek at the same time."

"Okay, so you have a long ways to go."

"It reads pretty fast, Tracey, but you're slowing me down. It's nine o'clock, and I would like to finish a few more chapters before bed."

"Okay, I promise I won't call you back anymore. But you do like it, don't you?" Tracey wanted to know. "I'm just nervous. I wonder what the public will think."

"It's good...a little bold, but very Tracey-like," she answered. "I just don't like what you mentioned about me."

"What did I say?"

"That I was an ugly duckling with an exotic look. What is that supposed to mean anyway?"

"Oh come on, Kay, you know it's not like that. You're beautiful."

"And why would you say I made you into a troublemaker? You were the instigator. I never picked fights with anyone. You would start stuff, and I was the one who ended up taking up for you."

"Kay, are you serious? We were kids. Some things you may not remember, but I do."

"I remember plenty, and thanks for bringing it up to remind me. I hated being teased as a kid, and I hated that school in New York."

"Hey, don't beat yourself up. I was a funny-looking kid too. I had to wear braces for my teeth, remember? Everyone said I had train tracks in my mouth." Tracey chuckled.

"I remember it, but I sure didn't see it written in the book, and I'm past the part when you're a kid."

"I didn't think wearing braces was important."

"But you obviously felt that mentioning I got teased when *I* was little was important, and made *yourself* out to be *my* savior, like you felt sorry for me. And thanks for putting down the fact that my parents bought me a Maximum. That was a nice ride," Kay complained. "Besides, you had no problems riding in it when your parents took the keys to your Ferrari."

"Kay, you're like my sister, come on. I didn't mean it that way."

"You never do." Kay rolled her eyes behind the phone. "But anyway, get off my phone so I can finish reading."

"I'm not hanging up until you tell me you're not mad at me anymore."

"I'm not mad. I'm just saying if you're going to tell the truth, it should be the whole truth, and not just *your* truth."

"I'm sorry."

"Bye, Tracey. For the last time, get off my phone."

"You forgive me?"

"Let me finish the book first and then I'll decide. I need to make sure you didn't say anything else bad about me."

"Seriously?"

"Bye, Tracey." Kay hit the *end* button on her phone. She flipped the pages to find where she left off. "Oh, here we are..."

In 1991, I was going into my junior year at The Carter Academy when my parents invited me and Kay-Kay to the premiere of *Boyz 'N the Hood* that summer. I didn't want to go; because I was afraid I would run into Zeek and Todd at the same time. Both of them wanted me to go with them to the premiere, but I lied and told them I was sick. Kay-Kay pressed me into going because she wanted to meet the cast, but I had already met them. They were filming across the lot from where I was shooting for a low budget movie.

"I see a future for you and Todd," Mom said, peeping her head back at me from the front leather seat as Dad's BMW approached the V.I.P. parking lot. "He's got his head on straight. He goes to church, and he's headed for college. That's the type of young man you need, not those thugs you dance with in those videos."

Little did Mom know Todd wasn't as innocent as she thought. Just a month before school had let out for the summer, I thought I was pregnant with his baby. We were praying for forgiveness in church, and then my period came. It was late. Instead of being repentant and thankful, we did it again. We didn't even care about the consequences.

"Dean, don't you think Todd is a pretty cool guy for Tracey?" Mom asked, while dad pulled up to the valet.

"I don't think any guy Tracey dates is cool." Dad cut his eyes at me through the front view mirror, then handed the valet his car keys.

"As a matter of fact," Dad continued, as we all got out of the car. "All these guys out here want one thing, and Todd is no exception, whether he's college bound or singing hallelujahs in church. You may think he's quiet and shy, but I think the boy is sneaky, and wouldn't put anything past him." Dad held my gaze so strongly that my stomach fluttered with nervousness. I looked away, and wiped my sweaty palms on the front of my shorts. I thought he suspected what Todd and I was doing when he and Mom wasn't home.

I managed to duck running into Zeek or Todd at the movies, but it was getting hard to keep up a relationship with both of them. Zeek began to demand more of my attention in the studio and celebrity parties. I was his trophy piece more than anything. He wanted to show that his ugly behind could pull a honey like me. Todd wanted my time too. He wanted to go to concerts, movies, bowling, and do real fun quality time stuff that couples did. I really liked Todd and I cared more about him than I did Zeek. When we were together I always felt like it meant something special, but with Zeek it felt like an obligation. Todd was the perfect gentlemen, he was respectful and polite, but Zeek was a very jealous guy, aggressive and demanding. I won't lie; I was scared of Zeek and what he might do to me if I broke up with him. Kay-Kay was scared of Zeek too, because he had threatened to punch her in the face when she told him in the studio that she didn't like his new record. I had no choice but to break up with Todd. It was for his protection and mine.

Todd didn't take the break-up too well. Neither did I. We cried in each other's arms, and stopped going to church because it was too painful to see one another. I promised myself if I ever met another guy like Todd I would love him for the rest of my life.

24

Todd starting showing up to my house unannounced. He made excuses to see me. He would claim that he stopped by to shoot basketball with my dad or my brothers, but then he would try to engage me in conversation with him. I kept warning Todd to leave me alone, because I was seeing somebody else, but Todd continued to follow me. He would show up at the same parties. He would come to my school and insist on walking me to my car. Every time I looked up, I saw Todd. One day while I was at the mall with Zeek, Todd boldly approached us as we were coming out of a record store. Zeek had just finished signing autographs for his new record. There were lots of people around, and Zeek didn't have any bodyguards. He was big enough to be a guard to himself. As we were leaving the record store, the fans followed us, and out from the crowd appeared Todd.

"So, is this the buster that you dumped me for?" Todd questioned me angrily; his fists balled in front us.

"Excuse me? You don't know me, partner!" Zeek stepped in front of me like a protector. I stood behind him, holding my shopping bags. I had to indulge a bit while Zeek signed autographs for hours.

"Yo' homey, you better step off!" Zeek shoved the skinny Todd so hard that Todd almost fell backwards. Next thing I knew, they were going for blows and trying to kill each other. I felt so embarrassed. I covered my mouth with my hand and turned my eyes in another direction. It hurt to see Todd on the ground and Zeek stomping him all over like he was an insect. Tears swelled in my eyes, and when I opened my mouth to cry for help, nothing came out.

"Come on!" Zeek yanked my arm when he was done. I'd squeezed my eyes shut; I couldn't bear to see Todd still lying on the ground.

We ended up in the studio, and Zeek acted like nothing had just happened. In fact, he started bragging to his boys and reenacting how he beat up Todd. They were laughing and slapping fives. I felt so bad for Todd.

"What are you still crying for?" Zeek shouted, standing over me while I sat in the studio chair.

"You want some of this?" he shoved a blunt in my face.

"No."

He sucked his teeth. "You gonna smoke this. Here, it'll calm you down!"

"No!"

"You yelling at me?" Zeek snatched me by my hair. "You want me to knock you out the way I did old boy? Huh?!"

I was too scared to put up a fight with Zeek, so I smoked the blunt and drank a forty. Hours later, Zeek followed me home to make sure I wasn't going to see Todd. Kay-Kay had called me on my cell to say that she heard Todd had gone to the hospital. She said Todd had suffered a small jaw fracture and bruised ribs. As soon as I pulled up in my driveway, Kay-Kay called back to say that Todd had been treated for his injuries and released.

[*I remember that day, and I felt so sorry for Todd. Zeek was one crazy dude!* Kay-Kay thought, sipping her tea.]

I remember seeing a police car parked at the entrance of the gate to our mansion, but I just assumed it was a security check. Sometimes LAPD would patrol our neighborhoods and make sure we were safe, but they never patrolled the poor neighborhoods unless somebody had been shot. I thought it was unfair to protect the rich and not the poor. Anyway, I walked in the house with my shopping bags from the mall, feeling like everything was moving in slow motion, even my legs. I had smoked before with Kay-Kay and a few of my friends, but never did I have anything as strong as what Zeek gave me. I was surprised I made it home. Zeek said I would be all right if I chewed some *Double Mint* gum afterwards. Sure, it hid the smell, and the *Visine* he gave me took the red out of my eyes, but I still couldn't hide how the chronic marijuana affected my thought process. When I walked inside, I could see two policemen with their backs turned to the corridor. They were standing in the living room straight ahead, talking to my parents and Todd and his parents. I spent the corner, and ducked around the tall Greek vases. I tried to hurry upstairs unnoticed. Then a lion appeared at the top of the stairs. I shook my head and it disappeared. When I looked down at my feet, I saw nothing but snakes crawling all around me. I started jumping up and down, and then they disappeared. I was high, high as a kite! I held on to the banister and steadied myself up the stairs. I was walking, but going nowhere. My mind was tripping. The high was in full effect!

Devin came out of the study room to the left of the stairwell. He was a cute, light skinned version of Dad, with long thick eyebrows, curly hair, and dark eyes. I loved Devin, but I could tell from the cartoonish grin on his face he was ready to rat me out.

"I'll give you some candy if you don't say anything," I hissed.

"I don't want candy, I want some money," he stated. I couldn't believe my little five-year-old brother was trying to extort me. I thought maybe it was still the high.

"What's wrong with you anyways? You look funny, why you keep blinking so slowly? Are you sleepy or something?" Devin asked, and I could hear my heart beating loud like it was going to jump out of my chest. I turned around and headed back up the stairs. I set my bags down once I got to the top of the steps, so I could catch my breath. I looked down the stretch of the hallway, and my bedroom seemed so far away. I didn't think I could take another step without passing out, but I grabbed my bags and took them to my room.

Devin opened my bedroom door. I was stretched out across the bed.

"Where is my money?" he persisted.

"I don't...I don't have any money right now. I just want to go to sleep, Zeek."

"Zeek? Who is Zeek?"

"I meant to say Devin."

"I'm telling on you." Devin ran out the room, and as tired as I was, I went after him.

"Mommy daddy! Tracey is here!"

I caught Devin just as he reached the steps, and I covered his mouth with my hand.

"Shhh...be quiet, and I will give you five dollars."

Devin held up both hands to indicate he wanted ten dollars.

"Okay ten dollars. Now if I uncover your mouth, you promise you won't yell?"

Devin nodded his head, and slowly I removed my hands from his mouth.

"MOOOOOM!"

"Tracey, is that you? Get down here right now!" I heard the sound of her high heels CLICKing rapidly towards me down the hall. I went downstairs reluctantly, and walked into the living room, where all eyes were on me. I spotted Todd sitting in between his parents with what looked like a chin strap around jawline. The police read to me what Todd had written down on the notepad about what happened earlier today at the mall, and demanded I tell them where Zeek was. I was scared to tell them what I knew, but they managed to pry a confession out of me. I can't remember what I said. To make matters worse, I do remember that Todd took a piece of paper and wrote down what we had been doing in the house when my parents weren't home. He even admitted that we thought I was pregnant once.

"How dare you!" Mom shouted, balling up the note after she read it out loud. I didn't see it coming, but she smacked the hell out of me! My chewing gum and my high ran out the door. I was alert now. "You slut! I didn't raise you like this!" She was about to hit me again, but Dad caught her hand just in time before the TKO.

"Come on, Connie, it's all right let me handle it from here. Go into the study room and see if Devin is doing okay with his homework."

Mom hesitated to leave, but not before she apologized profusely to Todd and his parents, and offered to pay for the damage that was done with a few extra dollars for hush money. Mom always hated bad publicity, so keeping them quiet would keep her good name. When Todd and his parents left, Dad did the unthinkable–he whipped me! I cried more from embarrassment than anything else because he whipped me with a long black belt. I couldn't sit down for a week.

Days later, Dad came into my room while I was on punishment. I was busy in front of the mirror, trying on new mascara. I don't remember what he said word-for-word, but the conversation started off with him telling me that Zeek had been arrested and charged with assault and statutory rape because I was under age. I was seventeen and he was twenty-one.

"Tracey, I can't protect you if you insist on messing around with these thugs," Dad warned me. "You need to focus more on other things like finishing high school and focusing on your acting career. Messing with those thugs will put you in the wrong lane. Is this the life you want for yourself?"

I glared at him through the mirror. "Dad, I can handle myself," I replied, blinking my lashes and admiring how beautiful and thick they looked with the makeup. "I'm doing just fine in school, and the movies and video gigs keep my pockets swollen."

"That's your problem!" Dad pointed. "You think you know

everything, but you don't."

I turned around sharply. "Dad, you don't know what I know. You guys are just a Bel-Air bourgeois couple living under a pompous rock," I argued. "You judge people who live in Compton, Crenshaw, Inglewood, and Watts, but you don't know that people from the hood have hearts. People from the hood got brains too. The only thing they lack is opportunity."

"And I guess you're going to save their lives by lifting up your skirt, huh?"

"What are you trying to say that I'm a ho?"

"I've seen girls like you who think it's cute to have a drug dealing boyfriend who use your face as a punching bag, then later buys you jewelry to make up for it," he stated. "You call it "love", but I call it a pimping."

"Dad I don't screw every guy I meet, so give me some credit." I turned my back to him and finished trying on my new makeup before the mirror.

"Then stop parading around like you do sleep with everybody. Demand respect from these guys and you'll get it. Stop dressing like a hoochie-mama, and show respect for yourself. Leave something for a man's imagination. You got it all...hanging out there, like it's cute." He stared me from head to toe. I was wearing a cut-off short jean skirt with a tie-up matching jean halter.

"I am cute. If you got it, you should flaunt it," I replied, adding lip gloss and smiling flirtatiously at myself in the mirror. He rested both hands on my shoulders and turned me around to face him.

"Look, Tracey, you're a pretty girl." He took the lip gloss from my hands and set it down on my vanity stand. "...And you're smart, but for some reason, you can't see that you deserve better. One day you're going to get hooked up with the wrong guy and he's going to drag you through the gutter. You'll pay a heavy price for the fame you're hoping for."

[I wish my father had a talk with me like that. Both of my parents were so busy with their own lives that when I told them I was moving out after high school, it was like telling them I was going out to buy bread. They could care less. Girl, you should have been more grateful for having parents who cared. I always told you that, Kay thought.]

Senior Year

I barely got through my junior year because my focus was off. However, by my senior year, I was making straight A's in all of my classes. I know it's surprising, but I wasn't a dummy in school. But I was flunking out in my social life. I couldn't see it back then, but you couldn't tell me nothing! I was the "it" factor! I was voted the most popular and attractive girl in school, but my parents were more excited that I was inducted into the Honor Society. My mother rewarded me for getting such good grades. She gave me tickets to see Digital Underground in concert. My brother Dean came home for the holidays from graduate school, and he and I went to the show together.

At the concert, we danced to "Humpty Dance", "No Nose Job", "Kiss You Back", and other hits by Digital Underground. I met a rapper named Tony Tee backstage. He opened up for Digital Underground that night with a little freestyle. He could rap, he had game, and I was down.

"Shawty, how old are you?" Tony Tee licked his lips as he stared me up and down.

"I'm old enough." I arched my back to poke out my chest so he could see my cleavage.

"I see." His eyes danced with mine, and then immediately bounced to my breasts and down to my exposed belly ring and tattoo right above my navel that said "Bad Girl". I had dyed my hair honey blonde all over and was attracting oodles of attention at the concert. Between my hair and my hazel eyes, and my body—BOOM! It was on and popping!

"Sis, you don't need to get caught up with a dude like Tony Tee. He's a dope rapper, but he's out there!" Dean warned me as we were leaving the concert. I ignored him and locked in Tony Tee's number in my cellphone.

What did he know? My brother was a geek. He was one of those types of dudes who was handsome but didn't know it until later in life. Clueless when it came to women coming on to him, and easily gave in, which was why he and Patricia kept breaking up; he didn't know how to tell other girls "no." Dean Jr. wore his heart on his sleeves and often fell hard for girls, but me? I knew how to play the game, and pick and choose who I would be with and who I wouldn't. I turned down plenty of guys, and I didn't consider myself a flunky like Dean was. If anything, I had the dudes coming for me. I didn't go after them. Kay-Kay would always say your brother is cute. Pah-lease! Dean Jr. was weak.

[*Wow, I didn't know that about Dean Jr. He is going to be mad with you. I agree that Dean is a fine brother. He's tall, dark, and handsome like his father. Smart and a little geeky, but it's kind of cute to me. I had a serious crush on Dean growing up, but he was your brother, and he had a girlfriend, so I had to respect that.*]

Tony Tee called me about a week later and we talked on the phone for hours. I realized that if we ever took it there, it would have been an unnecessary accessory to our friendship, so we remained friends. We continued to kick it at the clubs, he taught me how to ride a motorcycle, and sometimes we would chill at his house and watch movies. Next thing I knew, our faces started showing up in the magazines together like we were a couple. I milked the publicity of course!

Tony Tee was such a cool guy in the industry, and respected by many. He knew everybody from the west coast to the east coast, and he knew about me and Zeek. Tony Tee didn't care about my past, and I liked that he never judged me like the rest. Tony was sweet. He was the light in the room when everything around you felt gloomy. He had a boyish look that made him look like a teenager, although he was twenty-one. His rap music reached many people because he rapped about everything from growing up poor in Chicago to being homeless when he moved to California. He spit his life story on his tracks, and that was why he sold so many records; why women were after him, too. Tony was kindhearted, and he really cared about people. I knew we were just friends, but when people asked, I would say, "We're in love and we're an item." I just wanted to make all the other girls jealous. It was one of those situations where the publicity worked for me, and although we were just friends I didn't want to see him with anybody else. Eventually, my involvement with Tony Tee made my parents want to meet him.

[*That still amazes me how much the press ate that up when you guys were just friends. You played that one up hard, and showed your acting skills,* Kay-Kay laughed to herself.]

Dad lit into Tony Tee like a Christmas tree during their first meeting, and Mom followed suit, with grilling him with one question after another. They assumed by the way he dressed, with his pants sagging, tattoos all over his body, and lots of jewelry around his neck, that he was just another thug. Tony Tee proved them wrong.

"All I'm saying is, why y'all judging me 'cause I'm a rapper? I can't help what my profession is," Tony was arguing with Mom and Dad. It took several visits before they would ever get used to Tony or even like him. They were always debating about stuff, but eventually my parents admitted there was something special about Tony that they actually liked. I believe it was Tony's intelligence that won Dad over, and Mom was attracted to Tony's caring spirit for the disenfranchised. Tony and Mom actually connected when it came to helping the poor, since both of them were raised in the hood.

Tony insisted on paying for my senior prom and senior class trip to Jamaica. He also paid for my senior fees, class ring, and senior pictures. I remember *Right On! Magazine* had us on the cover, and one of the quotes said, "Rapper Tony Tee interrupts his tour to take his girlfriend, actress Tracey Michaels, to her prom". I was hung up on the part that said "Actress" more than anything else.

By summer, I graduated from The Carter Academy with honors. My family was so proud. I still remember the choir singing Boyz II Men's *End of the Road*. I was happy to be leaving The Carter Academy, though. I always felt ready to jump out in the world and explore, while my classmates feared what the future would hold. I was ready to embrace the unknown. The only thing about my graduation day that I missed was Tony Tee not being there, and Jet saying he was sick and couldn't make it. My whole family was there, including my grandparents on both sides of the family; Jet's mother came, but he was a no show. When I got home, I saw a red convertible Mercedes Benz, my favorite color. I swallowed my hurt and easily forgave Jet for not being there.

After graduating, I pursued my acting career full-time. My parents wanted me to go college, but acting took precedence over school. My parents didn't press the issue, but tried to support my goal.

"Just try to get some real acting roles that will showcase your talent and don't require you to take your clothes off," my parents insisted, referring to all the videos I was in, and the low budget films that would insinuate nudity. Once I had turned eighteen, it seemed like every director wanted me to show my body or do something sexual.

Nonetheless, I listened to my parents and decided not to accept those types of gigs anymore. It meant less money, so I hustled harder for as many gigs as I could to compensate for my high maintenance lifestyle.

I got a break later that summer, and landed a recurring role on the soap opera *Young & the Restless*. I played one of the main character's long lost sisters who was in and out of trouble. Art imitates life, and I played the role well, I must admit.

[*You failed to mention that I was the one who told you about the part, because I was hired as a stylist in one of the studios across the lot from CBS. I heard about the role from a friend. I told you to come and audition. When you got the gig we went out to celebrate. Girl, you are a trip! I don't know why you didn't mention that?* Kay-Kay shook her head in dismay.]

While taking a break from the set one day, Kay-Kay told me to check out this dope rapper who was cute and had mad rapping skills. She said his name was B-Money and he was from New York. He had moved to LA to pursue a music career. Kay-Kay was the hairstylist for B-Money's video shoot. (Girlfriend was rocking it in those days!) Anyway, I decided to check out the video, since it was across the lot from my studio. I saw this light-skinned guy with his hair cut close and a cute mustache and goatee, rapping hard on the mike while the cameras followed him back and forth on a premade stage for his video. His pants were sagging, and he wore a *Gucci* belt with a white T-shirt, with a matching jean jacket. At one point in his video performance, he pulled his jacket off. Both arms were filled with tattoo sleeves. The chains around his neck were long enough to jump rope with, and his diamond earrings nearly blinded you. Kay-Kay introduced me to this young man, who said his name was Bruce "B-Money" Benjamin. The half-Puerto Rican and half-black young man was indeed a cutie, but he was the quintessential thug that dad warned me to stay away from.

"I'm glad to finally meet you, Tracey. I been seeing you on TV and in videos and whatnot. You dope Ma, word up!" I could hear his New York accent coming out.

"Thank you," I blushed, twirled my hair around my finger.

He gritted his teeth. "Yeah, so uhm, you still messing with old boy."

"Who?"

"Zeek."

"No, he's old news."

"What about my man from Chi-town, Tony Tee?"

I shook my head. "No, he's my best friend."

Bruce stared me up and down while swirling a lollipop around his mouth.

"You single?"

"What do you think?"

"Don't play games with me, Ma, answer the question." It seemed like he was trying too hard to be tough, which was common with some of the pretty boys I've met through the years. It's like they're trying to overcompensate for being pretty, so they won't get "punked" if you come for them.

"I'm single," I replied, and Bruce kept staring at me with his eyes half-closed, and I didn't know if he was high or if he thought it was sexy to gawk at me like that. He reached for my hand, stroked it, and then kissed the back of it.

"Beautiful hands, Ma. You got your nails done and everything. They so soft," he kissed it again. That's when I heard someone clearing their throat loud, and I looked over my shoulder and saw a young woman sitting in one of the director chairs giving me the evil eye, and gritting on me.

"Guess that's my hint," Bruce chuckled. "I'll check you later, Ma."

"Oh snap! That's his girl?" Kay-Kay covered her mouth, feeling embarrassed. "Sorry Tracey, I didn't know she was his girlfriend. I thought she was one of the directors."

"That's all right. She can sit there and chick-watch all she wants to, but Bruce is more into me than he is with her.

[*You was workin' it that day, girl, I'll give it to you. You and Bruce wanted each other. You guys put the whole set on mute. Everything in motion stopped moving just to see how you guys would react to each other. There was chemistry that's for sure.*]

That next day, who came to my studio across the lot?

"Yo, ma, I was really feeling you yesterday, know what I'm saying?" Bruce approached me as I was reading over my lines.

"I brought you some roses, Ma," Bruce handed me a dozen red roses, attracting attention from my fellow cast members who offered to put the roses in a vase for me.

"Thank you," I blushed. "Why do you keep calling me Ma?"

"Because that's what you're going to be one day, my baby mother, know what I'm saying?"

I shook my head thinking he couldn't be serious.

"So check it, we going out this Friday at eight o'clock. Write your number and address down on this piece of paper." Bruce was straightforward, with no cut cards, and I actually liked that he was straight up about what he wanted. I didn't want to seem like an easy catch though.

"Say please." I raised one eyebrow flirtatiously and crossed one leg over the other.

He smirked. "I don't beg, but I plan to have *you* begging."

"Is that right?"

"Better believe it. You're gonna be my wife and my baby mama, know what I'm saying? You will have my last name and carry my seed as fine as you are."

"I've heard those weak lines before," I crossed my arms. "Tell me something new and maybe I'll be impressed."

"I'm telling you the truth girl. I'm going to marry you. Now here, write your number down cuz' I have to bounce."

I laughed at his cockiness, but I liked that he wasn't ready to give up and he bought me roses. "Here."

"Yeah baby!" he smiled at the piece of paper like he had just won a prize.

"So, how will your horse-faced girlfriend feel about you hitting on me like this?"

"Are you worried?"

I sucked my teeth and threw my nose in the air. "No, but I don't share."

He cracked a smile. I guess he liked that I was just as blunt as he was.

"I'll handle her, you just be ready for our date."

As he was walking away I said, "I'm the one who should be in your video anyway. I look better than those chicks you picked to be in your video. Besides, I'm a professional actress. People know me and my work."

He turned around, glared me up and down. "All right, I'll make you the main character, while the other chicks can pole dance or something."

"When do I start?"

After I finished taping, I went to the video set where B-Money wanted us to do a bedroom scene together right off the break. That's when I put my tongue in his mouth—*not written in the script,* but I did it to make his girlfriend jealous. B-Money's girlfriend jumped out of the director's chair and came at me. We went for blows. I guess she thought my hair was fake because she kept trying to yank it off my scalp while I was punching to get her off of me. Kay-Kay must have heard the commotion; she came running out of one of the trailers to help me beat this manly woman down. She saw me struggling to get the big heifer off me so she jumped in and took over. That's how we rolled.

[*Girl, that chick was beating the crap out of you! It had to take more than one person to handle her. She was hella' strong! Swinging you around like a feather in thin air. I remember your head was bleeding when the fight was finally over with, and you lost a few chunks of hair. Let's see...I don't see that part either.*]

"Man, y'all chicks are gangsters! I like that," B-Money said to us, smoking a blunt and blowing the smoke into the thin air. Never once did he try to break up the fight, now that I'm looking back on things. He and his boys just watched the whole time. B-Money didn't even see if his girl was okay.

"Girl, this winch is pressing charges against us. Did you get a subpoena to court? This girl is trippin', but I'll see if my parents can get us out of this," Kay-Kay told me by phone. We went to court, and the judge ordered me and Kay-Kay to serve forty hours of community service for the assault against Bruce's girlfriend. Thanks to Kay's parents we got a smack on the hand for what we did. While we served our time sweeping the streets of downtown Hollywood, I saw a newspaper on the ground that said, 'Judge Orders Up-and-Coming Actress, Tracey Michaels, to Forty-Hours of Community Service.'- Celebrity Times Newspaper. That's all it took for me to lose my job. I walked on the set the next day, and there was already another girl playing my part. I was so pissed! I tried hard to get another gig, but nobody wanted a troublemaker. That was the reputation that I had built for myself. I was Hollywood's bad girl in the worst way. From that point on, my life began to spiral downhill, while things were looking up for Kay-Kay. She moved out of her parents' house and bought a condo in the Franklin Towers on Franklin Avenue, not too far from Hollywood Blvd. She let her rapper boyfriend, Rock move in with her. (Kay-Kay had met Rock through our homey, Tony Tee.) Anyway, Rock gave Kay-Kay money to open her own spa and hair salon on Melrose Avenue. To keep some income coming in to pay my bills, I worked as a receptionist for Kay-Kay. My parents had already warned me that I was walking a fine line, and if I couldn't keep my career going or go to college, then I would have to leave. I had to find a way to make my own money somehow. Shoot, by then, my parents had cut off my allowance money since I was grown.

I gave Bruce an ultimatum; it was either his Director girlfriend or me. Bruce called one night and said, "Hey Boo, I told the trick it was quits, so it's me and you from now on." She got mad and told all the Hip-Hop presses that I stole her man. I didn't steal Bruce, he chose me.

"Yo' ma, come on tour with me!" Bruce kept begging me to join him on the road with his entourage. Truthfully, I finally gave in because I was bored. Like I said before, I hated being alone and having nothing to do. I wasn't getting any gigs because of the assault incident, and I was bored with answering the phones at Kay-Kay's salon spa. Kay-Kay had a career and a man, and we were spending little time together anyway. Against my parents' wishes, I packed my bags and hit the road.

While on tour, Rock was cheating on Kay-Kay the whole time. Every night he was taking a different girl to his hotel room. Bruce told me to mind my business and not say anything, but Kay-Kay was my best friend. We were like sisters. When I got back I had to break it down to her easy. She dumped Rock, and he blamed me. From then on when Rock and I would bump into each other he wouldn't speak to me. Eventually Kay-Kay took him back, and they ended up having a child together, a baby girl name Jazmine who is my precious goddaughter.

[Bruce was a dog too, so I hope you included that part, since you putting all of my business out there!]

We partied nonstop on the tour! We hit up every club, restaurant and bar in every city it seemed. When it rained we partied in the hotel rooms. We got high; we danced around the room, trashed the rooms, and got kicked out of many hotels for loud noise. I did get to know Bruce a little

37

bit better in between the partying, and especially when Bruce was high. He basically told me his life story. He had not only moved to Cali to pursue a music career, but he and his father didn't get along. He moved to Inglewood with his Puerto Rican mother and left his African American father back in the El Barrio community of East Harlem a.k.a. Hell's Kitchen. He told me his parents met when his father was in the military and stationed in California. They married and moved to New York, (his father's hometown). When his parents divorced when he was fifteen, Bruce's mother moved back to Inglewood. Bruce stayed in Harlem with his dad, while his two sisters moved to Inglewood with his mother. After his parents divorced, Bruce was between homes, from West Coast to East Coast because of visitation rights. He said he and his father stopped getting along so his dad basically kicked him out. Bruce claimed he had no money, and panhandled his way to California. Seriously? Yeah, right! That must have been the high talking. Anyway, I did feel a connection to Bruce. I think between the drugs, alcohol, and the sex we had on the road, I thought I was in love with him.

I met Bruce's mother right after the tour. "Ma-Ma, this is Tracey," he introduced us, barging into her house without a hello. "I'm going to marry Tracey one day." She laughed. She didn't know English well, but I'm sure she knew *that* was a joke. Bruce and I kept the lifestyle of partying at the clubs, shopping, going out to eat, and having fun for the rest of that summer. We had late nights out, and slept in all morning. I would sleep in so late that I would miss the few auditions my agent managed to find for me. After a while, I started ignoring my agent's phone calls. I would stare at my phone with the side eye when I saw her name pop-up on my caller ID and say to myself, "Winch, pah-lease." I was partied out most days, and too tired and hung-over to do anything for myself. Without noticing it, I was losing control of the game. My life began to evolve around Bruce and whatever he wanted to do. I was falling head over heels in love with Bruce, or so I thought. Looking back, I was more in love with his bad boy image, money, and fame. I loved his street credibility, and his toughness, and how he didn't take crap off nobody. People started calling us the Bonnie and Clyde of hip-hop, because I started acting just like him by being defiant, rude, and volatile. Profanity became my second language. I was arrogant, and treated service people rude by not leaving tips and being demanding. If I did go on an audition and didn't get the part, I cursed out the casting directors, gave them the "middle" finger, and spat at them. I was digging a deeper hole for myself.

[*Yes Bruce was definitely changing you for the worse. I tried to tell you he was going to ruin your career, but you accused me of being jealous so I left it alone. We didn't have much dialogue after that. I think we spoke sporadically during those times.*]

For me, Bruce defined what a man was. He had a pretty face, but a thug life mentality. Of course I would learn better later on, but it would take a long time to get there. Yet, I found myself attracted to the same rebellious type of guys over and over again.

[*Girl, you were a hot mess! I lived it with you, but I had my limits. Even still, I would not have put my business out there like this. Anyway, I'm going to bed. I'll read the rest tomorrow.*]

CHAPTER FOUR
BRUCE

"Yo man, what're you reading?" asked Bruce's cellmate Tommy.

"None of your business."

"You don't have to get ugly with me. It's just a question, homey."

"Like I said, mind your business, all right? No sense in making friends when I'm out this joint in thirty days, know what I'm saying? I wouldn't even be here if I didn't violate my parole."

Tommy laughed. "If you stop smoking them La-La's, your pee won't be dirty." Bruce gave Tommy the evil eye and turned his attention back to Tracey's book, *Riding the Waves.* It was true that he had been arrested again for having THC show up during his urine test with his parole officer. He knew he could easily get through thirty days though. Having been in and out of jail most of his life, serving thirty days was like serving three days.

"Now," Bruce sighed, resting his head against the tiny flat pillow on the lower bunk. "Where was I?"

My parents went on vacation at a dream resort in Belize, and they sent my six-year-old brother, Devin to stay with Aunt Peaches and her husband George. By then, Aunt Peaches and George were preparing to move to Chicago. Aunt Peaches was doing well as V.P. for the Freedom for Frieda Foundation. She was also a community activist, public speaker and drug counselor, and was making good money off of her series of self-help books. Yet, she always made time for family, so keeping Devin was not a problem. Anyway, my parents knew I wasn't home enough to be responsible to watch Devin, and they didn't trust me with him for that long. I had the whole house to myself and loved it. No parents breathing down my neck or a nagging little brother begging me to play with him. I came home whenever I wanted without being questioned about my whereabouts, and I let Bruce stay over every night. [*It would have been nice if you put in here what we did every day in the house.*].

Bruce came up with a so-called bright idea to throw a pool party. My backyard was packed with people, most of them I didn't even know.

Some people were in the pool, some were inside the house playing games in our entertainment room, and some in guest rooms. There was food, drinks, drugs, and alcohol everywhere. It was a madhouse, and I have to admit I felt a little nervous about so many people in the house.

[*I remember that party; it was dope.* Bruce cracked a smile.]

"You think Bruce invited too many people?" I asked Kay-Kay, as we sipped our drinks. Bruce paid for everything.

[*Yep, I sure did. I was a baller!*]

"Yeah, I think so, but how can we get them to leave?"

"I don't know," I shrugged.

About two hours into the party, we were all having a good, uninterrupted time, and then...

"What the hell is going on here? Y'all better get out of my house and my pool right now!"

I turned around, and nearly dropped my drinks. My mouth dropped and suddenly I felt like I couldn't move. My body froze in shock.

"Y'all got about ten seconds to get the hell out of my pool!" Dad waved his gun in the air, and people started jumping out of the pool and running to their cars. I was so surprised to see my parents back home so soon. I would find out later that they came back early because of a severe hurricane threat.

"Dean, please, please, put that thing away!" Mom cried. She wanted us out, but she didn't want Dad to *shoot* everybody out.

"You need to put that heat away, homes," Bruce said, talking slow. He was high as a kite. He slowly rose from the poolside chair and tried to tighten the towel around his waist. Because he was high, his hands weren't steady, so the towel fell to the ground. Bruce chuckled. I wasn't sure if he was embarrassed at first when he laughed, but I know I was.

"Bruce you dropped your towel," Kay-Kay picked it up and handed it to him. I couldn't move. I was so scared of what my parents were going to do next.

"To hell with the towel, I don't need it!" Bruce tossed it in the pool. My parents were still standing on the opposite side of the pool near the entrance to the house, watching Bruce's every move. Everyone else had rolled out, including the people who were inside the house.

"Ms. Cat, do you like what you see?" Bruce winked. Dad, who used to be a track star, literally jumped across the pool and tackled Bruce to the ground. We were all screaming as they fought.

"I'm calling the cops!" Kay-Kay tried to run inside the house, but Mom stopped her.

"No, don't! We can settle this ourselves!" My mother didn't want the bad press.

"Daddy, please stop, he's bleeding!" I cried.

"Get out!" Dad pointed to the back gate.

"Yeah I got your number, jack! You's a dead man!" Bruce shouted, pointing his finger as he slipped his swimming trunks on. "A dead man and I mean it!"

"You don't threaten me, boy!" Dad grabbed Bruce by the throat and slung him down to the ground.

"Dean, please stop, he's had enough!" Mom rushed over.

Dad got off of Bruce, who staggered to his feet.

"Are you going to be all right?" I helped Bruce get dressed, and Kay-Kay and I walked him to his car.

"Yeah, get out my way!"

"I'm sorry this happened." I found myself apologizing for something that wasn't my fault. I just felt so bad for Bruce, because Dad had really did him in.

My parents had it out with me so bad that my ears were ringing from them shouting. My Dad whooped me. This time was worse than the last and he said to Kay-Kay, "If you don't want your butt whipped too then I suggest you leave right now!"

I was screaming and crying so loud that my mother came into the room and pulled Dean off me.

"That's enough!" she cried. "We will not handle her like this! This is abusive, and I won't have it!" Looking back, I think the whipping reminded Mom of when Mason would abuse her. She was actually mad with my dad for a few days afterwards. She told him he shouldn't have whipped me so hard. Silence reigned over our house for about a week. Everyone was torn by what had happened. Mom broke her silence during breakfast one morning and said, "We need to see a family therapist." I thought *what a joke!*

[*Yeah, that is funny. Freakin' black Brady Bunch family seeking a therapist. Get outta here with that bourgeois mess!*]

* * *

The therapist's name was Michelle Larue. I didn't talk much at first. In fact, my mother did most of the talking for both me and Dad. As we continued to meet every Wednesday evening, somehow the therapist got me and Dad to open up. Dad admitted that he wanted me to move out. Mom wanted to give me one last chance to act right.

Devin wanted the arguing to stop and said, "My sister makes Mommy and Daddy sad." I remember it because it hurt my feelings. I felt like an outcast in my own house, like it was three against one.

"Thank you so much for being willing to share what has been going on with your family," Ms. Larue said during our final session. "Connie, I totally understand how you feel about Tracey," she began. "I am a mother as well. You have set standards for Tracey and rules that you expect for her to follow." Mom smiled, feeling good that Ms. Larue seemed to take her side. She crossed one leg over the other and threw her nose snobbishly in the air, as if to say *I told you so*.

"However, I do feel that you set the bar a little too high for Tracey."

Mom shifted her weight in her seat next to Dad. "Excuse me?"

"What I'm trying to say is, you and your sister were once like Tracey—a little wild and edgy, and now that Tracey is behaving the same way, you expect her to act differently. Sometimes wild oats are partly inherited."

"I expect Tracey not to repeat the same mistakes my sister and I made. I expect Tracey to use her head instead of what's in between her legs to succeed," Mom contested. "Do you know how embarrassing it is for me when people are whispering behind my back that my daughter is a tramp? You have no idea how that makes me feel."

"I understand," Ms. Larue nodded. "You have every right to feel hurt, but what I'm saying is that sometimes we can want so much for our children that we can push a little too hard. Now despite what you and your sister went through, Tracey never lived your life. She doesn't know what it's like to grow up and not have, because she was basically born into fame and fortune," Ms. Larue explained. "The problem I see with many children with celebrity parents is a struggle for them to find out who they really are. *You* know who Connie is and what Connie wants because you experienced the journey, but Tracey has not. She is still young and she is trying to find her own way while doing so under the Hollywood spotlight.

"And Tracey, while I understand that you're trying to find yourself, I do agree with your parents; you're going about it the *wrong* way. You have to realize the pain and hurt you're causing them. Being young is not an excuse for rebellion. I have read about you in many magazines, and it is truly sad. I have witnessed the talent you have as an actress, but you would rather do things for shock-value so you can get attention. In retrospect, what you're doing is crying for more love and personal attention. Do you feel like you're not getting it?"

"I don't do things to get attention because I don't care what other people think." I folded my arms and rolled my eyes to the ceiling.

"That is what you want to believe, but you're just putting on an act, and you're really good at it." Ms. Larue was laying into me. "Tell me this, what are you going to do when Hollywood moves on to the next young brood that are performing more dramatic and shocking things for the public than you?" I had no answers, so she continued. "You see, Hollywood is a place that forgets easily, but doesn't forgive easily.

"Now is the time to learn how to be Tracey Michaels. The *real* Tracey Michaels, whose mother and father raised her better than this role she's playing. Isn't that what you mean?" she asked Mom.

"That's what I mean, and maybe I have been too hard on her, but you're right I just know she can be better than the person she is right now," Mom admitted.

"That's what my wife and I have been trying to tell her," Dad chimed in.

"What you guys need to work on as a family is being united," Ms. Larue stated. "Being a united family means that you come together more often to share a common purpose. That purpose is to encourage in love by expressing affection, sharing feelings, and doing what will make the other person happy. You also have to have mutual respect."

"We know that," Dad chuckled bitterly. "But Tracey doesn't respect anyone, not even herself."

"Seriously, Dad?" I shot him a bitter look. "You guys don't respect *me,* so I don't respect you!"

"Now wait a minute, Tracey." Ms. Larue held up her hand. "Respect is not handed out like condiments; you have to earn it. Your parents brought *you* into this world, not the other way around. You're eighteen going on nineteen, and technically you can find your own place to live.

Just remember, even if you move out, you'll have to listen to somebody." Ms. Larue went on and on and then offered suggestions for us to do more as a family.

After seeing the family therapist, my mother tried to talk to me more often. We would go shopping together, get our hair done together, and do all the girlie pampering things that we liked. Yet, I still couldn't relate to her sometimes. I always felt inferior and inadequate when I was around her, like I didn't measure up to her standards. She was a very classy lady, smart, dignified, and a little conceited if you ask me. I often questioned how I measured up.

[*A little conceited? Conceited should be her first name. I can't stand her guts for what she did to me. If you look up 'bitch' in the dictionary, her face would be next to it! She ruined my career!*]

My mother did everything she could to try to bond with me, but I still felt there was a disconnect between us. Maybe it was in the way she corrected me when I talked because I talk really fast, and back then I used a lot of slang too. Perhaps it was something about the way she challenged my thought process, as if every feeling or expression I had was wrong, instead of just asking me why I felt a certain way about things. As giving as my mother was, at times she was selfish when it came to putting forth an effort to understanding *me* and actually talks *with* me without making me feel like one of her artists or clients. I didn't work for her, but she made me feel that way. For example, when I would tell my mother I needed to talk, she would put it on her calendar. She wouldn't drop what she was doing to listen to me, and I had to wait in line like everybody else. When we would talk, sometimes I just wanted her to listen and *feel* what I was saying. Instead, she was always teaching and preaching, instead of accepting the fact that we were having a conversation and nothing more. I didn't have to be told everything. For some reason my mother felt like she had to dot every *i* and cross every *t*, as if what she told me would stop me from discovering things on my own. I felt Aunt Peaches always kept it real with me more than my mother. She talked to me on my level, and she always listened without judgment. I often went to her about my relationships because I knew my mother would be quick to say something like, "He's a jerk! Get rid of him!" without considering the emotional attachments I might have to the person. I could go and on, but I don't want to throw my mother under a bus. I just had to remember that she lost her mother when she was a teenager. That was a time when most girls needed their mother for guidance and love. My mother didn't have that; she had to take care of herself. I know I wasn't the perfect daughter that a mother wished for and she wasn't the perfect mom, but at the end of the day we loved each other unconditionally, and that's what mattered most.

My family and I tried to put together the pieces to make our relationship better. Some days were better than others, but we were trying. We went on a three week vacation that included: Greece, Italy, and France. I loved it! That was the best part of the summer for me. Once we returned home, my parents were busy again, and they tried to keep me occupied too, by giving me responsibilities around the house. I also had to look after Devin. Every day my parents left me with some of kind of "to-do-list" and it was irritating me. I felt they should have hired help full-time. I wasn't the help. I was already wishing we were still on vacation, and that I didn't have to do the tedious crap assigned to me. For instance, I had to take my parents' clothes to the drycleaners, the cars to the car wash, and the dogs to get groomed. Another part of my responsibility was to pick up Devin from summer camp day every day. I had been doing pretty well with looking after my little brother until…

"Oh shoot, what time is it?" I woke up next to Bruce in his bed. Bruce had been banned from our property, and my parents resented the fact that we were still seeing each other. Anytime we wanted to be together, I had to go to his house. Despite how my parents felt about Bruce, his approval meant more to me than theirs. (My message to young girls is: If your parents don't approve of your boyfriend, please don't ignore them. That's a red flag! Listen to your parents, they know better. Trust me!).

I hurried and got dressed and sped the entire way home. When I got to the house, I spotted Devin peeping through the curtains from the den. When I walked in, he ran to the door to meet me.

"You're going to get it, Tracey!"

"Where's Mom and Dad?"

"In the living room," he pointed. He was "snaggle-toothed" now, with two missing teeth in the front of his mouth. Seeing his innocence made me feel bad for forgetting to pick him up. I walked down the hall to the living room with my head hung low. My parents were sitting on the sofa, and when I walked in, their eyes fixed on me. Mom's face was beet red, and her eyes were filled with tears. Dad was clenching his fists and drumming his feet against the floor. He started cracking his knuckles as I began to speak.

"Before you guys say anything, I just want to apologize." I spoke carefully, shoving my hands in the pockets on my shorts. "I'm sorry, I just completely forgot. I lost track of time."

"You're always sorry, aren't you, Tracey?" Mom stood up in my face. We're the same height, but her heels made her taller. "Well that's not good enough anymore!"

"You don't have to yell, I said I was sorry," I countered. "This was the only time I forgot to pick him up. I made a mistake, and I'm sorry."

"It's not a mistake!" Mom barked. "It's almost eight o'clock, and Devin was supposed to be picked up by six. What happened to you Tracey?!" Mom ranted. "I bet you were with Bruce doing only God knows what!

"The camp called us while we were in the middle of an important meeting, we thought something happened. We were worried about you and we were scared for Devin. Can't you see that? Can't you step outside of your own selfishness for once and see this was not a *mistake*!"

"Maybe I should lie on the altar and let you sacrifice my soul, then seeking your forgiveness would be good enough, wouldn't it, Mom?"

SMACK.

"Don't you dare speak to me that way! You have lost your mind, girl!"

I held the side of my cheek in shock.

"You gotta go," Dad abruptly stood up from the sofa.

"Yeah, get out!" Devin shouted.

"Devin, go to the game room and play. This is between us," Dad told him, and he took off running down the hall.

I was still rubbing the sting out my cheek when I questioned dad. "Did you say I have to leave? The last I checked, this was my mother's house, not yours."

"This is my house too. My name is on it, and if I say you need to go, it's time for you to go!"

"You're not my father!"

"Oh, so all of a sudden I'm *not* your father?" he argued. "Well guess what? I may not be your blood father, but I'm more of a father to you than Jet will ever be."

"My mother makes the money and you just live off her like everybody else. You don't do anything but that stupid personal training stuff. At least my father makes his own money."

Dad lost it. He tried to smack me, but I ducked just in time.

"Dean, don't! That's enough! She's had enough!"

"You're ungrateful, Tracey. You don't know half of what I've done for you. I may not have the money that Jet has, but I use what I got to take care of you. What's his excuse? It's my money that goes into this house just as much as your mother's. It's my money that pays your car insurance, phone bills, and credit cards because you don't have a job right now. It's my money that pays for your agent. An agent whose phone calls you ignore. So don't act like my money doesn't contribute to you or this family. Furthermore, besides money, I'm the one who is always there for you when your father isn't. I never missed any important events in your life, starting with your graduation. Now ask yourself, where was Jet on your graduation day?"

"He was sick!" I snapped.

"You think that was the truth?"

"Dean, don't go there, please don't talk about that," Mom intervened.

"No, let me tell Tracey the truth, since she thinks she knows *everything,*" his voice deepened. "I got news for you, baby girl." Dean pointed his finger at me. "Your father always claimed he was sick whenever you asked him to come to your graduation, school events, or whatever else was important to you, but he was never sick. He just didn't care to be there. He had you fooled because he's good at pretending, and you know what? The apple doesn't fall far from the tree, because you're good at putting on an act too."

I sucked my teeth. "Whatever!"

"Your mother didn't want me to tell you this, but on your graduation day, your father was four hours away in Las Vegas, gambling!"

"No he wasn't. He was sick!"

"Your father was in Las Vegas. As a matter of fact, he bought a second home there. He's a gambler. He is so addicted that he's about to

48

lose his wife and kids. Oh, and let's not forget all the extramarital affairs he's having. Jet is a loser who only cares about himself. He left your mother holding the baby bags for you while he ran off to college. *You* never mattered to him, but ever since your mother and I started dating you mattered to me," I could hear his voice cracking and I knew I hurt Dean.

"Even when Connie and I broke up, I still sent you birthday and Christmas presents, because I loved you that much. I knew I established a relationship with you, and despite what happened between me and your mother, I felt like you was my daughter." Dean blinked back tears. His mouth parted to say more, but he waved me off, and stormed out of the living room, deciding I wasn't worth another word.

"Mom, I'm–"

"No!" Mom held up her hand to cut me off. She walked away from me and reached for her Coach bag that was sitting on the sofa. "Keep your apology, Tracey. I'm sick of hearing you say you're sorry. It doesn't even sound believable anymore." She sniffed and wiped the small tears from her eyes. "You really hurt us this time. Here." She walked towards me with a check in her hand.

"What's this?" I took the check from her, and I could see it was already prewritten in my name in the amount of fifty thousand dollars.

"That was money we set aside for you to go to college, but you never went."

As I stared at the check, guilt came over me. "But Mom, I–"

"Just go, Tracey. What you do with your life is on you from now on."

[*That's a lot of cheese right there. Shoot, when I left my father's crib in New York, I had nothing but the clothes on my back when he kicked me out, know what I'm saying? I wish somebody gave me that kind of loot!*].

"You once said you would never kick your own family out on the streets, because Grandma did that to Aunt Peaches."

"I was a child back then, Tracey," Mom retorted. "I didn't understand. Now I know that patience eventually runs out. There are no more chances for you here. You are ungrateful and disrespectful, and we will not tolerate it anymore."

I bit down on my bottom lip, hung my head low, and shoved the check into my pocket. "If this is what you want...to see me out on the streets…maybe end up a drug addict or a prostitute, I will go." I slowly walked out the living room, trying to allow enough time for Mom to change her mind, but she never did. While upstairs packing, I called Aunt Peaches. (She and Uncle George had finally moved back to Chicago.) I explained everything that happened to Aunt Peaches, hoping she would understand once again.

"Girl, you better get off my phone with this mess. It's time for you to grow up and leave them hoodlums alone!"

"But Aunt Peaches–"

"Child bye. Don't try to win no Oscar from me, because I can't be sold on the drama. You're on your own with this one, girl."

CLICK.

I stared at the phone. I couldn't believe my Aunt hung up on me.

[*That's funny! I'm dying laughing up here! I mess with Peaches like that. Once a crackhead, always a crackhead. She was funny though. Cool peoples, with her watermelon head self. How does her body hold up that head? Does crack make your head big and your body shrink? I'm just saying.*]

I stayed with Bruce at his place for about a week, but I didn't like how he allowed his friends to come over whenever they wanted to. Bruce's house was in Hollywood Hills on Canyon Drive. It was way up the hills past the famous Hollywood sign. He paid good money to lease the house, but it was small, with only three bedrooms. I didn't like it at all. The best view was outside of the house, where you could see the whole city and the mountains in the distance. Inside felt like a closed-in cave. I was used to living in my parent's mansion with lots of space. I couldn't take Bruce's house anymore, so I reached out to Jet to ask him for money. It took weeks for him to call me back. I felt like I was going crazy living in a house filled with guys doing whatever they wanted with whomever they wanted, because Bruce allowed it. We barely had any privacy. I remember one of his boys walked in on us, and that was the last straw! When Jet finally called me back, I blasted him out about lying to me all those years claiming to be sick when he never came to my graduations, award ceremonies, and birthday parties, nothing. It really did hurt that he didn't show up, but I used that pain to get what I wanted from him by making him feel guilty. He ended up signing a lease for me at the Wilshire Luxury Apartments in Beverly Hills, and he put down enough money to cover one whole year's rent.

"You're on your own after this," Jet declared to me once he left my new apartment. I guess that was his way of saying he didn't owe me anything else, as if all I wanted was his money. I decided not to put up a fuss. I watched him leave my apartment without a loving goodbye. He didn't wish me well, nor ask if I needed anything else. He just left.

It felt good living in the Wilshire, and being away from the chaos at Bruce's house. During the 90s, celebrities like Drew Barrymore, Whoopi Goldberg, and Samuel L. Jackson were my neighbors. I only saw them occasionally though. Unlike me, they were "A" list actors, and I was on the "B" list. B-list actors didn't make millions; we were recognized for our years in the business, but not for doing good quality work that anyone could really remember. We didn't have any starring roles, and were lucky to be a supporting actor if the opportunity presented itself. I didn't know how I was going to make it with sporadic acting gigs, and an agent who had quit when the payments stopped coming from my dad. People don't realize it, but when you're an actor, you don't even get paid right away. It takes a few months before you receive your first paycheck. So as the gigs came every so often, that was how infrequently I got paid. It was different with music videos, though; you got paid within a few weeks from the record companies. But I didn't feel comfortable going back to dancing in videos, especially when I found out I was pregnant!

When Bruce came back from his European tour, he moved in with me. Almost immediately after he moved in, he proposed. I was ecstatic. I thought to myself, *I finally get to be a wife and a mom.*

"It's time for me to do things right for a change, know what I'm saying?" Bruce slid the rock on my finger before I even said yes. He didn't get on bended knee. He didn't read a poem or say anything romantic. I just woke up one morning and he announced it. "We're getting married." I had no say so in it, but it didn't matter because I wanted to be married. I thought later that evening we would get a limo and go have a nice romantic dinner, so I made all of the arrangements. I knew Bruce wasn't a planner, so figured I would help, and he would pay for everything. It was the same way when I had that big party at my parents' house. I arranged everything and Bruce paid for everything, and then invited all his friends.

"Nah Mommy, we ain't doing all that stuff," Bruce said, and he made me cancel everything. His idea of a celebration was having his friends over for drinks and getting high. *He* got high, not me. I stopped smoking and drinking when I found out I was pregnant.

While Bruce was having a good time with his "boys", I felt so isolated and out of place that I retreated back to our bedroom. I needed someone to celebrate with, but when I called my friends all of them had prior plans, including my Kay-Kay, who had dumped Rock and was now in love with a middle-weight boxer named Damien. Reluctantly, I called my Mom. We hadn't spoken in a couple months since I had moved, but I was desperate. I needed to hear the voices of people I cared about. Despite our differences, I loved my mother, and I needed her.

"Hello?"

I gripped the phone with both hands. I was a little nervous, since me and Mom had not talked since I was kicked out of the house.

"Hey Mom it's…it's Tracey."

"How are you?" she asked flatly.

"Okay, I guess. I'm staying at the Wilshire."

"Jet told me. He wanted to know why me and your father wouldn't co-sign for it."

I tried not to get caught up in why Jet had called my parents and questioned them about not getting me an apartment. They had taken care of me all my life and Jet signing for the apartment was the least he could do. For him to even complain about it was ludicrous, I felt.

"So to what do I owe this phone call at ten o'clock at night?"

I tried to rehearse it in my mind before I said it, but then I decided to just come out with it.

"I'm pregnant, Mom. You're going to be a grandmother."

There was a long pause, and I thought for a minute the line had disconnected.

"Hello?"

"I'm here, Tracey." She heaved a long sigh. "I guess this will be breaking news on *MTV* by tomorrow."

"Mom, I don't care about the news. I was hoping you would be happy for me."

"And Bruce is the father?"

"Of course, Mom. Who else would it be?"

"I had to ask, especially the way you change boyfriends."

"Well, it's Bruce's baby, and we got engaged tonight. We're getting married."

Silence lingered again, as if someone had pressed a mute button.

"Hello?"

"I'm listening, Tracey."

"So that's it, you don't have anything to say? You're just going to be quiet when I make a statement?"

"What do you expect me to say, Tracey?"

"I was hoping *congratulations* wouldn't be a stretch."

"Pah-lease, don't hold your breath on that." I could picture her rolling those green eyes of hers behind the phone.

"Fine, at least you heard it from me before it gets out, since that's all you seem to worry about—what other people think, instead of my feelings. Well here is the news flash—Tracey Michaels and famed Rapper B-Money are engaged and expecting their first child."

"And you're so proud, aren't you?"

"Why shouldn't I be?"

"You're marrying someone you've known for only five or six months. He crashes your parents' house and exposes himself to your mother, gets into a fight with your father, he's been in and out of jail his whole life, he degrades women in his music, and you want me to wish you well? Honey, if anything, I will pray for you."

CLICK.

When she hung up on me, I cried myself to sleep. I didn't feel better when I called her like I hoped. I felt worse. I felt like she didn't care and nobody was in my corner. I truly felt alone; even with Bruce and his friends around, I felt like it was just me against the world. No one understood how I felt and no one seemed to care.

Trey Donovan Benjamin was born on May 15, 1993. My family and closest friends were there to support me, but Bruce was on tour again. When Bruce came home, he assumed I named Trey after him and immediately started calling the baby "little Bruce". I told him I named the baby Trey as part of my first name and gave him Bruce's last name, Benjamin. Bruce was upset and insisted I get a blood test simply because

I didn't name our son after him. We got a DNA test, and of course Trey was 99.9 percent likely to be his child. "I wish the baby was somebody else's!" I remember my mother saying. She couldn't stand Bruce's guts.

[*What? You need to stop lying! I got a blood test, but not because of my son's name. You buggin' out! I got the test 'cuz some other dude was claiming he smashed while I was on tour in Europe. I didn't propose to you until after the DNA test came back positive that Trey was mine. You twisted around this part of the story. Get your facts right, Ma.*]

Despite Bruce's trust issues with me, and my reservations about whether or not he would be faithful, we drove to Las Vegas and got married. The ceremony was in a small chapel. It was just Bruce and I and our two best friends. My mother-in-law Gladys watched Trey for us. With fear and uncertainty in my heart I uttered, "I do," with a huge smile to hide what I really felt inside. I was hoping once we were married our relationship would get better, and that issues of trust would be a thing of the past. I was nineteen, Bruce was twenty-two, and neither one of us knew what we were getting into.

[*You ain't lying about that! My boys tried to talk me out of it, and I should have listened! They kept telling me I was blinded by your beauty, and they were right!*]

Even though Mom felt resentment towards Bruce for getting me pregnant, she came to our apartment every week. She showed me lots of motherly tips on how to care for Trey. The one tip that stuck with me was how to hold up his diaper to keep him from peeing in my face, which he kept doing until I got it right. Mom was tickled pink. She told me how Devin used to do that to her, and Dad would laugh too.

"He's going to be very close to you when he grows up, that's what it means," she said, then burst out laughing when it happened again. I hoped she was right, because my nose was starting to turn gold.

Mom and I grew very close during that time, thanks to Trey. She called me often, bought small gifts for me and Trey, and she came over and showed me how to cook. But, as for her and Bruce, they grew more distant. Bruce was always in the studio, on tour, in the clubs, partying, doing interviews, shooting videos and just basically rarely ever home. Many days, I stared at our family portrait, wishing those smiles were real and that we were one big happy family, but it was a façade.

[*Your mother was annoying as hell! I hated when she came over acting like she was running our crib. I never came home because I knew her snobby behind would be there!*].

When Bruce would come home, Mom would have to make him sit with Trey so I could finally get some rest. He insisted he wasn't good with babies, but Mom would make Bruce sit with Trey. She would make him take Trey out in his stroller, feed him his bottle, and change his diaper. "Tracey didn't make this baby by herself, and she will not take of the baby by herself. You're going to help her," I remember Mom letting Bruce have it! I love my mother for that, because when I complained to Bruce, he wouldn't listen. He would dump everything on me. When he claimed I pushed him too hard, he would then disappear for a few days and come back when he felt like it.

For the next four years, Mom helped me to take care of Trey, while I kept trying to save my marriage to Bruce or whatever it really was. It never felt like we were married. I was only reminded that we were married when I looked at my ring or when the bills came in both our names. We never had a honeymoon, and whenever I mentioned going on a vacation, Bruce seemed to get busier. When Bruce was home, he had the same boring routine—eat, drink, screw, and sleep. I felt like I was a trophy piece when we attended celebrity events and award shows together, I clock-watched when we had sex, and I requested the building's maid service to clean up his puke whenever he got pissy drunk. I was just there, and I felt like I had let myself go just to make him happy. Whenever I complained about Bruce not spending time with me and Trey, he would take us on shopping sprees. When I discovered empty condom wrappers in his car and accused him of cheating, he bought me a mink coat and blamed it on "his boys." When I threatened to leave him, he bought me a brand new car and diamond earrings. Bruce kept me floating through life with material things. I loved every minute of the high life, but deep down, I just wanted to have a happy, loving family. Looking back on those days, each time I accepted his gifts, I was only giving him permission to mistreat me.

[*Man, whatever! Ain't nobody have time to be playing Daddy and hubby, I was out there grinding and making money to keep you and Trey fed. You weren't working! You had it made, Ma.*]

It was my dad and my brothers who would teach Trey how to play catch, ride a bicycle, fish, and do all the things that boys were supposed to do, not Bruce. I felt like a single parent. To make matters worse, I had put my career as an actress on the backburner so I could take care of my son. I was once again living in the shadows of someone else's fame. At first it was my parents, Zeek, Tony Tee, and now it was my husband. I was always *B-Money's wife,* just the same as people referred to me as *Cat Morris' daughter* or *Jet's daughter.* No one knew me as Tracey Michaels, "the Actress." I always had to be connected to someone else. It was always like, *Oh yeah; Tracey does act, doesn't she? What did she play in?* No one remembered anything I had done up to that point. I'd starred in commercials since I was a kid and my resume of small acting roles on TV-sitcoms, movies, and music videos was nearly three pages long, but nobody cared. When people stopped me for autographs, it was because I was B-Money's wife or because I was Cat Morris and Jet's daughter. Not because I was a celebrity in my own rite.

[*You should have been happy with your life. If I had everybody taking care of me and buying me anything I wanted, I wouldn't complain. You were just never satisfied. You should have been proud to be my wife and have my seed, but that wasn't good enough for you. Any woman would have died to take your place, believe that!*]

Bruce had a baby by some other chick that lived in Georgia. He already had three other children, two daughters in New York by two different women (before we got together), and one with me, Trey. I was beyond upset when I found out Bruce got some other woman pregnant, and we had our first fight. I punched him upside the head when I found out from the woman, who called me, and then faxed me the proof that the baby was Bruce's. It was all in the papers, and I was humiliated. I shredded all of his clothes, dumped his shoes in the garbage, flattened his tires, and broke his cellphone. I kicked him out, and a month later he came crawling back begging for my forgiveness.

"I promise I will be a good father to Trey, and I promise I will be a good husband to you from now on." I let him come back home, but I didn't trust him. I made him wear condoms when we had sex, I followed him to the clubs, and to the studio, I checked his new cellphone often, but Bruce still managed to find a way to creep. I would find phone numbers in his pants pockets or lipstick in his car. It never seemed to stop. To make matters worse, the mothers of his other children were constantly calling the house all hours of the night demanding child support.

"I see you ain't wanting for nothing. You living good, and taking food from my daughter's mouth!" They would shout at me on the phone, and I would get into arguments with them. I changed our phone number a few times, but they found out what it was anyway each time they went to court. When I complained to Bruce that he needed to tell his accountant to make sure his *other* children's mothers got paid, he had the nerve to get pissed off at me.

"As long as you eatin' don't be worried about what I'm doing for other people. You and Trey are my family, so I ain't worried about them skanks!"

"But Bruce, the children are still *your* responsibility. You can't just ignore them and expect them to go away. They call here harassing *me* when you're out there doing whatever you want to do," I retorted.

"Just mind your business, Ma, okay? Just mind your business and that's it!" Bruce yelled, flopping down on the sofa and lighting up a blunt. "Besides, Ma, you need to start working anyway. Bring some paper in this house. Ain't nothing wrong with you!"

"You act like I haven't been trying. I'm not just sitting around!" I fussed. "Any gigs I get require a lot of time. Who will watch Trey?"

"I told you to hire a personal assistant."

"I don't want someone else raising our son. I know what it's like not having your parents around. My mother's assistant Cheryl practically raised me while my mother worked, and I don't want that for Trey, not at this young age. I don't want to miss the important milestones in his life."

"Well if acting ain't working out, you need to do something else. Maybe get a job like normal people." He exhaled a thick film of smoke, and I stepped back because I didn't want to catch a contact high.

"A normal job cannot maintain our lifestyle."

"If you stop shopping the way you do, it can. You don't need a purse that cost a thousand dollars; that's number one. And number two, you don't need to get your hair done every week, spa treatments every two weeks, pedicures, nails, and all that stuff. You breaking the damn bank, Ma, and it ain't cool!"

"You are too. You change cars like you change your underwear!"

"It's my money though. I can do whatever I want," he mumbled, as he eased back on the sofa. His eyes began to look smoky and blinked slow. I could tell his high was kicking in. I left him alone on the sofa and went back to my room. I didn't feel like arguing with him that night.

Bruce's affairs didn't stop with the woman in Georgia. It had gotten so bad that he stopped hiding it. I found pictures of him with other women, kissing them, hanging out with them in public. It was like he wanted me to see it. We argued so much about him cheating that sometimes we ended up fighting, and the neighbors would call the police. I would win when he was drunk, but when he wasn't I suffered a busted lip or nose. The crazy thing is, we would fight and then have makeup sex. "I love you baby, and I'm sorry. You're my wife and we in this together. We can work it out," Bruce would say something of that sort, and I would easily accept it. A part of me felt like I didn't want the other women to win him, but I was losing anyway.

[*You didn't have to bring all of that up. Why you gotta put our business in the streets? We had fights, but I never busted your lip or your nose. A lot of times you would charge into me, and when I would throw up my elbows to protect my face, it would accidentally hit you in the mouth. Now everybody is going to think I abuse women. I can't sell no records like that. This ain't cool Ma. When I get out I'm going to straighten you out for this*]

Bruce's next album flopped, and to make matters worse, a big West Coast versus East Coast rap beef started. Bruce felt caught in the middle of a rap music war. Bruce would go back and forth between making songs defending the West Coast rappers, and then the East. I think both sides felt betrayed by him because they wanted him to choose. One night while leaving a club after celebrating Bruce's birthday, shots rang out, and we all ran for cover. It was rumored that Bruce was the target. He started wearing a bulletproof vest everywhere he went and he bought vests for me and Trey. I discovered a gun in the nightstand drawer next to our bed and demanded Bruce get rid of it. "I don't want Trey to accidentally get a hold of that," I remember telling Bruce, so he hid the gun in his car. Our lives were changing; we were targets of threats, and I was afraid. The phone would ring at night and then stop and I knew it wasn't Bruce's crazy children's mothers. When Bruce went on the road, he paid his friends to keep an eye on us, but they turned their backs on Bruce when he couldn't afford to pay them anymore. These were the same guys who ate from our tables and went on shopping sprees with our money. Now that Bruce was going broke and needed a favor, they bailed out on him. During this time, Bruce started using drugs heavily, and it wasn't just smoking weed. I found traces of a white powdery substance and questioned Bruce about it, but of course, he denied it.

"You can't stay here if this is how it's going down. This is over the top, Bruce!"

"Come on, Ma, stop sweating me."

"Bruce, I'm serious. I don't do drugs, and I don't want this stuff in my house ever again!" I projected my voice, and he knew I was serious. He stopped bringing it in the house, but the police found a small bag of dope in his car and his gun during spot checks. Because Bruce had a prior record, and was already on probation for assaulting someone, he was facing five years in prison. I begged Mr. King, Kay-Kay's father to represent Bruce because I knew Bruce's other lawyer wouldn't have been able to get him off. Mr. King was able to get Bruce a deal where he would only serve one year in prison, with the agreement that he would enter rehab and perform 500 hours of community service (the equivalent of working anywhere for one year, performing forty hours a week). With good behavior, Bruce could be released within six months on probation.

[*You got a big mouth, Tracey! When I get out of jail, I'm gonna make you pay for this, and that's my word on my Mama! I'm gonna handle you! Why you telling people I did drugs, Ma? That ain't cool!*]

With Bruce locked up, money was running thin. The fifty thousand Mom gave me was long gone. I was grinding hard on auditions. Without money to pay an agent, I had no choice but to name drop and use my previous acting experience to try to get gigs.

"I'm Cat Morris's daughter. She's Vice President at BigStar Records."

"Yeah, um…we know Cat, she's good people, but you're just not good enough for this part," said one director.

"I'm Vernon "Jet" Michaels' daughter, you know he was inducted into the Hall of Fame last year?"

"Good for him, he was one heck of a player, but I'm sorry kid, this role is not for you," said another director. I couldn't even get a commercial!

To keep us from getting kicked out, I called my Grandpa Scott in South Carolina, and he wired us three months' worth of rent. I felt I owed Grandpa to at least go and visit with him and let him see Trey. He hadn't seen him since he was a baby. Grandpa paid for our flight, and Trey and I flew down south for two weeks. It felt like two years because I hadn't been there since I was a little girl. I was bored to tears, but Trey loved the farm and all the animals, and my grandparents enjoyed seeing their great-grandson.

Trey and I spent a lot of time with my family while Bruce was locked up. Bruce wasn't welcomed in my parents' house, not even after we were married. Trey and I usually spent the holidays with Bruce and his family when he wasn't on tour, but when Bruce was away we spent the holidays with my family. Now with Bruce in jail, I saw my family often. I missed them. I remember feeling a certain level of peace with Bruce being locked up. As crazy as it sounds, knowing he was in jail made me feel slightly secure that he wasn't cheating on me. I didn't have to stay up all night worrying about where he was or who he was with. I visited him while he was locked up and kept him up to speed with what was happening in the music industry and elsewhere. Bruce didn't look good, though. I wasn't sure if jail was eating him up, but he had let his hair grow into a wild curly bush, and he had these ugly blistery bumps on his face. I stopped hugging him during visits because he looked diseased. He kept scratching himself, and his lips had turned purplish blue. He kept asking me to send him some money, but I told him if I kept sending him money, we wouldn't be able to pay the rent. "Don't come back to see me no more until you send me some money," Bruce demanded, and it was like somebody else was talking. He wasn't the same Bruce. He was angry often, and sometimes I wouldn't hear from him for weeks.

Six months later, I was coming home from picking Trey up from school. I found Bruce in the living room that day when I got home. I knew he was coming home soon, but he never told me the exact date. His so-called friends picked him up from the jail.

[*Because I wanted to bust your chops! I heard you was giving up my goods, so I came home unannounced.*]

Bruce and all of his friends were playing video games in between drinking and smoking. They talked and laughed loud like a bunch of kids. I kicked them all out! I imaged the scene was probably similar to what my parents saw when I threw that wild party at their house.

"Why did you do that? We were just celebrating." Bruce got upset, and what should have been a warm welcome home turned into a heated argument.

"Stop it! I can't take it!" Trey covered his ears. That's when I realized something had to change. I wasn't sure what moves I could make but I couldn't have my son in an unhappy and unsafe environment anymore.

With neither one of us having a steady job, (since Bruce lost his record deal), Bruce and I fought often. During his six month stint in jail, I had reconciled my friendship with Kay-Kay, and starting hanging out with the girls from time-to-time. Now that Bruce was back home he tried to make me a prisoner. "Nah, Ma, you need to stay here with Trey. Wives don't belong in clubs without their husbands, know what I'm saying? That ain't happening." Yet it was okay for him to go to the clubs, although he claimed he was performing. Yeah right! Around this time, we were both doing our own thing. I wasn't going to sit on my hands anymore and wait for him to change, or allow him to control me. I kept my feelings inside as I plotted to leave him.

One day my wedding ring was missing, and so was Bruce. He had disappeared and then decided to show up about two weeks later, after I filed a missing person's report. He looked an awful mess. He smelled bad, his pants were dirty, his shoes were on the wrong feet, and his hair looked like a bird's nest. He was smelling funky and kept scratching himself as he talked.

"Why you call the cops? I saw my face all on the news. You didn't have to do that. You knew where I was!"

"You are on it!"

"What? You don't know what you talking about, Ma!"

"Bruce, I may be a girl from Bel-Air, but I hung around the hood long enough to identify a crackhead when I see one."

"Girl you trippin'. I been helping my man out. I just need a shower, that's all."

"Oh yeah? Helping your man do what, Bruce?"

"Get out my way!" he brushed by me and nearly took my shoulder with him when he bumped me. He went into the bathroom and took a long shower, but it didn't change the way he looked and behaved.

"You stole my ring so you could go get high, didn't you?" I asked when he came into our bedroom with a towel around his waist.

"I don't know what you talking about. I didn't steal nothing."

"The police called me because there is a serial number on the ring, Bruce. They said someone tried to pawn it. They brought it back to me, but I don't even want it anymore."

Bruce's eyes lit up. "You don't want it?"

"Why you say it like that? As if you're glad I don't want it."

"Nah, nah, it's not like that," he said. He crawled in bed next to me, but I slid to the furthest side of the bed, not wanting him to come near me. I forced myself to fall asleep. I hoped that when I woke up this would be a nightmare, and that my husband was not a crackhead.

When I woke up the next morning, the ring was gone again, and so was Bruce.

"Are you sure?" Kay asked me when I told her Bruce was a crackhead. (By this time, Kay-Kay had another daughter, and it was with Damien. She named her Dana.)

"I'm sure, Kay. I packed his things and dropped his stuff off at his mother's house. I can't live with a crackhead. I changed the locks, too."

"Good. You need to protect you and Trey." Kay-Kay gave me a big hug. I needed it. Seeing how easy it was for Kay-Kay to move on with her life after Rock, I thought I was making good strides to do the same with Bruce. Bruce was missing in action, and I told his mother everything that happened. His sisters translated it to her, and she was devastated. She kept crying, "Not my Brucey, not my Brucey!" I let the police know that Bruce was a crackhead who had stolen my wedding ring. They said they would be on the lookout for him, but so far, there weren't any leads.

I landed a main character role in a theatrical gig that was selling out all over California. The producer wanted to take the show on the road since it was a big west coast hit. He wanted to see how the play would be received on the east coast. The money was a guaranteed five thousand dollars per month for a six-month tour. All travel expenses would be covered, except our meals.

"I have to take care of my son," I told the producer.

"We would hate to lose you Tracey. You're the star of the show. I'm willing to offer you seven thousand a month, but the kid can't come with you on the road," he said firmly. I was desperate, rent was due, bills needed to be paid, and I had to take care of my son. As much as I hated to do it, I left Trey with my mother-in-law Gladys, and his two aunts. I felt horrible for going back on my word to never leave my child behind, but I was also starting to understand that maybe my mother was in similar situations when she left me with Cheryl. She was a single parent too, and trying to raise me as best she could. I didn't understand it until I had a child of my own. As a single parent, sometimes you have to make sacrifices that you don't always want to make, but you do it to survive.

While on the road I sent checks to keep the rent paid, and I sent money to Gladys to take care of Trey's needs. The time on the road went by fast, but I missed my baby. When I returned home, Trey had to make me stop kissing him and hugging him. "Cut it out Mommy," he kept saying.

When we got home, I noticed the lock felt loose when I used my key. Suddenly, I had a funny feeling in my stomach that something wasn't right.

"Wait here," I said to Trey once we were inside. Trey stood by the front door near our suitcases. I could hear the TV playing loudly from the back. As I tiptoed down the hallway, I could tell the sound was coming from my bedroom. I inched my way close enough to see inside. There was a naked woman lying in my bed. In *my* bed, like she paid for it. In *my* bed, like she lived there. My eyes shifted to a glowing light coming from underneath the bathroom door to my left. I quickly turned around and raced down the hall to the front door where Trey was. I picked up the phone and called the front desk security. I told them someone had invaded my apartment and they needed to come upstairs right away.

"We'll send someone up right away, ma'am, and call the police. You get out of there!"

"Baby, I didn't know you were home."

I turned around, and it was Bruce. He was wearing boxers, and no

63

shirt.

"Have you lost your mind?" I shouted. I guess the sound of my voice startled the woman, who came running out of the bedroom with her clothes in her hands.

"Tracey? Oh snap!" she quickly stepped into her pants. "I'm so sorry. Bruce said you guys were divorced!" She ran out the door, and nearly knocked over Trey.

"Baby, it's not what you think!"

SMACK.

I slapped Bruce so hard across the face, for a few seconds you could see my handprint.

"You got some nerve to break into my house and then sleep with another woman in my bed!"

"Girl, you must have lost your mind to hit me like that!" Bruce charged into me.

"NOOOO, STOP IT!" Trey shouted. "Leave my Mommy alone!" Trey rushed over and tried to pull Bruce off of me.

"Step off boy!" Bruce shoved Trey and he fell to the floor and started crying.

I could feel my blood boiling from my chest up to my head, and I fought Bruce with everything I had in me. I kicked, punched, but nothing seemed to faze him. He had been smoking that crack, and his eyes looked evil red as he returned body blows to me. I tumbled over and fell to the floor. I felt Bruce grab a handful of my hair.

"Going to teach you a lesson, you spoiled brat!" Bruce's nostrils flared and his face was red like a blazing fire.

"Get offa' me!" I tried to break free. I kicked and punched, but nothing I did seem to hurt him. He tightened his grip on my hair.

"STOP IT, STOP IT, YOU'RE HURTING MY MOMMY!"

Bruce dragged me by the hair out to the balcony of our tenth floor apartment. In one swoop, he held me over the balcony by my legs. I could see the entire city of Los Angeles upside down.

"Do you wanna die?!"

[*I didn't say that or did I?*]

"No, Bruce, please let me down!" I was screaming to the top of my lungs.

I could hear Trey shouting, "Daddy put Mommy down!" He was

crying, and I could feel the blood rushing to my head. Bruce and I had many fights, but he was going too far. I saw my life flash before my eyes as I hung. One wrong move and my body was going to splatter all over the concrete. I screamed, begged, and pleaded, and made promises I knew I would never keep, but Bruce would not pull me up. I kept lifting my head to keep the blood from rushing so hard to my head.

"God, please help me. I promise I will never date another thug again. Save me! Help me, Jesus!" I cried. Bruce laughed at my cries for help. "God, please get me up from here and I will serve you forever, I promise! I promise! Save me Lord!"

Next thing I knew, I heard loud voices shout, "FREEZE!" It was the cops. (I would learn later that the elevator broke, which was why they took so long to get to me.) One officer grabbed hold of me, while the other one grabbed Bruce and pinned him to the floor of the balcony with his gun pointed at his head. Bruce started fighting the officer, and I remember it took five police officers to try to pin him down to handcuff him. They had to pepper spray him. I was terrified, but the one thing on my mind was my son. I rushed to Trey's side and held him in my arms.

"I love you so much. I'm so sorry you had to see that." I wiped his tears and kissed him all over. He didn't understand why his father would do something like that to his own mother. "Everything will be okay from now on. You'll see."

Who would have ever thought that behind Bruce's pretty boy face was a man who was evil and vindictive? Women loved him and his tough boy image, and I was one of those young and naïve women. As I sat in the courtroom months later, the judge basically gave Bruce a smack on the hand for what he did to me. Bruce struck a plea deal for a lesser charge to attempted murder and was charged with second-degree assault. He was sentenced to five years in prison, with eligibility for parole after three years. When we left the courtroom, I just kept thinking about when my dad said to me when I was eighteen; *these thugs are going to drag you through the gutter, and use you dry.* That's exactly what Bruce did to me. He turned me into a totally different person. He abused me and used me, then tried to kill me. I only wished I had listened to my father. My message to the young girls reading this book is that it's not cute dating a thug. Thugs are not real men; thugs are boys who never had any real men in their own lives, so they put on a façade of what they think constitutes a real man. As cute as Bruce was, he was a young man who did not love himself. His father tried to raise him to be a man, but he didn't appreciate that tough love. Instead, he moved to California with his mother because he knew he could have his way. Her lack of discipline and Bruce's own selfish ways is what influenced him to become the type of person he was. As a young woman, you may not understand all of this, because I didn't when my parents tried to tell me, but sometimes you just have to trust that what your parents tell you is the best advice they can give. Your parents can see the future of where you may be heading, because they were young once too. As a young person, you only see the present, and the present is short-lived. You won't be young forever! Make wise choices now! I didn't, and look what happened to me.

[*Whatever! Now you want to be a preacher? Getta' here!*]

"Lights out, Benjamin!" the guards shouted. Bruce closed the book and tossed it to the side.

CHAPTER FIVE
PEACHES

Peaches was on a flight headed back to Chicago after giving a talk in Washington, DC at the National Women's Liberation Convention on behalf of the Freedom for Frieda Foundation. As soon as she got back to Chicago, she would have to do another speaking engagement at a local rehab center. Peaches' life was busy these days, as Vice President of the Freedom for Frieda Foundation and as Drug Counselor and Author. She stared out the window at the clouds before drifting off into a thirty minute nap. When she woke up, the flight attendant offered her lunch, and she accepted. Never in a million years did she think she would be flying first class, eating a lobster for lunch, and encouraging other people to get clean and sober. *Life is good, and God is great!* she often thought to herself. Now as for that niece of hers, Tracey, she was doing well until she opened up a can of worms by writing her tell-all book. Peaches made a mental note to call Tracey once she got settled into her home, which was only blocks away from her sister Connie. She didn't appreciate Tracey talking about her the way she did and constantly bringing up her past in a condescending way in her book. After Peaches finished her lunch, she pulled out her Kindle Fire and figured she would try to finish the book before she called her niece to give her final thoughts about it.

We got evicted from the Wilshire Apartments because Bruce had drugs on the premises and we brought bad publicity upon the apartment's owner. Me and Trey stayed with Tony Tee for a while. He was out touring most of the time, so Trey and I had the whole mansion to ourselves. Of course, the media read more into it. They printed that I had gotten back with my boyfriend, Tony Tee. The magazine articles made Tony Tee's girlfriend jealous of our relationship. Although it was platonic, the articles and my reputation for being a bad girl made her suspicious of me on the regular basis. After a while, I got tired of hearing her and Tony arguing behind closed doors. She was always complaining about us living with them. Kay-Kay offered to let us stay with her when I told her about it, but I didn't want to impose on anyone else. One day I packed our bags, left a thank you note for Tony, and moved back home.

The divorce between Bruce and I was nasty. I wanted it to be over with, fast. What I thought was supposed to be an open and shut case was getting ugly in the media and with Bruce. Bruce wrote hurtful letters from jail about how much he hated me for having him arrested, and talked about how *I* ruined his life. I couldn't believe he was blaming me for what *he* did. He called me ugly names so much that you would have thought they were my real names. I showed all the letters to my lawyer, who in turn submitted them to the judge. The judge ordered Bruce to stop harassing me or he would tag on another year to his sentence. I was having nightmares every night about being thrown over the balcony, but for some reason I never saw myself hitting the ground. In court, I testified about the emotional and mental anguish that Bruce caused me. Trey was also scared to fall asleep in his room alone. "My father is going to come, and he's going to kill us," Trey would say things like that, and I would put him in bed with me. Amazingly, with each other, we were able to fall asleep. We had to see a therapist during that time, and the reports were submitted in the case. My Dad was so furious about the after effects from what happened, and the letters that Bruce wrote to me that he decided to pay Bruce a personal visit in San Quentin.

[*We all did! Dean told Bruce to his face that he better not come near you again! He also told him to his face that he was a no good father, husband, and a no good man! Dean set it up so that Bruce got his butt kicked right there in prison!*]

While home with my parents again, there were always celebrities coming through, singers, movie/TV producers, and athletes. I asked them for work and some of them had me work as their personal assistants from time-to-time, which helped me to take care of my needs and Trey's, but for the most part I ended up working as a receptionist again at Kay-Kay's salon spa. Although I was living with my parents, they made it clear that Trey was *my* responsibility. So, when I needed a babysitter so I could go out, I had to find one; I couldn't ask my parents. They didn't bend their rules with me because I was grown and with a child. They made it clear that their money didn't mean my money, and their house and cars didn't make it *my* house and cars. What little money I made, I had to give them some of it for rent. When I didn't have enough money to pay my parents, I would clean the entire mansion- from top to bottom and run errands for my mother. I would also pick up Devin and Trey from school. At times I felt like a nanny, but I was happy we had a safe and loving home to live in.

It was 1998, and Devin was twelve and Trey was five. The two of them were growing up like brothers. Trey looked up to Devin and followed his every move. They did everything together—played basketball, swam in the pool, went to the movies, and practiced playing music together. Devin was a talented musician. Even at a young age, he could play several different instruments, so my parents sent him to a TAG school. Trey tried to follow in his footsteps by plucking around on the guitar or fooling around with the keyboards, but he didn't have the gift that his uncle had, although it was cute to see him try.

[*I remember those days, precious years. I loved that day when your mother had a talent show for the local kids at her house. Devin and Trey did their impersonation of the Men in Black, and dressed in black suits. Devin played the keyboards, while little Trey tried to lip sync Will Smith's rap. It was so cute. They stole the show!*].

I love my son, and I always wanted the best for him, but I remember one day he asked me for the new handheld Sony PlayStation. I knew those things cost just as much as the full game system and I couldn't afford it. The money I had earned from going on a tour when I was in a play was spent on legal fees in my divorce from Bruce, and to pay Trey's private school tuition. "If you had a real job, you could buy me a PlayStation," Trey said to me. I just cried. His words hurt. I know he didn't mean to say 'real' job, he meant a steady job with consistent money. His words did make me think about whether I should give up on my acting career. It wasn't working out for me. I felt like a failure and grew very depressed. I didn't feel like I was a good example as a mother, and I felt embarrassed that I had to come back home and live with my parents. Yes we were safe and yes my parents loved us, but I didn't feel like I was good enough. I'm sure Trey was smart enough to see that I wasn't handling my responsibilities as a mother too well. I should have been able to provide us with a new home. I should have been able to buy him all the things that he wanted. I was filled with guilt and shame. Maybe to Trey, it didn't seem like I knew what I was doing. After all, I didn't have a *real* job. Maybe I was being unrealistic chasing a dream.

Meanwhile, Kay-Kay was living the fabulous life. She and Damien had a beautiful wedding, and I felt happy to be her maid of honor. Yet, I would be lying if I said I wasn't jealous. She had the type of wedding I had always dreamed of. Kay-Kay and Damien also seemed very happy, and genuinely in love. I never felt that when I got married to Bruce.

Kay-Kay and Damien bought a nice home in New Port Coast, the Hunting Beach area. Kay-Kay was living the life we always talked about as kids, except I was living at home with my parents. I was still sleeping in the same bedroom since I was eleven years old, but I was twenty-four. All the redecorating I had done could not change that fact. I felt left behind, as Kay-Kay and everyone else I knew were pushing ahead. I felt like I was floating backwards and the shore kept moving further and further away. Considering whom my parents were, I felt I was supposed to be on top of the world! But I was twenty-four with a kid and living at home with my parents. This wasn't the life I pictured for myself. Even after my divorce was final, Bruce was so broke that I didn't get any alimony or child support. A house he owned in New York was foreclosed on, and the cars he had was repossessed. He didn't even own his songs. Bruce had nothing, and I had nothing. When the divorce proceedings were finally over, they escorted him back to jail. I left the courtroom feeling like I had wasted the past five years of my life on a loser. I could have spent those years at college or I could have pursued my acting career more seriously. After all the fights, arguments, affairs, drugs, and Bruce trying to throw me from a balcony, we had nothing! I walked out of the courtroom without a single penny for alimony or child support. The only thing I left the courtroom with was my maiden name. I cried in the limo back to my parents' house, as Kay-Kay held my hand. She reminded me, "You have Trey. He's the blessing from this." I knew she was right, but I wished I could turn back the hands of time.

While working at Kay-Kay's spa, I saw Kyle Lagers, an agent for top "A" list actors. To say I was desperate would be an understatement. I knew it was against company policy to solicit celebrities who came through, but after Kyle received his spa treatment, I handed him an 8x10 envelope that included my portrait and resume. I didn't think anyone saw me because I sat at the front entrance of the salon by myself. Somehow, one of the girls who worked as a masseuse saw me. She didn't hesitate to tell Kay-Kay.

"You can't do that, Tracey. If you start doing that, then everyone else will. If I let you slide, I will have to let everyone get away with that." Kay-Kay told me over the phone later that evening. It felt awkward being reprimanded from my best friend. It also felt uncomfortable to be working for her to begin with. I felt like we should have been partners with her business, not me working for her.

"Fine, it won't happen again." I hung up the phone, and Kay dialed me right back.

"Did you just hang up on me?"

"I thought you were through talking."

"Tracey, I'm your boss. You don't hang up on your boss. You *do* know that, right?"

"Well, you're not my boss anymore."

"Is that right?"

"I quit!"

"I thought you needed this job."

"I don't anymore."

"Well the next time things don't work out and you're in a bind don't call me asking if you can work here ever again!"

"Don't you worry I won't!"

CLICK.

[*Girl, you were stuck on stupid to quit that job when you needed it! Your ego is as big as your butt!* Peaches scrolled to the next page on her Kindle.]

To my surprise, Kyle Lagers called me the next day to come in for an interview. We had a nice conversation in his office. He was very cordial as we drank tea. He crossed one leg over the other, and then removed the thick scarf from around his skinny neck.

"Darling I have to be frank with you," he said, after I filled him in on my goals and where I wanted to be. Of course he already knew about me and my work in the business. He was Kyle. He knew everything and everybody, but he didn't know what my ambitions were.

"About what?" I swallowed the rest of my tea and set the cup down on the red table. Everything in Kyle's office was red except the walls. You knew right away what his favorite color was without having to ask.

"I have been watching you for a very long time, and darling, you are gorgeous."

I blushed. "Thank you, Kyle."

"But you're an absolute mess!"

My mouth dropped. "Seriously? Did you just say I'm a *mess*?"

"Obviously, darling, you're a mess. If Kyle Lagers is going to represent you, *you* need to clean up your act. My gosh, how could you ever be taken seriously being a video girl?" He laughed. "You played in low budget films, and did weak toothpaste commercials like you were a kid just starting out in the business—AS IF! Honey, no, *we don't do low figures* with Kyle, honey." He threw his nose up and puckered his lips. "And your reputation for bad boys is intriguing, but there is nothing they can do for you besides mess up your credit score, make you bail them out of jail, and have you paying their baby's mamas child support. Wasn't that the case with your ex-husband?"

"No, but—"

"Oh, never mind, you shouldn't have married him. My gosh, honey! You have no standards, and no standards equal low class, and low class means you'll only be known as a piece of trash."

"Stop it right there!" I threw up my hand and stood up abruptly from the red sofa. "I refuse to sit here and listen to you degrade me and throw me under a bus when I know I have worked my tail off to establish myself in this business!"

He raised his eyebrows. "Oh no, she didn't just curse me out." He held his fingers over his lips. "I know you better have a seat, as I do not like people standing over me, no ma'am, no sir, I am not having that. Thank you in advance. Be seated," He pointed for me to sit back down.

I slowly sat back down on the sofa, but I felt I had to defend myself. I respected Kyle, but he was about to make me lose it.

"Now darling, I can help you. I'm good at this." He shimmied his shoulders and I couldn't help but laugh. "First, you need to turn your mistakes into fortunes by making them work for you instead of against you."

"I'm not following you."

"Write it. Tell the world how you became a hot mess, and make them feel sorry for you. Let's face it, America loves sappy stories, and it will sell."

"But people know enough about my life as it is."

"So they think." Kyle crossed one leg over the other. "You got secrets that nobody else knows, I'm sure. Tell it and sell it. Trust me, it will make you rich and famous, honey. In the end, people will see your drama in a whole different light. You'll look less like a hoodrat and more like a child star who became a diva."

"I'll give it some thought, but–"

"You'll start writing it now, and by the time you're finished, you'll be the cleaned-up actress that I plan to turn you into. Big movie executives will see your talent and take you seriously. Right now you're a hoodrat in fancy clothes, let's just be honest. But, once Kyle hooks you up, you'll be a masterpiece. You'll not only have the style, your mannerisms will change, your taste in men will change, and your associates will all change. You'll become an international star, when I'm finished with you."

"You're sure about this?"

"Positive! Write the first few chapters, and I will shop it right away and get you a publishing offer you won't be able to refuse. But, it must be honest, it must be juicy, and it must be filled with exaggeration!

"For now, we'll create *good* press, so you can show Hollywood you're changing. For starters, I have seen your acting work, and I think you're good, but not great. So, you're going back to school to hone your craft. It will be fantastic for the press. I can foresee the headlines now- 'Newly Divorced Actress Tracey Michaels Takes Steps to Clean up Her Act by Going to College to Earn Her Degree.'"

"I don't have time for school."

"Of course you do, darling, you don't have a job. Now is the perfect time to become better at what you do."

Kyle laid out an entire plan to get me going. I felt unsure about his suggestions, but on the other hand, I was desperate. I started writing my life story as soon as I got home. I didn't give it much thought, really. I tracked down some of my old journals that were still under lock and key beneath my mattress. I typed every single night and found that it was actually therapeutic for me to write it. When I was finished the three chapters, I emailed them to Kyle. I didn't know what to expect, but after a few weeks passed, Kyle called me with an offer, just as he promised. *Calidream Publishing* was willing to pay me a ten thousand dollar advance to finish writing the book, and afterwards, they would get thirty percent, and Kyle and I would split the rest.

Everything was happening so fast for me. It seemed like only a day had passed when I was a down in the dumps, and the next thing I knew, I was being treated like royalty in a matter of months. Kyle escorted me to a few celebrity events, I walked the red carpet with famous people I didn't know personally, and dined on caviar and fine wine with the elite. Honestly, I felt out of my league at first because I was used to hanging around a different crowd, mostly rappers, B-list actors, and hangers-on. Most of the people at the parties often asked about my parents. They never asked how I was doing since my divorce or how my son was coming along. I could see the peculiar look in their eyes that said I didn't belong there. They were just being nice to me because of my parents, and that Kyle was their agent too.

"Your former associates were fast-money and easy out of the game celebrities," Kyle would say to me. He was right. Most of the people I knew didn't last long in the business. In fact, I had heard that Zeek couldn't get another record deal after he got out of jail, and he was back in the streets selling drugs. Tony Tee had changed up his rap style and started recording gangster rap music and hanging with the wrong crowd. We were all riding in different lanes by then.

"Darling, fame is not about being known by your peers, it's about being known everywhere you go by everyone," Kyle would say as he would continue to teach me a new way of thinking. I had the game backwards, and all that time, my mother was right. It's funny how a stranger can tell you something and you believe them over your family.

At any rate, I applied to USC and majored in Dramatic Arts. When I got accepted, my parents were so happy for me that they agreed to pay my tuition as long as I stayed out of trouble and earned good grades. Kyle was so nice to me that he kept the maintenance up on my Mercedes, took me on shopping sprees, and bought clothes and toys for Trey. He told me I didn't have to pay him back. "When your book is released I'll get my cut then, and when you earn your first movie role, I will get a cut as well." I was so happy to have my bills being paid for and going on auditions that I just signed the contract with Kyle without thinking. My mother told me, "Have a lawyer to review that contract just to make sure everything looks legit." I insisted that Kyle was cool, and I felt confident that he knew what he was doing. I felt like the old Tracey again. I was in style, and my son had his needs and wants taken care of, so who was I to question Kyle for pulling me out of a rut? Even if I had a passing thought about his business dealings, I quickly dismissed them when I looked at all the things he was buying me and Trey. Now whenever I visited my friends, I felt like I fit in. I could talk about the lasted trendy things because now I had them.

In the meantime, school hadn't started yet, and I told Kyle I wasn't having any luck auditioning for potential blockbuster movies. I was going against big named actors like Angela Bassett, Loretta Devine, and Sanaa Lathan.

"Let's just go back to doing commercials," I remember telling Kyle over the phone.

"You most certainly will not. You'll continue to audition for the roles I say you will. No client of mine does commercials. If you think small you'll always be small."

"But I'm not as good as those other actors!" I protested.

"Just be patient, there's a method to my madness. Your image cannot be cleaned up overnight"

"But Kyle, seriously, this is crazy!"

"Listen, darling, by sending you out to audition for a part you may not get is still sending a message to the casting directors that you want to be taken seriously. The more they see you auditioning for major roles, the more likely they are to break down and give you a small part in their film."

[*I loved me some Kyle. That boy was flaming brighter than a blow torch, but he knew how to work the business in his favor, that's for sure!*]

Kyle was right! I landed quite a few small roles in three different blockbuster movies that summer. Although I would only say one or two lines in each movie, the point was getting the face time. In between my acting gigs, I became Dad's secretary, and started scheduling appointments for his clients. To my surprise, dad had a very busy schedule, and he made pretty good money helping his clients. While we worked together, I began to feel guilty about the way I had treated him. I remember the day he was showing me files of his new clients and how I should label and file their medical information. My mind drifted to the day I told him he wasn't my father and my eyes began to tear up thinking about it.

"...and then you can attach their photograph in the corner of the file, like this," Dad was showing me. "See?"

I nodded, fought back tears.

"Are you okay?" Dad asked. I just threw my arms around him and hugged him. "You're not pregnant again, are you?"

"No," my voice was smothered against his chest as tears streamed down my cheeks.

Dad tilted my chin up to face him. "Is Bruce still harassing you? Because I'll put some more guys on him in prison to knock his head off again if you want."

I shook my head. "No, Dad. I just wanted to say thank you for giving me the job."

He hunched his shoulders. "This is nothing," he chuckled.

"I wanted to...I want to also tell you that I'm sorry for saying you weren't my dad, because you are. You're the best father I've ever had, and I love you very much."

"Oh sweetheart, I got over that. I know you didn't mean it."

"I see why Mom married you. You have a good heart."

"Is there a tape recorder around here or a hidden camera somewhere? I mean, where is all of this coming from?" he wondered with a slight grin.

"It's real, Dad, now come on and finish telling me what to do and I'll take care of everything for you."

My Dad was typically on the neat side, but not when it came to paperwork. I had to reorganize his file cabinets, create folders and labels, and file the paperwork on his clients. I answered the phones and ran errands for him during the day. I was basically my Dad's secretary. His office was on the first level of the mansion and down the hall from Mom's office. Dad paid me four hundred dollars every week, which I thought was cheap, but looking back on it now, he was teaching me responsibility. I used the money he gave me to pay for Trey's private school tuition. I was glad to be paid, and happy that Dad was flexible when I had to go on auditions. I didn't have that same flexibility when I was working for Kay-Kay.

Speaking of Kay-Kay, we had stopped speaking to each other for a while after I had abruptly quit. She would hang out with her other friends, and it was weird because I would run into them while I was out with Kyle. Kyle would say, "You don't know them. They are beneath you. They're hoodrats, so keep right on walking, honey." That's what I did, turning up my nose and let Kyle escort me to the V.I.P. section of whatever venue we attended. Through Kyle I became friends with a lot of rich and famous people. We didn't click the way I did with Kay-Kay, though. The conversations I had with them were shallow, which made me miss Kay-Kay that much more.

"You need to get out and date, or at least be seen with a hot prominent cutie," Kyle suggested to me one day, while I was in his office. I was telling him that I missed my friends. I felt like I didn't have a social life. He wanted me to fake like I was living "the life" and that I had quickly moved on when inside I was still hurting. My divorce had failed and now my relationship with my best friend was crumbling too. It was my fault, but Kyle didn't give me time to marinate in feelings of guilt, so I pushed them aside. Getting famous and rich was our goal. I believed Kyle was "fixing" me, and once I had it all that everything would be just fine.

"My Dad is a personal trainer, you know. He works with the NBA, NHL, and NFL."

"Athletes, huh? That's perfect. Just make sure he's cute, rich, and smart. Pick someone who is clean cut, gives to charity, and loves children. This will look good for you."

"Well dang, Kyle, you make them sound like projects. What if I happen to like him?"

Kyle tilted his head to the side. "Darling, don't go falling in love just yet. It's premature, and it will make you look like a skank."

"I'm not looking to fall in love. I just need some companionship right now. Nothing serious."

"If you say so." He twisted his lips. "Just don't forget your photo-shoot is tomorrow."

"Geez Kyle! I don't plan to act that soon. Give me some credit," I playfully hit him on the shoulder.

"Fine, but just remember what I said, no more thugs for you. That's the rule."

"Bye Kyle. I got this!"

After my photo-shoot the next day, I went straight home. Usually, I would stop on Rodeo Drive to see if I could catch a sale, but my feet ached, and my eyes were still bothering me from all the cameras flashing. I could still see speckles of light in my eyes when I walked into the house. As I slid off my heels, I heard loud laughter coming from Dad's office. I walked down the stretch of the hallway and took a quick peek in the doorway of his office. I saw the most beautiful man I had ever seen. He was laughing loud with pearly white even teeth. I took another peep, checking him out without him noticing me. He was sitting in the chair in front of Dad's desk wearing a nice beige suit and a soft blue shirt and tie. I was thinking maybe the guy played for the Lakers or the Clippers or he could have been a baseball player for the LA Dodgers or Angels. Whoever he was, he was having a good conversation with my dad. I thought about what Kyle said too—*make sure he isn't a thug, and he's clean cut.* I peeped my eyes around the doorway and from what I could tell from the surface, this guy seemed decent. He had a very polite and pleasant look on his face. Feeling curious, I stepped back into my heels, and I knocked on the door. Although the door was opened, I didn't want to walk in on their meeting.

"Excuse me, is it okay if I come in?" I asked.

"Sure, come on in, sweetheart," Dad said, sitting behind the desk with his arms folded. A stack of papers and what looked like some type of brochures were on his desk. The guy in the suit shifted his eyes from Dad to me, and instantly our eyes locked in on each other. He had the sexiest pair of eyes that I'd ever seen. They were big, dark, with long lashes. His eyebrows were thick, with a natural arch. He had a fresh haircut that was tapered on the sides and wavy at the top. I didn't recognize him from any of the profiles nor did I recall seeing him on TV, but he was handsome. He wasn't a pretty boy like Bruce. He had a very masculine look, with broad shoulders and big feet.

"Oh, Keith, this is my daughter Tracey. Tracey, I would like for you to meet Keith Smith." Keith stood up from the chair, and it seemed like he kept rising and rising. I thought his head was going to touch the recess lights in the ceiling. He extended his long arm down to shake my hand

and I could see his muscles protruding under that suit. He must have performed five hundred push-ups a day with muscles like that. He wasn't bulky, but had a built like he worked out often. He was hairy from what I could tell, from his hands, and the five o'clock shadow along his jawline. I loved him instantly. I know that sounds cliché, but Keith was so handsomely beautiful.

"It's nice to meet you, Tracey. I've seen you on TV, but you're much more beautiful in person." His voice was saxophone deep and sexy. For a moment, my knees buckled as we held steady eye contact with each other. His hand shake was gentle, but firm enough to seem sincere. In that one touch, I could tell he wasn't a stranger to hard work.

"Thank you, Keith. It's nice to meet you too." I returned the same flirtatious smile he was giving me. "I don't recall Keith being on your schedule, Dad."

"Oh he's not on the schedule, honey; I was just sealing the deal on our new gardening contract."

My eyebrows curved upwards. I was confused. "Gardening contract?"

"Yes," Dad replied nonchalantly, as he signed a few documents.

I shifted my gaze back to Keith, who I caught staring at my legs. "So you're not…you're not a baller?"

Keith shook his head, chuckled. "No, does that surprise you?"

"Well, you're just so…"

"Tall?"

"Yeah, about six feet, six inches?"

"Six-four actually, and I used to play basketball in high school, but now I just play for fun."

"Oh." I scratched the side of my temple, feeling a bit puzzled as to why this hunk of a man decided to be a grass cutter.

"I'm a professional landscape artist," Keith spoke confidently, as if he was reading my mind. "I see an ordinary yard, and I draw up plans to turn it into a paradise for my clients."

"And he's good, too, honey. You should see these brochures and the pictures in his portfolio." Dad walked from behind his desk with a big leather black portfolio in his hand.

I waved him off. "Uh…no thanks I take your word for it."

"Well suit yourself." Dad handed Keith his portfolio back. "Keith is starting tomorrow, so if you hear noise first thing in the morning, just know it's Keith and his workers redesigning our lawn."

"Thanks for the heads up." I then turned to Keith. "It was nice to meet you."

"You too Tracey."

I thought to myself as I left office, *Dang. A landscape professional and not a baller?* I was shocked. I knew if we ever dated that Kyle would never approve of him! But I quickly dismissed his occupation and tried not to think about what Kyle thought. It had been a year, and I needed some TLC.

[*Listen to your hot tail! That's how you always got into trouble! Keep your legs closed sometimes.*]

I caught up with my dad in the kitchen minutes later. He was pouring Keith a glass of iced tea.

"Dad, can I ask you something?"

"Shoot."

I thought about it for a minute, twirled my hair around my finger. "Is Keith single?"

Dad twisted his lips and gave me a look that said, *'don't even think about it'* before answering, "He's not your type, Tracey."

"I saw the way he was looking at me, so I must be his type."

He shrugged. "You're a pretty girl; that's why he was staring. But personality-wise, you're not his type."

"You still didn't answer my question."

"Tracey, Keith is a religious man."

"I believe in God too."

"No, no, you see, Keith's a *practicing* Christian, and I don't want you to contaminate him."

"Dad!"

"I was trying to put it politely, but you pushed me. Let's face it, you've been around the block a few times sweetheart, and I think Keith is looking for a woman who is active in church like he is. At least that's what I gathered from several conversations we've had in the past."

"So you know this guy?"

"We've had some interesting conversations at the gym where I used to train. Nothing special, just men talk that's all."

"Dad, let me take Keith his drink. Maybe I'm wrong about him and I need to give him a chance."

"But—"

"Dad, I got this. Even Christian men need love." I winked, grabbed the glass of iced tea from Dad, and headed out of the kitchen down the hall to his office...

"So how long have you been in landscaping?" I asked, offering Keith the iced tea. I sat down slowly on the black leather sofa in the lounge area of the office and crossed one leg over the other. Keith's eyes dropped right to my thighs, and I didn't try to pull my skirt down to cover it either.

Keith swallowed hard and cleared his throat, "Three years." Then he wiped a few sweat beads from his forehead.

"You okay?"

"Uhm...yeah. I'm cool." He finished the tea, and unloosened his necktie. "It's uh...a little warm in here, don't you think?"

"I'm just fine," I slid in closer to him.

"You seem pretty young to have your own business."

"I never believed in working for somebody else."

"Well how did you come up with the money to start your own business?"

"It's a long story, but God has been good to me."

"Yes God is good!" I threw up my hand. "Praise him!"

"So you're a believer?" his eyes widened with excitement, like he had won a prize.

"Who, me?"

"Yes, you."

"Of course. If it wasn't for God, I wouldn't be here."

His lips curved in a big smile. "Amen."

"So what made you give your life to the Lord, sister?" Keith rested his arm comfortably behind me on the sofa.

I cleared my throat. "Uhm...well...I'm not quite dedicated yet." I slapped my hand on his lap, and gently squeezed his thigh. All I felt was muscle.

"What's holding you back?" He slid my hand off his lap.

"Hmmm, I'm not quite sure, but I will get there soon enough."

"There's no time like the present, Tracey."

"Yeah man, I hear you. So um...are you single? Dating? Engaged married?"

"Whoa, slow down!" he laughed. The whole time, I was thinking my dad was right. Although Keith was twenty-eight, he came across like he was a man in his thirties.

"So, is it true that you officially divorced B-Money?" he raised a curious his thick eyebrow.

"Yep, and I've moved on." I assumed Keith heard all about me through the media like everyone else. "You know Keith I'm not the same girl I was when I was with B-Money. I'm headed in a new direction in my life. I could use all the help I can get."

"Let God lead you, Tracey," his eyes dancing with mine.

"I believe he is leading me right now. He's telling me that you and I should go out."

He blushed. "You move pretty fast, don't you?"

"Like you said, there's no time like the present."

"Listen, Tracey." He stared me from head to toe. "I think you're a very beautiful young lady but–"

"But what?"

"How about we try being friends first. Get to know each other, and then decide if we really want to take things to the next level."

I looked at him and thought, *this guy is weird. Normally, I didn't have to be this forward with any guy.*

"Isn't that why we should go out? Duh?"

He laughed. "Eventually. I just think that keeping a safe distance will help me to see if you're just as beautiful on the inside."

"Okay if that's how you want it," I was thinking it was the strangest thing. "So, what do you need to know about me that you haven't already read in the media?" I asked. Why did I do that? This Negro grilled me with questions to the point I felt like I was being interviewed for *him*. I had to flip the script and ask him questions. The longer we talked, the more we learned about each other. But I was sick of the Q and-A's after the first half hour. Either we were going to hook up or we weren't. I didn't need to know his life story to determine if I wanted to sleep with him or not, because I knew I did. I'm not sure how he felt, but he was acting like I had to earn him. He had the game all wrong. I was not a woman to beg and I didn't like that he was trying to challenge me. He was a gardener! I felt he should have known better than to tell me to slow my road. I was a diva! I told guys how high to jump and they jumped.

My parents popped in and joined part of our conversation for a little while. Keith ended up staying for dinner. He met my brother Devin and my son Trey. I found out many things about Keith. He was originally from the Bay Area in Oakland, but moved to L.A. after his business took off. He considered landscaping a big dream of his, but I considered it thinking small, like Kyle would say. I thought, *who dreams of doing yard work? Seriously?* Keith mentioned that certain things happened in his life that made him dedicate himself to God, but he never said *what* those things actually were, and at that moment I didn't probe. I know it was in poor taste, but in my mind I was imagining what Keith looked like naked in my bed; while he talked about the gospel and praised his church. It didn't even seem real that a guy so young and handsome would be devoted to God like he was. My parents were hung on his every word and seemed delighted by the way he spoke. After a while, I started clock watching, and then I excused myself from the scene all together.

Keith and I kept in touch after that evening, but he was moving way too slow, and I needed my bed warmed. Since there was no commitment between us or a romantic relationship, I started dating. I got the heat I wanted occasionally, but in a weird way, I found myself comparing my dates to Keith and ended up feeling unsatisfied because they didn't measure up.

"Your dates are failing because you keep picking whack dudes," Keith would say. I knew he was a little jealous, it was kind of true. They were whack!

"Let's not talk about those old ladies you said who like you at your church," I would counter back.

"I don't know why that is. I'm twenty-eight, but women in their forties and fifties are always approaching me," Keith laughed. "I respect my sisters, but I prefer to file for social security around the same time, know what I mean?" We cracked up laughing. That's how most of our conversations were–cordial, but funny. I wasn't a phone person until I met Keith. I preferred face time, so I could read facial expressions and gestures. Strangely, our conversations on the phone, emails or instant messaging seemed to be drawing us closer as friends, despite the fact that we were moving at a snail's pace. Within a few months, I began to look forward to seeing messages from him on my email or voicemail, and when I didn't receive one, I called him. I was breaking my own rule about not ever calling a guy unless it was a return call. We would talk on the phone for hours and sometimes I would fall asleep on the phone or he would fall asleep. I even called Keith while on my breaks at the studio, and he would call me on his lunch hour. Never in my life did I actually have lengthily conversations with a guy, except Tony Tee, but he was like my brother. Keith and I left no stone unturned and talked about everything it seemed. He invited me to his church often, and eventually I gave in and went a couple of times. Keith even convinced me to call Kay-Kay and apologize to her.

"You want *me* to apologize?"

"Yes, too much time has passed, and she's your friend. Finding a good friend is like finding a diamond in the ruff. You should rekindle your friendship and appreciate the treasures you have," Keith said to me, during another midnight conversation. I couldn't believe I actually followed his suggestion and called Kay-Kay the next day. Keith made it seem so easy to do. His reasoning was so honest and the things he would suggest for me always seemed to make sense.

"I'd like to meet Keith, because if he could convince you to apologize, he must be someone really special," Kay-Kay said, after accepting my apology.

"You can meet him tomorrow at church. I promised that I would come and visit again, and bring Trey. You guys should come. I miss seeing you anyway."

To my surprise, Kay-Kay, her husband Damien, and my godchildren came. I never in a million years thought Kay-Kay would actually join a church, but Keith persuaded her to do it the very same day of her visit. For me, I can't say that I was focused on anything spiritual, really, but I loved seeing Keith's role in the church and how he helped his parishioners run the church. Everyone there seemed to love Keith, from elderly women to the small children. Keith also lent a hand to some of the disabled ones, helping them to sit down or to get into their vehicles. Some of the women who liked Keith gave me the evil eye so often that I could feel their burning stares through my clothes. Keith never left me feeling alone when I visited his church. I know I had Trey there with me,

Kay-Kay and her family, but Keith always introduced me to a new face. He also explained how the church operated. Keith definitely had a zeal for God, and I admired his faith. He persuaded Kay-Kay to join the Bible study group, and she did that too! I thought she was faking the funk at first, but before long, she was going to Bible study every Wednesday night faithfully. Damien and I were the odd ones out. We had to gradually find our own way. During this time, it was definitely God who helped me and Kay-Kay rekindle our friendship. I felt empty without Kay-Kay, like a part of me was missing. It felt so good to have her back in my life again.

It was like any other date I had. I came home tired after dinner and dancing, and then I would reevaluate if I wanted to go out with the guy again or not. A couple of dates Kyle had set me up with, and they were literally "setups!" The guys Kyle introduced me to were so arrogant and snobbish that I couldn't take it. Tonight's date was no different, it failed. I kicked off my heels and crawled into bed after midnight. There weren't any messages from Keith, so I called him. It took a while before he answered, and I prayed he would answer despite it being late.

"I guess we must have been on each other's mind," Keith finally answered. I knew he was looking at his caller I.D. because he didn't say hello.

"If I was on your mind why didn't you call?"

"I figured you were still out on your date. So, how did it go with Raymond?"

"You mean Ricky?"

"Yeah, that dude or whatever his name is."

"The restaurant was nice, but the conversation was so boring that I was rehearsing lines to my next gig in my head."

Keith laughed. "I told you he didn't seem like your type from what you told me about him."

"He talked about himself the whole night, and then had the nerve to think he was going to get some. Pah-lease. That pencil headed geek. He was not about to get my sweetness that's for sure. He got the bill to my dinner and that's about it."

"Well, it's time you go out with a real man. How about I take you out to see *Armageddon?*" he asked. I held the phone away from my ear and stared at the receiver for a moment. I couldn't believe he was asking me out. After all, we had been talking for a few months now. I had started school and everything, but I still made time for Keith. I never had that type of friendship with a guy besides Tony Tee, and I loved having Keith as a friend. Yet, I tried not to show too much excitement to Keith asking me out, but I was really happy.

"You know that movie is *not* about the Bible, don't you?"

"Of course, it's just an action flick."

"Whatever! Seriously? You expect me to believe that?"

"You seem to think because I'm a Christian that I'm a fanatic. I don't take everything literally. I know how to chill and have fun, live life."

"Show me, and then I will believe you."

"All right doubting Thomas. What time shall I pick you up?"

Keith and I went out on our first date. I thought he was going to pick me up in a *Sanford & Son* red pickup truck, but he picked me up in a silver Acura SUV with dark-tinted windows and shiny 22-inch rims. I gave him a few cool points mentally for having the latest wheels. I was still pushing my black '95 Mercedes convertible that Bruce bought me.

Keith opened the door and helped me to step up and get inside. The smell of cherry tree air freshener greeted my nose, and I loved it. I was used to guys' cars smelling like weed, beer, or some other woman.

"These are for you." Keith reached behind his seat and handed me two dozen yellow roses.

"These are beautiful. I never received *yellow* roses before."

"I'm a different kind of guy. Most dudes give girls *red* roses, but the fact that I gave you yellow will always make you remember me, and how special our friendship is. At least I hope you will." He winked those big sexy eyes at me. I smiled, thinking about how romantic the gesture was.

After the movie, we went out to dinner all the way out in Malibu, about a 45-minute drive from my house in Bel-Air. We both knew we liked seafood, so Keith made reservations for us at *The Open Shell*, a five-star restaurant overlooking the beach. It was so beautiful. I remember it to this day.

"How did you find such a nice restaurant like this?" I was surprised that a landscape guy knew about classy places. I imaged Keith taking his dates out to franchise restaurants, which I couldn't stand. I preferred elite places that your average Joe didn't know about or couldn't afford.

"I have a few clients out here, and I actually live about five minutes from here. I own a condo further up the hill." He pointed.

"I totally misjudged you, Keith."

"I know. I could tell. I kind of like showing bourgeois people why they shouldn't prejudge others."

My eyes widened. "I know you're not calling me bourgeois."

"You don't think you're bourgeois?"

"Uhm…no, I do not."

"Pah-lease!" He cracked up. "You're like a black valley girl. *Seriously? Are you serious? That's totally not cool, really? Me? I wouldn't be caught dead wearing that ugly dress she's wearing! Bourgeois? Not even!*"

I fell out laughing. He'd impersonated me so well that he could have won an Oscar!

After dinner, we walked along the beach holding hands, and he draped his suit jacket over my shoulders. We talked about everything it seemed, and then we sat down in the sand. I sat between his long legs and leaned my head back against his chest as he cuddled me in his arms. We stared at the waves crashing into the huge rocks and gazed at the moon and the stars in the dark sky. It was so peaceful and tranquil that I felt like I was in heaven. The moment felt surreal. I had never experienced anything so romantic.

"What are you thinking about?" Keith whispered softly in my ear as a light breeze blew through my hair.

"I'm thinking this is the best date I have ever had in my life."

"Scooore!" he pumped a fist in the air.

"I'm serious." I looked over my shoulder at him. "But I am scared."

"Why?"

"You want the truth?"

"That's always best."

"I have a habit of like totally screwing things up, and I seriously don't want to break your heart."

"That's why we're taking things slow." He tightened his hairy muscular arms around me. We gazed at the moonlight reflecting off the waves. I started thinking about all the conversations Keith and I had, and out of those discussions, I felt there was something missing. After going through so many bad relationships, including a tumultuous divorce with Bruce, it was hard for me to trust what I was feeling for Keith. He almost felt too good to be true. I promised myself that I would never give my heart to another guy again unless I was absolutely sure of the man he was. Keith seemed too perfect, like he didn't have any flaws, except annoying me sometimes when he quoted scriptures for everything.

"You never told me some of the things you used to do before you became a Christian." I slowly stood up and turned around to face him. He stood, and dusted off the sand from his pants before taking hold of my hands.

"I told you all the things I felt was important for you to know."

"Yeah I know your favorites and your dislikes. I know you're the youngest of four boys, and you never knew who your father was. I know you're from the Bay and all of that. You know about me, Bruce, my son, and of course you know my family, but who is the *real* Keith? I want to know what he was like before he became a Christian."

Keith gently pulled my hair behind my ears, and then kissed my forehead. "Why is my past so important to you?"

"You're hiding something." I gave him a playful shove and walked away. Keith quickly caught up with me and took hold of my hand.

"You don't want to know the truth about me," He said, pausing, as he kneeled down, picked up a rock and tossed it out into the water.

"Then why would I ask?"

His facial expression began to change from a look of contentment to uneasiness. He looked at me with an unfamiliar stare like he was afraid.

"It's getting late. I should take you home." He tried to steer me towards the truck, where he had parked at the top of the hill, but I let go of his hand.

"You can't run away from your past; it's always there, Keith. If anyone knows that, it's me."

Keith heaved a deep sigh, and slowly pulled me into his arms, and held me.

"Every day, I look at my son and I'm reminded of Bruce," I gazed into his eyes. "The older he gets, the more he looks like Bruce and less like me. Although we're divorced, it's like he's there in the physical form of Trey. I don't regret my son, but every day he is a reminder that me and Bruce happened."

"I understand, but some things I just can't talk about Tracey." I could see tears forming in his eyes, as I reached up and stroked the side of his face.

"Sometimes the past hurts, but it gets easier to deal with when we talk about it. It's the best way to let it go."

"When we first met, you asked me if I played ball, and I did play basketball for a long time, but never professionally," Keith began to explain. "I wanted to be like my brothers, so I joined a gang instead of accepting a basketball scholarship. I started slanging and moved my way up the ranks. I became a connected man. If I told one of my boys I wanted somebody dead, they would be killed by the snap of my fingers. I had lots of money, cars, women, and I owned a few drycleaners. I'm not proud to say this, but I ran a brothel with a few pimps too." As he explained, I remember thinking to myself, there was no way that *this* Keith used to be a pimp and a drug dealer.

"One day, I got caught slipping. I cheated on my girl with one of the women at the brothel. The hoes...I mean the girls set me up. They were jealous of my girlfriend because I gave her the best of everything. To make a long story short, when I got back to my house, I caught my girlfriend flushing keys of dope in the toilet. She was yelling, "This will teach you not to ever cheat on me again!" I lost it. I hate to think about it now, but–"

"But what?" I stared at him, feeling nervous and anxious. I had never heard a story like his before. It sounded like a movie.

"I was enraged Tracey and...I beat her up. I beat her up pretty bad."

"Oh my gosh!"

"I ended up doing three years in San Quentin."

"Wow, I...I don't know what to say." I stepped back from him. In disbelief I walked back to the spot where we had been sitting. When I looked up, Keith was approaching me and he sat down slowly next to me. We sat silently for a while, and I remember this eerie feeling I had in my gut about him.

"I have to ask what you did to your ex-girlfriend." I hoped that Keith wasn't an abusive man, and what happened had been an isolated incident.

"I would rather not say."

"You *need* to say it and let me judge if we'll continue our friendship."

"All I know is that she ended up with a broken jaw and fractured ribs."

"WHAT?!"

He dropped his head. "I still feel bad about it, Tracey. It's not easy for me to talk about. You have to know that."

"What happens if I make you mad?"

Keith's big eyes gazed into mine, and then looked away. He stared out at the ocean, watching the waves crash into the big stones.

"I already paid for what I did Tracey. I served three years. Not a day went by that I didn't think about what I had done to her. When I got out, things didn't get any better."

"What happened?"

"The dope she flushed in the toilet had to be paid. Those guys were hunting for me. I was a wanted man. My boys turned against me, and my girl ended up having a baby with my best friend."

I shook my head in disbelief. The story was getting deeper by the minute.

"So did you pay the guys back their money?"

"I would have paid them if I had it, but I was fresh out the joint. No job and no connect."

"So how does your story end?"

"They knocked down my mother's door. I was hiding in the closet in her bedroom. I was on my knees, praying to God asking him to forgive me for everything I had done. I prayed and I said to God that if he saved my life, I would give him mine forever. I was only twenty-three years old, but I made a promise if God kept me alive my life was his from that day forward."

"And then what happened?" I was hung on his every word.

"They found me in the closet. It was like they knew exactly where to look. The strangest thing is I had a gun in that closet, but for some reason I could not reach for it. It was like something was holding me back. I was frozen."

"And?" My heart raced with anticipation.

"The door opened, and they shot me up."

"WHAT?!"

"See," He lifted his shirt. Buried underneath his hairy chest, I could see indentions from the bullet wounds. I counted at least ten. I gently ran my fingers over his healed wounds.

"Everyone in the hood thought I was dead. They were shocked to see me when I got out the hospital. There was a minister who came and prayed with me every day in the hospital with my Mom at my bedside. His name was Sonny. After I healed, rehabbed and all of that good stuff, I got baptized and never looked back. It was Sonny who came to me like a messenger from God. I lived in the basement of the church, and I took care of the grounds as a way to show God I was thankful. Sonny told me I was good with landscaping, and that I needed to get my license and move out of Oakland. He gave me startup money, and once things picked up, I packed my bags and moved out here. I never looked back. I never asked God for anything, except to bless me with a wife and kids. I want my own family you know?"

"I understand," I held his hand. "So, whatever happened to the guys who shot you?"

"They're dead I guess. You know how it is. It's an endless cycle."

"And your brothers?"

"Locked up on some gangbanging stuff."

"How did you get involved with that stuff in the first place? I mean, it doesn't seem like you have the personality to get into that type of stuff, like seriously, I'm totally shocked!"

"Girls like ball players, but they prefer the dudes with money. Now that's enough about the past," Keith stated, he looked exasperated. "I hate the person I used to be, but I love the man I am now by God's mercy and grace."

I smiled. "At least now I know why your faith is so strong. You're a walking miracle, Keith."

"God can change you too if you let him."

I blushed. "I take your word for it."

"Remember, when you told me you screamed for God to save you off that balcony and that if he saved you, you would serve him?"

"Well, I was caught in the moment. All people cry for God or their mother when they're afraid."

"If you say so, but I think God is calling you. You should listen to his voice."

Brian McKnight was singing, *The Only One for Me* from Keith's CD that was playing during the ride back to my house. I thought a lot about

Keith's story. It was an awful lot to take in, but I felt really special that he shared all of that with me and trusted me with it. Keith reached over and held my hand while keeping his eyes on the road. I was surprised at how affectionate he had been throughout our date. Normally, he seemed to shy away whenever I touched him. I guess after knowing me for a few months, he finally felt comfortable with me. Now that I knew his story, I hoped he would be even more affectionate.

"Here we are, the BIG house," Keith chuckled. I pressed the password to get through the gates. We drove up the hill and Keith parked his truck out front of the roundabout driveway with the fountain in the middle. The censor lights illuminated around the whole mansion. It looked so pretty. I lived here all my life pretty much and still loved it.

"I hope you had as much fun as I did." Keith walked me inside and we stood in the corridor holding hands under the dim lights of the chandeliers.

"I had a great time. Thank you." I stood on my tip toes and kissed his cheek. That's when he stepped in closer to me. He smelled so good, and looked so good, that the simple touch of his lips against mine excited me. I couldn't control myself anymore. I grabbed hold of his face and rushed my tongue into his mouth. He quickly pulled away, and I felt embarrassed.

"Patience," he whispered, and then he kissed me very slowly and gently. It was passionate, but tender. Sweet, but gentle. Slowly, Keith pulled away, and I lie to you not, I felt dizzy when he stopped kissing me. I thought *What is this guy doing to me?*

"I know a secret place in here we can go to right now if you like." I circled my finger in the palm of his hand.

He grinned. "I want you to understand something."

"What's that?"

"When we make love it won't be rushed, and we won't have to do it in hiding, because we'll have God's blessing on our marriage."

I wanted to strip him naked right then and there.

"I should go."

"Nooo, Keith, please."

"We have to control ourselves."

"Seriously? You're going to leave me hanging?"

He gently stroked the side of my face. "I promise to make up for every moment like this. See, you're use to the quickies, one shot tricks and bangs, but baby I promise to show you what love feels like."

"You can show me now."

"Goodnight my love," he tenderly kissed my lips and left.

He left me standing there in the corridor, holding my purse, feeling hot and aroused, and there was nothing I could do about it. I felt like a little girl who just had her candy taken away.

"Seems like you had a good night."

I turned around. It was my mother's voice calling out of the near darkness. She was wearing a robe and drinking something hot from a mug.

"Yeah I guess," I pouted.

"You all right? Would you like to come into the sitting room and talk about it?" she asked. I thought about it for a moment and decided I needed to calm myself somehow.

Mom and I sat down in the sitting room to the right of the corridor. I told her all about my date with Keith and our overall friendship, relationship or whatever it was. I didn't share his story, of course, but I talked about our general relationship.

"…and despite the fact that Keith is a good man, I don't know if I can be in a relationship with him like this."

"What do you mean?"

"Okay, if I tell you the truth, you can't judge me. I just need you to hear me as a woman. Promise?"

"I promise."

"Keith believes in waiting until marriage before you have…well, you know."

"Sex?"

"Exactly. While I respect Keith and his beliefs, that's not who I am. I believe if two people are responsible adults, they should be allowed to have sex. If they happen to be in love, that's an added bonus."

"I see."

"Mom, please don't think I'm sleazy. I'm just being honest. I have strong feelings for Keith, but I don't want to marry him just so we can have sex. Marriage is a serious commitment, and after what I just went through with Bruce, I'm definitely not ready to get married again."

"That's a tough decision to make, but I don't want to see either one of you get hurt."

"I know. That's why this is so hard for me. I know Keith wants me, and he keeps teasing me. That doesn't make things any easier for me."

"Honey, you need to be honest with Keith like you're being with me. Don't string him along knowing you have strong reservations about being committed. He shouldn't flirt with you either. It's unfair to play those kinds of games, it's dangerous."

"So what should I do Mom?"

"Letting go of each other now doesn't mean you won't have a future, especially if it's meant to be. Sometimes love is about timing. When your Dad and I got together, the timing was right. Before then, I was too busy chasing my career. I had to get to a point where I understood what really mattered to me. Think about what's really important for Tracey right now, in this moment."

"Mom, I don't want to lose Keith as a friend. We're just getting started."

"You can't have it both ways Tracey."

"Well, I guess I have a lot to think about."

"It will work out for the best," she hugged me.

"Thanks Mom. I love you."

"I love you too. It's time we go to bed. And you, my daughter, need to take a cold shower first."

That was one of the best conversations I had with my Mom. I don't know what made her open up and want to talk about men and relationships. Maybe she saw that I was becoming my own person. Maybe she was trying to help me not to make the same mistakes I had made in the past, like marrying Bruce. I don't know, but it felt good to be friends with my mother. From that moment on, we would continue to talk openly about everything, and not just men. I saw my mother as more easygoing most of the time. Occasionally, some of her views were still a little condescending, but I could live with our differences. She had the right to be her own person too. I was just happy that we were talking *to* each other and not *at* each other anymore. As for me and Keith, I gradually avoided taking his phone calls and responding to emails from him. I was getting really busy with my career and taking care of Trey. I stopped making time for Keith on purpose. I was hoping that somehow

Keith would take the hint, but he kept calling. I had no choice but to be more direct about what I wanted…

CHAPTER SIX
DEAN JR.

Dean Jr. was running on the treadmill in the exercise room of his brownstone home on Garfield Place. He was listening to the audio version of Tracey's book while he worked out. He texted Tracey and told her that he didn't like the fact that she painted him as a gullible man who was weak-willed when it came to women.

"Sorry bro didn't mean it that way. Love ya!" She texted back.

Dean shook his head, put his phone back in the pocket of his shorts, and continued to jog on the treadmill. He hit the play button on his iPod again, and put his headphones back in his ears so he could finish up the book...

Keith and I met for lunch in Beverly Hills a few weeks later, so we could talk face-to-face. While we ate sushi and drank Coronas, we had small talk at first. I told him I was busy filming for a new show called *For Your Love,* starring Holly Robinson-Pete. Between acting, school, and taking care of Trey, I was pretty busy.

"...I also did a couple of photo shoots for *Hype Hair* magazine, see?"

His lips curved a handsome smile at my portfolio. "Beautiful."

"Kyle also got me a cosmetic contract. I have my own makeup line, called TGM. I created the logo and everything. Can you believe I'm now Tracey Gina Michaels Incorporated? I'm a brand now. Isn't that great?!"

"That's great, but I really miss seeing you, Tracey." Keith slid his hand across the table and rested it on top of mine. "Sounds like you've been pretty busy. No wonder we've hardly had time to talk."

I slid my hand from underneath his. I tried to be all business with him. "So, how are things for you?"

"Thanks to your parents' referrals, business is doing great."

"That's good, I'm proud of you!"

"My staff was so excited. It means they'll all get a pay increase."

"I bet they were excited. They probably worked minimum wage anyway, right?" I laughed.

"Tracey, come on, don't be so shallow."

"I was only kidding!"

"Well, I've been thinking since we've been working so hard, why not do something fun together this weekend? Have you ever been rock climbing?"

"No, but I heard it's fun." I took a sip of my Corona with a straw.

"Let's do it." He clapped his hands. "Let's go rock climbing this Saturday. I'll pick you up at seven. We'll get there early before it gets too hot and humid."

I cleared my throat. "Uhm…actually, that's not a good idea right now."

He hunched his shoulder. "Why not? Are you busy this weekend, too?" he asked, and I could hear the desperation in his voice since I had been turning him down a lot lately.

"Keith, there's something I need to tell you, and it's hard for me to say." I placed my hand over my heart.

His expression grew concerned. "Just say it, Tracey."

I took a deep breath. "I think we shouldn't go any further than just being friends. We shouldn't date anymore."

Keith leaned back in his chair and looked the other way.

"I'm sorry, Keith." I patted his hand. "This may sound cliché, but it's not you, it's me. I'm not ready to get married right now. I just got a divorce a year ago, and I know you're hoping our relationship will lead to that. Knowing that's how you feel, I need to step out of your way so you can find someone who can give you what you want." Each word I spoke made me feel like I was throwing darts at a good guy for no reason. The solemn look on his face and the way he kept avoiding eye-contact made me feel even worse. Keith rubbed his chin in thought, puffed his cheeks out, and slowly blew out air from his mouth. I watched as he blinked back hurtful tears.

He howled, "Okay, if this is what you want, I have to respect how you feel." I wanted to jump across the table and hug him and tell him that everything would be all right. I felt so bad. It was the same familiar pain I felt when I broke up with Todd back in high school. Now I was giving another nice guy the axe. Another good egg was leaving my nest.

The ride back to my house was a silent one, and as usual, Keith was playing Brian McKnight. I glanced at the yellow roses in my lap that he brought me, and I felt so bad. I wasn't sure what I was giving up. I started to question whether or not I was doing the right thing. I wish I could take back what I said and fix things so both of us could be happy.

"If you ever need anything, Keith, I mean anything, please call me." I told him sincerely, as we stood outside of my house. I planted a soft, gentle kiss on his lips that I would remember forever. Keith held two fingers over his lips as if he was savoring the moment. I reached up and cupped the side of his cheek with my hands. His eyes opened and he stared at me intensely, as if my touch warmed his soul. I attempted to kiss him again, but he slowly stepped away from me.

"Take care of yourself, Tracey. Be blessed."

"Thank you, Keith. You do the same."

My heart hurt, and some nights I couldn't sleep. That's how I knew it was a mistake to let Keith go. For the short period of time that he was in my life, he helped me mend my friendship with Kay-Kay; he helped to better my relationship with my mother, and made me care just a little bit about spiritual things. I never met anyone who encouraged me to change for the better; they usually brought out the worse in me. In the coming months I tried to bury my pain behind my career. Mom was no dummy, she noticed it and said to me, "Baby, I know it hurts to love someone and have to set them free, but if Keith ever comes back to you, he's yours." I was hoping one day he would. I hoped that he understood I wasn't ready for marriage, but that it didn't mean I wouldn't ever be. Like mom said, timing was everything.

My career was really taking off in the months that followed. With a steady flow of acting jobs coming in, I saved up enough money to move out and get my own place. Since I was still attending USC, I wanted to live closer to the campus. I found a nice luxury apartment on Scott Road in Burbank. It was twenty minutes away from USC. While it wasn't like the Wilshire, it was still a very nice complex, with evenly aligned palm trees along the sidewalks, and plenty of good parking spaces on the streets. The amenities were awesome. There was a washer and dryer in every unit, free cable, an outdoor pool, and a full gym. It wasn't a high-rise apartment, because I'd been afraid of heights ever since Bruce tried to throw me from a balcony. My apartment was on the second floor of the three-story building. It was a very spacious two-bedrooms with a den, lots of countertop space in the kitchen, plenty of closets, and a walkout balcony with a beautiful view of the swimming pool out back. When the landlord handed me the keys, I couldn't believe I finally got something I could call my own. I had cleaned up my credit report, and didn't need anyone to cosign for me nor pay the security deposit. Signing my name on the lease felt better than signing autographs.

[*Yeah, I remember when you moved. I was home for the holidays and we all helped you to move out,* Dean said to himself as he jogged on the treadmill.]

Right before my family left, after helping Trey and I get settled, I felt this overwhelming feeling that I was no longer a child anymore. I was a grown woman who would be living on her own for the very first time. I wasn't married, I wasn't moving in with a roommate or a boyfriend; it was going to be just me and my son. It felt kind of scary at first, I won't lie. I was already feeling lonely.

"Mom, Dad!" I called out to them, right before they left. My brothers continued to head out to the car.

"What's wrong, honey?" Mom anxiously wanted to know.

"Oh nothing's wrong Mom, it's just that…" I fidgeted around with my new apartment keys in my hands, trying to find the right words to say. "I'm going to miss you."

"We'll miss you too honey," Mom and I hugged.

"Thank you both for raising me to be the woman I am now. I know it wasn't easy, and I'm truly sorry for all the heartache I caused you guys. But look at me now." My eyes gazed the room. "I have my own place, and I'm finding my way!"

"We're very proud of you, Tracey."

"Very proud, and we're also very glad that you're gone."

"Oh, Dad, you always got jokes."

"Just make sure you set the alarm every night, and watch your surroundings. I know this is a quiet neighborhood, but always look over your shoulders both day and night."

"I will, Dad." I hugged him.

When they left, I sat down on the sofa with Trey next to me. He was flipping the channels with a remote in his hand, searching for cartoons.

"It's me and you from now on buddy. Mommy will take good care of you with my *real* job, okay?"

"Okay," he answered, but his attention was on the TV more than me.

I walked into my bedroom to call my friends and share the news. I gave them my new address and phone number. There were two people who I really wanted to share my happiness with–Keith and Kay-Kay. I purposely saved the best for last. Calling Kay-Kay was easy, but I was hesitant with Keith because we hadn't spoken in months.

"Hello?" Damien answered.

"Hi Damien, it's Tracey. Is Kay-Kay home?"

"Hey, Tracey. Sure, hold on."

"Keyshia!" I heard him yell in the background for her, and she picked up the other end.

"Hello?"

"Hey Kay, how are you?"

"I'm good. I'm up here doing Jazmine and Dana's hair for church tomorrow. You coming?"

"No, it's time I find a new church home. You know I moved this weekend."

"Oh yeah that's right. How did everything go?"

"Girl it's too quiet."

Kay laughed. "Get used to it. You're on your own now, girlie. Just you and my godson, Trey."

"I know, right. Who would have thought?"

"So, I read about you and Keith's breakup today in *Sister2Sister* magazine."

"What? How did we end up in there?"

"Ask your boy Kyle."

"I didn't know anything about that magazine. He's supposed to ask me first before he goes to the press about anything."

"Well, it's no wonder we haven't seen Keith as much at church. When he is there, he acts like somebody died. He doesn't say much and hangs his head low. As soon as services are over, he dashes out the door."

"I'm sorry to hear he's taking it so hard. Maybe calling to give him my new address isn't a good idea, huh?"

"That's up to you, but I don't see your point unless you plan on seeing each other again. That back and forth stuff can play on a person's emotions, and Keith already seems more down than up."

"Why are you just telling me all of this?"

"You've been busy filming. Besides, what difference does it make?"

"You're right," I sighed behind the phone. "Anyway, let me call Kyle and find out how my relationship with Keith got out to the press."

"Good luck with that."

I called Kyle right after I hung up with Kay, but I got his voicemail, and decided I'd speak with him in person some other time. Against Kay-Kay's advice, I called Keith anyway, but he wasn't home so I left my new contact info on his voicemail. I hoped he would call me back, but he never did.

["*Part Three,*" the audio voice said, and Dean let the book play from there while he took a break, so he could drink some water.]

One Year later...

It was the year 2000, a year that was supposed to be Armageddon for all of mankind. Yet when we all woke up the next day, we were thankful that life was exactly the same as it was before. I know I was. At that time, I was a junior year at USC. Trey was in the second grade, and I had just finished filming *Remember the Titans,* where I played one of the football player's girlfriends. It was my first major movie. I was proud to have met such a wonderful cast, as well as work with Denzel Washington. I had also written half my book by then, and requested an extension with the publishing company. I finally got rid of the 95' Mercedes, and bought a white 2000 Trident Iceni convertible for a hundred thousand dollars. I used the advance money from my new makeup line to purchase it. I'm kicking myself now, because that was too much money for a car! Yet, I had to have it, and I was the first amongst my celebrity friends to buy one. And oh boy, did it attract a lot of attention! When I pulled up in front of the red carpet during the premier of Remember the Titans, Trey and I could barely get out without the cameras flashing in our faces. Even the valet guy was excited to go park it for us. I was living the life, and had little time for dating anyone seriously. But every time I heard a Brian McKnight song, I thought about Keith Smith. I tried calling him a few more times, but I didn't leave messages anymore. The last time I called him, I was shocked that his phone number had been changed, to "non-published number" the operator said. I thought to myself, *seriously! You're not the only one disappointed that things didn't work out, but I was hoping we could still be friends. Geez!*

After the movie premiere, the next day was back to normal. I woke up early to get ready for class, and to get Trey ready for school. We sat down ate breakfast together, and then headed out. I opened the door and I was surprised to see Tony Tee since I hadn't seen him in a while. He came over when I first moved, but it had been over a year now. I was even more surprised by who was with him. I didn't need to see his eyes through the dark sunshades to know who he was. From the nose downward and by his cocky stance, I knew.

"Whatcha looking all scared for, Ma?" He still called me Ma. It used to be a term of endearment, but now it made my skin crawl. "I just came to see my son, if that's all right with you," He said it like a demand and not a question.

I slid Trey's jacket on, "Trey, this is your father."

"He know me!"

"Trey, you remember me, don't you?" Bruce removed his dark shades, and rubbed the top of Trey's head. "Yeah, you my little man so don't ever forget that. You're my only son, you know that? You got half-sisters so you gonna have to look out for them one day, all right shawty?"

"Okay," Trey said under his breath.

"You want me to take you to get a pair of them new *Jordan's* homey?"

"Yes," Trey murmured. He rocked side-to-side nervously as he held his backpack. I could see the fear in his eyes. He was only agreeing with Bruce because he was scared.

"Come on, let's go shopping," Bruce grabbed his hand like he was a little kid, but Trey wasn't a little boy anymore. He was seven and growing tall.

"Bruce, Trey has school today, what are you doing?!" I stopped them at the door and snatched Trey away from him.

"I'll take him to school after I take him to buy some kicks. Ain't nothing wrong with him being a little late, is it? I mean, I ain't seen my son since I been up in the joint, so give me a break, Ma."

I took Trey by the hand. "Trey, go to your room and watch TV, okay?"

"Okay," Trey hesitated, and then looked over his shoulder. "Mommy, do you want me to call Granddad? He used to be a cop, you know."

"Everything is okay. We'll be just fine," I declared. Trey walked out the living room and down the hall to his room.

"Bruce, you're not welcome in my house, and I need you to leave right now before I call the police!" I had tried to keep calm with Trey around, but with him out of sight, I lit into Bruce.

"You ain't gotta get all nasty Ma, know what I'm saying? I'm leaving, but I'll be back to see my son."

"I don't want you to come near me or my son ever again!"

"Your son?" he barked defensively. "He's my son too, and don't you ever forget that!" he pointed his shades at me as if he was about to throw them.

"B, chill out, man. Just go ahead and leave. Wait for me in the car," Tony said to Bruce, who took his time in leaving out. My heart was racing fast. I was feeling anger and fear at the same time, and one of those emotions was about to take over.

When Bruce left, I lit into Tony like fireworks. I didn't appreciate neither one of them just showing up at my place.

"...and you got some nerve to be hanging out with Bruce after all the terrible things he did to me!"

"We're label mates. We plan to make music together and that's it. Besides, he's *your* enemy not mine."

"Tony you just broke the code to our friendship. I thought you would be more loyal to me than this."

"Tracey, you're like my sister. I would never betray you. Bruce just wanted to see his son. What's the big deal?"

"I don't care! Bruce knows he's not supposed to just show up at my house! I have a restraining order against him."

"I'm sorry, Tracey. I didn't know. It won't happen again. I swear!"

"Look, I'm late for class and Trey is late for school, so please just leave and don't come back. As a matter of fact, lose my number."

"Tracey, when we get there?"

"Just now," I opened the door for him to leave.

"But Tracey—"

I threw up my hands, not wanting to hear any more excuses. I opened the door, and Tony took the hint and left. I peeped out my window and when I saw them drive off, Trey and I headed out.

I told my lawyer what happened later that day after class, and he sent Bruce and his lawyer a reminder letter that Bruce was to stay away from me, as per court orders. Also, Bruce could only have supervised visitation with Trey, which meant that his probation officer or a social worker assigned by the court had to be with him. From then on, we didn't have any trouble out of Bruce until I heard the lyrics to Bruce's new song...

"Tracey was supposed to be a fan, but she trapped me to be her man/had my baby, then she got lazy/flipping out on me and going all crazy/She was my ride or die chick turned into a trick/all she saw was dollar signs like the hoes on Sunset..."

Kyle and I sued Bruce for defamation of character, and ordered a cease and desist. My mother heard the song too. Trust me, it was raunchier than that, and I don't want to repeat it. My parents were both furious. Mom got so angry that she made sure Bruce would never release another album after that. What little money he made from that one record, I took it when I sued him for child support.

"Why you trying to ruin me, Ma?" Bruce snatched me by the back of my hair. I was right in the middle of auditioning for the movie *Baby Boy,* which was scheduled to be released in 2001. To this day I'm not sure how he got pass security.

"Hey, it's not going down like that!" one of the guys who had already been cast in the movie shoved Bruce.

"This is our beef, homey. You ain't got nothing to do with this here, homes!" Bruce shoved him back, and next thing I knew they were fighting on the set, and I didn't get the part. The studio thought I was going to bring trouble. Bruce was supposed to stay away from me by court orders. Not only did he come near me, but by grabbing my hair, he was charged with assault. He was forced to serve his remaining sentence of three years, plus they tagged on another year for him violating his parole by putting his hands on me. I was happy Bruce was back in jail, but Kyle was totally upset that I didn't get the part in the movie. In fact, a part of him acted like it was my fault. "Now I have to fix this mess. Get it together girl. I can't keep cleaning up your mess!" he argued with me. We went back and forth until I just hung up the phone on him. We didn't speak for a couple of weeks after that. It didn't matter to me how Kyle felt. I was just glad that Bruce was back where he belonged. Obviously, Bruce loved jail because he stayed in trouble. He got a kick out of harassing me. He was always on some get back "*ish*", so now he was back in the slammer. He had the nerve to write a letter to Trey talking about I made it hard for him to be a father. Seriously? I threw that letter in the trash! Bruce needed help!

By 2002, I'd done it! I earned my bachelor's degree in Dramatic Arts from the University of Southern California. Despite Bruce trying to hold me down and put me down, I moved forward with my life. I never thought I would see myself with my own place, car, and a college degree. My parents were so proud! We all went out to celebrate. We partied on Dad's boat as we cruised to Catalina Island. We had an awesome time!

Not all good times last unfortunately, just a few weeks after graduating, Kay-Kay called me while I was on the set for the movie, Drumline. I had earned a small role in the movie as one of the dancers in the band. I tried to ignore my cellphone, but it kept vibrating. I knew it must have been important. The director allowed me to be excused, and I was glad he was nice about it.

"Kay-Kay, have you lost your mind? This had better be important. I'm filming Drumline with Nick Cannon."

"Tracey!" her voice cracked. "It's bad news, girl. It's bad!"

"What is it? Did something happen to Jazmine or Dana?"

"No, they're fine." She burst out crying.

"Is it Damien?"

"No, it's...it's Tony Tee. He's dead, Tracey. He was killed in a drive-by shooting!"

"Noooo! You can't be serious!"

"I'm not playing. His manager was at my shop when they called her. The word on the streets is that Bruce had his boys to put a hit on him, Tracey."

"What? But why would he do that?"

"Because he and Tony had a beef before Bruce got locked up again and Tony came out with a stupid diss record about Bruce," she explained, crying at the same time. It took me a minute to get myself together. The last time Tony and I had talked was when I kicked him out my house. We hadn't had a chance to reconcile our friendship. I felt terrible. I don't remember what steps I took next, but I remember being at Tony's funeral a week later, bawling my eyes out.

[*That's the life he wanted to live. Tony Tee was never a thug. I could see he was just trying to be someone he was not, when he switched record labels.* Dean Jr. moved from the treadmill and started bench-pressing weights.]

At the funeral, there were tons of people. My family came and showed their support as well. At the repast, held at the Beverly Hills Hotel, it was just as crowded as the church. Special music selections were played by well-known music artists while guests ate fancy finger food like it was a wedding reception. Afterwards, guests were offered to share expressions to the family, and we each stepped up to the podium. After I said what I needed to say, I sat down with my head hung low. I was waiting for the day to be over. My heart ached so bad, it felt like I had been hit with a ton of bricks. I felt sick to my stomach. Tony and I never had a chance to reconcile our friendship. His death made me see how important it really was to put aside differences and learn how to forgive others. I clung to Kay-Kay's hand and she squeezed mine. She felt just as sad. The three of us used to be so close. Now it was just me and Kay-Kay.

"Hello everyone, my name is Keith Smith…"

I lifted my head to make sure my ears heard correctly. And there he was, the tall, handsome man I had met a few years ago in my father's office. He had grown a fuller mustache and goatee. I figured he had to be thirty-two or thirty-three by then.

"I met Tony Tee a few months ago when he asked me if I thought his backyard had enough room for a swimming pool," Keith said, and everyone started laughing. "I said, you have enough room for a swimming pool, but if you think I'm going to install one, you got the wrong guy." More laughter followed; my own included. "I just want to say that in the short time that I knew Tony, he seemed like a guy with a big heart and he was really smart. The conversations we had led me to believe he wanted to do something different with his life. He mentioned he wanted to try his hand at acting or host his own TV show, but he seemed too afraid to do it. He was worried about his "boys" and what the fans would think. I told Tony, I said, listen man, if God is for you, let no man on this earth hold you back. Do what you feel is right."

"Amen!" People shouted and applauded, including my parents.

"One day we shall all meet Brother Tony again in paradise," Keith concluded.

After the repast, we all headed to our vehicles. I tried hard to see if Keith was around, and finally spotted him talking to my parents in front of their Mercedes. With so many attendees, we got separated when leaving the hotel.

"Come on, Trey, let's go say hello to Keith. Do you remember Keith?"

"Yeah, he's the gardener for my grandparents." Trey ran over to Keith and almost knocked him down, as he was talking to my parents. Keith gave him a big hug and a high five.

"Well it was good seeing you, Keith, keep up the good work," Dad was saying.

"Bye Dad, bye Mom," I waved, as they got into their cars, leaving me and Trey standing in front of Keith.

"So, what's up, Trey? You're all grown up now, my man. How old are you?" Keith asked him in between taking glances at me. Trey was growing; it was amazing how tall he'd become over the last two years.

"Nine." Trey poked out his chest a little. He was a little show-off.

"Trey, go tell Jazmine and Dana goodbye before they get in the car with their parents," I said to him.

"All right. Peace out, Keith!" he threw up the peace sign with his fingers. We watched Trey run off.

"How are you?" Keith and I both asked each other at the same time.

"I'm okay I guess, you?" A part of me was still thinking about Tony and the other part of me was happy to see Keith.

"I'm taking this loss pretty hard."

"I'm sorry. I know he was your friend," Keith reached down and wrapped his arms around me. He smelled so good and I felt comfortable being in his arms. In those few seconds it felt like we had tuned out the world around us. I wanted him to hold me forever. His sexy saxophone voice, whispered in my ear, "Let me know if you need anything." I parted my lips to say *I need you,* but nothing came out because…

"Keith, we should get going now." A woman wearing a purple dress with matching pumps seemed to appear from the crowd of people who was searching for their cars on the parking lot. She looked much older than Keith, and I was surprised, because he said he never wanted to date a woman who was much older than he was. She looked like she was ten years older than him.

"Tracey, this is my fiancée Hope. Hope, this is Tracey."

"Hi Tracey. Aren't you the actress from *For Your Love?* "

I forced a smile. "Yes, that's me."

"I heard they're cancelling the show though, right?"

"It's already cancelled. We taped our last episode last month. Now I'm finalizing a new film that will be out later this year, called *Drumline.*"

"Such is the life of a Hollywood star. I guess sometimes you never know when your next paycheck will come," She laughed.

"For some of us it's not a job. It's a career that pays good money. That's my Icenti over there. Some people call them Aston Martins. *Such is the life of a Hollywood Star, right?*"

Keith cleared his throat, breaking the tension between us. "Well, um…I'm happy for you, Tracey, I knew you always had it in you." Keith said, giving me another hug. "I know Drumline will be a success." To this day, I wonder if he hugged me on purpose in front of Hope.

[*Of course he did, sis!* Dean laughed to himself as he continued to work out].

It hurt to know that Keith was engaged to be married. When my mother called me later that day to see if Keith and I reconnected, I told her about his engagement. "Are you going to be okay?" she asked. I lied and told her it was no big deal. "I'm totally over Keith."

[*Dean pressed the fast-forward button, tired of hearing about Tracey and Keith. He skipped through a bit more of her brooding to the chapter titled,* My Big Break!]

Months later, Kyle called me with more good news. He had gotten me an audition for *Ice Cube's Barbershop.*

"You need to hurry to the studio now," Kyle shouted anxiously over the phone.

"Now?"

"Yes, right now, as in the present. I know it's last minute, but as soon as I found out about this, I begged the casting directors to audition one more girl for the part of Terri Jones. You need to be there in thirty minutes, because they're already packing it up. They're waiting on you, so knock 'em dead girl!"

I called one of my girlfriends from USC, and she agreed to come over to my house to keep an eye on Trey. Trey was old enough to be home alone, but I didn't trust him yet. He was still very immature for his age.

"All the best, girl." My friend gave me a hug.

"Thanks!" I donned my helmet and riding gear for my motorcycle. I knew the quickest way to get to Studio City was to ride my motorcycle, and take the back way through the hills. I sped off as quickly as I could. If you have ever driven in Hollywood Hills, you know there are tight winding roads. Therefore, I felt driving my motorcycle would help me maneuver with ease. Suddenly, there was a truck coming towards me on Laurelwood, full speed, and it didn't look like it was going to shift to my left to make room for me. The street had a narrow two-way lane, so it was either I was going to hit the trashcans lined along the side of the houses or hit the truck. I swerved and hit the trashcans that went flying in the air, but one of the trash barrels got caught underneath the wheel of my motorcycle. I flipped in midair. I remember flying off the bike, and I could see that I was going to land on the front windshield of the truck. I threw up my arms, but the whole front part of my body went through the front glass windshield, and my lower body crashed into the hood, then I blacked out.

When I came to, I was in the hospital. My parents were holding my hands praying over me. They told me that Keith had stopped by, and they showed me the 'get well' flowers he had bought me. The only thing I could remember was the doctor telling me I broke my collar bone, both of my legs, and had a concussion. I didn't remember seeing Keith at all.

I was in the hospital for two months before they released me. The swelling on my brain had to go down first. I felt depressed because I wasn't able to work. I missed seeing my son regularly. He was staying with my parents, since I wasn't able to care for his basic needs--cooking, laundry, cleaning, driving him to school, etc. He came to visit me on the weekends. He would sit and play *Connect Four* or *Uno* with me, but it wasn't the same. I was supposed to be his mother, but I felt like a patient he was visiting. I felt he was getting closer to my parents than with me. I hated the fact that I couldn't do for him. Each time he left my side, I felt a piece of my soul leaving with him. The loneliness began to set in, and I felt like a prisoner in my own home. I found no joy in watching TV because I knew I was supposed *to be* on TV or starring in a movie.

The guy who drove the delivery truck was arrested for reckless driving, and Kyle made sure my lawyers sued the company he was working for. They paid my medical bills and loss of wages. The funny thing is, when I look back, all of my bills *were* paid for. I just didn't see any extra money coming my way.

I requested a new physical therapist because the previous therapist seemed like she was causing more harm than good. While I waited for my new therapist to arrive at my house, I thumbed through magazines and cut out all the articles about my accident. While looking through the magazines, I discovered that the part went to somebody else. I was so upset that I didn't hear the doorbell ring. The caregiver told me my new therapist had arrived.

"Hello."

My gaze shifted from the magazines to the man walking through the door, wearing an all-white medical uniform. I stared at him and blinked twice. Couldn't believe who it was. I thought my mind was playing tricks on me. After all, I had suffered a concussion, and had occasional laps in memory.

"Noah? Noah King?"

"It is me." He smiled, a set of pearly whites against his dark chocolate skin. "How have you been? Not too good I see," he said, leaning down to hug me.

[*Oh boy! Not Mr. ladies' man, Noah!* Dean thought, as he continued to listen to the book while he did some stretches.]

"Thanks for coming to visit me. Did Kay-Kay tell you where I lived?"

"No, my job did. I am your new therapist," he smiled.

"Boy, you are not about to rehab my legs. You're like my little brother. We grew up together. Are you sure you know what you're doing?" I was freaking out. I didn't think Noah had the experience. I'd watched him grow up, and now the little boy who Kay-Kay and I would call Steve Urkel was a grown man. A handsome man at that!

"Did you not request a new physical therapist? I am that guy," he said sincerely, and I could hear a little bit of his Nigerian accent. Noah's was always heavier than Kay-Kay's for some reason.

"Seriously?"

"Yes." He pulled back the long locks of his hair into a ponytail. "I am serious. My goal is to help you to walk again. I understand your muscles just need to be retrained. It starts with your torso and upper-body, where your injuries were initiated. It will be very painful at first, but I will be as gentle as I can. Each day will become a bit easier. I promise," he said, and I chuckled at the fact that he never used contractions when he talked.

"Well," I set the magazines aside. "You sound like you know what you're doing."

"I did not study at Oxford to waste my parents' money, you know. Now, I am going to give you a massage."

I laughed out loud. "You're serious?"

"Tracey, stop asking me if I am serious. Come on, lie back and relax. We do not have all day."

Noah didn't waste any time in helping me. His strong hands massaged my legs and inner thighs. At first it felt like a medical routine, but from that day forward, when he would massage me, his touch felt sensual. I knew I wasn't going crazy from the meds I had to take. Noah was flirting with me and purposely trying to excite me. What can I say? It worked! The attraction between Noah and I grew stronger with each visit. Noah tried to come off as *all business* with me, but we started having conversations that were not related to anything medical. In a matter of weeks, Noah had me back on my feet. I walked with a cane at first, and then I no longer needed it. I was back to normal again. The only thing that reminded me that my injury even happened was the occasional migraines and the scar on my forehead that I covered with makeup. But hey, I made it through that accident alive, so I felt blessed.

"Tracey, you think maybe you and I can go out some time?"

"So it's true, huh?"

"What is true? What are you talking about?"

"You volunteered to be my therapist so you could wean your way to asking me out. I'm not stupid. I know you saw my name on my medical files before you accepted this assignment."

"Maybe part of that is true, but I really was doing my job. You are the one who started flirting with me. I would be lying if I said I did not like it."

"*Me* flirting with you? You're the one who started giving me all of those sensuous massages!"

He cracked up laughing. It was a loud goofy laugh that kind of reminded me of Keith's.

"One date."

"Okay, one date and I will not be fresh."

"And you can't tell your sister or she will kill me!"

He held up his hand. "I promise. One date. I will not tell, and I will not be fresh."

One night out with Noah led to several nights out. We had too much fun together not to go out again. We went out to the reggae clubs and bumped and grinded all night on the dance floor. To this day, when I hear Sean Paul's *Get Busy* I think about how much fun Noah and I had dancing. Noah knew he looked good too, because he would always wear his shirts half buttoned so his chest was exposed. All of the women would stare at him as if he was a Greek god. Taye Diggs had nothing on this man's body. He was chiseled!

Noah and I secretly dated each for weeks. Whenever he called me when Kay-Kay was around, I would send his call straight to my voicemail. After all, Kay-Kay used to have a crush on Dean Jr., and I told her I would knock her teeth out if she ever dated my brother, but there *I* was secretly dating her younger brother, Noah.

[*That's cute that Kay-Kay had a crush on me. I kind of knew it by the way she stared at me. I could never see us as a couple, though. Not because she was much younger than me, but Kay seemed to have a little chip on her shoulder. I don't like my women feisty.*]

"You and my brother have been rolling pretty tight these days," Kay-Kay said to me while we were out shopping at *Saks*. I had lost a lot of weight since my accident, and I couldn't fit any of my old clothes.

"We're just kicking it." I walked away from her and searched the racks for a cute skirt.

"Uh-huh, sure." Kay caught up to me. She was fishing hard and I was trying not to be the bait.

"I'm totally serious. We're good friends, and nothing more."

"Listen." Kay took hold of my arm like a mother does her child when she tells her not to touch something. "I know things didn't work out between you and Keith, but don't be desperate, Tracey. Noah is my brother. Don't be disrespectful."

I snatched my arm away. "Desperate? I'm far from desperate. If anything, your brother has his nose wide open for *me*."

"Then why lead him on if you know he likes you and you don't feel the same way about him?" Kay was hot on my heels. I couldn't turn around good without her being right up in my face demanding answers.

"I'm not leading him on. We know where we stand."

"Tracey, I just don't want you to hurt my brother. I've seen the way you dog out guys, and I don't want my brother to get his heart broken. He's very sensitive Tracey. When he gets hurt, he can be very spiteful."

I rolled my eyes to the ceiling.

"Tracey do you hear me in there?" she tapped my head.

"Stop it, Kay, cut it out!" I smacked her hand away.

"Answer this one question, and I want the honest truth."

I heaved a long sigh. "What is it?"

"Did you sleep with him?"

CHAPTER SEVEN
NOAH

Noah flipped to the next page on his iPad as he lay back in bed next to his sleeping fiancée. Thinking about Tracey tonight made him put some serious loving on her that made it much better than it had been for months. Noah glared at his fiancée; he could hear her faintly snoring. He smiled, and then continued to read Tracey's book…

My relationship with Noah made me feel like a teenager again. Noah was twenty-five, a few years younger than I was, but filled with vigor and life. We had this physical attraction to each other that was unexplainable. Yet each time we came close to taking things all the way, I turned him down. I was torn between my friendship with Kay-Kay and my relationship with him. What was a girl to do? Each time, it was getting harder to resist Noah, and one weekend we caught on fire!

Noah and I had just come from taking Trey to see the movie *Spider Man*. Trey was tired from an eventful day out. I was tired, myself. I kicked off my shoes and sat down on the sofa. Noah wasted no time to start kissing on me.

"Tracey. I love everything about you. I think you are an intelligent and talented *wo-man*." (I loved the way he said *wo-man*.), he continued to kiss me up and down my neck, working up a heat inside of me that I wasn't sure I could turn down.

"Noah…we…we…shouldn't," I panted heavily as he continued to kiss me down to my belly button. I wanted him so bad my body ached.

"But…but…" I gasped. "You're my best friend's little brother."

"Little brother?" his head jerked up from my lap. "There is nothing little about me. I am a man!"

I pushed him off me, stood up patted the wrinkles out of my cropped pants. "But I promised Kay-Kay I would not lead you on, so we have to say goodbye."

"Goodbye as in goodnight, or goodbye forever?"

I groaned. "Noah, I like you a lot, but I can't keep my promise to Kay-Kay if you keep kissing me like that. I just think we should be friends. I don't want to hurt Kay-Kay."

"My sister does not control my life!" he snapped. "I am a man. Nobody controls my life but me."

"Maybe you ought to take that up with Kay and help her understand."

"I will, but I want you. I want you right now!" He pulled me with force into his arms.

"And then what Noah? Let's say we bang each other's brains out, then what? Are you going to expect this to go somewhere? I can't commit to you."

"We can take our time Tracey, but tonight let me love you. Please! I am begging you. Just let me love you for tonight."

"I'm sorry Noah, but I can't. My friendship with Kay-Kay means the world to me."

[*What? What is this? This is lies! All lies! We made love that night! You did not write it in this book because of Keyshia!* Noah felt his body heating up in anger. He tossed his iPad to the side and crossed his arms. Yet, a part of him wasn't ready to give up on it. He was sure that somewhere in the story Tracey would confess what he hoped for.]

Mom and Aunt Peaches wrote a screenplay loosely based on their lives in Cabrini Green, called *A River Moves Forward*. The casting director wanted Mom to come by the studio to critique the lists of actors within a couple of weeks, but Mom had someone else in mind.

"What's this?" I asked when Mom came to visit me.

"It's the script for A River Moves Forward. I'd like for you to play me," She said, and my eyes widened with excitement at first. I didn't know what to say.

"Well?"

I looked away for a moment, pushed my afternoon lunch aside. Suddenly, I felt overwhelmed. It would be my first major film, in a starring role on a major cable network. I knew I was supposed to be happy about it, but I wasn't. I had mixed feelings.

"I can't."

"Why not? Is your schedule too busy?"

"It's not that," I stood up from my dining table and walked over to the living room to sit down.

"Well what's wrong?" Mom joined me on the sofa, rested her arm behind me.

"If I accept this role, you'll be *giving* it to me. I want to earn it so I can feel like it's mine."

"You're serious?"

"Yes, Mom. I want to audition for it like everybody else. You've done so much for me my whole life. People always think that children with celebrity parents don't have to work hard, but I want to prove them wrong."

"Go for it. Make me proud."

Noah still didn't like the idea of being just friends, but when I called and told him I was auditioning for a very important role, he agreed to help me rehearse my lines to A River Moves Forward.

"Noah you're pretty good at this," Kyle said, watching us rehearse at his mansion one evening.

"Do you really think so?" Noah beamed a big smile.

"Honey, yes, Kyle doesn't lie. You need to ditch that medical uniform and stop by my office tomorrow for a photo-shoot."

Noah blushed. "Acting is not my thing. It is Tracey's."

"Oh gosh! And listen to your beautiful accent, '*it is Tracey's*'. And that body of yours is to die for!" Kyle crossed one leg over the other. "Honey, we can make you a hot commodity. And you don't have to worry about acting with a body like yours, okay? I see potential. I also see a lot of chemistry between you and Miss Tracey, and I like it. I suggest at the next event you and Noah walk the red carpet together. Everyone will wonder who this gorgeous man is." I laughed at Kyle's suggestion at that time, but I never knew just how serious he really was.

When we left Kyle's office, I got a phone call that the studio wanted me to stop by for my second audition. My first audition was a monologue off the top of my head. The second audition was for the parts I had rehearsed with Noah. By the third audition, the casting directors had narrowed it down to me and another actress whose film credits were much longer than mine. I was so nervous that I couldn't sleep that night when I went home, but when the phone rang, I jumped up and answered it.

"Tracey, congratulations and…"

I didn't hear anything else. I just knew the part was mine. I started screaming in the phone. "Thank you thank you!" I danced around my room. My schooling and experience had paid off. It didn't matter that I went against someone else whose resume outshined mine. At the audition, I was the one who nailed it!

[*We went out to celebrate that night,* Noah recalled, as he was reading. *We also celebrated when we got back to your house, too. But where is that? I do not see it!*]

We filmed right on the turf of Cabrini Green and the surrounding areas. It was a hood like no other, and I didn't see how my mother and Aunt Peaches could have ever survived living in Cabrini. I was scared every day going on the set. There were gangbangers near who watched us film, and even with the police there I still felt nervous. Noah was right there by my side every day. I felt more protected with him near than I did with my security guards, and the police. My mother and Aunt Peaches actually connected with the people in the community. It was like they weren't even scared. I remember there were kids who drew my mother's name on T-shirts and they called her a hero. Months after we filmed, the mayor added a cross street to North Sedgwick, called Morris Place, in honor of Mom and Aunt Peaches.

The following year, 2003, the movie A River Moves Forward aired on cable television. The movie received great reviews, enough for me to earn an Emmy nomination. Kyle suggested that Noah escort me to the awards ceremony, so there we were sitting next to each other inside the Shrine Auditorium. Trey sat to my right and Noah set on my left. When Ellen DeGeneres announced the nominees for best new actress in a primetime movie, I squeezed Trey and Noah's hands. Kay-Kay and Damien sat opposite of Noah, and they both looked at me and smiled. I was so nervous that I couldn't keep my legs from shaking. I looked down the aisle and my parents gave me the thumbs up.

"And the winner is...Tracey Michaels!"

I couldn't believe my ears. Noah kissed me smack on the lips and told me congratulations. As I made my way towards the stage, Kay-Kay jumped up and hugged up. I saw my parents walk down the same aisle towards me and they hugged me too. We all stood there and hugged, before the camera directors hurried me to the stage. Kyle was already standing on stage waiting for me. To this day, I can't remember how he got to the stage so fast.

"Seriously?" I spoke into the mike, staring at the Emmy, and the audience cracked up laughing. They knew I made that word famous. "Thank you so much. I honestly didn't expect to win this, but I thank everyone who voted for me. I don't…I don't know what else to say. I'm totally in shock. I didn't even prepare a speech. I thank my parents, who never stopped believing in me, my brothers who have always been my protectors. My Aunt Peaches who always tell me to just be myself no matter what. I thank my son, Trey. Baby this *is a real job.*" (The audience laughed). I fought so hard to keep at this craft for you and for us. Together we did it!"

"Tracey, the clock is running out," someone whispered in my ear.

"Okay, I have to wrap it up. Oh…and how could I forget, my amazing manager, Kyle Lager. I thank my BFF Kay-Kay, and her brother Noah who helped support my career. And, thank you to all my fans!"

Kyle stepped to the mike when I was finally finished, but the music started playing and nobody heard him. We were quickly escorted backstage.

"Gee, thanks a lot Tracey!" he snapped. "I prepared a speech in case you won."

"Sorry."

"From now on, I want you to prepare a speech. Keep it brief and save some time for me to speak as well."

"Fine, Kyle. Just chill out."

He stormed off angrily. I couldn't believe he was that upset with me.

After the ceremony, we all went out to dinner to celebrate, and I did a special toast to thank my mother and Aunt Peaches for sharing their story with the world, and allowing me to play a part in it on screen. It was an incredible night for me. To think about it today still gives me Goosebumps.

When I got home that evening, Noah and I climbed the stairs to my apartment on the second floor. I felt like I was walking on clouds. I kissed my trophy all the way up the stairs, even though it was fake. The real one would be shipped out to me once they engraved it.

"Look, your fans are already leaving gifts at your door," Noah said, walking a few steps ahead of me. He picked up what looked like a vase, and when he turned around, my mouth dropped from what I saw.

"I know, it is amazing to you right?" Noah smiled, seeing my facial expression. I remained speechless, as I stumbled to get the key into the door.

"Here, hold it while I open the door," Noah took the keys from me.

"You should read the card." Noah removed his coat and walked towards the sofa and sat down while I deactivated the house alarm.

"Whoever it is has poor taste, because I would never send a woman yellow roses. Who does that?" Noah laughed, as I sat down next to him and ripped the envelope open, not caring if my nails got messed up. Noah slid his arm behind me and looked over my shoulder as I read the note.

Tracey,

Congratulations on your Emmy. You were always a winner in my book.

Keith Smith.

My heart fluttered, and my palms began to sweat.

"Who is Keith?"

"Uhm…just an old friend," I tucked the card in my purse. "Noah, maybe we should call it a night, I'm really tired," I yawned, stretched my arms to the ceiling.

"I was hoping we could perhaps pick up where we left off last time." he tried to kiss me but I turned my head.

"Let's just catch up some time tomorrow."

"What time?"

"I don't know. I'll call you, okay?" I remember hurrying Noah out of my apartment. With my back to the door, I caught my breath and listened to Noah's footsteps and the sound of his car driving away. I dashed to the phone in my living room to dial Keith. When I picked up the receiver, I realized I didn't have Keith's new phone number. I leaped from the sofa and ran through my whole apartment, trying to find the slightest bit of evidence of Keith's contact information. I found an old business card with his business phone number on it inside one of my old purses.

"Shoot!" I shouted to myself. "It's almost midnight. He's not at work now, and if I leave a message, he won't get it until tomorrow." I started to pace the room. Then an idea popped in my head to call my parents. I knew they would have his number, but then my mother would be nosy and want to know why I was calling Keith this time of night. I was losing my mind. I sat down to catch my breath. Despite my physical attraction to Noah and the amazing chemistry we had, Keith had a *Krazy Glue* grip on my heart that wouldn't let go. After all of this time, all of these years, I still loved Keith Jamal Smith. My heart was beating so fast that I could feel it in my throat. I paused to collect my thoughts and get a grip on myself. I wondered *What if the roses were as platonic as his visits to me at the hospital during my motorcycle accident? What if he's married? I shouldn't be freaking out and feeling like this about him if he's married.* One thing for sure, it was a good thing Trey was staying the night with his grandparents, or he would have thought his mom was going crazy!

I dialed my brother Devin on his direct line. "You want me to do what?" he asked, projecting his voice higher. He was a teenager now, no longer the little brother who used to snitch on me all the time and chase me around the house with his pet lizard.

"Please Devin, it's important. Check in Dad's office, I'm sure Keith's number is in his rolodex."

"Tracey, you are trippin'!" He griped. "You want me to get out the comforts of my bed while I'm having a good convo with my girl, and then go all the way downstairs to Dad's office to find some dude's phone number? I mean, can't you find somebody else for your booty call?"

"Seriously? This is NOT a booty call!"

"Yeah right!"

"I would do it for you."

"No you wouldn't."

"Okay, you're right, I totally would *not* do that for you, but you're not me okay? So just do this one favor for me. Do it because you're better than me. You're much nicer, kind, loving, giving and...."

"Go on, keep gassing my head up."

"Devin, just do it!"

He heaved a long sigh. "Look, I will do it this time, but don't call me again asking me no bull crap like this. Now hang up, and I will call you back with the number."

"Thank you so much, Devin, I love you!"

"Yeah right. I want a hundred dollars next time I see you."

"You got it! I promise!"

I paced the floor and waited for Devin to call me back. As soon as the phone rang I answered it. Devin told me the number and I jotted down all three; Keith's home, cell, and his work number again. I took a few deep breaths and sat down and dialed Keith's number. It had to be close to one in the morning by then. Keith's home phone rang a few times, and then I got his voicemail. I really didn't want to leave a message, so I prayed he would answer his cellphone instead. "Please God, let him answer. I love this man, and please don't let him be married. Please let him still love me!"

"Hello?"

Thank you God! I said to myself. That familiar deep voice sent chills all over my body.

"Keith?"

"Yes."

"Hi, it's Tracey."

"Hello Tracey, how are you?" he asked, I could hear faint music in the background and what sounded like air.

"I'm fine, and you?"

"I'm good, just on the road right now. Can I call you when I get home or tomorrow, since it's pretty late?"

"Uhm…wait a second, how far are you from where I live?"

"About ten minutes or so, why?"

"You should stop by and see me. I mean if you're not tired that is."

"I'm not tired, but I do think it's kind of late, don't you?"

"No, not at all. I feel too good to fall asleep."

"Alright. I'll be there in ten minutes," he replied, and just hearing his voice brought back so many memories of all of our late night conversations. I ran into the bathroom to freshen up a bit.

Although Keith said ten minutes it was really twenty, and I felt myself dozing off on the sofa until the sound of the doorbell woke me up. My excitement to see him returned, and I slowly got up off the sofa and walked to the door still wearing my evening gown. There he was, standing on the other side of the door, looking breathtaking. This was the first time I saw him wearing something other than a suit and tie. He was dressed down in a pair of black jeans and a *LA Raider's* jersey with black Timberland boots.

"Hi," we spoke at the same time. I invited him inside, and I could feel his eyes following my every move as we sat down on my sofa. Tamia's song, *Officially Missing You* played softly in the background.

"Why are you up so late?" Keith asked, stuffing a piece of bubble gum into his mouth. I stuck my hand out, and he gave me a piece before shoving the pack back into his pocket. He smelled so good. I could tell it wasn't the same cologne he used to wear, but it still smelled nice.

"I don't know. I was excited about tonight, I guess," I answered, blushing nervously. I wanted to ask him what kind of cologne he wore, but I didn't want to make it seem like I was flirting. I sung Tamia's song under my breath. I felt so nervous I couldn't look him in the eyes.

"You look beautiful. That dress really fits you." I could feel his big handsome eyes on me, as I looked off, twirling a string of my hair around my finger.

"Don't act shy," Keith gently tilted my chin towards him, and I blushed.

"You still have the same beautiful smile."

Each time he complimented me, the more nervous I felt. I usually felt confident.

"So, who was the guy that was sitting with you and your family at the awards?" he asked, sliding in closer to me, erasing the space between us.

"Oh, that was Noah. Kay-Kay's brother. He's a really good friend."

"A good friend, huh?" he smirked at first, then blew a big bubble and popped it loudly.

"Yes, he's been very supportive of my career. He also helped me to rehab my legs after the motorcycle accident. If it weren't for him, I don't know how I would have recovered."

"God would have healed you. It didn't have to be Noah, but it would have been somebody."

"Why are you hating on Noah?"

He rolled his eyes at me, and I loved how he couldn't hide his jealousy.

"Why'd you call me? Why you didn't call Noah?" he asked, stretching out his long legs before him.

"Maybe I wanted to see you so I could look you in the eyes and ask you why you sent me roses when we haven't spoken in a long time? I mean, did you even know I would win?"

He blew another huge bubble. Popped it.

"Well?"

"I believed in you. I always have, so I had the roses sent in advance."

"Aw that was so sweet. Thank you!"

"You're welcome."

"What're you doing out this time of night anyway?"

"One of my boys had a bachelor party tonight."

"Not your bachelor party? I'm shocked. Whatever happened with you and Hope?" I noticed he wasn't wearing a wedding band.

"If you must know, we broke up."

"Why? And don't say the past is the past."

He laughed out loud. No doubt he remembered how often he used to say that to me whenever I asked him personal questions.

"Why?" I pressed him.

"I don't know, Tracey. Maybe I wasn't ready. She sensed that, and I didn't want to lie about it."

"But all you ever talked about was marriage. I thought that was what you wanted."

His eyes locked with mine, and he said, "I only talked about marriage with you." I didn't know what to say. I was at a loss for words. Next thing I knew his lips were kissing mine.

"You still look beautiful," he gently caressed my cheek.

I returned a soft kiss to his lips, and that's when he cupped my cheeks and slowly slid his tongue into my mouth. The old Keith I knew would have pulled away, and told me to have self-control. This Keith gently sucked down on the tip of my tongue and held it. I eased back until I was lying down, and Keith lay on top of me. His mouth took over mine as he kissed me deeply and passionately. I glided my hands up his shirt and let them travel wherever they wanted to go. Keith shivered from the pleasure of my touch as I nestled in his warmth. I found the zipper on his jeans and quickly pulled it down. He was more than ready for me. He moaned softly from my touch, and then returned his lips to mine. I wanted him to take me right then and there. With Tamia singing in the background, setting the whole mood, I was ready.

"Hold on, I'll be right back," I slipped from underneath him, and I went into my room. When I came back with a condom in my hand, Keith was sitting up on the sofa with his clothes fixed.

"We can't do this," He exhaled as he stood up from the sofa, and his face was still flushed with passion. "I need to bounce."

"Keith, please don't leave." I took hold of his hand.

"We've been down this road before, Tracey."

I heaved a long sigh, unsure of what else to do. I shook my head upset. "We get stuck in this hot passionate place and then we don't do anything about it. You know what, just go," I tossed the condom packet on the table, and walked to the door. I opened it for Keith to leave, but he closed it shut. Keith took my hands and pinned them against the door and started kissing me around the tender spots of neck, and licking me around my ears. I tried to fight off his passion by turning my head away.

"Keith, please stop."

"Tracey, I love you, and that's never going to change," He gazed into my eyes. He looked drowsily in love with me.

"I love you too." Our eyes danced with each other. "I love you so much that it hurts to think about not being with you."

"I don't want to lose you again, Tracey," He started kissing me again, as he simultaneously unfastened his belt.

I pushed him off me. "And I don't want you to make love to me knowing you'll only wake up in the morning regretting it," I stepped away from the door.

"You'll regret it won't you, Keith? Tell the truth."

He shrugged his shoulders, and a look of uncertainty came over his face. "I don't know."

"Why don't you come pray with me," I walked from the door into the living room and sat down. I don't know what came over me.

"Now?" Even Keith looked shocked, as he fastened his pants back.

"Yes, right now." I patted the vacant spot next to me on the sofa.

Keith's eyebrows puckered, as he slowly walked over and sat next to me on the sofa.

"I want you to pray that we both control ourselves until we're married."

His lips curved a slight smile. "What are you saying?"

"I'm saying, I love you and I want us to be together no matter what."

Keith beamed with excitement. "You're serious? I mean, I don't want to push you into a commitment if you're not ready."

"Well I'm not saying it's going to be easy for me, but I am saying I love you enough to try. That's all I can promise."

He took hold of my hand. "Let's pray."

[*How could you spend months with me and then dump me for Keith in one night? This is unbelievable! You wrote all of this stuff about Keith and did not mention anything about us! This is unfair! I deserve better than this, Tracey! I am going to tell the world our truth. You watch and see!*]

Keith and I continued dating. We picked up where we had left off. We did everything together, and the press ate it up. 'Tracey dumps model boyfriend, Noah and gets back with the choir boy.' Despite winning an Emmy, they seemed more interested in my personal life than my career. They hid in bushes and snapped pictures when Keith and I went horseback riding, skiing in the Colorado Mountains, movies and dinner. The cameras were even there when we took Trey go-kart racing or to the carnival and the circus. We had no privacy, and I told Keith to never say anything to the cameras. Just smile and keep walking.

We flew out to Oakland where Trey and I met Keith's family. Surprisingly, the media wasn't anywhere in sight. Maybe because Keith was from the hood. Keith showed me his old stomping grounds by pointing out the corners where his runners used to sell drugs for him, and he showed me the houses where he ran the brothels. It was still hard to believe that such a religious man used to be a dealer and a pimp. As Keith continued to show me around, Trey hung out at Keith's mother's house with his younger cousins and played. Keith and I strolled the neighborhoods as Keith greeted his old friends. I was the celebrity in my own rite, and I signed a few autographs and snapped pictures with the people in Oakland. But Keith was well-known too, just in a different way. He knew so many people that it made *my* head spin. They acted like Keith was the mayor of Oakland, and surrounded him with warm welcomes. I was amazed that Keith was so humble about the love he received from his community. People respected him, and I felt honored to be by his side. I wasn't a trophy piece the way I had always felt in previous relationships, I was Keith's woman. He made that clear upon introduction, "I would like for you to meet my lady, Tracey." I felt special each time he said it.

"Well she's a beautiful woman just like her mother," one guy replied to Keith after being introduced to me.

Eventually, we went back to Keith's mother's house and had dinner. She was a very nice woman, but she seemed more excited that I was a celebrity. She asked about my parents a lot, and she also invited her friends over. "I told y'all she was staying the weekend with us," she said to her girlfriends. They were gawking at me like they couldn't believe I was actually there. They seemed even more surprised at how normal I was. "You like collard greens?" Mrs. Smith asked me. I tried to hide my laugh when I replied yes. When I told her my mother was coming out with a soul food cook book, she almost fell backwards out the chair in disbelieve!

We decided to visit my hometown, Chicago a few weeks later. I showed Keith out to the best restaurants in town. I also showed him where I'd lived when I was little…

"This is the house that Mason set on fire. You can't tell, can you? They did a good job rebuilding it. There's a small family that lives there now," I explained to Keith. While in Chicago, we visited my Aunt Peaches and Uncle George. Keith loved Chicago, and he thought Aunt Peaches was funny.

"Niecey, you done good girl. He's a looker. He's spiritual. Got his head on straight, don't mess that up. You mess that up and I'm gonna mess you up. I'm serious," Peaches said to me privately before we left. Aunt Peaches was a trip.

About a month or so later, I earned a role in the remake of the movie, *Fame,* and had to fly out to New York to film. Keith came with me, and we stayed with Dean Jr. and his family while I was filming. Keith had the chance to get to know my brother and his family. We also went to one of the Knicks games together, and Keith was so excited.

"Man, I never thought I would ever see a game up this close. Floor seats at the Knicks game. This is great, man. Thanks," Keith slapped hands with Dean. After the game, Dean introduced us to Allen Houston and Kirk Thomas. They signed the basketball to Keith, and gave him a couple of free jerseys. Even though Keith was a Laker's fan, he felt overjoyed meeting a couple of stars from the NBA.

"Man, I wished I had stayed at it and kept playing. That could have been me on the court," Keith awed.

By that summer, my mother had retired from BigStar Records, and we were having our last family reunion at the big house in Bel-Air. They were putting the mansion up for sale, and planned to move back to Chicago. The backyard barbeque was filled with family and old friends, and a few celebrities among them. As the evening wound down, and the sun began to set, Keith took the microphone from the deejay, and got everyone's attention.

"I just want to say thank you all for the food, the good times, and for embracing me as part of the family. As you all know, I've known this family for quite some time, and you guys have become like my own. I don't think nothing will solidify our family bond better than me asking this beautiful woman right here, if she would be my wife."

My mouth dropped.

"Tracey," Keith approached me. "Will you marry me?"

"Say yes Mom!" Trey shouted. Everyone cracked up laughing. (We have the whole thing on video. Maybe I should post it on *YouTube*. It was hilarious!)

"Yes," I cried.

Keith got down on one knee and placed the ring on my finger. It was beautiful. It wasn't forced, and we didn't celebrate it with a bunch of thugs the way Bruce had celebrated when he and I got engaged. It was special. Five months later, we were getting married. Kay-Kay helped me to find the best wedding coordinator who could put it all together within a short amount of time. Keith and I couldn't wait any longer to be together.

Our wedding day turned out beautiful. It was just the way we wanted it. I have a thing for balloons so we had balloons everywhere! They were red and white to match our color theme. The musical selection was by none other than Keith's favorite artist, Brian McKnight who sang, *Love of My Life* to our first dance. Booking Brian was part of my groom's gift for Keith.

Our honeymoon was in Jade Mountain, St. Lucia, and it was Keith's gift for me, because I always wanted to go there. It was a tropical paradise. In our honeymoon suite, Keith loved me from head-to-toe and did not disappoint. He gave me all of him, and I gave him all of me. We made love for hours, and couldn't get enough of each other. As soon as we caught a second wind, we were making love again. I loved Keith with my whole mind, body, and soul. Our love joined together was explosive, and so powerful that as I write this I feel excited all over again. Keith was so romantic, passionate, and gentle. He showed me things that blew my mind away. With Keith, I understood what it meant to make love. It wasn't just physical; it was mental, emotional, and spiritual. My mother once said that love was about timing, and she was right. God blessed me with a man who loved me and my son unconditionally. He never abused me physically or verbally like Bruce nor try to control and manipulate me like Zeek. Keith was a blessing. I finally came full circle with my life by not only marrying the man of my dreams, but earning my degree, starring in major movies and I was drawing closer to God. Everything was looking up for me. My journey to here was like riding the waves, and I finally sailed to the right shore.

[*This book stinks! You made me look like a handbag! I read this book all the way to the end for nothing! You mentioned me like you promised, but you left out a lot! I will show you! I will show you that you cannot get away with using people! You will see!*] Noah turned off his iPad and forced himself to go to sleep.]

Part Two

CHAPTER EIGHT
TODAY-2013

"Wow, you've had quite an amazing journey, Tracey," Autumn Whitman said, as I briefly talked about my book on her show, *Women's Plights*, here in New York. After years of delays and changing editors, I finally published, Riding the Waves. Now I was a guest on Autumn's show, as part of my book tour.

"So, how long have you and Keith been married now?" Autumn asked, as I sat on the sofa across from her.

"Next week will be nine years." I blushed, still feeling very much in love. (The audience applauded.)

"So, you're thirty-nine with three children now. Tell us about the kids," Autumn said, as the production crew flashed a family picture of us on the screen.

"Aw!" heaved the audience.

"They are adorable. They look just like their dad. Wouldn't you all agree?" she asked the audience, and they clapped in unison. My children's dark hair and big, long-lashed eyes glowed on the screen.

"So are the children in show business?" she asked.

"My son Trey is a sophomore at my alumni school USC, and he's studying business, but he produces music on the side with my brother Devin Dollarz." Younger ones in the audience cheered when I mentioned Devin's name. "My daughter Alexis just turned six, and my son Keith Jr. is five. My kids have a modeling contract with an international clothing line, but they only model during the summer, when school is out. Keith and I want them to live as much of a normal life as possible."

"Getting back to your book, congratulations on making the *New York Times Bestsellers* list."

(Audience applauded)

"Thank you."

"However, you have received criticism, particularly from the Christian community who felt your book was edgy. Do you agree those remarks?"

"Part of the reason I wrote Riding the Waves was to show people my struggles to find my own identity. I also wanted to show the youths out there why they shouldn't follow the path I took with drugs and alcohol, driving under the influence, and dating guys who just weren't good for me. I showed there was a price to pay for every decision that I made. As far as the Christian community is concerned, I respect how they feel. Everyone has a different conscious towards certain reading materials, but let's face it, my life story was not rated PG! I think the synopsis indicated that."

(The audience applauded in agreement).

"That's true." Autumn nodded, and then she took a sip of her coffee.

"Let me ask you this. Keith is studying to be an Ordained Minister at Pepperdine. How did he feel about you releasing this book, knowing that you would talk about your former "bad girl" behavior?"

"Well…" I paused and giggled a little. The audience laughed with me. "Naturally, he had some reservations about it. He's a man who likes to push ahead and not bring up things from the past, but I started working on this book project before we got together, and I was under contract to finish. So here it is."

"In terms of your career, I know you have done some really good movies within the past five years, two of which were blockbuster hits where you co-starred with some of Hollywood's heartthrobs. Do you think the path you're on will ever measure up to the legacy of your parents?"

Here we go. The media always bring up my parents. Isn't this my interview? Sheesh! I tried not to frown or give Autumn the evil eye.

"After all, your mother earned a star on the Hollywood Walk of Fame and–"

"I try not to compare myself to my parents." I cut her off before she laid out a long list of their credentials. "Our journeys are very different. I'm here because I've earned the right to be here, and I think my legacy will express my own originality and uniqueness."

"Understood. So tell us, what projects are you currently working on?"

"Right now, Kay-Kay and I started *Divas of L.A.*, a reality TV show where I'm executive producer, and Kay-Kay is co-producer. In fact, part of this interview today will be aired on the show when it debuts next week."

"Congratulations to you, Tracey," Autumn smiled. "Now in case our audience and our viewers at home may not know that Kay-Kay is no stranger to Hollywood. She's the stylists for many Hollywood celebrities, including Tracey. She also runs her own salon spa in L.A."

"And more importantly, she's been my BFF for thirty years," I added.

"Really? Wow, that's awesome. I didn't realize it had been that long!" Autumn's eyes widened behind her fake blue contacts.

"Well, I promised the audience I would let them ask questions, so let's start with Linda from Maryland," Autumn stated. Linda stood up in the audience. She had a microphone attached to her blouse.

"Hi Tracey. First I just want to say that you're very beautiful in person. Kay-Kay does an amazing job with your hair and wardrobe."

"Thank you Linda." I smiled, showing my new pearly veneers. "Kay-Kay is sitting three seats down from you, actually."

"Oh my gosh! It's Kay-Kay!" Linda's face flushed red with excitement and her belly jiggled. "I didn't even know." She covered her mouth, embarrassed. The audience laughed, and applauded when Kay-Kay stood up. She was wearing a white shirt with a black scarf tied around her neck. Her hair was pinned into a nice bun, and she wore dark framed glasses, a plaid skirt, and boots with thick heels. She sashayed up and gave Linda a hug. The audience clapped.

"Wow, okay, now where was I," Linda caught her breath, and the audience laughed with her. "I enjoyed reading your book, Tracey, but I just couldn't get past the fact that B-Money tried to throw you from a balcony! I was like oh my gosh, this dude is crazy!" The audience laughed, but mostly because of Linda's animated spirit. "I was wondering if you still talk to B-Money. I mean, what is your relationship with him today?"

"Honey, we don't have one."

Someone shouted from the audience. "I know that's right."

"Next question." Autumn pointed to another woman in the audience. She looked middle-aged and wore a wig that was too big for her tiny face...

"Tracey, I was wondering if you had any regrets about some of the things you've done in your life. As a mother myself, I got upset by the way you treated your parents. You were really rebellious and disrespectful. If I were your parents, I would have kicked you out a long time ago and not let you come back again."

"BOOOO!" heaved the audience.

"Don't *boo* her you guys. Everyone is entitled to their own opinion," Autumn tried to calm the audience. "Go on Tracey, please respond."

I cleared my throat. Clearly this woman was taking *my* life too seriously. The truth of the matter was, I was *not* her daughter; she needed to get over herself and have several seats.

"I can understand how you feel, but my parents were very understanding, kind, and loving. They knew I was trying to find myself and make my own way in this business. During those years, it was challenging for all of us. I know I hurt them a lot, and I have since made amends with my parents. I believe I showed my remorse in the book. What's important now is that our relationship is ten times better than what it was back then."

"That was a good question that she asked," Autumn mentioned. "Last year, you and your mother were on the cover of *Essence* magazine for the Mother's Day issue. In the magazine, you guys talked about how much better your relationship has gotten over the years. Miss, maybe you could check out that article online," Autumn stated to the lady. She nodded her head and slowly sat back down in her seat as Autumn invited another lady in the audience to ask a question.

"Tracey, you mentioned earlier that you don't have a relationship with B-Money, but do he and Trey have a relationship? Also, how did B-Money feel about you writing this book?"

"Trey hasn't seen B-Money since he was probably seven years old. My husband adopted Trey when we got married. In fact, he doesn't even have Bruce's last name anymore. As far as the book is concerned, B-Money signed a contract giving me permission to talk about our relationship in this book, but I'm not sure how he feels about it. Frankly, it doesn't matter to me what he thinks. I spoke my truth about it."

A woman sitting near the exit sign asked, "I want to know whatever happened between you and Noah King. In your book, Noah seemed to disappear after you and Keith got back together."

"Let me interject for a second," Autumn interrupted. "For our audiences at home, you may know Noah King as "Bison", the model and actor, but in Tracey's book, she uses his real name. Back then, he was a physical therapist. Here is Bison's cover shoot for Valentine's day this month." (The picture of Noah flashed on the screen.)

"WOO-WE! YES, BABY!" The audience roared when Noah's picture came up on the screen. His locks were past his shoulders, and he still had an amazing body. The picture showed him standing in the waters of a jungle, wearing only a pair of boxers. I knew this was a marketing ploy from Kyle.

"Well, Tracey, What *did* happen after you got back with Keith? Did you break up with Noah, or keep your chocolate *and* caramel?" Autumn teased. It wasn't a question that had been prearranged like the others. My mind searched for the right words to answer that question, because I knew the world was watching. Most of all, I knew Keith would probably see this.

"Noah and I were still friends after Keith and I got back together. We don't hate each other. We practically grew up together, and I'll always be appreciative of Noah's support. I think he's a great guy, and I'm happy for his success."

"But Tracey, we all know that Noah liked you as more than just a friend," Autumn probed more. "In your book, it's like he's crazy about you. Someone with that much insatiability cannot switch gears and say, 'let's go grab a beer.' Let's keep it real."

(The audience laughed).

"From my perspective, Noah is like my brother. He knows I'm married with children, and that I love my husband very much. I believe Noah has always understood that we could never be anything more than friends."

"Tracey, let me stop you right there. My producer just found this tweet on *Twitter* from Noah. He writes, 'If you are watching *Women's Plight*, Tracey Michaels claims her book, *Riding the Waves*, is the honest truth. What she did not mention was the love affair we had while she was engaged to Keith. To call herself a Christian these days is blasphemy.' That's the end of the tweet. So, what do you have to say about that Tracey?"

"Whoooa!" The audience seemed to go into an uproar like this was the *Jerry Springer Show.*

My mouth dropped. I wanted to jump out of my seat and run off the set. I felt my body shake, so I crossed one leg over the other to try to keep them still. I clapped my hands together so no one would see them shaking unsteadily.

"Tracey, how do you respond to that?" Autumn asked, over top of the audience going crazy. I took a deep breath and I smiled to try to hide my anxieties.

"Wow, I'm just as surprised as you guys are." I nervously scratched the side of my temple, and pulled my hair behind my ears. "I'm at a loss for words, and I have no idea why Noah would say that. My account of things is quite different."

"Well folks, there you have it. Whether something happened between Tracey and Bison, we'll never know. Well Tracey, thanks for being a guest on my show today. We wish you all the best."

"Thank you for having me."

"All of our guests will receive a free copy of Tracey's book. That's our time folks!" Autumn shouted over the theme music.

After the show, I took pictures with some of the guests. Then my security whisked me off into the back of my limo where Kyle and Kay-Kay were already inside waiting for me.

"I can't believe your brother said that, Kay," I told her, as I stepped into the limo, sat down, and removed my leather gloves and coat.

"I can't believe it either. I just called him and left a message for him to call me back," Kay replied.

Meanwhile, I sent Noah a text message...

'Noah, your comments on Twitter was distasteful. I thought you would've moved on by now. I know I have. I love Keith and I love my family. If you have an issue about my book, we can discuss it like adults, not on social media, so keep my name out your mouth!'

"Noah's comments are good publicity to your book," Kyle expressed, taking a sip of tea that had already been picked up for us by the driver.

"Who cares about publicity Kyle? I don't want Noah telling people stuff like that," I argued.

"More publicity means more money, whether it's good or bad. See, people are talking about you guys on Twitter now. You're a trending topic," Kyle leaned in to show me his phone. "People love good gossip, and it's obvious they love the two of you. This will be good for Bison. This will also be great for your book!"

"Kyle, will you shut up? Tracey is hurt by my brother's comment.

You should be comforting her, not telling her how she can cash in on a cruel rumor," Kay-Kay snapped.

Kyle's jaw dropped. "Horse face, you better saddle up them lips!"

Kay-Kay's eyes tightened and her lips formed a tight seam. "Horse face? You little walking drag queen midget! You don't care about anybody but yourself!"

"Honey I don't do drag, but I do *queen. And you,* my dear, need to check yourself, okay? Because I'm not the one you want to mess with. Got it? Good. I'm done." Kyle snapped his fingers.

"Why you little–" Kay-Kay quickly reached over me and snatched Kyle by his coat.

"Kay, stop it!" I shoved her back in her seat. "Kyle, you knock it off too with the name-calling. You guys are like my children." I cut my eyes at Kay, and then gave Kyle a sharp look. "Now we need to chill out and get it together before we do the *Jay Leno* show next. The last thing I need is my manager fighting with my BFF."

CHAPTER NINE
KEITH SMITH

Keith was putting on a show for the elementary school kids in the inner city Los Angeles. He and basketball all-star Tyson Marshall from the Los Angeles Clippers volunteered to speak with the children. They read stories to the kids, played with them, and did basketball tricks in the school gym. This was all part of the foundation Keith and Tracey started to help at-risk kids.

Keith did a few hands tricks with the basketball, Globe Trotter style, and the kids laughed. When it was Tyson's turn, he performed a complex variety of dribbles before finally running the ball up court to do a 360-dunk. The kids applauded and cheered for him much louder than Keith. Tyson continued with one acrobatic dunk after another, driving the kids crazy, until it was time for them to go back to class.

"Show off!" Keith joked as he and Tyson headed out of the school building after the program had ended.

"Don't hate on me, old man!"

"I still got my jump shot though. My knees may not let me dunk, but the "J" is on the money," Keith bragged.

"If you say so."

"On the real, thanks for hooping with me, man, I appreciate your support for these kids." Keith slapped hands with Tyson. When they hugged like brothers, Keith spotted a copy of Tracey's book sitting on the passenger seat inside Tyson's car. Tracey's book seemed like it was everywhere he looked. He couldn't ignore it. It was all over different websites, posted on social media, and he heard about it on the radio, and TV. Yet he never expected to see her book in the car of an athlete. To him, it seemed like mostly women had been interested in it.

"I see you got my wife's book," Keith acknowledged with a head nod.

"My girl gave it to me. She said, 'baby, you need to read this book,' and I just finished it today. I'm glad you reminded me that it was sitting there." Tyson unlocked the door, reached inside and grabbed it. "I brought it with me so you could ask Tracey to sign it for me."

Keith shrugged. "Sure, no problem."

"It's a good book, man, but I'm shocked you would let her put it all out there like that."

"She was under contract."

"So have you read it?" Tyson raised a curious brow.

"I already know her story." Keith tossed his backpack onto the seat of his Hummer.

Tyson scratched the side of his temple and rubbed his chin. "So um, let me ask you something, man."

"What's up?" Keith leaned against his truck and folded his arms.

"Did you ever ask Tracey about that cat, Noah?"

"Is this about what he tweeted the other day? If so, I don't believe that mess for one minute, man," Keith waved him off.

"I do. When I read Tracey's book, she never mentions Noah again after she won the Emmy and got back with you. He had feelings for her so I know he didn't just disappear. She should have said what happened between them after that."

"Maybe there was nothing more to say. She got back with me so obviously I was the chosen one."

"You better put that Bible down for a minute, my man, and read what your wife is putting out there. Look at this right here." Tyson leaned in and turned the page to the middle of the book. "You see these pictures, right?" Tyson thumbed through them. "All of them are different pictures from Tracey's childhood and important events in her life and all that stuff. Now look, right here before the portrait picture of your wedding day, she put a picture of Noah on the last page *with* his shirt off, posing. Right underneath it says, *what could have been*. He got the whole page to himself."

Keith grinned, laughed lightly. "It's just a stupid modeling picture, man, so what! And maybe they would have happened if we hadn't got back together. So what!"

"He's on the whole page though, Keith!" Tyson chuckled in disbelief. "You don't see a full picture of them other dudes up in here. She was married to Bruce for what? Four or five years? Only one small picture of him is in here. Why you think that is?"

"What are you trying to say man?" Keith asked, pointedly.

"I'm saying maybe Noah's comments were right. Maybe her relationship with him was more than what she said in her book."

"Why should that matter to me? I'm the one who got the prize. She's *my* wife."

"You forgot the part where Noah said he was banging her even while y'all were engaged. Remember that part on his tweet? She was still messing with the dude."

"So *he* says."

"All right homey, maybe you're right." Tyson slapped him a five. "Maybe it's nothing. Remember this, dawg, your wife is an actor. Pretending is her career. If she wanted to, she can fake it with you forever. I'm just saying....let's hope I'm wrong."

"You *are* wrong!" Keith was sure he was.

Keith tried to dismiss what Tyson was insinuating about his wife during his ride to pick up the kids from school, but Tyson's words kept ringing in his head like an alarm that wouldn't stop. *Your wife is an actor...she can fake it forever.* He turned on the radio to try to change his thoughts—put his mind someplace else. Jill Scott and Anthony Hamilton were singing *So in Love,* and Keith sung along until the song went off. A non-interesting program came on afterwards so he turned to another station.

"So we're back, and we're here talking to B-Money on Hot-93 on your FM dial," the radio host was saying. "...And we're talking about B-Money's ex-wife Tracey's bestselling book, *Riding the Waves.* B-Money was just saying there is truth to Noah's Twitter tweet from the other day. Yo' B, tell us what proof do you have about Noah's tweet?" *This thing is really blowing up,* Keith thought to himself. Keith reached out to press the button to turn the station, refusing to hear anymore until he heard his name, and decided not to turn just yet.

"... and Tracey was still seeing Noah while she was engaged to church boy, know what I'm saying? I saw them one night, walking hand-in-hand coming out of a club in L.A. They looked at me, and Tracey's mouth dropped when she saw me because she knew she was guilty. I never said a word, though."

"Okay so they were holding hands. That's not a big deal," the radio host said.

"Hold up, Ma, pump the brakes and let me finish," B-Money countered. "That wasn't the only time I saw them together. I saw them again like a month later. This was after old boy proposed or whatever, cuz' it was on *Entertainment Tonight*. They were sitting in the airport, looking googly-eyed at each other. Now, she was supposed to be getting married. Why was she still seeing Noah? And why were they flying together to Paris? Tell me that!"

"Maybe we should have Tracey on the show to address these accusations. We don't want to be responsible for gossip," the radio host stated.

"The only thing Noah is trying to tell y'all is don't believe the hype. That's what I been saying too. Tracey exaggerated stuff in her book, and she also left out a bunch things too, like how she even cheated on me when we were married. Tracey is a tramp. She's no Christian, pah-lease that's some funny stuff right there!" Bruce laughed. "She just married that dude because her manager Kyle told her it would look good for her image, but Tracey not the settling down type of chick. Real talk."

Keith turned the radio off and slid in his favorite Fred Hammond gospel CD. He could feel his temper rising from Bruce and Tyson's accusations. He knew that Tracey was seeing Noah during their time apart, but he recalled that she always said they were good friends. He wondered why after all this time, Noah would come forward and make those statements. After all, he seemed quite happy being the ladies' man these days as a model. This was the type of drama that Keith knew he didn't want for him and Tracey, especially now that he was trying to become an ordained minister and eventually have his own church. They had been doing just fine without the press in their faces until Tracey's book was released. As he questioned the puzzling rumors about his wife, his phone starting ringing. It was Tracey. He needed a minute to think, so he hit the *ignore* button and continued driving, singing to Fred Hammond, and praying. His business cellphone started ringing, and it was Tracey again. He hit *ignore*, but Tracey kept calling both phones— He finally decided to answer, thinking it must have been an emergency.

"What's up babe?"

"Where are you?" She sounded frantic.

"Headed to pick up the kids from school. Why?"

"Thank God!" Tracey shouted in relief. "Keith had a fall on the playground and busted his lip on the monkey bars."

"Is he okay?" Keith pressed the gas paddle and started driving way over the speed limit down the highway.

"The nurse said he will be okay, but she was worried that she couldn't reach you, so she called me. I've been totally freaking out, because I'm still in New York and you weren't answering your phone. I just didn't know what to do!"

"Just relax, honey, everything will be okay. I'm almost there. If the nurse said he's okay and he just busted his lip, then he'll be fine. It's all part of growing up and being a boy." Keith eased up on the gas, and his shoulders relaxed after Tracey gave him more details.

"But where were you, Keith?"

"I had the charity event at the school in Crenshaw for our foundation today, remember?"

"Oh yeah, I forgot. Sorry. How did it go?" Tracey asked, pausing to blow her nose in the background.

"It was pretty good. The kids were excited to see Tyson. He signed basketballs and a few jerseys for them. He also made a generous donation to the foundation, so we can keep helping public schools."

"That's great baby," Tracey pulled the phone away from her ear and sneezed several times.

"Sounds like you're getting sick out there."

"A little bit. The transition from California out here has gotten to me. It's cold here, and I heard it's snowing in DC. We're headed there tomorrow, and then Chicago will be our last stop. The ten city tour will be complete," Tracey said, sniffing behind the phone and sounding stuffy.

"Make sure you take care of yourself. You can always reschedule the two cities for a later date."

"I don't want to disappoint the fans. Besides, I'll be heading overseas soon, and after that I have a movie to film. If I cancel, I won't see my fans in DC and Chicago for at least a year," Tracey explained. Keith was trying to hold back from bringing up everything that was going on. He wanted to wait until she got home so they could speak face-to-face about these accusations between her and Noah. It was a good thing Tracey moved right along in the conversation and starting talking about something else other than her book.

"Well, I hate to cut you off babe, but I'm here at the school."

"That's okay, kiss our babies for me."

"I will."

"I love you."

"Ditto."

"Ditto?" Tracey chuckled. She knew Keith always said ditto if Tracey did something to upset him.

"When we get there?" she questioned.

"Don't worry about it. We can talk when you get home. Just take care of that cold, all right?"

"Fine."

Keith hung up. For a second, he stared at the phone, thought about calling her back by voice-recognition and apologizing for suddenly acting so distant, but decided not to.

Keith picked up the kids from school, and KJ was just fine like he thought. He drove to their home in Malibu—a beautiful five-bedroom home sitting up in the mountains. Just two years ago, they'd had a modern home in L.A., with only three bedrooms, a pool, and a very nice yard that he'd designed. The lawn was picture perfect, with plush green grass, a playground set, sandbox, and beautiful flowerbeds that lined the wooden fence. Tracey was offered a two million dollar advance for her tell-all book and a signing bonus for her reality TV show. Next thing he knew, they were buying a new house in the Malibu Luxury Estates. It was filled with more luxuries, such as an indoor and outdoor pool, tennis court, basketball court, and a miniature golf course. The estate sat on five acres of land, and the contemporary style mansion overlooked the ocean. The view was amazing, but Keith and the kids felt like they were far away from civilization. Every time Keith drove home, he felt like his house was further away from the city.

"Daddy, can I go swimming in the pool after this?" Alexis asked, while they were going over her math homework.

"No, it's getting dark out, and you have school tomorrow," he replied, thinking about just how much he missed the simple things in life. The pool was nice, and so was the Jacuzzi, but his wife wasn't there to share it with him. She had been gone for two weeks, but to Keith, it felt like two months. He was used to her being away when they first got married, but things were different now that they had kids. He couldn't just pack up their bags and travel with her. The kids had school, and hiring a tutor wasn't an option they wanted to take.

"Will Mommy be home tomorrow?" Alexis asked, she was always

filled with questions. It was as if every thought that came to her mind, she had to ask him a question with it. Keith watched her count on her fingers, and he was just noticing that she had gone a whole day with her ponytails lopsided.

"No, but she'll be home soon," Keith answered, his thoughts continued to travel elsewhere. Keith always pictured himself having a stay-at-home wife while he went out and made the bread. Now he was feeling like a house husband. Tracey insisted he quit his landscaping business, but part of the reason he'd never quit was he didn't want to feel like he was living in the shadows of his wife. He wanted to feel like a provider, a husband, a man of purpose. As he stared at Alexis' lopsided ponytail and glared at KJ's busted lip that he gave him an icepack for. He was reminded that he was a good father, but he missed the joint effort that it took to raise kids. He remembered the day he sat Tracey down to discuss her career ambitions; the response wasn't surprising.

"Kyle said people will soon forget about me if I don't get back out there soon. Besides, it's boring just staying at home doing nothing all day," Tracey had complained after the children were old enough to walk. She was ready to jump back into her career.

He warned Tracey, "Seek the kingdom first, then take of home, and everything else will come. God takes care of his own, but you need to be balanced. No one said to stay at home and do nothing. You can run your brand from home, and travel ever so often, but the constant "on the go" and taking on all these projects that keep you away from us. That's not healthy for our family." Tracey had insisted she was being balanced, but Keith didn't put up an argument. He knew enough about his wife to know that she was the type who had to learn the hard way.

"It's time for bed, guys, let's go. You did well on your homework assignments. Your teachers will be proud," Keith walked the children upstairs to their rooms.

"Goodnight," Keith said. "Put your pajamas on."

"But Daddy, we didn't take a bath," KJ protested. He smiled, revealing his two missing teeth.

"Yeah Daddy, you forgot to give us our bath, and we stink!" Alexis added. Keith shook his head, grinned at his animated children. He loved how they looked like him, but felt they could be dramatic like their mother.

"All right, let's get you guys ready for your bath. Sorry I forgot," He said to them. "Daddy is just a little tired that's all."

"It's all right Daddy, when Mommy gets home soon she can help you."

"Yes," Keith nodded. "She sure can."

CHAPTER TEN
TREY

Trey tried to be discreet as possible as he tiptoed up the wide spiral staircase and down the hall to his bedroom. He tried to remember which part of the floor squeaked, and he stepped over those sections. His heart raced as he got closer and closer to his bedroom. His body jerked when he heard the sound of a door opening behind him. He stopped, and slowly looked over his shoulder and spotted his six foot-four, muscular stepfather, with a bat in his hand. His hazel eyes widened with fear.

"Boy, I thought you were an intruder!" Keith shouted, then he relaxed his arm and the bat hung down at his side. "Aren't you supposed to be in school? You have classes tomorrow, right?"

"Dad, wha-wha-what are you doing with a bat? You're a preacher!"

"I'm protecting my family! You're lucky I'm not packing a gun the way I used to!"

Trey rested his hand over his heart as he gasped to catch his breath. "You scared me, Dad!"

"Serves you right," Keith snapped. "Man, you should've at least called to say you were coming home."

"My bad, I got out the studio late tonight, so I missed the curfew." His cellphone started ringing and he pulled it from the clip of his pants.

"Don't answer that. We need to talk."

"About what?" Trey wondered, shifting his weight from one foot to the other and folding his arms. Keith stared his stepson up and down. He was taller now, a young man, but skinny. He was sort of a lanky kid with a cute pretty boy face.

"You thuggin' out on me, is what. Look at you, pants sagging, and all these chains around your neck. And what's this, a tattoo?" Keith grabbed his arm and read the calligraphy of Trey's name with a microphone underneath.

"I'm an artist now, Dad. I have to represent, like Uncle Devin said. I can't be going around looking like a geek when I throw up gang signs."

"Gang banging is not your life, boy!" Keith shook his head in disgust. "It's not how your mother and I raised you. Didn't we have this conversation before? Didn't I tell you about my life and what happened to me? I could have been dead, man. I could have died in them streets, and here you are trying to live a life that's not even yours."

"Dad, this is me. I'm grown up now, know what I'm saying? It's time you and Mom accept that I changed, that's all."

Keith scoffed. "Changed into what? A *wangster*? Man you bucked from this bat and you calling yourself a gangster? If I had a gun you would've peed your pants."

"See, you got jokes, but I'm making money." Trey pulled out a stack of hundred dollar bills from his pocket. My single is out now, and my whole CD is about to drop. I'm blowing up Dad!' Trey flashed a half smile.

"Trey, listen man," Keith rested his hands on Trey's scrawny shoulders. "I don't want to see you end up hurt out here. One thing about the game is that you can't start late. Them busters out there on the streets been banging since they were kids. You can't be rapping about banging when you're not a real gangster. You don't want to get shot or end up in the cage like I was."

"Oh here we go again," Trey exhaled, rolled his eyes toward the ceiling. "You always preaching, Dad."

"And here you are not listening. I'm trying to tell you to stop being something you're not and quit making music that doesn't apply to you. You were born in wealth. You went to private schools, you never slung dope, you never owned a Low Rider, and you're not part of a gang. You're a sophomore at USC, studying business."

"Wrong!" Trey shoved Keith's hands off his shoulder. "I *was* a sophomore. I'm dropping out. It's time I take things to a whole new level with my career. I wasn't gonna say anything about it tonight, but I haven't been to classes in three weeks. I been busy promoting my music."

"Is that what you really want, Trey? To drop out of school? Ruin your future?"

"I'm not ruining my future. My future is now. My next single off my CD will air tomorrow. It's a diss track to Bruce Benjamin, my sperm donor, since he dissed my mother in his new song. I'm dissing him. He may not have said her name, but I know he was talking about her."

"WHAT?" Keith's eyes popped. "Are you crazy? That's how Tony

Tee got killed over a beef, and it's rumored your father had him killed!"

"I'm not worried about that. I had to defend my mother. The track is called *Has Been,* because that's what Bruce is. Check it, this how my song goes... *you ain't never been a father to me—a has been, all you did was implanted the seed—a has been, my mother married a deadbeat— has been, you went to jail and they set you free—a has been. But I'm putting you in the grave with these—has been, when you see me bow down to ya knees- has been, take these bullets cuz they came from me— has been. And if I see you—*"

"That's enough, man, I don't need to hear that crap!" Keith shouted. "You can't release that. I'm telling you now you're asking for serious trouble!"

"Too late Dad. BigStar Records will play it tomorrow."

"You signed with them? Tell me you didn't sign a deal with them without even talking to us about it first."

"I signed the deal, Dad. I'm grown. It's a two-album deal. They even gave me an Escalade as part of the signing bonus. It's outside," Trey grinned ear-to-ear with excitement. "They said, 'your grandmother Cat Morris was a legend for this company, and we see a legend in you and your Uncle Devin, your producer,' so they let both of us have whatever we wanted."

Keith groaned in distress. "Fine. This is going to break your mother's heart."

"I plan to tell her when she gets back. Or you can tell her."

"It's your life, man. This is your decision, you tell her yourself," Keith retorted. "But, one last thing. You can't stay here anymore. I don't want trouble to follow you into this house and endanger everybody else. This home is blessed. In my house we serve the Lord, and all that worldly stuff you can take that with you when you go."

"That's cool. I kind of figured you would say that since you're trying to become an ordained minister and all. I just came to get my stuff. Uncle Devin already told me I can stay with him if it went down like this."

"Let me share this scripture with you, man, and I want you to always remember it."

Trey giggled nonchalantly. "Go ahead, I'm listening."

"First Corinthians 10:12 says, *"Even if you think you can stand up to temptation, be careful not to fall.'*

"Okay, what does that have to do with us and this conversation?" Trey twisted his mouth in doubt.

"You may think you're at the top of your game, son, with all the fame, riches, glory, and girls. But like gravity, what goes up must come down, so be careful how you land."

CHAPTER ELEVEN
BARRY JOHNSON, AKA "BJ"

BJ didn't feel like being dragged out into the cold to go to the bookstore for an autograph of his own cousin's book. Yet, his wife, Sandra told him it was a good idea to show Tracey support while she was in town.

"After all, we missed seeing her during the holidays because she was busy filming a movie," Sandra pressed BJ.

Reluctantly, BJ climbed into his black *GMC Denali* truck, and drove his wife and children downtown to see their cousin, Tracey. It wasn't like he wasn't interested in supporting his cousin, but he couldn't understand why people were so obsessed about the lives of celebrities, as if they were gods.

"I can't wait to get Tracey to sign my book for me!" Bianca beamed a smile from the back seat.

"You read that book?" BJ cut his eyes at her from the front view mirror.

"Yes, and it was soooo good, Dad. You should read it!"

BJ took a glimpse at Sandra. "You let her read that junk?!"

"It's not *junk* BJ. Tracey left a positive message in her book for young girls, and now Bianca knows what *not* to do with her life."

"Humph, I already been telling her what *not* to do, and so have you. What makes it so special coming from Tracey?" he challenged. "Oh I get it, because she's a star right? Pah-lease! She made a mess of her life, and now all of a sudden she's got all the answers? If you ask me, she's just cashing in from her drama. You guys are suckers for falling for it!"

"You're such a grouch BJ!" Sandra contested.

"I'm not a grouch. If I'm going to read something it will be educational, and something that will feed my mind in a way that will be productive for my life. You guys get a kick out of living vicariously through other peoples' lives. That's why people watch so many reality shows, but really they should focus on their own lives. Everybody wants to air out their dirty laundry to the world for a buck. I don't have time to waste on that mess."

"BJ, you're so judgmental. When was the last time you examined your own life?"

"Don't go there with me Sandra," BJ cautioned her. "Not in front of the children."

She sucked her teeth. "Fine, let's drop it. Anyway, there's the book store right there!" Sandra pointed. BJ saw a long line wrapped around the corner.

"All right, I'm going to drop you and Bianca off right here. Me and Junior are going across the street to the sporting goods store. If I were you, I would skip the line. Tell them, Tracey is your cousin. I'm not trying to be downtown all day long."

Sandra and Bianca hurried inside the store, while BJ had to find a parking space inside a nearby garage. BJ always knew that if it weren't for his Aunt Connie, his cousins would not have the success they have today, and neither would his mother. He stepped out the truck, catching a glimpse of his reflection in its shine. He smiled proudly, feeling happy that he didn't have to capitalize on his Aunt's fame and fortune like other family members had. He paid for his truck with his own hard earned money from working as an architect. Although he felt grateful for his Aunt Connie taking care of him as a kid, he never asked her for anything as an adult. He felt good that it gave him an edge over his cousins. He set the alarm, and then he and Junior headed to the sporting goods store.

"Dad, I meant to tell you that Grandma Peaches called."

"Oh yeah?" BJ asked, while sorting through the fishing rods. He was ready for the spring. This Chicago winter was a rough one so far. He missed riding out on his boat catching fish.

"Yeah."

"Excuse me?"

"I meant yes sir. She called and asked if you were coming to hear her speak tomorrow at the Hope Center over in Roseland."

"Nope," BJ replied quickly.

"Yeah," Junior mumbled, as he tossed around a basketball in his hand. "I figured you would say that."

"Then why did you mention it?"

"Because she called. You said to always give you your phone messages."

"Well, tell her I'm not coming if she calls again."

"Yes sir."

BJ and Junior headed to the bookstore afterwards. As soon as they walked in, they had to squeeze by a crowd of fans waiting for Tracey's autograph. They maneuvered themselves through the crowd until they could see up front. BJ spotted Tracey sitting behind a long table, signing book after book for each customer, and smiling to take pictures. Behind her were Sandra and Bianca talking with Kay-Kay and Tracey's manager.

"Go tell your mother I'm ready to leave," BJ said to Junior, and he excused himself through the line until he reached his mother. He whispered in her ear, and when Sandra looked up and saw BJ on the other side, she motioned her hands for him to come over and join them.

"Come on!" Sandra hissed, and BJ slowly walked over.

"Hey Cuz!" Tracey smiled when she saw BJ approach the table.

"Hey, how is it going?"

"It's going great!" Tracey smiled, looking out at the crowd. "There's nothing like hometown love."

BJ forced a smile. "It was good seeing. Take care."

"Hey, you want a copy?" Tracey called after BJ.

"Nope," He replied, and Sandra glared at Tracey's happy expression. She watched it turn from a look of excitement to disappointment. She couldn't believe BJ dissed his first cousin like that.

"I'll be right back," Sandra whispered in Tracey's ear, and then hurried to catch up with BJ who had walked down the Home Improvement aisle where there were books about remodeling and building things.

"BJ!" Sandra shouted, loud enough for him to hear but no one else. He turned around slowly just before taking a book from the shelf.

"Yes?"

"That was so rude. I think you owe Tracey an apology."

BJ pushed the brim of his glasses over his nose. "What for?"

"You shouldn't have declined her offer in front of all of her fans."

"Sandra, I don't care about those people. If I don't want to read Tracey's book then I simply don't want to. I'm not going to change up because of a group of fans. I'm not her marketing tool, and neither are you. In fact, I'm ready to go. I didn't want to come here in the first place. Now let's leave."

"You are so wrong, BJ. You know, I tolerate a lot from you. I deal with your stoic attitude all the time, but this time you are wrong!" Sandra stormed off to tell the children it was time to go.

The ride home was a silent one. Sandra and Bianca were upset about BJ's actions. Junior was used to tense moments like this, but he wished his father would lighten up a bit.

During dinner that evening, they ate quietly not saying a word, and BJ loved peace and quiet, only when it wasn't intentional. He pondered over the way he behaved at the bookstore, and could see how it hurt Sandra and Bianca's feelings. He didn't want to, but he went out and bought Sandra flowers, and Bianca a gift card from the music store.

"From me to you," he said to Sandra right before she got in bed that night.

"You can sit them on the nightstand," she wept.

"I think they're nice," BJ stared at the flowers, and smiled.

"BJ, is this your way of apologizing again?"

He shrugged his shoulders, said nothing, changed his clothes and got in bed.

"Your mother called again. You should go hear her talk tomorrow."

"If I do, will you stop being upset and move on?"

"I shouldn't have to strike a barter with you about something like that. Peaches is your mother."

"I called Tracey. She accepted my apology, why can't you?"

Sandra sucked her teeth, pulled the covers over her head and forced herself to fall asleep. *He just doesn't get it,* she thought to herself.

Roseland was one of the toughest gang neighborhoods in all of Chicago. BJ served in the Iraq War fresh out of high school as a US Marine for twelve years, but never saw a war like the ones in his hometown. It wasn't the gangs in the neighborhood that made him hesitant to go inside, the Hope Center, it was…well…he couldn't put his finger on it exactly. He just figured he would go as a way to make peace with his wife. Sandra had been begging him to see his mother give talks for years. Since she was still upset about how he acted at Tracey's book signing, he felt she would want to hear that he did something good, especially for his mother.

A young lady at the door to the center handed BJ a program and directed him down the hall to a big room. His eyes scanned the room, and he noticed what seemed to be nearly a hundred folks of different races, genders, ages, shapes, and sizes. All of them sat in folding chairs and faced a small wooden handmade stage, as BJ tried to discretely make his way to the back of the room.

"There's a seat right up here," whispered a man with a scrubby beard who looked heroin sick. He pointed to a chair that was empty in the row in front of him. BJ looked at the chair, and back at the man. BJ kept moving towards the back of the room. *I don't want to sit near you addicts. People may think I'm sick too,* BJ thought to himself, as he sat by the window. He removed his hat, and placed it on his knee as he crossed his leg.

As Peaches spoke, BJ felt amazed by the power she had over the room. She commanded attention, and you couldn't hear a pin drop as she spoke. What was amazing to him was the articulate way she used her words, whereas in regular conversations with people she used slang and spoke immaturely. He couldn't believe how professional and mature she sounded. BJ held his hand under his chin, and began to wonder, *Somebody else may have written her talk.*

"…And we often hear that people become drug addicts for different reasons—some will say they were trying to self-medicate, and others may say somebody introduced them to drugs. Maybe they tried it for the first time as recreation and liked it. Each one of us has a story behind how we became hooked on drugs. I know I had every reason to explain to people why I got hooked on heroin and crack cocaine. I kept telling people it was *because* my father was physically abusive to me, and *because* I felt my mother didn't love me. I always found a way to justify why I kept doing wrong, and why I kept abusing myself. I thought it was okay to hate me, because nobody else cared, but you see, God cared. I just couldn't see it at the time."

"Amen!" someone shouted from the audience.

"We all have choices. Life itself is a choice. You can choose to live or die. With the help of a counselor, my beloved sister, and my son, I found joy in wanting to live," Peaches stated. "You see these pictures," Peaches pointed to a poster board of her mug shots sitting on an easel next to the podium. "That woman didn't want to live. She didn't know how to live.

She stole from people to support her drug habit. She abandoned her baby boy so she could get high without him being around. She ended up in jail several times. This woman had a death wish, but today I stand before you as living proof that there is a God. I have made the choice to want to live again without making any excuses, and I've been clean for over thirty years now."

The whole audience stood up and applauded.

"Ladies and gentlemen, we all have choices, but today I want you to make a better choice than what you did yesterday. Take it one day, one hour, and one minute at a time, but make the right choice. Pray for God's strength, and never give up in your fight to live!"

After the talk ended, BJ watched at a distance as people hugged and thanked his mother for her words of encouragement. He donned his hat, slid on his dark shades, and made his way towards the exit.

"BJ!" Peaches called when she spotted him heading out. He wished he could run somewhere and hide. Panic came over him, and his palms began to sweat, as he saw his mother maneuvering her way through the crowd to get to him. An older lady unconsciously stepped in front of BJ, blocking his path to the door. *Dag! Now I'm stuck unless I push her out my way!* BJ thought to himself.

"Thank you for coming, baby!" Peaches approached him, throwing her arms around his neck, before he could manage to leave the room. His stomach rattled from the awkward feeling, and his heart still felt the same familiar wall of an emotional disconnect.

"So you are Peaches' son. I know you must be so proud of your Mom!" the Director of the Hope Center shook his hand, and she was so loud that everyone else heard her. Others started approaching BJ with their sentiments. Some of them reached out to shake his hand, but he frowned, and patted their shoulders instead.

Peaches stood on her tiptoes, whispered in BJ's ear, "Hate the disease of addiction, but not the person." She could see BJ's uneasy facial expression, and the condescending way that he looked at everyone. Just as he attempted to respond...

"BJ!" a familiar voice called him from behind, patted him on his shoulders.

BJ turned around. "Uncle Hank, what are you doing here?"

"Just came to hear your mother speak. Good job up there, Peaches."

Hank gave her a hug, and kissed her cheek. "I'd love to stay and chat, but I have a run to make," he said. "I'll call you later." Hank smiled flirtatiously. Hank no longer wore the infamous patch over his eye. Years of cosmetic surgery had fixed his face, and he had a glass eye now, but he wore glasses to help deter people from staring at his eye.

"See you later BJ," Hank shook his hand.

"All right, see ya," BJ puckered his eyebrow and frowned his lips. He was baffled by Hank being there.

"Do you feel like grabbing some lunch?" Peaches tugged on BJ's arm, he was busy gawking at Hank as he walked out of the center.

He turned around to face her. "What?"

"I said do you feel like grabbing some lunch?"

BJ twisted his lips. "No. I'm going to the gun range."

"Still got all that anger balled up inside of you, huh?"

"Peaches save your soppy pretenses for your speeches. You're much better at that than pretending to be a mother."

"The Smith family may have raised you but I'm your mother. Can't no piece of paper ever change that," Peaches countered. "You can hate me for the rest of your life BJ, but your hate will never change the fact that it's my blood that runs through your veins. There's nothing fake about that!"

"Don't remind me," he turned and walked out of the center. Peaches buttoned her coat, and followed him out the door.

BURNP, BURNP.

A white Cadillac pulled up to the curb.

"That's Andre; he's right on time, and never misses a beat."

BJ stared at the young man behind the wheel, and then cut his eyes at his mother.

"What?" Peaches crossed her arms.

"What do you mean *what*? You're going out with a boy? He barely looks twenty-one is what!"

"What's it to you? You don't even claim me as your mother."

"That has nothing to do with it. You're sixty years old going out with a kid. You ought to be ashamed of yourself."

"Well I'm not," Peaches countered. "Anyway, I would thank you for coming, but you never wanted to be here, so I can't." Peaches stepped in the car, slammed the door, and told Andre to speed off. BJ watched them drive off into the distance. He had seen his mother with one boyfriend after another since her divorce from George several years ago, and he never liked any of them. He really felt upset that she was now dating someone who looked just a few years older than her grandson.

"Say my man, I got that new book, "Riding the Waves", said a homely looking man who looked like he was trying to hustle almost anything to get his next fix. BJ turned his attention from the Cadillac driving away to the man holding up his cousin's books in his face.

"See, she signed her name and everything, and dig this man, she's from the Chi. You have to support a young lady from our hometown. I'll sell them to you for twenty dollars. You can even give your girl one."

BJ snatched the books from him, and glanced at the signature. He knew it was fake. Tracey didn't spell her name with an "i." He also noticed that Michaels was spelled Michels, and Smith was spelled Smeeth. The signature read Traci Michels Smeeth."

BJ turned up his nose, and tossed the books at the man who barely caught them before they fell to the ground.

"Okay, how about two for ten dollars, then?" the man followed him down the street."

"Get a job. Get a life."

"Okay, two for five dollars, that's my final offer."

"How about you get out of my face before I snap your neck into five different pieces."

"Well just let me hold twenty dollars until tomorrow."

"Say What?" BJ turned around sharply with his fist balled, and the man took off running. This wasn't how BJ planned to spend his weekend, but he kept thinking to himself if Sandra didn't forgive him after all he had been through today, he would have to figure out something else.

CHAPTER TWELVE
WELCOME HOME

There is no place like home! The ten city book tour was awesome! I'm so happy to have so many fans across the country who supported my book. I did radio, talk shows, and interviews for magazines. I swear I didn't want to see the public for at least another year, but I knew that wasn't going to happen. BJ called me to apologize, while I was on my private jet flying back home. I guess you can call it an apology. He said, "What I did was not right. It won't happen again." I was like, "OK." Then he just hung up. BJ has had some serious anger issues since he was a child. The man needs therapy! I don't see how Sandra can handle his temper after all of these years. She claims he wasn't that way when they met in the military. She said he was just really shy. BJ didn't even tell her that he was adopted until they were about to get married. And how desperate was Sandra that she didn't know a lot about BJ's past before she married him? Don't get me wrong, I think Sandra is a sweet person, but marrying my cousin BJ is like Olivia Pope marrying Huck on *Scandal* it's the craziest relationship I ever heard of!

Anyway, I stepped out of my high heels and climbed the stairs with my luggage in hand. I could feel the circulation in my feet again, as my arches relaxed, but where was a bellman when you needed one? I opened my bedroom door, and right away I noticed a beautiful vase filled with yellow and red roses on my nightstand. My lips curved a blushing smile. I missed my Keith so much. I rolled my luggage into the closet and paid it no mind. I'd shopped everywhere I went and brought back twice as many clothes and shoes for me and my family. I rushed back into the room, and picked up the beautiful roses, inhaled its natural perfume scent. I read the card that had a computer generated inscription— *Welcome home! We missed you! Happy Belated Anniversary! Love, Hubby, Alexis, and KJ.*

"Aw, this is so sweet," I held the card over my heart. I missed my babies, and a part of me felt guilty for being away from them for so long. I reached in my Chanel purse for my cellphone and voice dialed Keith, while I got undressed.

"Hey you." He answered on the first ring, and I could picture his handsome face beaming behind the phone.

"Good morning, my Pookie."

"Good morning to you! Glad you made it back safely," he replied. "We tried to wait for you, but I didn't want the kids to be late for school, and I couldn't hold up the guys on this new project I'm headed to."

"I'm sorry. You must have missed my text message saying we were running behind."

"No problem. I'm just glad you made it back safely, thank God."

"Me too, and hey, thanks for the beautiful roses. Happy Belated Anniversary."

"Always."

"And I appreciate your support while I was gone."

"No problem, but we may have to consider hiring a little help like you suggested. Our lives are pretty busy right now."

"I'll start making the calls so we can interview for a nanny."

"Sounds good. We can talk more about that later on. More importantly, how are *you* doing?"

"I'm okay. I was actually hoping you wouldn't mind turning around and coming back home for a quickie with your wife," I said flirtatiously, talking to him on speaker. "I owe you a belated anniversary present."

"Hmmm…sounds good, but I'd rather have an all-nighter instead of a teaser."

"That's too bad, because right now I just took all my clothes off, and I'm totally naked. All I need is my husband to walk in and join me. And then, I can show him how much I missed him."

"Whoa now, don't make me have an accident out here on the road."

"Come home, baby," I whispered seductively. "The roses are lovely, but I got something even better. We can have a quickie now, and then go for round two later tonight."

"Let me show the guys what to do first, so they can get started. Then, I'll see you in about thirty minutes."

"I'll be waiting. *Muah!*"

I took a quick shower, slipped into my *Victoria Secrets* lingerie and crawled into bed. My pillows felt so good that I tried not to fall asleep so I could stay woke for Keith. Minutes later, I heard feet trampling up the stairs like there was an emergency. I sat up in bed, fluffed out the curls of my hair with my hands, and then Keith appeared. He stood at the entrance of our bedroom, and rested his muscular arm against the door panel, trying to catch his breath from running up the stairs. His breathing slowed down and he stared at me with a seductive look on his face. He could pass for an older brother to model *Christian Keyes*, except Keith had a thicker build, and he was taller. He was still in uniform, wearing dark navy pants, boots, and a light blue short-sleeve shirt with the company logo that said *Smith's Landscaping*. He was handsome as the first day I met him in my father's office, and I wanted him right then and there.

"Are you going to stand there all morning or join me?" I pulled the covers back to reveal my red G-string and bra. His eyes brightened with excitement at the sight of me. He loved seeing me in red. I called him over to the bed with my pointing finger. He immediately rushed over and started kissing me with an uncontrolled passion. Our lips never left each other, except when I pulled his shirt over his head and tossed it on the floor. He unfastened my bra and dove in. I slid his boxers past his waistline. He quickly wiggled his legs to slide them all the way off. The sight of Keith's nakedness always instantly made me hot. He propped my legs on his shoulders, and traced his tongue along the smoothness of each one, then returned his lips to mine. He wasted no more time on foreplay, and entered my soul. He thrust his love deep inside of me causing my back to arch and a loud moan to gasp from the pit of my stomach. As he made love to me, I gripped the sheets from his pleasure. His rhythm intensified, and I dug my nails into the small of his back and embraced all of his manliness. His face formed a tight scowl as he worked me with a vigor that I'd never experienced with him before. I tightened my legs around his waistline, and kissed him deep in the mouth as my love came down in a speedy an intense fashion. I hugged him tight as my body shook underneath him like an electric shock.

"Oh Keith baby!" I moaned. A slight grin formed on his face.

"You like that huh? Well big daddy is not finished yet," he teased. In what seemed like a one hand trick, he turned me over and loved me from behind as I held on to the bedpost. Keith tightened his grip around my hips and worked me until I felt his body tense up and jolt, followed by a loud moan that escaped his throat. And then we collapsed next to each other on the bed and tried to catch our breath.

"Wow!" he gasped for air. "That was so good baby!"

I shifted my weight closer to him and snuggled in his warmth.

Keith kissed me deeply in the mouth. He slowly pulled away, kissed my forehead, asked, "You okay?"

"I'm wonderful now that I'm here with you," I stroked the side of his face. "So, where did that tiger come from?"

"Did you like it?"

"I loved it. I should make you hold out on purpose next time."

"You better not." He squeezed my butt with his big hand. "You've been gone for a month a half. I know you didn't expect me to be tamed when I'm used to getting it on a regular basis."

I laughed. "So what were you doing while I was gone?"

"I took a lot of cold showers."

"Yeah right!"

"I did. Shoot, now I see why the bible says, 'do not deprive each other of it, but let the husband give to his wife what is right and the wife unto her husband.'"

"Well I gave, received, and I am fully satisfied." I kissed his lips.

"So what did *you* do while you were away?"

"I was well-behaved. I didn't have time to even think about sex as busy as Kyle had me. As soon as I lay down to sleep, it was time to get up and do another interview or a book signing."

"So you didn't think about me?"

"Of course. I missed you a lot, but I tried not to think about it too hard so I could get through the rest of the tour. To be honest, I thought you were mad with me."

"I wasn't mad it's just that all the rumors and…"

"Shhh…" I covered his lips with my hand. "We're not going to bring the drama to our house. This is a blessed home."

"I know it is, but I just want you to know I love you."

"No ditto?"

"No ditto. I love you, Tracey. You do know that right?"

"Of course. I love you too," I said, as we intertwined our hands with each other.

"Good. Let no man come between us, Tracey. For what God has yoked together…"

"Let no man tear it apart."

CHAPTER THIRTEEN
DAMAGE CONTROL

I fell into a deep sleep after Keith left to go back to work. When I woke up, it took a while for me to realize I was in my own bed, especially after being on the road. For a minute, I wondered if I had dreamt about me and Keith until I spotted my G-string and bra under the covers. I got up out of bed and went into the bathroom. I ran hot water in the Jacuzzi bathtub and slowly inched my body into it. The water came up to my neck, engulfing my body, opening up every pore. I allowed the water to saturate the tenderness from Keith's lovemaking, and slowly released the clip from my hair. It dropped down in wavy ripples from the steam of the room, and I sunk down deeper into the tub. It felt so good that I allowed my whole body to sink under. Every muscle in my body relaxed, and I felt so good.

Ding Dong....

My body jerked forward, and water fell heavily from my face as I caught my breath. I looked around the room, bewildered as to who could be ringing my doorbell. I wiped the access water and soapy suds from my eyes. I grabbed my towel, and quickly dried off, then slipped into my robe.

Ding Dong...

I ran down the spiral staircase and opened the door. There was a man wearing a short fur coat, blue jeans and black boots. He had his back turned to me.

"May I help you?"

The man slowly turned around, removed his sunshades.

"You may."

My mouth dropped. "Wh-wh-what are you doing here? How did you find out where I lived?" My voice trembled.

"Come on Ma, you called me over here so quit playing games. You know what time it is. You always call me after Keith leaves."

I stepped back. "Bruce, I don't know what you're talking about or what kind of games you're playing, but I have a restraining order against you. I'm calling the cops!" I tried to close the door, but Bruce stuck his foot out.

"Wait a minute, Ma, hold up. I'm not gonna hurt you!" he said, sounding unnatural. "You called me over here so I came. Are you changing your mind now?"

"Get out right now!" I ran to grab the phone in the den.

"Fine, fine, I'm leaving," he threw up his hands. I followed him to the door while I was holding the cordless phone to my ear.

"Yes, this is Tracey Michaels-Smith and I have an intruder here on my property that won't leave. Please hurry and get here!" I hung up the phone, and then realized I forgot to tell them my address because I was so scared.

"Come on, Ma, don't be that way. We loved each other at one time. We weren't always enemies," Bruce reached for my hand, and I smacked it away. That's when I spotted a tall man with a video camera. He stood from behind one of the rose bushes out front, and aimed the camera directly at us.

"Get out of here! You're trying to set me up!"

'Muah!' Bruce cut me off with a kiss that I didn't see coming. He and the camera guy took off running. I hurried and dialed Keith while I waited for the police to arrive.

"...and that's what happened," I explained everything to the police, as I held on tightly to Keith's hand. He kept huffing and puffing, and shaking his head in frustration. I made sure I was fully dressed by the time they arrived.

"We'll try to track him down, Mrs. Smith. However, we must be honest with you. It may be his word against yours. And if he's got video footage, he can easily manipulate it to his advantage if we don't find him soon enough."

"But I have a restraining order against him," I cried. "He should be arrested immediately when you find him!"

"According to our records the restraining order expired seven years ago. Looks like you didn't extend it."

"Are you saying this dude can impose on me and my family whenever he wants to?!" Keith snapped.

"No Mr. Smith, we're not saying that. In this case, you have no real evidence that Bruce broke into your home. We didn't find any fingerprints, broken glass, nor any marks or bruises on your wife, and you don't have any items that are missing from your home," the officer explained.

"We see situations like this all the time," the shorter officer chimed in. "Sometimes when a marriage ends, the ex can start harassing his/her former spouse. Sometimes, the ex may even make the whole story up."

"I'm not lying!" I screeched. I couldn't believe the police officer would even think such a thing.

"Look, if my wife said Bruce came here on his own and without permission then that's what happened," Keith defended me. "We just need you guys to do your jobs. We're the victims here, all right?"

"We'll patrol the area and be on the lookout for anything suspicious tonight and over the next few days. If we find Bruce, we can question him, but we can't just lock him up without any proof. I doubt very seriously if a guy like "B-Money" is going to confess to anything either. His record is as big as the acres of land you have. I'm sorry this happened to you guys."

"Fine! Just go!" I rushed to the door and opened it, and the officers slowly walked out apologizing along the way. I locked the door shut and rejoined Keith in the den. He was pacing the room back and forth, and cracking his knuckles.

"That punk got some nerve to just come up in my house and violate our personal space!" Keith shouted. "He doesn't know who he's messing with, that's for sure!"

"It's over now, baby," I exhaled noisily. "The cops said there's nothing they can do," I ran my fingers through my hair in frustration.

"It's not over!" Keith stormed out of the den, and ran up the stairs. I was surprised to see him so angry like this. I ran behind him, because I was afraid of what he may do.

"Keith baby! Wait!" I ran down the hall to our room. "Where are you?" I called, searching our room, and then I found him inside his closet.

"What are you doing?"

Keith brushed pass me, took off his uniform and put on a black hoodie, blue jeans, and started lacing up his sneakers.

"Where are you going?"

"I'm gonna look for Bruce, that's where I'm going!"

"Keith, seriously? You're taking this way too far!" I stood in front of the bedroom door as he started to leave out.

"Move, Tracey!"

"Keith, I'm not going to let you go after Bruce. I won't. You'll have to hurt me before I let you go out here and do something stupid!"

"Suit yourself!" Keith easily picked me up, walked me over to the bed and dropped me.

"Keith! Keith!" I got off the bed and chased him down the stairs and grabbed him before he reached the front door.

"Baby, please don't do it. Don't go after Bruce. Please!" I tugged at his waist, trying to pull him back, but Keith was too strong. He easily broke free from my hold.

"You're a man of God, Keith!" I cried, and Keith stopped short of walking out of the door. "Remember your relationship with God! Remember your promise to do His will. Think about what you would lose if you go after Bruce. You won't have me, and you won't have your kids. You'll be back in jail, Keith. Do you want that?! Do you?" I panted out of breath. I was doing everything I could to try to stop him from making a horrible mistake. Keith bit down on his bottom lip hard. He started cracking his knuckles in frustration again. He glared at me, and then rolled his eyes to the ceiling.

"Baby, no harm came to me. See," I opened my arms wide. "God made sure of that. He protected me. He's going to always protect me as long as I do what's right. He'll protect you too, baby. Where is your faith in Him? Huh? 'Vengeance is mine, said the Lord!'"

Keith heaved a long sigh, and then he quickly grabbed me and hugged me tight. I felt the squeeze of his big arms.

"I love you!" he cried.

"I love you too. I love you so much. God will take care of us. He always does. Trust in him."

Keith blinked back tears of rage. "I know that. It's still *my* job to protect you and I should have been here. I should have stayed home from work like you wanted me to!"

"You didn't know that was going to happen, and neither did I. Don't go beating up yourself."

"Man if my kids was here too I would've....oh man, I feel like, I feel like...dammit I wish I was here!" Keith said through clinched teeth, as he thrust his fists into the air as if he was striking Bruce. "I would've knocked him out and stomped his face in the floor. Who the hell does he think he is? Messing with *my* family!"

"Baby please, please calm down. You have to calm down, you're scaring me. You don't curse. This is not you. Please calm down," I took hold of his hand and eased him over to the stairs, where we sat down on the bottom of the staircase.

"We have to go pick up the kids from school in a few minutes. You really need to calm down, okay?" I gently stroked the side of his face. "Bruce tried to set me up. He's just mad he didn't win the lawsuit against me about my book, but I'm going to make sure that whatever video footage he got won't spread. I'm calling my lawyers and I'm calling Kyle."

"If he and Noah are willing to go through these extremes over a book, then maybe I need to take a break from my studies and read it myself," Keith stated, rapidly tapping his feet against the floor. "I need to see why they're so pissed off about it."

"Baby, no need to trouble yourself," I stroked his back. "You have enough on your plate with your online theology classes, work, ministry and home. It's nothing to be concerned about right now. Read it later when you're calmer."

He puffed his cheeks, and then blew out. "Maybe I will, but I know one thing."

"What's that?"

"When we get back from picking up the kids, I'm calling a security company to come out here and put cameras everywhere. I want 24-hour security- two men on deck at all times. I want another bodyguard on *you* and not just when you have events, but whenever you go out. I want bodyguards with our kids too. They can sit in the classrooms with them, and watch them at all time."

"I get it babe. We'll tighten our security that's for sure."

Keith stood up. "Let's go pick up the kids."

"All right," I set the house alarm before we left out. When we stepped outside, our eyes canvased every nook and cranny of our surroundings. It was upsetting that a situation like that with Bruce made me paranoid and afraid all over again.

I called my lawyer and told him everything that happened. He said he would do everything in his power to make sure the video was not released. I called Kyle too, but I got his voicemail, and left a message. This certainly wasn't what I expected once I returned home, and definitely not the reaction I anticipated simply because I wrote a *book*. Seriously?

I watched Keith walk out of the school building with our kids in each hand. As soon as they got close enough, I got out of the Hummer.

"Mom-meeee!" they ran towards me and I picked them up, hugged and kissed them. I loved to surprise them whenever I returned home. This was the love and affection I missed so much. This was home. This was how my return was supposed to be.

"We missed you mommy!" KJ kissed my left cheek, and Alexis kissed my right.

"I missed you guys too. Let's celebrate with some pizza tonight, how does that sound?" I offered.

"That sounds awesome mommy!" KJ kissed my cheek again.

"Yeah, and let's order lots and lots of pepperoni on it!" Alexis added.

"You can order anything you want on it."

"Can I put *Cheerios* on top too?" Alexis giggled.

"No, girl. Don't be silly. And what happened to your hair?" It was just as lopsided as it could be. One ponytail was much fuller than the other one, and the part was crooked.

"Daddy jacked me up is what," she frowned.

Keith and I burst out laughing. Alexis was too mature for a six year old.

"What do you know about being "jacked up?" Keith asked, laughing. "Is that what you're learning in private school? We need to transfer you."

"No Daddy, I was only kidding."

Keith and I cracked up laughing again. For a brief moment our eyes locked in on each other, and our smiles slightly faded away. We both knew what the other was thinking. What happened earlier was still lingering in our minds. We knew we had to do everything in our power to keep our family protected and safe.

CHAPTER FOURTEEN
SISTERLY LOVE

Connie and Peaches decided to go out for a Sunday brunch at Pierre's Gourmet Restaurant when Connie was stopped by two paparazzi right before she went inside.

"Cat Morris, it's good to see you. We wanted to get your thoughts on your daughter's tell-all book!" A microphone was shoved into her face.

"No comment."

"But Cat," the taller reporter stood in front of Pierre's blocking the door. "Your daughter's book is becoming an international bestseller. Do you feel she's exposed too much about your parenting, or a lack thereof?"

"Excuse me!" Peaches shouted. "Didn't my sister just say no comment?"

"Does 'no comment' mean that you're disappointed? Do you feel like your children's behaving badly will ruin your legacy?"

The cameras started to draw the attention of passerby, and the people inside the restaurant were all wide-eyed and curious by what was going on.

"Don't make me hurt you!" Peaches threatened with her fist balled.

"Stop it Peaches, don't!" Connie stepped in front of Peaches, and pushed her back. "Listen, if I comment, I want you guys to keep it moving after this so my sister and I can enjoy our afternoon brunch."

"Absolutely, Cat. We understand." One of the reporters put a recorder up to Connie's mouth while the cameraman steadied the lenses on her face. "Just tell us your feelings about Tracey's book, and your son Devin making a diss record about Tracey's ex-husband."

"I don't feel my daughter's book will ruin my legacy in any way. The book is about *her* life and the way *she* viewed those events as happening. Second, I don't approve of Devin making music that speaks bad things about anyone, and he knows that. Neither do I approve of my grandson rapping to the songs that my son has produced. I hope all of these young men will call this whole thing a truce before someone gets hurt. Now you gentlemen have a lovely afternoon."

"Just one more question."

"I'm finished guys. Really, please respect my space."

"Have a good lunch Cat," they respectfully left her alone.

"I can't believe you bothered to answer their questions," Peaches stated, once they were inside and had placed their orders.

"They were causing a scene. I figured it was the quickest way to get them out of my hair."

"Oh trust me; I know how you could have gotten them out of your hair," Peaches threatened. "With these." She balled up her fists.

"Peaches that's ridiculous!" Connie retorted. "You're a mother and a grandmother, just like me. You can't go around fighting people. Besides, didn't you learn that God hates violence from today's service?"

"Yeah but I'm not God. I don't have his patience."

"Then pray for it. Now be quiet. The waiter is coming over with our salads and iced tea."

"Anyway, speaking of Tracey's book," Peaches began eating and when she looked up Connie was praying over her food. "Oh yeah, I almost forgot," Peaches bowed her head and prayed. "As I was saying, what's going on with these rumors? Have you talked to Tracey?" Peaches stuffed her mouth with salad.

"I've talked to Tracey several times. She admitted that Kyle made her exaggerate some things so the book would sell. She apologized for making me out to be a hard-to-please mother, because I'm far from being that way. I was tough on her, but not as critical as she exaggerated in her book. One thing for sure, she said she will never write another one. Not about her life or anything personal at least," Connie explained. "I told Dean we should fly out to California next week, because this thing has snowballed into something huge! Now Trey and Devin made that stupid song about Bruce, which will only feed the fire. It's a hot mess, and Tracey admitted she's responsible for things getting out of hand. I just wish she didn't listen to Kyle so much. He's controlling and manipulative. All Tracey can see is dollar signs, so she keeps working with him. If it were me, he would have been fired a long time ago."

"My thing is, if you're gonna write a book about your life, don't be so blunt about other peoples' personal business. Shoot, I called her on the phone and cursed her out about what she said about me! Talking about I may have been bipolar when I got out of jail. Is she crazy?"

"I told her that wasn't right. I talked to her about what she said about other people in her book too. You know I gave my children the world and look at what I'm getting back in return."

"I hear you Sis."

"Dean Jr. is the only one who never gave me any trouble."

"That's true. So what did Dean have to say about you guys going to Cali to intervene?"

"You know Dean. *'Let them handle their own business. We can't keep running to their rescue.'*"

"Dean is right. It's time for you to cut the strings and let your children find their own way, Connie."

"Hold on a second. This is Devin. He calls me every Sunday at the same time."

"See what I mean. We can't have a decent lunch without you dropping everything to talk to your children. Devin's a Mama's boy, anyway," Peaches rolled her eyes, continued to eat her food.

"I love you too….all right now…bye-bye."

"What's going on in Devin's world?" Peaches asked.

"Oh he was just checking on me. He said he's going to email me his schedule. He and Trey have a tour coming up soon."

"How is it that you know more about his schedule than Andrea does?"

"I do not."

"She called me last week complaining about Devin not telling her where he's been or where he's going. Listen Sis," Peaches pushed her finished plate to the side. "The reason Devin hasn't married Andrea yet is because you're his wife. The boy has that Oedipus complex."

"He does not!" Connie shook her head. "Anyway, enough about my children, what's going on with BJ and your grandchildren?"

"BJ still needs anger management classes. As for my grandchildren they are fine, but I hope they'll turn out just like Sandra and not my son. I can't do anything right in his eyes after all of these years."

"He'll come around. Don't worry."

"Yeah when I'm dead!"

"Oh stop it!"

"Anyway, I don't even want to talk about BJ. It makes me upset that he can't forgive me."

"One day he will, but anyway, I don't want to upset, so let me tell you about my class reunion at Lakeview High last night…" Connie went on to explain everything to Peaches and how all of her former classmates were doing. In between the conversation, Peaches ordered dessert, and the waiter served them cranberry sorbet.

"And Smokey is dead. Ray told me that he was shot by a group of loan sharks."

"Whaaat? So what about Ray's sister May?"

"She is still the same old May. Ray said he sent her some money to fly out here to Chicago for the reunion and she spent it on something else. She's still the same May—a money hungry opportunist."

Peaches shook her head in disgust. Hearing about Connie's reunion just made her think about Cabrini Green.

"It's hard to believe that just six minutes away from here—we used to live in the Projects." Peaches glared out the window at the dense thicket of expensive condos, high-rises, and stores that had replaced Cabrini Green.

"I know. I hardly recognize our old neighborhoods anymore. Leo's Pizza is gone now, too. I thought they would never close Leo's," Connie said. "Remember we used to collect used soda cans and trade them in for money, just so we could get a slice of Leo's Pizza?" Connie laughed, recalling the memories.

"Yes, and we had to split that one slice three…ways," Peaches remembered.

"Yeah…the three of us…" Connie repeated in an undertone. "Baby would probably be forty-one years old. Just two years older than Tracey."

"I know. It's still hard to believe sometimes," Peaches shook her head, recalling the memories of their sister Gina "Baby" Morris. "At least we know where Tracey got her writing skills from."

"That's true. I never thought about it that way. Plus her acting skills are from Baby too. You know, Baby was always walking around the house pretending and playing make-believe," Connie added.

"Those were the good old days."

"Well, we're still here my sister," Connie clicked glasses with Peaches.

"Now you pay the tab. The waiter is on his way over."

"Oh no my dear. You won't stick me with the bill this time," Connie quickly grabbed her purse. "Meet you back at the car."

"Hey! Hey Connie you can't do that? Just because I'm the oldest doesn't mean you can stiff me like this!"

The waiter set the tab on the table. "Whenever you are ready Miss."

Peaches flipped open the bill. "Sixty dollars?"

"Yes ma'am," the waiter smiled.

"Sixty dollars? Shoot, all I had was rabbit food and a sorbet that wasn't nothing but Italian Ice in a fancy bowl. I could have bought this crap from the grocery store for twenty bucks!"

"Is there a problem?" the waiter asked.

"Nah, ain't no problem. See, I got a black card," Peaches proudly held it up and stuck it inside the fold of the bill.

"Thank you ma'am. I will be right back."

"Mm-hmm you kinda cute," Peaches grabbed the young man by the arm and stared him from head-to-toe.

"What's your name?" she asked.

"Leo."

"And I bet you roar just like a lion, don't you?"

"Excuse me?" he turned up his nose.

"How old are you, Leo?"

"I'm…thirty-two," His voice shook nervously. Peaches leaned forward across the table, and whispered so no one else could hear.

"Listen here, Leo. I think you're a nice-looking young man, but these young girls can't give you what I can. I will have you sucking your thumb like a baby, and you'll be writing checks to pay my bills. You understand what I'm saying?"

He stepped back, and turned his top lip into a frown. He couldn't believe this woman, who looked old enough to be his grandmother was hitting on him.

"I understand if you're a little shy, but I'm too old for games. So you want to go out some time?"

"I'm gay."

"Dag! Always the cute ones!"

CHAPTER FIFTEEN
DOMINO EFFECT

Keith pulled up in front of the Peterson's estate in Baldwin Hills, and noticed cameras set up outside of the home. He assumed Mr. Peterson, the Governor of California was about to speak to the news crew. He was used to seeing cameras outside of his elite clients' homes. He parked his company van outside of the gate, and he and his work crew stepped out of the van with their landscape equipment and supplies. Next thing he knew, the camera crews were running towards him.

"Keith, is it true that your wife, Tracey is having an affair with B-money?"

"Is the video that B-Money released something that you were aware of?"

"Is it also true that this isn't Tracey's first time cheating on you?"

"I don't believe that–" Keith attempted to answer, but the questions kept coming.

"If you don't believe it then why is Bison stating that he slept with Tracey when she was supposed to be engaged to you?"

"I don't know, but–"

"Hey! Hey! Get off of my property!" Mr. Peterson came running through the gates and Keith never felt so relieved in all of his life. The muscles in his shoulders started to relax as he finally exhaled a deep breath. He was used to the media when he was with Tracey, but without her he felt nervous and unsure of what to say. Mr. Peterson turned to Keith, patted his shoulders. "It's all clear now. You guys can go on about your business here."

Keith and his crew entered the gates and immediately got to work. Keith couldn't believe what had just happened, but he tried to focus on the job at hand. He and his crew treated the lawn, cut the lawn, trimmed the shrubs, and planted new flowers just the way Mrs. Peterson wanted them to. After they were finished, Mr. Peterson swiped his credit card through the Square on Keith's phone.

"Thank you for your business Mr. Peterson and I apologize about the camera crews I didn't know they would be here."

"That's all right. One way to get rid of reporters is to pretend that you're going to run them over with your car," Mr. Peterson laughed. Keith didn't see the joke in it, but he smiled out of courtesy. "See ya next time kid!"

Keith didn't bother to mention the reporters to Tracey. Besides, she had been telling him to ignore all the rumors anyway, so there was no sense in bringing up something as if he couldn't handle it.

The paparazzi didn't stop harassing Keith for the rest of the week. Everywhere he went someone was shoving a microphone to his face for a comment. Yet, there was one place he felt he could always find solace, and there wasn't a camera in sight–church! Keith sang his heart out in the choir as his family cheered him on from the front pew. When the services were over, he went to the back conference room to help count the collection money for the day. Meanwhile, Tracey and the kids were busy helping clean up the church now that service was over with.

"Are you guys almost finished?" Pastor Richardson entered the room. His deep bass voice echoed across the room. It was just as big as his stature.

"Almost, about five minutes," Keith replied.

"No rush, but Keith I would like for you and Chris to train Larry here with the accounts," Larry entered the room with a big smile on his face.

"No problem Pastor, so would you like three of us to count the money from now on?"

"No, I'm pulling you off the accounts from now on."

"Does this mean you're ready for me to give my first practice sermon?" Keith beamed a smile, and Chris slapped him a five.

"No, but it does mean that Larry will take over the accounts with Chris and Sam will handle our youth ministry from now on. Not you."

Keith looked at Chris who shrugged his shoulders. He was just as clueless as to why the Pastor was saying that to him.

"Is there a problem?" Keith stood up from the conference table.

"Don't question me in my own church, boy."

"I'm sorry, I didn't mean it that way, but I'm just trying to figure out what's going on."

Pastor Richardson removed a book from the inside gown he was wearing, and when he placed it on the table, Keith saw that it was

Tracey's book.

"We can't have this kind of thing going on," Pastor pointed to the book.

"Chris, Larry, can you guys excuse me and Pastor Richardson please?"

"They don't need to excuse themselves," Pastor Richardson stated, projecting his voice. "You're a hypocrite, and I suggest you repent of your sins before I have you removed from the church."

"I don't know what you're talking about, but I'm far from a hypocrite."

"I can't have you leading the youth ministry when you're a poor example of what it means to have a holy courtship," Pastor Richardson stated. "This book that your wife put out goes into plenty of details about your indecent and lustful behavior. It's no wonder you asked Sonny to marry you instead of me. He always approved of your courtship. I didn't."

"Look, I don't know what Tracey said in that book, but–"

"Then I strongly suggest you read it."

"So, am I being demoted here?"

Pastor crossed his arms and gave him a stern look.

"Fine, but the only hypocrite I see is you."

"I beg your pardon."

"I helped you to build this church when it sat on the corner in a rundown house. Now it's a big sanctuary with a huge parking lot. My wife and I gave you the money to build this place. Now that you got what you wanted, you're kicking us out."

"Heathen money is what it was."

"Really?" Keith looked the Pastor eye-to-eye. "Then sell it since you think it's heathen money."

"Get out!" Pastor pointed to the door.

Keith looked over his shoulder at Chris and Larry who both looked afraid to come to his defense. They didn't know where all of this was coming from. They always looked up to Keith.

"I'm sorry it came to this. Maybe I was out of line and I meant no disrespect, but I ask you to please pray about this Pastor Richardson. Please see the truth in this matter and let us settle things as men, as Christian brothers."

Pastor Richardson shook head. "I vouched for you and Tracey, but I can no longer carry the load of your sins. The church is disappointed in both of you. I suggest you check the road you're walking on. Your path is crooked, starting with your wife."

CHAPTER SIXTEEN
ONE LAST CRY

Keith could feel Tracey's hand stroking his back underneath the covers, and he shifted his body closer to the edge of the bed further away from her. When he didn't respond, Tracey slid her body closer to him and wrapped her arms around his waist, allowing her hands to travel wherever they wanted to go. She flicked her tongue to lick his earlobe. He knew what Tracey wanted as she teased the outskirts of his ear with her tongue. He tried to fight off the good feeling by allowing his mind to recall the video he saw of B-Money kissing her while she stood in the doorway of their home. He also thought about the photo of Noah in her book. Every time he saw a magazine in the store, there was another picture of Tracey with Bruce or Noah. Although she claimed the photos were old, the public didn't know that. Keith felt embarrassed and humiliated at work, and even more embarrassed by Pastor Richardson a few weeks ago. He hadn't returned to the church since, and he told Tracey they needed to find a church closer to home.

"Tracey, get off of me!" He shoved her.

"Baby, what's wrong?"

"I'm not in the mood." He got up to check the new security system. The extra security pad in their room by the door was all lit up, which meant the alarms had been set. He shifted his gaze from the security pad to the monitor above it. The monitor captured pictures every three seconds from the outside surveillance cameras surrounding the house. He wished they had the system sooner, like back in February when Bruce had first invaded their home.

"I'm leaving for the international book tour in a few days. I just wanted us to spend some private time together. Now that we have a nanny, I was hoping we could have date nights and go out somewhere, but you don't want to do that. Even while we're at home, you don't want to watch a movie, play games in the entertainment room, and you barely even touch me. You've been preoccupied with your studies lately, but you still have to make time for me. I'm your wife," Tracey reminded him, as she sat up in bed, watching him check the alarm. "The bible says that a man ought to treat his wife the same way Jesus treats the congregation or something like that."

Keith quickly turned away from the security pad, and gave her a sharp angry look. "What do you really know about the bible, huh? When was the last time you picked one up besides at church? Have you ever read it for yourself?"

"There you go judging me again. How do you know I don't carry a bible with me on the road? Anyway, that's not the type of conversation I want to have right now. I was just hoping I could make love to my husband before I leave the country. I don't see what's wrong with that."

"You always want your way that's what's wrong with *that*," Keith glanced at the digital clock on the nightstand that read 2 A.M. "We can discuss this tomorrow. It's late."

"No, let's talk about it now. It's obvious that something has been bothering you. It's not like you to not talk to me or want to be with me."

"I may not be talking to you, but I've had plenty of conversations with God."

"Really?" Tracey folded her arms. "Well, let me in on the discussion."

"Is sex your angel? I mean, do you think making love to me every night is going to make me stop thinking about all the trouble your book has caused? You're trying to cloud my judgment, but I'm not stupid."

"I don't know what you're talking about."

"You know what I'm talking about. I'm talking about Bruce and Noah."

"Seriously? You know they're just upset, but like my brother Dean said, this will all blow over soon. Remember he called and told us that?"

"Even if it does, it may not change the facts."

"Facts? What facts?"

"I read your book."

Tracey's eyes looked like a deer caught in headlines.

"That's right. I just finished it tonight as a matter of fact. That's why I've been in my office for the past few weeks with the door shut. I wasn't just studying, I was reading," Keith crawled back in bed and yanked the covers on his lap.

"Well I...I'm glad you finally read it."

"Then why do you look so surprised?"

"I didn't know you were reading it that's all."

"Yeah well, I can see why Bruce and Noah are angry, because I'm pretty pissed myself. I didn't appreciate you telling the world I used to be a drug dealer and a pimp before I became a Christian. No wonder people in church were raising their eyebrows at me, giving me funny looks. I even lost my church privileges because of what you wrote in your book!"

"What? Since when?"

"Since a few weeks ago now."

"Pastor got some nerve to demote you! I see the way he looks at me and other sisters."

"You shouldn't wear short skirts."

"Whatever. He's a man—an imperfect man. We're all sinners. Jesus called sinners, not saints. That's really what I'm trying to say."

"You're missing the point, Tracey, because you're thinking about your own selfish reasoning. The point is if *I* wanted people to know those things about *me*, it was *my* right to tell them, *not* yours!" Tracey folded her arms and pouted, but Keith refused to play into her 'victim' mode.

"When I told you I was a *connected* man that meant I knew people who were deep in the drug game. You quoted almost everything I said verbatim in your book. Why do you think I check the security systems every night? It's not just because I'm worried about you and your safety, but mine too, as well as our kids. It's all because of what *you* put in your book. To you those are "just words". Remember you said that? You said you couldn't understand why people were upset about *words* in a book. Well guess what? Words have started plenty of wars, baby! And you wonder why Bruce and Noah are trying to destroy you?!"

Tracey dropped her chin to her chest. She looked away from Keith and fought back her tears.

"Another reason I'm upset with you is that Pastor Richards read the book too. He didn't take away my privileges because of my past with selling drugs and pimping women. He judged me for what I did with you when I was supposed to be a Christian then. I was supposed to set an example, but I was going to your house in the middle of the night like I was making a booty call."

Tracey cut him a surprised look, as her mouth dropped.

"Oh yeah, Pastor read the book too."

"I'm sorry. I didn't know all of this, Keith. Why didn't you tell me?"

"Would it have made a difference? You're still promoting the book, still going to meet your international fans. This is what you want—to be a star at any cost." Keith shook his head. He stared at her for a moment, searched her hazel eyes for truth, but wasn't sure what he saw in them anymore. "You have to understand Tracey that everything you do is about *us,* not just *you.* What you do, what you say, and what you don't do is a reflection of *us.* That's what marriage is. People don't separate the two of us; they see us as a unit. So your book made *us* look bad before the church. Now *we* need to fix this or find another church home."

Tracey looked away and swallowed hard. She felt like she was shrinking in her own skin with each word that Keith spoke.

"One more thing about your book that I got a major problem with is you, Bruce, and Noah, and all the rumors circling about your relationship. I asked God to show me the light. Show me if my wife has been unfaithful to me during my marriage or before. And each time, something about you and Noah or something about you and Bruce suddenly showed up in the news. Now, look at this, it popped up on my phone right before bed," Keith reached for his cellphone, and showed her the headlines from an entertainment news website. "It says, 'Noah had his turn on the Autumn Winters show today. He told Autumn that he and Tracey had one last tango in Paris right before she got married," Keith read. "So, what's up with this? Is it true?"

"I'm a celebrity, there's always going to be news about me, good or bad."

"I know all of that, and some things the media says about you are just nonsense. What I don't understand is Noah's ploy for revenge. I can see clearly that Bruce just wants to make another hit record, but Noah is at the top of his game. He has no reason to lie about anything or hurt you, which makes me wonder if he's telling the truth."

Tracey stepped out of the bed. "I have to go to the bathroom."

Keith quickly stepped out of bed and snatched Tracey by the arm before she reached the bathroom door. "Did you sleep with him when you were supposed to be my fiancée?" he demanded an answer. Tracey snatched her arm away then rushed into the bathroom, quickly shutting the door behind her.

"I deserve to know the truth, Tracey. I would rather hear it from you before God reveals it to me," Keith shouted outside of the bathroom door. When the toilet flushed, water ran, Tracey slowly opened the door and came out. She walked pass Keith and sat down on the bed, and he joined her. His eyes followed her every gesture from her darting eyes, to her biting down on her bottom lip like she was emotionally pained.

"Look at me."

Tracey shook her head no, as tears began to stream down her cheeks. Keith's lips tightened and his eyebrows drew in closer. He gave Tracey a stony look of concern and worry, as she began to speak.

Tracey sniffed, and wiped her tears. "Noah was my physical therapist. We became good friends during that time, and there was a physical attraction—a chemistry we had."

"I read all of that," he said sharply, rubbing his goatee trying to calm himself. "Get to all the parts that Noah claims you left out."

"Noah and I were friends…friends with benefits, so…we did have sex a few times before you and I got back together."

"And was one of those *few* times in Paris?"

"Well…" Tracey hesitated. "Kyle suggested we go to Paris for fashion week. My makeup line TGM Cosmetics had just started, and Noah was new to the modeling scene too, so we all went–me, Kyle, Noah, Kay-Kay and Damien. We all went out partying after the show, and I got drunk."

"Go on." Keith started cracking his knuckles.

"I went to my room to lie down, and I woke up with a hangover. I was very sick, so we flew back here to the states. That's just about all I can remember."

Keith stood up abruptly. "Tracey, do you think I'm stupid?"

"No."

"Are you trying to play me? Tell me the truth!"

"That's what happened, Keith."

"You're lying, Tracey! Stop lying!" his veins between to twitch at the temples. "You're acting. Don't play a role with me. Tell me the truth!"

"I...I can't!" She cried.

"Then it must be true, isn't it?" Keith insisted, as his nostrils begin to flare. "You cheated on me. You cheated on me when you knew we were engaged to be married!"

"It wasn't on purpose, Keith. I swear it wasn't. Noah took advantage of me. He knew I was drunk," Tracey howled. "I'm sorry, baby. I'm so sorry." Tracey tried to hug Keith.

"No, don't touch me!" Keith shoved her hands away and stepped back. "Nobody has sex by accident. I don't care how much you had to drink!"

"But Keith–" Tracey grabbed his arm.

"I said don't touch me dammit!"

SMACK!

Tracey fell backwards onto the bed. She held her hands over her cheek. The initial sting suddenly felt like fire all over her face. Silence suddenly came over the room. The only sounds were Tracey's whimpering tears and Keith's heavy breathing. He stared at what his bare hands had done to his wife. Keith felt the scene was all too familiar. He had done the same thing with his ex-girlfriend years ago during a heated argument. His anger became mixed with guilt as he rushed to Tracey's side.

"I'm sorry, baby," Keith gently stroked Tracey's back. "I didn't mean to hit you."

She gazed into big chocolate eyes, and somewhere inside there she saw that he was sincere.

"I had been drinking, Keith," she sniffed, wiped her eyes as she continued to explain. "Noah walked me to my room. It started with a kiss and then you know the rest. I regretted it ever since," she expressed. Her lips quivered with each word she uttered.

"Just go ahead and kill me, Keith, because right now I feel like dying anyway." She looked into his eyes and could see the pain she had caused him. He could see that she was hurt too. Keith got up went into the bathroom and shut the door.

"Oh God, why?!" he cried. Tracey could hear him crying like someone had died. She lay across the bed and cried just as hard. She cried so much that every part of her body felt weak. She cried at the thought of losing Keith, she cried for hurting him, and she cried because she regretted not telling him the truth.

The sobbing from the bathroom stopped, and Tracey eased herself off the bed and approached the door. She hesitated to bother him at first, but she wanted to make sure he was all right. She lightly tapped on the door, but didn't get a response.

"Keith, please open the door," she begged. Keith opened the door slowly, quickly wiped his tears so she wouldn't see them, but his eyes were red with sorrow. She hadn't seen him cry since their wedding day, but those were tears of joy. Tracey wrapped her arms around his waist tried to hug him, but Keith wouldn't budge. He stood like a statue, resenting her touch, resenting her hold, the way she smelled, and how beautiful she still looked after all the crying. It meant nothing to him in that moment. She had allowed another man to sex her, to become one with her. He tried to block out what he envisioned, but he couldn't.

"I'm sorry Keith. I'm so sorry for hurting you," Tracey wailed. "I love you. I love you so much. I didn't tell you because I knew this would happen. I knew it would hurt you as much as it hurt me."

"Please let me go," he told her stoically. Tracey slowly released her arms and followed Keith over to the bed. They sat next to each other.

"Do you still love Noah?"

"No, I never loved him. I cared about him. It was just one night, Keith—a night that shouldn't have happened. Noah is making it out to be more than that in the press, and that's the truth. He's been in love with me since he was a little boy, and he never got over me. He thought after that night in Paris that I would break up with you. I told him I was still going to marry you, and he got upset," Tracey explained. "When I reached out to him about my book, he said he would only agree to it if I told the truth. I told him I would. I showed him the draft, but, after giving it some thought, I knew the only reason he wanted me to tell the truth was to try to break us up again. So, I didn't go into details."

"Was he strapped?"

Tracey nodded her head. "Yes, he wore a condom."

"And was he...was he better than me?"

"What?"

"You heard me, and you know what I'm talking about."

"Of course not! With you it's always about love."

"And have you...have you slept with him or any other man since we've been married?" Keith found it hard to ask those words, but he felt he needed to know.

Tracey looked him directly in the eyes. "No, I haven't, and that's the truth. I've only been with you. Bruce is lying. Those pictures on the Internet are all old pictures. Look, my hair is dyed black now. The pictures that Bruce posted, my hair was honey blonde. I haven't had my hair that color since Bruce and I divorced. That video of him kissing me, as you know, was a setup as well... So, no, I have not slept with Bruce either, or anyone else for that matter."

Keith rose to his feet and fought back his tears. He felt himself getting worked up again. Just thinking about Tracey being with another man angered him. His heart ached, and he couldn't stop the throbbing pain he felt in his head.

"Why, Tracey? Why couldn't you wait until we got married? Why did you have to cheat on me? And then you had the nerve to say at the end of your book that you had finally done something right. Really?"

"Keith, you're the only man I ever loved in my whole life. I *never* loved any other man as much as I love you. To find you was a blessing!"

"You didn't love me that much, since you slept with Noah!" he choked. "You stood before the altar of God and lied. And for nine years you knew about this, and not one time did you ever tell me the truth. The fact that it never bothered you is what hurts me the most."

"It did bother me, Keith, I've been regretting it for a long time, but you need to know that it didn't mean anything to me."

"There you go again, thinking about yourself. Just because it didn't mean anything to you still didn't give you the right to hold back the truth, Tracey! And then you had the audacity to act like Noah and Bruce was just making this stuff up. Bruce said he saw you with Noah several times while we were engaged. So you were still seeing him after Paris?"

"No. Those were lies, Keith. I only saw Noah at Kyle's office or celebrity events. If Bruce saw us, it was in those places and it wasn't the way he's making it out to be."

"How am I supposed to believe you when all this time you're walking around like you were innocent in all of this? You coached our family and friends to be on your side against these rumors, when all along it was true about you and Noah. That's wrong, Tracey! Can't you see the deception in that?" He shook his head. "And for what? So *you* could get what *you* wanted. Forget everybody else!"

Keith walked away from her and went into his walk-in closet. He started removing his suits off the racks and tossing them on the bed. When he found his suitcase, he sat it on the bed and made his way to the dresser.

"What are you doing?" Tracey asked, frantically.

"I don't know who you are anymore. I can't trust you." Keith started emptying out each drawer, tossing his socks and underwear inside his suitcase. "You played me for a fool!"

"That's not true!" Tracey protested. "It wasn't like that, Keith."

"You're so selfish, Tracey. You would rather live a lie for nine years than to tell the truth. What's the matter with you?" Keith zipped the suitcase. "Why did you marry me, huh? Did you marry me because I was something different? A good *catch*? As your boy Kyle would say. I guess I was cleaned up enough for you. I loved kids and gave to charity, is that why you married me? Because I helped clean up your bad girl image?"

"That's not true! And that's not a fair thing to say!"

"You ruined me like Delilah did Samson. I lost my respect from the church, my friends, and... probably even God himself. I married you knowing you weren't saved, but I should've known better. You were just as worldly as they came, but I tried to see past all of that."

"You're so wrong, Keith!" Tracey barked. "I married you because I loved you. I still love you with all my heart. I didn't ruin you. I tried to help you. I'm paying your tuition for Divinity School, and when you tried to quit, I was the one who told you the church needed you. When your mother was sick, I made sure we flew out to Oakland to care for her. But you were so busy caring for the church that you wasn't going to bother until I forced you to."

Keith shook his head. "That's crap and you know it!"

"It's not crap! You think you're so perfect, but you're not. The reason you're so pissed off about my book is because *you* pranced around the church acting like a know-it-all and a goody-two-shoes. The reason the church was shocked by what I wrote is because you never let them see the side to you that's human!"

"That's enough!" Keith pointed.

"Are you going to hit me? Smack me around like you did the women in the brothel you ran when they didn't have your money?"

"No, but don't tempt me."

"Tempt you? Did I tempt you that night you came to my house after I won the Emmy? I left out the other parts and what you did to me while my hands were pinned against the door or have you forgotten?"

"I remember what I did. It was the only way to calm you down. As I recall, we both tempted each other. You called me at almost midnight remember? You started it, and I just thought I would help put the fire out. Obviously that one time wasn't enough because you still went out and cheated on me anyway after we got engaged."

"Well I'm sorry I cheated on you, but you need to realize it was *before* we were married. I know that doesn't make it right, but I tried to be faithful to you. I waited a long time to be with you. Frankly, you didn't always help with my celibacy."

"You can't justify that you cheated on me Tracey. Even if we got a little carried away at times, I was always with you. I didn't creep out on you, so to accuse me of making you sleep with another man is ridiculous!" He sat down on the bed and slid on a T-shirt and a pair of shorts and sneakers. "You don't have self-control. That's your problem," he argued. "Everything you do is impulsive, and then when things blow up in your face, you blame everybody else."

"So you're just going to leave me now that I told you the truth. You don't want to try to work things out? Are you serious?" Tracey questioned with her arms folded, and feet tapping against the floor.

"Right now, both of us need to cool off. It's better if I take my leave. Give myself time to think."

"Fine, that's just fine," Tracey fumed. "What am I supposed to tell the kids while you're *thinking*?"

"Just tell them...tell them..." Keith was at a loss for words.

"You want to lie to them, don't you? And the reason you want to tell them a lie is because you don't want to hurt them. That's why I lied to you, for the same reason, but you can't see that."

"Look, I'm done arguing here. I'm leaving," He slung his bag over his shoulder and grabbed the suitcase with his other hand. "I'll be in touch later to let you know where I'm staying."

CHAPTER SEVENTEEN
LIFE IS A REALTY SHOW

Kay-Kay

Tracey cried the whole plane ride to London like somebody had died. Kay-Kay told Kyle to cancel the trip two times on behalf of her BFF. Tracey was so depressed she barely talked to anyone.

"When we get to the hotel, you need to grin and bear it, honey, because the cameras will be rolling everywhere. I need you to smile and wave your hand like a beauty pageant queen, and be nice to everyone," Kyle said to Tracey as she sniffed and blew her nose when they got off the plane.

"It's okay, Tracey, we can talk some more once we get to the hotel, okay?" Kay-Kay hugged Tracey, and Tracey squeezed her tight like she didn't want to let go.

"WE LOVE YOU TRACEY!" The fans shouted. They had been waiting for Tracey's arrival. They stood outside of the London *Westminster* Luxury Hotel, waving poster pictures of her and copies of her book in the air. The media also surrounded the hotel, and cameras flashed as Tracey quickly put on her dark shades and waved her hand with a forced smile on her face. She scribbled her name on a few pictures and books that fans managed to squeeze through to her, then her bodyguards and the London police rushed Tracey, Kay-Kay, and Kyle inside the hotel.

"Bags over there, darlings!" Kyle directed the bellmen. Tracey and Kay-Kay sat down on the plush contemporary style sofa and kicked off their high heels.

"And what is this?" Kyle pranced over to the living room, where Tracey and Kay-Kay were resting their feet. "Get up right now. Darling needs to be ready by nine o'clock for a press conference. We have three hours to get her ready. Understand?"

"She'll be ready. We just need to take a load off for a minute, so chill out," Kay-Kay replied.

"I beg your pardon? Her makeup alone can take an hour, and you need to get started with her hair. You're her stylist. You don't get paid to sit on your behind, okay? We have several interviews and lots of bookstore signings this week. Darling is also scheduled to do a meet and greet for fashion week for her summer makeup line. This is not a vacation for you, so let's be clear about that!" Kyle snapped his fingers.

"Look, you don't give me orders. Nobody orders me around. You're not my boss. Tracey pays me, not you. So you go and take care of what Kyle needs to do and mind your own business!" Kay-Kay argued.

"Three hours, and I'm not going to repeat it. She cannot be late!" Kyle abruptly turned around and walked out of the room. Seconds later, the door swung open.

"Oh darlings," Kyle walked back in. "Room service is here, and they're on time, just like I asked them to be. You babies will need your energy, but don't eat too much; it creates a fat gut. Bye-bye."

Kay-Kay slowly got up from the sofa. She approached the white clothed table that was filled with an array of assorted fruits, muffins, and bagels. Pitchers of orange juice, milk, and a side pot of coffee were perfectly lined outside of the centered platters of food. Kay-Kay helped herself to a little bit of everything. When she looked up, Tracey was groaning and massaging the sides of her temples.

"Tracey, I can fix you a plate."

"I'm not hungry," she mumbled, and lay back against the pillows on the sofa, and propped up her feet.

"You have to eat, Tracey. Here, you have to eat, because I have to get set up and get you ready."

"I need a bath and some sleep," Tracey moaned.

"Are you sure you're up for this? I mean, I think it's bad timing that we came here," Kay said. "You're going through a rough separation right now. You should be back home with your kids and trying to work on your marriage."

"I just need a good nap. I'll be fine."

"Well, I know Kyle will be upset, but I don't care. You should go in the room and lie down and sleep for as long as you want."

"We have to get ready."

"Tracey, you're my girl, and life goes on even when the fame and fortune is gone. It really does. Family is more important. You're important too. You're burning the candles from both ends trying to please everyone, mostly Kyle. He's pushing you so he can fatten his own pockets. Why do you think his other clients have left him?"

"I don't want to think about that right now. My head hurts too bad from all that crying I did on the plane."

"I understand. I'll lay off, but you should seriously reconsider hiring another manager. Not just for your own sake, but mine too. I can't work with Kyle around, and I'm not going to take him much longer. Go ahead in the room and rest. Forget Kyle."

At the press conference, Kay-Kay was sitting to the left of Tracey and Kyle sat to her right. Tracey and Kay-Kay talked about their reality show, Divas of LA, and then Tracey talked about her makeup line, and her book. She also talked about new movie offers she'd received, and answered each question with ease. Kay-Kay knew it was just a matter of minutes before the heavy hitting questions would come. It all started with rumors about Tracey and B-Money supposedly sleeping together. They flashed the picture of B-Money kissing her while she stood in the doorway of her Malibu home in a bathrobe.

"Those rumors were proved false. B-Money fabricated the whole thing," Tracey replied.

"So it really was just an act like Kyle said. He mentioned it would be part of season two for your show, Divas," One of the reporters mentioned.

"What?" Tracey and Kay-Kay gave Kyle a stern look.

"Next question, please!" Kyle clapped his hands.

"We also heard from Kyle that Bison is here in the UK for fashion week as well. Is it true that now that you are separated from your husband, you and will Bison will reunite, and that will be part of season two as well?"

Tracey's mouth dropped, and so did Kay-Kay's. Kay-Kay and Tracey looked at Kyle who simple shrugged his shoulders. He leaned into Tracey and whispered, "I'll explain later, but just answer as best you can."

Tracey looked at the reporters with cameras flashing, and TV cameras filming her every move, and replied nervously, "I, um…I had no idea that Bison would be here. I'm here because I'm scheduled to do an international book tour, and to promote "TGM" my makeup line, that's it. There won't be any reunions of any sort. Not on my part."

"We just received word that Bison is here, and he said he's willing to come out on the platform and speak about your love affair with him during your engagement, and you plan to reunite as part of season two. Do you wish to speak on that before Mr. Bison approaches the platform?"

"No-she-does-not!" Kay-Kay shouted into the microphone, and then leaned over and pointed to Kyle. "This was your doing wasn't it?"

"I beg your pardon?" Kyle's mouth dropped.

"You heard me."

"Please be silent guys," Tracey uttered in a whispered to Kay-Kay and Kyle, but the microphone picked it up.

"Tracey, please answer the question," the reporter insisted.

Tracey swallowed hard. Took a deep breath and exhaled in a way that made the top of her curls flow to the side of her face.

"Tracey, isn't it true that you and your husband separated because he learned about your affair with Bison?"

Tracey thought about it, and she didn't want Noah to come out on the platform and speak his own truth about things. He had already done that in the states, and she felt it painted the wrong picture of how things happened, so she parted her lips to answer.

"Don't say a word if you don't want too Tracey," Kay-Kay hissed, but when Tracey let go of her hand she knew her friend was about to speak.

"The real reason my husband and I separated is because...I did have a one night affair with Bison," Tracey answered, and the whole room sighed.

"Oooooh!"

Cameras flashed so much after her statement that all Kay-Kay could see was spots and floaters. She couldn't believe her ears. After all of this time of defending her best friend, the rumors were true. Kay-Kay didn't know if she wanted to hit Tracey or hug her. Her heart felt shattered like broken pieces of glass.

"For me...it was just one night," Tracey continued. "It was a night that should not have happened. I have regretted it ever since. I guess for

Noah, or Bison as you guys call him, that night meant a lot more, because here we are, nine years later, talking about it as if it happened yesterday."

Kay-Kay suddenly felt an urge to get up and leave the conference room, but she decided not to draw attention to herself.

"Tracey, are you saying your affair with Noah was nine years ago? And not during your marriage?"

"I was not married, but engaged to be married. It was nearly a decade ago really. Bison felt a need to mention it to the world since I decided to omit it from my book to protect my family."

"So Bison is a home wrecker you would say?" asked another reporter.

"I didn't say that, but you did."

(The media laughed).

"Is there any chance that you and your husband will reconcile?"

"Only God knows the answer to that. In my heart I know I still love my husband and I believe he still loves me."

"And if he doesn't take you back, will you and Bison get together?"

"No we will not."

"Do you think Bison talked about your affair because he still has strong feelings for you?"

"You can ask him when it's his turn, but guys I'm done with the questions for today. To my fans, I'll see you soon. To my children back in the U.S., mommy loves you! Thank you guys for this interview," Tracey quickly waved good-bye to the press, and existed the platform.

Tracey was slouched down in the back of the limo with her sunshades on. Kay-Kay couldn't bear to look at her anyway. She kept staring out the window wishing she was back at home with her family.

"I'm sorry Kay. I'm sorry you had to find out that way, and I'm sorry I told you that Keith and I separated because of my career. That was just a partial truth, but I know it was still wrong. That's why I've been crying this whole time. I was tired. Tired of hiding, tired of thinking I was protecting the ones I loved, but all along, I was hurting, holding that in."

"You're not the victim, Tracey. What you did was wrong!" Kay-Kay snapped.

"I know. I'm really sorry," Tracey reached for Kay's hand but she snatched it away, and rolled her eyes.

"You told me you would never sleep with my brother, but you did it anyway. You have a hard time keeping your word, *and keeping your legs closed!*" Kay fussed. "When will you grow up, Tracey? You can't go around sleeping with every good-looking man and expect for people to respect you. You screw them and then leave them high and dry. That's why Bruce and Noah are angry with you. You used Bruce for his money and fame, and then you used my brother for sex. Now you're having a pity party? Pah-lease! You are wrong on so many levels that it doesn't make sense!"

"I'm not that girl anymore, Kay. I made a mistake. What happened between me and Noah was years ago. I've found God now, and I'm a much better person."

Kay-Kay twisted her lips. "Pah-lease, you may have found God, but you haven't let him into your heart. Otherwise, you would've admitted the truth a long time ago!"

"I'm sorry, Kay. You're right about everything. I'm not going to argue with you. I was wrong, and there's nothing I can do to fix this."

"This is so exciting!" Kyle laughed. "I'm taping you guys arguing on my phone. This will be good for next season too. The ratings are going to skyrocket!"

"Kyle, don't tape us!" Tracey shouted. "Speaking of which, you will not use that video footage from Bruce to put into next season either!"

"Driver, let me out here please. I'm going to have drinks with friends. Be ready for your book signings tomorrow darling," Kyle said, ignoring Tracey all together.

"I'm sick of him!" Tracey sucked her teeth, but Kay-Kay wasn't paying her any mind. She was still upset and didn't say another word the rest of the ride back to the hotel.

"Kay-Kay, I'm sorry I hurt you. You're my best friend. Please talk to me," Tracey begged, once they were back in their hotel room.

"You need to hire another stylist after this tour."

"But Kay-Kay, I need you!"

"No you don't"

"I do," Tracey held her hand. "I need you to help me to figure out something about Kyle. I need to make sure I'm right about things."

* * *

NOAH

Nobody was speaking to each other. The lunch table was quiet, making Noah feel uncomfortable. He was glad they were all having lunch together before his fashion show tonight, but the silence was irritating him.

"Who arranged this quiet meal?" Noah asked, and Tracey and Kay-Kay both looked at Kyle.

"What? Was this a bad thing? You guys needed to talk, right? Hash things out?" Kyle asked, stuffing his mouth with food.

"Why are cameras here?" Noah asked.

"It's part of Tracey's reality show, for season two," Kyle replied as Tracey and Kay-Kay continued eating without saying a word.

"I do not think the cameras should be here," Noah said to Kyle.

"Why?" Tracey put down her fork and stared directly at Noah. He was captivated by her beautiful hazel eyes and felt goosebumps all over his arms. After all of this time, he still found himself very attracted to her, despite the fact that her stare was cold and uninviting.

"I just think lunch should be just between us, not the public."

"You embarrassed me and ruined my life. And now you want to hide?" Tracey barked, and Noah didn't like the sound of the tone in her voice.

"You are telling the world your book is the truth, but you left out many things about us, Tracey."

"Has it ever occurred to you, Noah, that maybe I left those things out because they didn't mean anything to me, and that I didn't want the people I love to get hurt behind something that happened nine years ago? Almost ten?"

"I beg to defer," Noah retorted, wiping his mouth with a napkin. "The only reason you did not mention our love was because you did not want to be responsible for your actions. You never do."

"Noah, you can think whatever you want, but you and I happened a very long time ago. You need to get over me. That's your problem!"

"Is it?"

"Yes, you're not over me. Just so we're clear, Keith never took me from you because my heart was always with him."

"That is what your mouth says, but your actions said something else."

"Noah, even if Keith and I had not gotten back together I wouldn't be with you. You're immature and spiteful. You're just a boy who never grew up."

"Boy? How dare you call me a boy? Was I a boy when you had your legs wrapped around me begging for more? Who was the boy then, huh?"

"Ooooo, honey," Kyle instigated. "Tell the truth, shame the devil, honey!"

"And was your heart with Keith when you had your legs wrapped around me in Paris, was it?" Noah disputed.

"I was drunk that night, and you took advantage of the situation. You couldn't have me any other way, and you knew that," Tracey argued. "You need to let go, get a life, and move on!"

Kyle shifted his gaze to Noah, but Noah didn't have a response.

"I just hope you're satisfied that you broke up my family. Now, my children are wondering why their parents aren't together. I hope you're happy Noah!" Tracey slammed her fork down on the table, and shook her head in anger.

Noah cleared his throat. "I am sorry for hurting you and your family, Tracey. I never would have mentioned us if you had told the truth like you promised. It was the only reason I agreed to you writing about me. I never like to hurt a family, and especially children."

"Look," Tracey heaved a long sigh. "We need to just squash all of this mess. I'm woman enough to say I apologize for hurting you, Noah. And to you, Kay-Kay, my best friend and my sister, I apologize for lying to you. The three of us grew up together. It may take us some time to get back to that happy place, but I'm willing to work hard to gain you guys' trust again and friendship. I'm willing to work just as hard to get my family back together because my children don't deserve this."

Kyle started clapping. "Great speech, you get an Oscar for that. Mr. Cameraman, did y'all get that?" Kyle laughed.

"Kyle, I want you to know that I prayed all night long last night, and Kay-Kay and I talked until the sun came up."

"Good for you, honey."

"Yeah, and we really wanted the cameras to be here today, that's why we agreed with you that we could film for the show," Kay-Kay added.

"Cool. It's going to be a great season two."

"Hold up," Tracey threw up her hands. "They say every show should end with a bang or a great cliffhanger."

"That's right," Kyle paused, and sipped his drink.

"It was you who told Bruce where I lived, and you gave him a record deal in return. You even promoted his diss track about me. Although he doesn't say my name, the world knows he's talking about me. Now, my son and my brother did a diss track about him. Meanwhile, you're sitting back loving all the drama by playing a puppet master with peoples' lives."

"What? I don't do business with thugs!"

"Of course you do. My mother blacklisted Bruce from making records, but as soon as she retired and others took over, it was easy for you to get him a deal. But guess what? My mother still has more respect and power than you ever will. She emailed me the paperwork last night, which showed that you signed to be Bruce's manager."

"Oh hush! You don't know a thing about this business honey, so keep your trap shut!"

"I'm smarter than you think, and I learned from the best in this business– my mother," Tracey countered. "You see, I already figured out there had to be a reason for this back-to-back drama. It all started after I got engaged to Keith. Kay-Kay and I figured out it was no mistake that Noah just so happen to be in Paris that night that *you* got me drunk. *You* asked Noah to walk me to my room that night. Why?" Tracey asked.

"I don't know what you're talking about. Guys, turn those cameras off!"

"No, keep the cameras rolling!" Tracey demanded. "Of course you'll say that now, but the reason you set up the whole thing was because you didn't want me to marry Keith. You only intended for him to help clean up my image, but I *never* dated Keith for those intentions. I loved him from the moment I laid eyes on him, and you knew if you didn't break us up that would take me off the market. Being a single sex symbol in the business is more attractive than being married in this business, right? Isn't that what you used to always tell me?"

"Look, I made you the superstar you are right now, and this is the thanks I get!" Kyle abruptly stood up and tossed his napkin on his plate.

"Oh no, you don't get off the hook that easily," Tracey stood up. "You don't get to walk away and quit. Kyle Lager you are fired!"

"YES!" Keyshia clapped her hands. "Did you hear that *darling*? She said, *you're fired*, so walk your narrow behind on out the door!"

"No wait hold up. I'll see you in court Kyle."

"For what?"

"For stealing money from me after all these years. When I was hurt in that motorcycle accident, the court documents stated I won two hundred and fifty thousand dollars, but I never saw any of it. My new accountant got back with me last night, and he said my bills only came up to a little over fifty thousand dollars that year."

"Whatever, he's lying!" Kyle threw up his hand.

"Oh wait, I'm not finished yet. Not only do you owe me the rest of that money, but you're in breach of contract."

"Breach of contract?"

"That's right. I never signed permission for you to put Noah's picture in my book. Our contract stated that all images had to be approved mutually. You called and had the publishing company to throw in those pictures of Noah after I had already signed off for them to go to print. You lied to them and said I agreed to the photos. Therefore, you'll owe me every penny from the percentage you earned off my book. Plus I'm suing you for ruining my marriage and my reputation. Should I continue?"

Kyle threw up his nose and stormed out the door.

"Cut! That's a wrap!" The cameraman gave Tracey the thumbs up.

"Wow, the next time you guys decide to film me, at least give me a script," Noah wiped the sweat from his forehead. "I did not know what was going on. You really cursed Kyle out!"

"Noah, life is a reality show. You didn't need a script," Tracey told him. "Besides, Kyle had it coming."

He gave her a hug. "Maybe you're right. Say listen Tracey, I am really sorry for hurting you and your family. I hope that when the show airs, Keith will finally see the truth."

"I hope so too. For now, it feels good to have you guys back."

They did a group hug.

"I guess I need to check my financial statements to make sure Kyle did not get over on me too."

"You better!" Kay, urged him.

"And find a new manager," Tracey added.

"You guys sound just like my big sisters."
"We are!"

CHAPTER-EIGHTEEN
CROCKED ROAD

Keith wasn't sure why he kept hanging out with Tyson and his boys at the clubs every Friday night, but he tried not to think about too much about it, as he downed his fourth shot of Tequila. He was starting to feel like he was floating, and he felt good. He snapped his fingers and bopped his head to the loud music thumping throughout the club. The guys were going crazy over the women pole dancing to the beat, and Keith was right amongst the crowd of men cheering on the women, and tossing up dollar bills, making it rain.

"How about we go back to your place, big boy," one of the strippers whispered in his Keith's ear as her breast pressed up against his face.

"Oh yeah!" Keith smiled, half drunk. "Hooow about weee go in the back, like...like right now!" His speech slurred.

"Give me five minutes," she said. She spun around the pole and did a few more acrobatic dance moves, collected more money and slowly exited the stage while her girlfriend took the next set.

"Go for it!" Tyson slapped him on the back.

Keith staggered for a minute then he caught his balance as he made his way through the crowd. It was very dim down the stretch of the hallway, and he had to balance himself against the wall.

"Right in here honey," the stripper called him. Keith followed the glowing light from the dressing room. The music kept thumping in the background, and he could feel its vibrations and hear the faint cheers from the guys out front. He snapped his fingers to the beat, and made his way to the door.

"Come on in," the stripper called him with her pointing finger. Keith peeped inside the room and there she was lying on a sofa naked.

"Alright leeet's geeet it popping!" He shouted. He had already picked up Tyson's slang, and didn't care.

"I don't think so!" Keith heard a man's voice from behind, and turned around. He couldn't really make out the guy's face at first.

"Say maaan what's up with you? I came here first!" Keith shoved the guy who stood the same height as him.

"Keith it's Sonny!"

Keith squinted. "Sonny?"

"That's right it's me. Pastor Richardson told me he tried to talk to you but there was no getting through. I've been trying to track you down, but I never thought you would be here until your neighbor told me you were frequenting these kinds of places now," Sonny's eyes scanned the room.

"Pastor Richardson never came to talk to me. He's lying. He-he-he kicked me out the church, man. Now leave me alone. I got business to handle with this lady here," Keith turned his attention to back to the stripper and helped her up off the sofa. "Get dress. We're going to my crib."

"No way. Not now and not ever. You're drunk and you've lost your mind, brother," Sonny stepped between them, as the woman was getting dressed.

"Man, step off before you get dealt with!"

"Calm down Keith," Sonny warned him. "As for you young lady, this is a married man and he's coming with me," Sonny tugged at Keith's arm and hurried him out the door.

"Shoot! The good ones are always taken!"

Keith woke up on his sofa the next morning with a blasting headache. His head ached so bad that he could barely open his eyes.

"Drink this, it will help," Sonny offered him a hot cup of coffee. Keith stared at the mug and then lifted his eyes to the man handing it to him. A part of him kept thinking he had been attached by this man the night before. Suddenly, Keith jumped up and grabbed Sonny by the shirt and they tussled to the floor.

"You're trying to rob me!"

"No, calm down! I picked you up from the club! You're still drunk!" Sonny tried to shove him off, but Keith kept punching him.

"I said calm down!" Sonny pulled out his gun.

"Sonny? It's you man?" Keith slowly turned him loose, and backed away.

"It's me!"

"Man, what're you doing with a gun? You're a preacher."

"It's not real, and it's not loaded. See," Sonny squirted Keith in the face.

"Aw man," Keith wiped the water from his face. "What are you doing here?" Keith staggered to the sofa and flopped down.

"You need to sober up first and then we can talk. I think someone may have slipped something in your drink last night. You're hallucinating. Go get cleaned up and rest. We'll talk shortly."

Keith went to take a shower while Sonny took a nap in a chair in the living room. He had been watching Keith all night to make sure he was okay. After Keith took a shower, he took some medicine for his headache and laid down in his room.

Hours later, there was a knock at Keith's front door. Sonny waited to see if Keith would come out of his room and answer it, but when he didn't, Sonny went to the door himself.

"Is Keith home?"

"And who are you?" Sonny stared at the young man wearing sagging pants and jewels around his neck, wrists, and big rings on his fingers.

"Tyson," He replied, smacking on his gum like a cow and adjusting the bandana around his head.

"Keith is resting."

"Tell him his boy stopped by to check on him."

"His boy?" Sonny questioned, pushing his dark framed glasses over the brim of his nose.

"Yeah, no homo, but uhm, we're cool like that. Who are you?"

"I'm Sonny."

"Oh yeah, you're the Reverend dude who married him and Tracey."

"Reverend *dude*? I told you my name was Sonny."

"Yeah whatever. You look like Roger from *What's Happening*," Tyson laughed.

"Do yourself a favor Tyson. Seek help. Seek God."

Tyson burst out laughing. "You must not know who I am, Reverend."

"I know you're a ball player, but besides that you're a lost soul."

"Man, you don't know me to judge me."

"Speaking the truth is not judgment. You look like a slave with all those chains around your neck, and a jailbird by the way your pants are sagging. You're an insult to our people is what you are."

Tyson twisted his lips. "What are you man?"

"It is not *what* I am. It is *who* I am," Sonny stared Tyson eye-to-eye and did not look away until Tyson looked away first. "Don't come by here again. You're poisoning a good man."

"Whatever Reverend. Tell him I stopped out. I'm outta here. I don't need a sermon," Tyson smirked, waved him off and went about his way. Sonny shut the door, and when he turned around, Keith was standing in the living room.

"So Tyson came by to check on his buddy, huh?" "What has gotten into you, Keith?"

"I don't know what you're talking about. I'm straight," Keith shrugged, sat down and turned on the TV with the remote.

"I'm not going to waste anymore of my time here. I need to head back to Oakland. My flight leaves in exactly two hours."

"Who told you to come?"

"Your mother and your wife."

Keith's eyes widened. "My wife?"

"Yes. The last I checked Tracey was still your wife."

"So that's what the paper says."

Sonny reached for the remote on the table, turned the TV off and sat down in a chair across from Keith.

"Brother, I need to remind you that you are not a free man. You're still married by law and before the eyes of the living God."

"And?"

"Listen, Tracey has expressed even public repentance for her sins. Have you not seen her press conference that she did overseas?"

"I don't watch TV much. I'm rarely here."

"Anyway, I have talked with Tracey and I believe she is genuinely sorry for what she has done. I know that she misses you and she still loves you. She may not be as strong as you are in your walk, but she's never stopped trying to do the right thing."

"It's too late for all of that man!" Keith snapped. "She screwed that dude, Noah, and made me believe she was saving herself for me. Do you know how that makes me feel? She put my business in the streets and everything. I can't trust her anymore.. Do you know how much this hurts?"

"Brother, you're like my son. Listen to me, you may feel like you're getting back at her from what you're doing, but you're only hurting yourself and your family. Most of all, you are disappointing God."

"I take care of my kids. I still spend time with them no matter what. I just don't have anything to say to her right now."

"That's not enough. You made a promise before God and his angels that you would love Tracey in sickness and health through good and bad times."

"Sonny," Keith abruptly sat up and looked him in the eyes. "Tracey stood there in front of all of those witnesses and told the world she loved me knowing she slept with another man. That's deceitful Sonny! So for you to come all the way out here from Oakland and try to tell me that I need to forgive her is ridiculous!"

Sonny heaved a long sigh. "Need I remind you that you have done worse things?"

"I wasn't married."

"Neither was Tracey."

"Yeah well she promised."

"She kept the promise and married you, but she broke the trust. Yet, she's asking for your forgiveness and you're turning your back on her the same way Pastor Richardson turned his back on you. How is it that you want this man to forgive you and overlook your sins, but you cannot forgive the sins of your wife? Who is more important? Doesn't the word of God encourage us to take care of our own household first? You're not doing that. You're being a coward about this. The first sign of trouble in your marriage and you pack your bags and run? That is not what a mature Christian does," Sonny expressed. "Tracey mentioned you told her you were taking a time out. That time is up brother. You need to let go and return home to your family before things get worse."

The phone started ringing interrupting the conversation. Keith answered it. Sonny walked off to the kitchen to grab something to drink, but he overheard Keith talking on the phone.

"Yeah Trey, you can stop over and get whipped on *NBA2K*," Keith laughed. "Alright. Yeah well uhm…tell your mother I said hi too. All right man. Peace."

Sonny sat back down in the chair, cracked open a soda, and took a few swallows before he spoke again.

"So, what's your solution my son?"

"For what?"

Sonny gave him a blank stare. He wasn't about to play any mind games.

"I don't know Sonny," Keith hunched his shoulders. "I'm hurting man. Every time I see her when I got pick up the kids, I just think about how she let some other dude hit it, know what I'm saying? I'm just keeping it real."

"Listen to you. You even sound like that no good Tyson that you hang out with."

"Well at least he's a loyal friend."

"He's a kid, a loser, and you're a forty-three year old man running around here acting like you don't know God or have a family who needs you!"

"What do you want me to do Sonny?"

"It's not about what *I* want you to do. *You* know what to do, but you're allowing your pride and your ego to block out the spirit of God that's trying to direct you back on the right course."

"It's my life, and I'm not that kid you saved years ago. I'm a grown man."

"You're not a kid but I can't tell by the way you're acting. You've lost your way, Keith. The road you're on now is crooked, and if you don't straighten up soon you'll lose everything. I'm through talking," Sonny donned his hat, and put on his jacket. "May God help you, son."

Part Three

CHAPTER-NINETEEN
SHOWBOATING

TREY

Trey just came from seeing his dad, and whipping him in videogames. He decided to go shopping on Rodeo Drive afterwards. He ended up spending over two thousand dollars on an outfit he felt he needed for his show tonight. He walked out of one of the stores texting one of his girlfriends who was complaining about him not calling her back.

"Dang, watch where you're going!"

He looked up from his phone, not realizing he almost bumped into a group of girls walking by.

"My bad. Sorry," He looked back down at his phone, and texted the girl back.

"Oh my gosh, it's Trey Mikes!" One of the girls screamed, suddenly realizing who he was.

"Oh my gosh, can we have your autograph?!"

"Hold on a second," He stuffed his phone into his back pocket, and searched his front pocket for something to write with. "I don't think I have a pen."

"Just take a picture with us, pleeease!"

"No problem." he blushed.

"You're such a showoff."

Trey looked over his shoulder.

"Jazmine?" he smiled ear-to-ear. He didn't see her walk up behind him. She had veered away from her friends.

Trey approached her. "How've you been?"

"Just fine, thank you," She sneered.

"Oh my gosh, Jazmine, you didn't tell us you knew Trey Mikes!"

"I know him. We grew up together," she replied nonchalantly. It had been a while since Trey had seen Jazmine. She was still tall and slim like her mother, with the smoothest coconut brown skin. She was sporting micro-braids and had them pulled up in a ponytail. She was rocking that old school 80s look with her hot pink leggings, black boots, and a matching cut-off top that showed her belly ring.

"I can't believe you never told us you grew up with Trey Mikes!" one of her friends said.

"Our mothers are best friends," Jazmine informed them.

"So what're y'all doing on Rodeo Drive? Shouldn't you be shopping at Crenshaw Mall?" Trey chuckled.

"Ha-ha-ha, you got jokes! Don't act like we never shopped there as kids before our mothers blew up and made it big," Jazmine rebuked.

Trey laughed.

"Y'all go ahead. I'm taking a ride back home with Trey."

"Say what? How're you going to volunteer my services? You don't know where I'm going after this."

"Don't matter, open the door. You can take me home."

He shook his head. He couldn't believe she just bum rushed him like that. He opened the door to his new Lamborghini Aventendor. Jazmine waved goodbye to her friends, who were in awe as they drove away. Jazmine knew she would have to explain why she kept her celebrity a secret. Everyone knew that her mother and Trey's mom were famous best friends and business partners.

Trey adjusted the bass louder on the stereo as Rihanna was singing "Pour It Up." He rolled the windows down, leaned back, and cruised down the street, making heads turn. When he spotted paparazzi, he slowed down a little and flashed a smile at the cameras.

Jazmine rolled her eyes to the ceiling. "You're such a show-off!"

"What? I can't hear you!"

She reached over and turned the radio down.

"I said you're such a show-off!"

"Don't hate."

"I'm not."

"You still mess with that nerdy dude? What was his name, Peter?" he laughed.

"Ha-ha-ha, very funny. No, his name wasn't Peter, it was Joe, stupid. And, if you must know, we broke up."

"I can see why."

She sucked her teeth. "Excuse me?"

"I said," He leaned forward and turned the music down some more. "I can see why. You have a stank attitude, girl."

"I do not."

"You do. That's why I never–"

"Never what?"

He looked away. "Nothing. Don't worry about it."

She turned the music back up and starting dancing. Trey thought she was being wishy-washy; one minute she was giving him attitude and the next minute she was dancing like she wasn't mad about anything.

Trey sped down the highway, jumping lanes, testing out how fast the Lamborghini could go. He glanced over at Jazmine and saw her hands gripping her seat and her body tensed up. He drove up close on the car in front of him like he was going to hit it, then quickly spun the wheels, and darted into the next lane.

"Trey, what're you doing? I've had enough of your crazy driving!" Jazmine panicked. "You're gonna get us both killed!"

He burst out laughing and eased up on the gas paddle.

"It's not funny, see what you done?"

"What?"

Jazmine pointed in the side view mirror at the flashing lights of the highway patrol cars fast approaching them.

"Aw man!" he slammed his hands against the steering wheel. The cops were almost catching up to them. He pressed his foot on the gas and fled down the highway, passing the exit to get off and head towards Jazmine's house. He kept going until it looked like he lost police. Finally, he got off at the Santa Monica Boulevard exit, and then made a U-turn to head back towards Jazmine's.

"You jerk!" Jazmine got out the car and slammed the door, once they arrived at her house.

"I bet you won't be hopping in my car next time," he laughed.

"You could have killed us! We could have gotten arrested, fool!"

"Aw look at you pouting. You look cute when you're mad, you know."

Jazmine hurried to her front door, pulling her keys out of her purse. Trey thought about what happened for a few seconds, and then got out of the car.

"Hey, hey Jazmine," he rushed up to her. "I'm sorry, okay? I didn't mean to scare you. Real talk."

"Wipe that funny smirk off your face, then," she rolled her eyes.

"You can at least look sincere about it."

He opened his eyes wide and put on a Frankenstein monster expression. Jazmine tried not to laugh, but couldn't resist.

"You're so stupid!"

"You coming to my show tonight?" he asked, following her inside.

"I don't have tickets."

He twisted his lips. "Come on, you couldn't call me and ask me?"

"If I wanted tickets I could buy my own. I'm not one of your begging fans."

"So are you saying you didn't want to come?"

"I don't know. I don't want to sweat you like that."

"I thought you knew me better than that. Here," He reached in his back pocket and handed her two V.I.P passes. "I want you to be there and see me. Bring one of your friends with you."

She felt unsure. "But you never cared if I came to one of your shows before."

"Yeah well, come tonight. I want you there," He winked.

"You're just giving me these tickets so I won't snitch on you for driving so crazy."

"Nah it ain't like that. I want you to come." He watched the corners of lips curve a smile.

"That looks beautiful."

"What?"

"Your smile. You should do that more often."

"Thanks."

"You're not just a fan, Jazmine. I haven't forgotten about you since we were little kids."

"I can't tell. You're always up in some other girls' face."

"They don't mean nothing to me though," he gave her a quick kiss on the mouth. "You do. Always remember that, alright?"

She blushed. "All right. I'll remember."

"I gotta go."

"See you tonight."

After Trey left Jazmine's house, he headed to Malibu to visit his mother. He drove along the Pacific Coast Highway (PCH) up into the hills that overlooked Zuma Beach. He loved how his mother's house reminded him of a private paradise, but there was nothing around except beaches and mountains. Trey drove up the hill, entered his password to get through the gate, then drove around the circular driveway and parked behind his mother's BMW. She had traded in her Incenti Maybach after his little brother and sister were born. He remembered her saying to his dad, "We need a bigger family car since it's no longer just me and Trey." He missed his parents being together.

"Treeeey!" Alexis jumped up and down with excitement when Trey walked in.

"How did you know I was coming in?" He picked her up, swung her around. Her ponytails blew in the air like long spider legs.

"I was looking out the window," she replied as he propped her up on his hip. With his other hand, he lifted his little brother KJ, and leaned down enough so he could crawl onto his back.

"What's for dinner?" "Mac n' cheese!" KJ shouted in his ear.

"That's not all we're having, KJ," Alexis said, talking to him across Trey's shoulder like they were riding a horse. "We're having mac n' cheese, calorie greens and..."

Trey raised his brow. "Calorie greens?"

"Yeah."

"You mean collard greens?"

"No, stupid, it's calorie greens," she insisted.

"What else?"

"Stop interrupting me. Now I have to start over," Alexis whined.

"That's okay, we're here now. I can find out myself. Hey Ma."

"Hi Trey." They hugged and kissed each other. Trey sat down at the island while his mother was cooking. The kids sat down at their table.

"You look tired, Mom. Why didn't you let Clara, the new nanny, cook today?"

"As strange as it may sound, I missed my own cooking. I wanted to see if I still got it," she winked. "Now I know what your grandmother meant when she used to say she wanted to eat her own food."

"Sure smells good."

"My mac n' cheese is almost done, the greens are simmering, and the baked chicken should be done in a few more minutes," She said, stirring the greens. "Are you sticking around to eat?"

Trey shrugged his shoulders. "I guess I can."

"Good, your grandfather called. He's coming over for dinner."

"Really? I didn't know he and Grandma were in town."

"I'm referring to your Grandpa Jet?"

"Whaaat? Get the—fudge outta here!"

"Watch your mouth."

"I said "fudge", Ma," he laughed. "Anyway, what made him want to come over? I haven't seen him since I was a kid."

"He saw your grandmother at their forty-first high school reunion, and told her he really wanted to see me."

"That's cool. I'll say wassup to him. Break bread and all, but I can't stay long. I got a show tonight at Riser's."

"Kay-Kay and I used to hang out there all the time. I still remember when Jodeci performed there. I thought they closed that place down."

"They renovated it now. It's nice. Got three floors and everything," Trey informed her.

"You be careful, Trey. It's a fun little spot, but it's kind of rough in that area. That club is right across the street from a rundown bridge. A lot of crimes happened over there. That's why they shut it down in the first place," she cautioned, while simultaneously stirring the greens in the pot.

"We'll have bodyguards with us Ma don't worry."

"And I hope you won't perform that song 'Has Been'."

"But Ma it's a hit. I have to give the fans what they want."

"Trey, I know I'm probably sounding just like my parents when they used to preach to me, but on the real, watch your back. It's not a game out there. And please don't perform that diss track about Bruce. It's rumored he had my best friend Tony Tee killed for rapping something bad about him in a song, so be careful. Bruce is crazy, and I don't want anything to happen to you!"

Trey gritted his teeth. "I got this, Ma. I'm good. Don't worry."

"I'm only saying this because I love you, Trey."

"I love you too Ma and I hear you. Trust me on that," Trey grabbed an apple from the fruit bowl in front of him.

"Have you heard from Dad?"

"He comes by and gets the kids, but you know we don't say much to each other. That's not my choice either. Half the time Clara is the mediator between us. When I see his number I let her answer the phone and she relays the message to me that he's coming. Sometimes she drops them over his house, and then he'll drop them off back to me. That's how it's been."

"I did tell him that you said hello when I went over to play some game videogames with him today."

"Trey, you need to stay out of our business. You know I didn't tell you to say that."

"I know. I just want ya'll to get back together. I know you still love each other right?" he asked, smacking on the apple.

Tracey turned off the stove, and turned around to face Trey. "Of course we do. That kind of love doesn't easily go away, but–" She stopped in the middle of her sentence when she saw Alexis and KJ had their eyes glued to her. They were hung on her every word.

"Alexis, KJ, go play in the entertainment room," Tracey said to them, not wanting them to hear the conversation about their dad. When they walked away she continued.

"Anyway, it seems to me that your dad is having a good time clubbing and hanging out with strippers like he's a single man. I don't foresee us getting about together any time soon."

"I asked him about that, and although he didn't deny it, I don't think he's sleeping with other women, Ma. If he was, I would have knocked him out," Trey made a fist. "I could tell he misses you though. He's just being stubborn about the whole thing."

"Childish is more like," Tracey countered. "Anyway, that's enough about me and your dad, what's going on with you? You better be wrapping it up out there. I see the way those girls are all over you in them videos."

"Come on Ma," Trey chuckled. "That's my business."

"It's *my* business too. Don't make me a grandmother Trey. I keep seeing you posting a different picture on *Instagram* every week with a different chick. And how old are they? Some of them look like they're pushing forty like me!"

"I like 'em older sometimes."

"Boy, you are not Usher, stay in your own lane. Date somebody within your age group."

"Yeah well, I may settle down one day. I got somebody in mind, but she need to get her attitude right."

"Somebody as in Jazmine?" Tracey raised her brow.

"How you know that?"

"Your Mama knows everything boy. I don't miss a beat. She's had a crush on you since you were kids."

Trey blushed. "So what has she been saying about me?"

"That's between me and her, but I will say you need to make up your mind about who you want. You don't need to be like Bruce and think you can have all the women you want to. You see where it's gotten him. He's got kids all over the place and can't take care of any of them."

"That won't be me, Ma. I promise."

"Fine, but like I said, don't make me a grandmother. I'm not ready, and she better not be old enough to *be* your mother either."

"Alright Ma, I got it."

"Mommy, me and Alexis heard the doorbell ringing," KJ ran into the kitchen.

"Yeah, and I peeped out the window and it's a man with grey hair and he's wearing a suit. Maybe he's a Jehovah's Witness. Can I ask him for a Watchtower and Awake magazine?"

"That's probably your grandfather."

"I'll go answer it, Mom," Trey said. "Alexis, how you know about Jehovah's Witnesses?" he asked, as they headed to the door.

"Because, when me and KJ were staying the night at Daddy's house, they came by on Saturday morning and gave him the magazines. I saw it for myself. "

"You're too grown, you know that," Trey tickled her.

"Yeah because I'm six, and I'm tall."

Trey cracked up laughing, then answered the door.

CHAPTER TWENTY
SECOND CHANCE

I was worried about Trey. I hope he listened to what I just said to him about performing tonight at Risers. I didn't raise him to be a rapper, but I do understand it's his choice. Of course it's not that I have anything against rap or rappers, because I love rap. It's the business aspects of the music industry, and rap culture that can get ugly, especially when artists start beefs with each other.

Speaking of the business, I've been managing myself since firing Kyle. I didn't think I could handle it on my own, but I managed to get a two million dollar deal to expand the Divas brand by doing spin-offs of my reality show. In the fall, there will be Divas of New York, next spring will be Divas of Chicago, and next summer will be Divas of D.C. Each reality show will be filmed in its self-titled locations, showing classy divas in those areas and the different things they have to deal with on the regular basis. Season two with *Divas of LA* is complete. Kay-Kay and I agreed that we would take a backseat after season two, and allow other divas of LA to take over for season three. We're still producers for the show, however. The network already sent us a three hundred thousand dollar advance. We split the money evenly as partners since we both came up with the original idea. My mother taught me well. She used to always say that branding was good business. I'm also the owner and President of Divas Incorporated and Kay-Kay is Vice-President. Aside from Divas, I also have my brand, Tracey G. Michaels Inc. and my cosmetic line. If I never film another movie or TV show again, I know my kids will be set for life, and that's all that matters to me. Who knows, I may even run my business from home. It will give me more time to spend with my kids.

Anyway, I could overhear my children greeting my father at the door, so I left out the kitchen to greet him. I was still in shock that Jet called me to say he wanted to come over for dinner. I had not talked to my father in nine years. He was upset that Dean walked me down the aisle on my wedding day, we hadn't spoken since.

"...And you got tall, boy, look at you!" Jet was saying to Trey. For a man who was almost sixty years old, he wasn't aging too well. His hair was now whitish-gray, his cheeks sagged, and his droopy eyes made him look like he was in his seventies or early eighties. Gone was his athletic build; he had a big potbelly now and rocked side-to-side like a penguin when he walked on his cane towards the living room. I offered him to sit down.

"Tracey, you weren't lying when you said you were out in the hills of Malibu," he chuckled, and his belly shook when he laughed.

"I love it out here. It's beautiful, peaceful, and quiet."

Trey cleared his throat. "And boring."

"Oh hush, boy! Go set the table for dinner."

"Come on Alexis and KJ, y'all can help out your big brother."

"So, where's uh…Keith?"

I bit down on my bottom lip, unsure of how to answer that, but I decided the truth was better.

"I don't know we're separated right now."

"Oh, yeah, well um…I thought I heard something like that. I wasn't sure if it was true."

"Well anyway, would you like to come into our dining room and have dinner now?"

"Sure." He slowly rose to his feet, and I had to give him a hand as he balanced himself on his cane.

After dinner, Trey put the kids to bed for me, and then he left. I joined Jet in the living room where we sat drinking hot cups of tea.

"So, my mother said you were at the high school reunion back home in Chicago."

"Yeah, it was nice."

"So did you drive up from Florida?"

"I haven't lived in Florida in quite some time, baby girl. I got a house in Vegas."

"Oh really?" I thought to myself, *So Dean was right. You did have a house in Las Vegas, and after all this time, you never came to see me or your grandchildren knowing we are just four hours away?*

"I lost my house in Miami and moved to Vegas after Sabrina and I divorced back in 2000. I had a house in Chicago, lost that one too, but it doesn't matter. You can only sleep in one bed, right?"

"I guess so...I mean...what happened?"

"Well baby girl, I'm not proud to say it, but these days it feels good to just tell the truth." He paused, looked off in thought. "I made bad investment deals and got caught up in heavy gambling debts too." As he went on to talk about some of the things he had been doing over the years, I noticed some of the resemblance we had in the shape of our noses, eyes, and cheeks. Despite our genetic similarities, I felt no connection with him the way I had with my stepfather, Dean. Jet continued to talk about himself and all the people he used to know who lived in California, and I started feeling impatient. I felt the need to cut him off.

"Me and Jim Brown used to hang out together too," Jet was saying.

"So, why are you really here, Jet? Do you need some money?"

"Honestly I do."

"Figures."

"Now wait a minute baby girl, hold on. I really wanted to see you," he asserted.

"I don't know if I can help you or even if I *want* to help you."

"Look, I understand how you feel and I'm sorry for not being there for you like a father should. All the things you said about me in your book were true. I hated to admit it to myself, but I was a deadbeat dad. There, I said it. I'm not proud of it, but it was true. Still I'd like a second chance to be a better father to you."

"I'm not looking for a father, Jet. I have Dean. When I needed you, you were never there. You missed all the important things in my life," I expressed with agitation. "Scratch that, you didn't *miss* anything, you just didn't come!"

"Look, baby girl, I'm sorry. I didn't know how to be a good father. Your mother and I had you when we were just kids ourselves. I told your mother I wasn't ready to be a father, and she should have gotten that abortion like I asked her to!"

"What? You asked mom to abort me?"

"I'm sorry Tracey. I didn't mean for it to come out that way. What I'm really trying to say is I was too young, and I didn't know how to be there for you."

"I bet you were there for my half-brother and a half-sister weren't you? You forgot about me, your first-born! My mother had to raise me by herself!"

He heaved a long sigh, reached for the cup of tea on the table, and drank some more before he spoke again.

"I didn't think you cared if I came around or not, Tracey. The only time I heard from you was when you needed money."

My eyes bucked in shock. "That's insane! Don't try to twist this on me and make yourself a victim!" I stood up from the chair.

"All right, calm down, Tracey, okay? I'm still your father. Show me some respect by not standing over me, yelling like I'm a small child. Sit down." He pointed to the chair across from the sofa. I didn't realize I was getting so worked up.

"Now listen, I'm not going to sit here and be your punching bag. I know you're angry and you have every right to be. I wasn't a good father to any of my children. Not you, Vernon Jr., Stephanie, Mickey, Greg, Yolanda, Rene, Thomas or Malik."

"Jet, you fathered all of those children?"

Jet looked slightly embarrassed. "I remarried after Sabrina, and had five more children. Malik, who is the youngest, is by an ex-girlfriend whom I never married. Hell, they all cleaned me out dry. I couldn't even pay the debts I owed because every single one of them wanted child support," he explained, bitterly. "I've been getting by on my football pension and occasional broadcasting gigs."

"Sorry to hear that," I uttered, but I'm sure I didn't sound sincere.

"I did some good things in my life too, Tracey. Whenever you called me, I gave you whatever you wanted, didn't I? I bought you those Ferraris, I got you an apartment in Beverly Hills, and whenever you asked me for something, I gave it to you. I never told you no. Did I?"

I thought about it for a moment, and he was right, but he was missing the point. "Dad I would give all of those things back just to have you in my life, just to experience what a real father and daughter relationship is like. Dean did the best he could with me, and I love him for stepping in to take your place, but he's not my biological father. You are! It hurt me for a long time that you weren't there for me. Now here you are after all this time, asking for my help. If I give you the money, are you going to disappear for another nine years? Will I ever see you again?"

"I hope so, but I don't have much time left, baby girl."

"Come again?"

"If I'm lucky I'll live another couple of months if I stay like this," he replied solemnly, stared at the floor. "I'm dying, Tracey. My kidney is failing, and I need a transplant right away. The doctor's found a donor, but I don't have the money to get the surgery done. I'm two months in the hole on my mortgage, and the bank is threatening to foreclose on my home. Child support payments are behind, and if I get pulled over the police would lock me up for the warrants I have for not paying." I held my hand to my mouth. I couldn't believe all of what I was hearing. I took a deep breath and tried to remember that this man was still my father. I could turn him down, but then I would regret it if he died.

"Okay." I held up my hand. "I almost feel like I need a drink right now, but I need to pray. Just give me a minute." I walked out of the living room and stood in the foyer and I prayed silently to myself. I asked God to show me what I should do. Minutes later, I walked back into the living room and Jet looked up at me with those brown puppy eyes that my Mom once told me she loved about him. I'm sure they were cute during his heyday, but now they kind of looked sad. I didn't know if he was putting on an act, but he looked like if he blinked that tears would fall down his cheeks at any moment. I sat down and crossed one leg over the other. I relaxed my shoulders, took hold of Jet's hand, and asked, "How much money do you need?"

"For all my debts? Well I don't know exactly."

"Throw out some numbers and we'll see what I'm working with."

"About a hundred thousand dollars at least. Maybe a hundred fifty thousand, so I'll have enough to get out the hole with my mortgage, have the surgery and get caught up on my child support payments," he answered.

"Wow!" I gasped for air. "I don't know about that."

"I understand. Whatever you can do. I'm not trying to put you in a bind baby girl."

"Listen Jet, the best I can do is pay for your surgery and keep your house from being foreclosed on, but as for the child support payments, those are *your* children. You should ask the judge to lower the payments or tell them you can't pay what you don't have."

"I understand," he lowered his head, and then lifted his eyes to watch me write him a check for seventy-five thousand dollars.

"Thank you, I really appreciate this." He stood up and hugged me.

"Call me and let me know the date of your surgery so I can be there for you."

"I promise I will."

I was praying inside that Jet wasn't lying. When he left, I felt more insecure about our relationship than ever before. I felt like I had just been had. *God I hope I'm wrong about Jet.*

CHAPTER TWENTY-ONE
HEAT— R.I.P

"So you just gonna act salty all night?" Devin asked Andrea. They were eating dinner at the dining room table. Andrea kept rolling her eyes and sucking her teeth because Devin told her Trey had a show at Riser's Nightclub tonight. He wanted to be there to support his nephew, especially since he'd produced Trey's debut CD.

Andrea pouted. "I'm tired of being stuck in the house every weekend with Leah while you get to go out and have all the fun. Why can't I go with you? I would like to support Trey too. My mom said she could watch Leah."

"Because you don't need to be up in the club. Let me handle this grown man business, all right? All you gotta do is keep looking pretty and take care of home, know what I'm saying?"

Andrea slammed her fork down on the table next to her plate, slid her chair back, and stood up abruptly.

"You're a chauvinist pig!"

"That's not chauvinist. I bring my money home to you and let you spend it on whatever you want. How is that chauvinist? Any other woman would be happy to be in your position."

"I'm not any other woman, I'm your fiancée, Devin."

"Look, I'm not having this crap tonight," Devin argued. "We been together too long to keep talking about how I handle *my* business. And I wish you quit complaining about our relationship to my mother and Aunt Peaches. If you ain't happy, you can get to steppin!"

"Maybe I will!"

"What?!"

"I said, maybe I will." She looked at the fifty-thousand dollar engagement ring on her finger, snatched it off, and slammed it down on the table like it cost fifty cents.

"I'm stepping, and I'm taking Leah with me."

"Yeah right. Whatever you say." Devin twisted his lips in disbelief, thinking about her previous threats to leave him, but she never did.

* * *

By the time, Devin, Trey, and their entourage pulled up in front of Riser's Night Club, Devin had smoked a few blunts and drank a forty-once of beer. Andrea had made him mad tonight, and he felt like he needed something to calm his nerves.

"TREEEY! WE LOVE YOU, TREY!" the girls screamed from the lines outside of the club.

"DEVIN! THAT'S DEVIN DOLLARZ, OH MY GOSH!"

Their bodyguards fought their way through the crowds to escort Trey and Devin inside to the V.I.P. section on the third floor. A few company executives from BigStar were already there to meet them. A big cake surrounded by champagne glasses awaited them. The microphone-shaped cake was decorated in Trey's name.

"Congratulations! Your single is now platinum!" The executes toasted up. Trey and Devin were excited, and they drank a few glasses of champagne.

"Congratulations, Trey." Jazmine stood up from the lounge sofa and kissed his cheek. He smiled, feeling happy she actually came.

"What're you doing here?" Devin sneered.

"Oh it's cool, Unc, I invited her and her friend," Trey said, and then he kissed Jazmine on the lips. "Thanks for coming."

"I gotchu," Jazmine flirted.

Devin pushed himself in between them. "You don't have time for them hoes. Save your energy for the stage."

"Yo, chill out Unc!"

"Hoe? Who you calling a hoe?" Jazmine replied angrily.

"Don't pay him no mind. He's a little blazed right now," Trey said to her. "Come on, let's have some cake."

The club was pumping Jay-Z's "Tom Ford", and Devin sat down on the other lounge chair next to the groupies that his bodyguards let enter the V.I.P. room. The girls were all over him, sitting on his lap, grinning in his face, and touching all over him. Devin loved every minute of it.

"Trey it's time for you to go on stage," said Trey's manager.

"Go do the thing, nephew! Kill 'em!" Devin shouted, lifting his third glass of alcohol in the air to cheer him on. He could barely keep his eyes open.

"I'm gonna bring the house down, Unc. This one is for you, bro! You're the best producer in the business, homey!"

"No doubt!"

Devin got off the sofa to take a look at the action downstairs from the VIP booth window. He watched his nephew perform "Has Been" and a few other songs from his CD. The audience went crazy. When Trey finished performing, he joined the ladies on the dance floor. They formed a circle around him and danced to Robin Thicke's "Blurred Lines". He looked over his shoulder and spotted Jazmine leaving out. She rolled her eyes and sucked her teeth at Trey was dancing with other girls. Devin laughed at her jealousy, and then turned his attention back to the dance floor. He spotted his bodyguard Darnell walking through the crowd on the dance floor like he was trying to find his way through the maze. As Darnell was maneuvering people out of his way, Devin saw a group of guys rushing towards Trey from the opposite direction. He blinked twice and rubbed his eyes to make sure he wasn't hallucinating. Sure enough, it was a group of guys in black hoodies and dark shades, rushing towards Trey like they were after him.

"Yo' Tim, Gary, Reggie, let's go downstairs quick! I think something's about to jump off!"

"Call security!" Trey's manager told one of the executives from the record company.

When they got to the dance floor, Devin saw commotion coming from the crowds, and people started screaming. Devin watched a guy wearing a long black trench coat and dark shades snatch Trey's chain off his neck like he was the leader of the guys wearing the black hoodies. It was hard for him to make out his face with everything happening so quickly, and with so many people around. Darnell chased the chain snatcher out of the club. A melee broke out, and fans that supported Trey started throwing chairs and bottles at the group of the guys. Devin ran full speed ahead towards Trey, even stepping on people who had fallen to the floor. Tim threw people out of his way so he could get to Trey. Trey was throwing blows with one of the black hoodie guys, and then out from amongst the crowd, a bottle flew up in the air, and smashed into Trey's face. Tim picked Trey up easily like a toothpick and rushed him outside to the truck. Trey was bleeding from the nose and mouth. The guys in black hoodies started running out of the club when the security officers of the Club came for them. Devin ran out of the club after the guys, but his high slowed him down and they got away.

"Let's get 'em!" Devin pointed towards the black SUV, as he and his bodyguards, entourage, and Trey hopped into their white Escalade. They chased the black SUV down the highway. Devin watched Tim pull out his gun. He started shooting at the SUV, but the driver of the SUV kept going. They followed the SUV off the next exist and down an alley. That's when Devin heard sirens, but he wasn't sure which direction it was coming from. The SUV fled down the alley, and quickly turned the corner. There was so much smoke from the SUV spinning dirt that Tim made a wrong turn during the chase, and they ended up facing a dead-end inside the alley.

"Just get out this alley so we're not trapped when the police come!" Devin shouted. Tim sped out of the alley in reverse, and got back on the highway.

"There they are right there man!" Devin shouted, navigating Tim from the backseat.

"Look one of those fools just leaned out the window!" Gary yelled. That's when they heard shots, and bullets piercing through the metal of the Escalade and hitting everything within its path.

"Everybody get down!" Devin shouted, with his head slightly lifted enough to see that his bodyguards Tim and Darnell were shooting back at the SUV.

"Yo' Devin, I been hit!" Gary said, holding his shoulder.

"Tim, quit following them busters and let's get Gary and Trey to the hospital. We'll get those suckers later, man!" Devin commanded.

"All right, I think we lost them anyway," Tim stated, glancing over his shoulder at everyone that was in the back of the truck. He headed towards the hospital on Beverly Boulevard, which was off the next exit. As Tim approached the hospital, he had to make a U-turn since it was located on the opposite side of the street. As soon as he turned around, they heard shots going off again.

"They're back, Devin, what're we going to do?!" Trey's voice was shaking in fear and his hazel eyes looked terrified.

"Everybody just stay on the floor!" Devin covered his ears and ducked his head. It seemed like neither his bodyguards nor whoever was in that SUV was going to run out of ammo any time soon. Devin felt like he was in the middle of a warzone, and thought about his cousin BJ. He wondered how he would have responded to a situation like this since he knew a lot about war and often talked about survival techniques.

"Oh God, please get us out of this!" Trey started crying real tears. "I want my Mommy. I want my Dad. Oh God, please help us!"

"Calm down, Trey. Everything will be all right, nephew," Devin said to him.

"Trey why you crying like a little b—"

"Reggie, shut up, man. Don't diss my nephew like that, homey."

"Heavenly Father, please hear my prayer and help us."

"Oh man, is he back there praying?" Darnell laughed.

"Hold tight, Trey and Gary, I'm going to get you guys to Cedar-Sinai Hospital now," Tim shouted. Slowly Devin crawled off the floor when the shooting stopped. He was pretty banged up from taking nosedives to the floor.

"I just wanna go home, man," Trey wiped his eyes.

"We'll get you home. Just let the doctors see you and Gary first," Devin patted his shoulders. Trey got up off the floor, and made his way to the seats all the way at the backend of the truck.

"Say man, those fools are back. They're headed straight towards us!" Tim pointed. The SUV pulled up on the side of the Escalade, and the back window rolled down. A light skinned guy, who looked familiar to Devin, leaned out the window with an A-K47 aimed right at the truck.

"Who's the *has-been* now?"

"It's B-Money, everybody duck!" Devin dove to the floor. Shots sounded off like fire crackers. Suddenly, the Escalade crashed into three parked cars, slinging everyone inside every which way. Devin slowly rose to his feet when the shots stopped. He spotted the SUV speeding down the street. It went through a red light and then crashed into an oncoming car. All the guys inside the SUV hopped out and ran. Devin wanted to get out and chase after them, but instead he turned his attention to the guys inside the truck.

"Is everybody all right?"

"I been hit!" Tim shouted, holding his neck, as he leaned over the steering wheel.

"Me too, I think I took one in the side!" Reggie groaned. There was a loud thump, and when Devin looked over his shoulder, and noticed that Gary had fallen over against the door. Devin rushed to his side, taking his jacket off so Gary could hold the jacket over his wound.

"Devin, I hit my head from the crash, but I think I'll be okay," Darnell stated.

"And Trey! Where's Trey?" Devin called. He reached for the light switch in the roof of the truck and turned it on. He could see glass everywhere, blood, seat cushions with bullet holes all through them. It looked like a warzone inside the truck. There in the midst of it was Trey, who lay motionless in the backseat of the truck. "NOOOOO TREY TREEEY!" Devin rushed to his side.

"Are you guys all right in there?"

Devin looked over his shoulder, and saw that it was a group of doctors asking if they needed help. The doctors had ran down the street to their rescue after they got word of hearing gunshots and people running into the hospital to report the car crashes and shootings.

"My nephew has been shot, please help him!" Devin cried, fighting back tears. "Trey, please stay with me man, please!"

Devin and Darnell waited in the lobby while the doctors worked on Trey, Gary, Tim, and Reggie. Devin started pacing the room huffing and puffing, trying to catch his breath, but he couldn't keep calm.

"I need to call my sister, man!" he cried. "But I don't know what to say, homey. Tracey will kill me if Trey dies, man!"

"Calm down, Devin, he'll be all right, man!" Darnell said, trying to comfort him.

Devin searched his pocket for his phone. "Dag man, I don't have my phone. I think it's in the truck."

"Shoot, we ain't going out there. It's too much heat out there. The cops will be all over us. Hell, it's just a matter of time before they come in here looking for us and asking questions. Shoot, I'm sitting here trying to think of what I'm going to tell them."

"Where's my son? I heard he's been hit?"

Devin turned around and noticed the man questioning the registration clerk was B-Money. He wasn't wearing a black hoodie. In fact, he was wearing a white T-shirt and blue jeans. Devin thought to himself, *Is this dude serious? This man just shot up our truck and now he's coming up in the hospital like he didn't have anything to do with it!*

Devin glared at Darnell and noticed he was slowly withdrawing his piece.

"Not here, man," Devin cautioned him. He and Darnell studied B-Money's every move. B-Money turned around, and at first he looked surprised to see Devin and Darnell. His facial expression turned from shock to a cold stare, and then suddenly B-Money's lips curved a smile. He walked over to Devin and Darnell. Devin couldn't believe how crazy he was!

"Hey, I'm glad y'all here, man. Is Trey gonna all right?" B-Money asked cordially. Devin lost it. He grabbed him by the throat and starting choking him. B-Money fell to the floor and started red, but Devin wouldn't let go. He squeezed and squeezed until he could see the veins popping out in his neck.

"Hey, hey, hey none of that in here! Y'all take it outside!" The hospital security guard standing near the front doors responded swiftly. He and Darnell had to pry Devin's hands off B's throat.

"Y'all get out of here!" the officer shouted, after freeing Devin's hands.

"I got it from here!" Darnell told the officer, he waved a fake police badge. Darnell shoved B-Money out the back way of the hospital.

"Man, get...get...off me!" B-Money said, gasping for air. Darnell discreetly shoved his gun at B's side, and B-Money stopped resisting, and walked with him out the back. Devin waited until the security guy took his eyes off him. He eventually turned his attention to an attractive lady with a sick little girl. He then quickly eased by him and out the back door of the hospital, which led to an alley.

The alleyway stank. They were the menaces in the shadows and had no business being there. Fear settled deep in Devin's chest and something inside of him was telling him to go back in the hospital to be by Trey's side, but the other side of him wanted revenge.

"That's for trying to kill your own son!" Devin said standing over B-Money with his fists balled after him and B-Money fought man-to-man. B-Money was gasping for air.

"I'mma get you for this! You's a dead man!" B-Money threatened, trying to crawl back to his feet after Devin beat him up. He tried to stand but he felt weak and dropped to his knees in pain.

"Finish him, Devin. You need to finish him, or he's going to come back for you, homey." Darnell tried to hand Devin his gun, but he looked away.

B-Money starting laughing sarcastically. "He ain't got the heart to finish me! He's a rich mama's boy! He don't have the heart! Finish me, chump!" Bruce challenged, spitting blood.

Devin hungered to shoot him, but could hear his father's voice in his head, loud, as if he was standing right there. *Never kill your fellow man unless it's self-defense.*

"Why did you do it, man? Why? Trey is in there dying, man! He's your son! *And* you shot my boys!"

"How was I supposed to know which way the bullets were going to fly? Huh? I didn't know!" Bruce yelled, still on his knees, because he felt too weak to move.

"But you knew your son was in that truck, you idiot!" Devin kicked him in the side and he tumbled over to the ground.

"I bet you set Tony Tee up to get killed, didn't you?"

"So what! I would've killed you too but the bullets flew the wrong way! I didn't mean to hit my son. Those bullets were meant for your sorry–"

Devin punched him in the mouth before he could finish.

"This is too much conversation." Darnell lost his patience, cocked the gun and aimed it at Bruce's head.

"Darnell, wait, man, don't do it!" Devin cautioned. Darnell gritted his teeth at Devin, grabbed a stale potato near the dumpster, and covered the barrel like a silencer.

"I don't want any part of this Darnell. B-Money ain't worth killing, and going to jail for."

"You can leave, man, but I'm going to handle this here!" Darnell rolled his eyes at Devin. As soon as Devin turned his back to walk away, he heard one muzzled shot go off. He paused in his tracks, looked over his shoulder, and Bruce's body stopped moving on the ground. His arms and legs were spread out before him, his head cocked to the side, and his eyes looked off into oblivion. Darnell cleaned off the gun and threw it in one of the dumpsters, and then ran down the opposite end of the alley. Devin tried to go back through the basement door of the hospital, but it was locked. He had no choice but to walk around the front.

"Where did you just come from?" one of the officers on the scene stopped and questioned Devin.

"Taking a walk."

"You must think we're stupid. You're coming downtown with us for questioning," He shoved Devin against the police car and immediately cuffed his wrists, and searched him for weapons.

"But my nephew has been shot. I need to call my sister. I can't just leave him by himself!" Devin panicked.

"Tell us her number and we'll have the doctor's call her, but you're coming with us, *now*!"

CHAPTER TWENTY-TWO
THE CALL

I wasn't sure if I was dreaming when the phone rang. I knew it wasn't time to get up for church yet. I finally realized I wasn't dreaming when the phone kept ringing and wouldn't stop. My body jerked forward. I glanced at the glowing green neon light on the phone. When it lit up, it said, 'Cedar Sinai Hospital'. I quickly grabbed it.

"Hello?....what? NOOO!"

When I got to the hospital, the media was standing outside of the hospital doors, and so were Trey's fans. Many of them looked like they had camped out outside with their signs saying, 'I love you Trey Mikes' and T-shirts with his face on the front. I was escorted inside by my bodyguards and led to ICU by one of the nurses. My bodyguards stood outside of the family waiting room. "Dr. McCormick will be in soon to talk with you," the nurse said. I walked inside the quiet room that had a sofa, one round table and chairs, and a big window that overlooked the whole city of Angels.

"Keith!" I rushed towards him; he was sitting down on the sofa. He stood up and hugged me. He was wearing a gold chain with a big medallion, a throwback jersey with a T-shirt, and both his ears had diamonds in them. He was dressed like a thug again, and I didn't like it. Each time he came to pick up the kids there was something new about him, but in a bad way if you ask me. Keith was going backwards. The last time I saw him, he had gotten tattoos on each shoulder with our kids' names in a fancy script. I tried to look past it, and not mention it, especially not now.

"I'm so glad you're here!"

"Of course," he embraced me. He still smelled good. He always wore nice colognes. I just wanted him to stop being childish, and get back to the old Keith I knew and loved. As I hugged Keith, I spotted Devin standing at a distance near the window. I turned him loose.

"Devin! Devin, what happened?" I rushed over to my brother's side. When Devin turned around all I saw was dried up blood all over the front of his clothes.

"Wh-wh-what happened?" My mouth dropped. He looked a nasty mess.

He shook his head, spoke softly but hesitantly. "A fight broke out at Risers and—"

"I knew it! I had a bad feeling about you and Trey performing at that club!" I shook my head, ran my fingers through my hair out of frustration and feeling antsy. "What happened, Devin?"

"It's a long story, but Trey was shot."

"Oh my gosh, this is not happening right now!" I started to pace the room. "You're not telling me this you're not! I'm dreaming and I'm just waiting to wake up. Tell me you're lying Devin! Are you serious?"

"B-Money and his crew shot at us. Trey is in ICU, and my boys got hit too."

"Devin, how could you let this happen? You're Trey's uncle!"

"I'm sorry, Tracey," Devin blinked back tears. "We didn't go there looking for trouble. They sought us out. You gotta believe me!"

"Yes, you are sorry! Trey wouldn't be in this situation if *you* didn't produce that diss track in the first place! And I bet he performed that song, didn't he?" I shoved Devin so hard he almost lost his balance.

"Ay, girl, you better stop tripping, all right? I don't want to hurt you!" Devin stepped in my face. He was taller than me now, but I was ready to knock him out.

"Hurt me? Boy, I oughta' knock the hell out of you!"

"Tracey!" Keith jumped off the sofa and stepped between me and Devin before we went for blows. "Calm down, you guys need to be sensible right now!" Keith looked at me sharply, and then shifted his gaze to Devin like he was the referee amongst us. Devin walked away and sat down in the chair at the round table near the window.

"There's more," Devin lamented. "But I'm not gonna say until Tracey calms down."

"What do you mean there's more?" I started towards him.

"Tracey, calm down and let Devin finish." Keith eased me back, and sat me down on the sofa. "Hear him out, Tracey, all right?"

I huffed loudly. "Yeah, all right. Whatever!"

Devin glared at me, and I watched his mouth move slowly when he said, "B-Money-is-dead." I burst into tears.

"Hold on baby, everything will be all right," Keith tried to hug me and comfort me.

"No, no, don't. I can't believe this!" I cried, dropped my head in my lap. "My son is in ICU and now you're telling me that Bruce is dead?!" My chest shivered up and down.

"It was a shooting, Tracey," Devin explained. "Everybody got hurt. I got called down to the police station, and they questioned me, and then..."

I heard some of what Devin said, and pretty much lost it after that. I jumped from the sofa.

"If my son dies, I will disown you as my brother, and I mean it!" I shoved Devin's head back. "This is all your fault! I hate you for this, Devin! I hate you!"

"No, you're wrong!" Devin pointed at me, as Keith held him back from approaching me. "This started because of YOU and that crap you talked about in your book!"

"Seriously? You did the diss track not me!"

"Man, you know what? I'm done with this!" Devin threw up his hands. "I risked my life tonight for Trey! You weren't there so you don't know!"

"You risked *your* life, huh?" I barked. "Then why is he and your friends the only ones fighting for theirs when you're walking away without so much as a scratch? You always get what you want, don't you, Devin? Well, that's my son in there fighting for his life and if he loses it, you're not family anymore, so you may as well stop calling me your sister!"

Devin stormed towards the door. He nearly knocked the doctor down as he was walking in.

"Uhm...good morning." The doctor swallowed hard and looked over his shoulder as the door slammed behind him. His face started turning red as he approached us with caution. Obviously, he could see he was walking into a heated situation.

"You must be Mr. and Mrs. Smith?" he asked. I grumbled a faint *yes* under my breath while Keith shook his hand. The doctor introduced himself as McCormick and asked us to sit down at the round table. My head ached with anger and my heart was filled with pain. I was angry at Devin, worried about Trey, and had mixed emotions about Bruce's death. There was no time to process any of it at the moment; I had to listen to the doctor's prognosis about Trey.

"I'm sorry to have to meet with you like this, but I'm the surgeon who operated on your son Trey," Dr. McCormick explained. His crystal blue eyes stared at Keith and I with a seriousness that made my stomach flutter with anxiety. I started rapidly tapping my nails on the table and Keith kept rubbing his beard as Dr. McCormick explained Trey's situation.

"Trey was shot several times, and one of the bullets pierced his left lung. He's lost a lot of blood, but we've given him dextran to build up the volume in his system, which helps his blood to build back up, so far it's working just fine without having to do a transfusion," he explained. "There were some other injuries as well- a broken nose, and a busted lip that we had to stitch." My head started spinning as Dr. McCormick went into all the details.

"Doctor what're the chances for our son surviving this?" Keith asked, and I wished he hadn't. I couldn't bear to hear it. I wiped my sweaty palms on the front of my pants.

"At this point we have to wait and see," the doctor replied solemnly. "We'll have to see how he recovers from the surgery. He's very critical because of the wound to his lung and loss of blood. We're also hoping that he won't have any internal bleeding from the gunshots. We have him under a 24-hour watch. The machine is doing most of the breathing for him at this point. But he's not unconscious, he's just very weak, so he may not talk much," the doctor said. "Please be assured that Trey is receiving the best care here. After the nurse checks his vitals again, you are more than welcome to come back to see him."

"Thank you, Doctor." Keith shook his hand, and as soon as the doctor left, I cried in Keith's arms.

The ICU room felt cold. I approached Trey's bed slowly. Wires and tubes were running all through him. I hated to see my baby, my firstborn, lying in a hospital bed trying to survive. I could see bruises on his face from the fight he had gotten into, and the stitches on his top lip. His face was swollen, and both eyes were black from him having a broken nose. He didn't look like my child. I could only imagine how rough the night must have been for him. It was hard to believe this happened to my baby.

I had just talked to him yesterday and he was in good spirits, now he was fighting for his life. As I stood over him, I started thinking about the day he was first born and how I cradled him in my arms. He was a tiny little thing. He weighed six pounds, and was nineteen inches long. I remembered his first day of school and when my dad taught him how to ride a bike. I recalled how handsome he looked when Keith and I got married. He was the ring bearer, and Jazmine was my flower girl. I smiled to myself as I thought about my wedding day as a family, but my proudest moment was Trey's high school graduation and when he got accepted to USC. He never got into any trouble, nor gave me any. We talked openly about everything and he never kept things from me because we were close. Trey had so much potential, and I wish he had stayed in college and finished. He was a bright kid. As I thought about our life together, that's when I felt a need to pray for my son. With my eyes closed, I took hold of Trey's hand, and prayed hard like I had never prayed before.

"Father God, I know I've done some horrible things in my life and I've had to pay the price for those things, but Trey was the opposite of me. He was well-behaved and he listened to us. The only time he stopped listening was when it came to his music ambitions. This is a horrible price to pay for fame and fortune. Please give Trey another chance at life and a chance to live the way you see fit. And Father, help me to rid my heart of this anger and forgive my brother Devin just as you forgave me. In Jesus' name, Amen."

As the word about Trey traveled, more people met outside of the hospital, and the doctors felt compelled to issue a statement on Trey's condition so they would go away. I also had my publicist to speak on our behalf and to thank the fans for their support. This was going to be a long journey…

CHAPTER TWENTY-THREE
MAMA'S BOY

Dean and Connie stood in Trey's room staring at him as he breathed with the help of a machine. They had just flown in on their private jet with Peaches and Dean Jr. Dean asked BJ if he wanted to come, but he refused. Dean didn't waste any time begging BJ, nor did Peaches. They hopped on the plane and left.

"I always told Trey and Devin, if you die, do you want to be remembered for what you *had* or what you *did*? What kind of legacy do you want to leave behind?" Dean was saying to Connie as she wiped the tears from her eyes. She and Dean had practically raised Trey like their own son. "Both of them trying to be thugs like they're from the hood were just ridiculous!" Dean shook his head in disgust. He hated to see Trey laid up like he was.

"Hang in there my son," Dean stroked the top of his curly hair, and then Connie leaned in and kissed Trey's cheek.

"God is with you," Connie whimpered. "We love you and we're right here with you," she stroked his hands.

"Come on, let's go now. I think Peaches and Dean are ready to see him next," Dean said to Connie since only two people could be in the room at a time.

As soon as they left the room, they spotted two police officers questioning Devin, and next thing they knew he was pinned to the wall outside of Trey's room in the hallway. They cuffed his wrists.

"Hey, hey, wait a minute, what's going on?" Dean and Connie rushed towards them.

"Your son is going to jail is what!" The officer sneered.

"Why? He didn't do anything!" Connie cried.

"Devin, what's going on, son?" Dean asked feeling puzzled.

"I didn't do it Dad. I didn't. Please believe me."

Dean and Connie watched the officers escort Devin to the elevator and out of the hospital.

"Connie, you go and tell the family I'm going down to the police station."

"I will, but I'm coming with you, Dean. He's my son too."

"Connie, there's a lot going on right now. You should stay here and support Tracey."

"Dean, I'm coming with you," Connie insisted.

"Fine, let's tell the family together."

Dean and Connie walked into the family waiting room and explained everything. The room was already tense, but the air became so thick that Tracey started crying about Devin going to jail. Her tears made Connie cry, and the two hugged each other. This was too much.

Dean turned to his eldest son. "Dean, you stay here with Tracey and Peaches while your mother and I go see what's going on with Devin."

"I got it covered Pop," he nodded.

"I'm coming too," Peaches grabbed her purse.

"Look, somebody needs to stay here with Tracey," Dean urged.

"It's okay Dad. I'm only going to stay here for a little while longer. I need to get back home to the kids. Kay-Kay is watching them since I let the nanny have a few days off, but she has a flight to catch to Atlanta," Tracey explained.

"I'll go and watch the kids," Keith said to her. "You can stay here as long as you like," Keith kissed Tracey's forehead. "Keep me posted on everything. Stay strong," Keith got up and headed out.

"Fine," Dean nodded, giving Keith a cold stare as he walked by him. He didn't like the way Keith had been carrying on lately and he was quite disappointed in him. "Anyway, let's go before they start processing Devin."

While in route to the police station, Dean said to Connie and Peaches, "Just let me do all the talking."

As soon as they walked into the police station, Connie rushed ahead of Dean and approached the officer behind the front desk.

"My son Devin Wilson is here and we need to see him now," Connie demanded. "I don't know why you would embarrass me and my family at the hospital like that, but I want answers and I want them now!"

The heavyset officer behind the desk twisted his lips into a frown, said nonchalantly, "Have a seat over there with the rest of those folks and we'll be with you in a minute."

Connie looked over her shoulder at the people who were half-sleep, slouched down in their chairs or preoccupied with handheld gadgets as if they'd been waiting for hours.

"I will not have a seat. I want to see my son now!"

"Connie," Dean stepped in front of her.

"What Dean? They need to let us see our son!"

"Connie, have a seat like the man said, *please*," Dean was starting to feel a little irritated as he watched to make sure that Connie and Peaches sat down.

Dean turned his attention to the officer behind the desk. "How you doing today my man?"

"Work ain't hard," the officer smirked. "I'm Devin's father."

"I know who you guys are, but you have to wait like everybody else. Ain't no special treatment around here for stars."

"I can respect that. Who's working my son's case?"

"Lead Detective Stevenson, and when he's done I'll let you know."

"Listen, Officer uhm–" Dean read the badge on his shirt. "Vincent. I'm sure you have a family room in this building somewhere right? Can we just sit outside of Detective Stevenson's office?"

Officer Vincent thought about it, and looked Dean over. He didn't seem like any of the cocky celebrities he had met before.

"Alright, take the elevators to the eight floor. Homicide is room 871."

"Homicide?" Dean looked bewildered.

"Yes sir. I'm afraid so."

"And what floor did you say it was on again?" Dean asked, feeling embarrassed by the minute.

"Eighth floor is homicide."

The word *homicide* echoed through Dean's head bringing back hunting memories of when he worked as a detective.

As soon as they stepped off the elevator, there was a room filled with cubicles facing them. The phones were ringing off the hook, officers were moving about with paperwork in their hands. It was as if they weren't there.

"Wait here," Dean said to Connie and Peaches. Dean spotted Stevenson's cube from the nameplate on his desk.

"Excuse me," Dean tapped on the wooden panel of the cube. He noticed Detective Stevenson gathering papers off his desk.

"I'm here to see my son, Devin Wilson."

"You need to have a seat. You can wait in conference room four."

"I understand. I just wanted you to know we're here since no one has acknowledged us."

"I got it. You're here. So what. Have a seat in room four," Stevenson gritted his teeth and rolled his eyes at Dean.

"You don't have to be rude," Dean said to him calmly.

"I'm not being rude. You're the one who's at my desk unannounced."

"Point taken."

"Dean is everything okay with Devin?" Connie pressed him.

"I asked you guys to wait over there." Dean pointed to the chairs near a window.

"I need to know what's going, Dean," Connie insisted.

"Go grab some coffee or a soda or something and let me handle this," Dean reached in his wallet and handed Connie a twenty dollar bill.

"I don't want anything to drink. I'm staying right here until I find out what's going on with my baby!" Connie grieved. Dean hated when she got out of control emotionally like this. It made him nervous and worried about *her.* They were all sleep deprived, jet lagged, angry, frustrated, and worn out by everything that was going on. Now this!

"Connie, I think Dean's right. Let him handle this," Peaches said to her. "Come on, let's go to the Starbucks." Peaches carefully took hold of Connie's arm, and steered her away. She knew how sensitive Connie could be about her children, especially Devin.

Dean turned his attention back to Detective Stevenson, who was searching his desk for something. He folded his arms, asked, "What's the real story here, my man?" He knew all too well that detectives don't call you in for questioning a second time unless something fishy is going on. Devin had already explained everything to his parents when they arrived at the hospital, or so they assumed. Stevenson shuffled more papers around on his desk, and underneath the piles of files was a videotape. He grabbed it to take with him into the interrogation room.

"We have more questions for Devin." Stevenson held up the tape. "I'll be right back. Have a seat in waiting room number four like I said."

* * *

237

Dean reluctantly went into the waiting room, and tried to think about what could've been on that videotape. Connie and Peaches joined him minutes later with their cups of coffee. Each minute that passed made Dean more concerned for his son, and it didn't help that Connie kept asking him questions about what was possibly going on inside the interrogation room.

An hour later, the door to the waiting room swung open, and in walked Stevenson. He was chewing gum as he casually approached the long table where the family was sitting. He sat down in the chair with a cocky expression on his face.

"Thank you guys for your patience. I know you're anxious about what's going on, but I'm afraid to tell you that Devin is being charged with second-degree assault and contempt for holding back evidence in the murder of Bruce "B-Money" Benjamin. His arraignment will be tomorrow, and that'll determine if the judge will allow bail or keep him retained in jail until his trial."

"Will he have to stay in jail?" Peaches interjected.

"I don't know." He shrugged his shoulders and continued to pop gum. "I mean, it's likely the judge will allow him to post bail since he doesn't have any priors. From talking to him he doesn't appear to be a threat to society either, but it depends. I'm not a judge."

"Oh my gosh!" Connie covered her mouth in shock. "Not my baby!" She shook her head.

"It's gonna be all right, Sis." Peaches hugged her.

"I'm not sure what Devin told you guys, but after further investigating the shooting of Mr. Benjamin, we discovered the hospital had a video camera in the back of the building which records cars coming out of the garage. However, the camera just so happened to pick up the whole murder scene of Mr. Benjamin in that same alley. Devin assaulted Bruce, which he'll be charged for, and then he fled the scene when his bodyguard shot and killed Mr. Benjamin," Stevenson explained. He turned the page inside his file, making sure he told them everything. Connie started crying uncontrollably, so Peaches took her out of the room. When Connie and Peaches left the room, Dean pulled out a chair that was closer to Stevenson and looked him directly in the eyes.

"How much time is my son looking at if he's convicted?"

"Depends on the judge. Could be ten years, could be five."

"Well I know the maximum sentence in the state of California for second degree assault is five years," Dean stated. "But I hope he'll do the minimum of three."

"Did you look that up?"

"I'm a former police officer who still keeps all his contacts. I had my people in Chicago do a little homework for me."

"Oh yeah?" He smacked on his gum like a cow. "Good for you. You ever think of coming out of retirement?" Stevenson asked, starting to relax.

"Never. I'm the happiest I ever been in my life." Dean pulled out of stick of gum and chewed it very slowly. "The only thing I miss is helping the community and keeping them safe. I didn't do my job just to feel like a bully over others. Seems like that's what most cops are into these days, especially with our young folks."

Stevenson chuckled bitterly. "You think I'm bullying your son?"

"You better not be," Dean popped a bubble so loud that it echoed through the quietness of the room.

"I hear you, man. Say, listen, your son is a good kid, man, but he messed up when he lied to us and held back information. If he had been upfront, things could've been different."

"I know the rules."

Stevenson leaned back in the chair, crossed his arms. "What do you say we wipe this thing clean? You and Cat Morris sitting on a goldmine in Chi-town, and my daughter's tuition is going up next school year, know what I'm trying to say?"

Dean chuckled in disbelief. "Grease your palms, huh?"

"Something like that." His lips formed a crooked, devious smile.

"Well look here, jack, I was never a dirty cop then, and neither am I a *retired* dirty cop now," Dean told him, leaning across the table and looking him dead in his beady eyes. "I'm not proud of what my son did, but *he* was the one who broke the law; we didn't. Whatever time the law decides he'll serve is what he'll do. It's the only way he'll learn from this."

Stevenson smirked. "Yeah, okay. We'll see if you tell me those hero lines when the judge sentences him to ten years." Stevenson stood up to leave the room.

"The only thing I ask is that you let us see Devin before you take him away to jail."

"And if I say no?"

Dean threw up his hands. "That's your choice, man."

Within a minute or two, Devin walked into the room with his head hung low. He was wearing a black T-shirt with a microphone on the front, and blue jeans. He had gone home and cleaned himself up before his parents had arrived in town. Although he felt clean on the outside, on the inside he felt dirty for lying to the police. As he sat in front of his father, he felt like he was shrinking in his seat by the way his dad was staring at him. Dean didn't know if Devin could sense his disappointment as he studied his every move. His son's hesitation to look at him spoke volumes nonetheless.

"I'm looking at hard time, dad, I can feel it," Devin finally spoke. He shuffled his feet underneath the table, and twirled his thumbs around in a circle. "I know I let you down, and I'm sorry. I wished this never happened."

Dean cut to the chase. "Did you tell your bodyguard to kill Bruce?"

"No sir. I didn't want anything to do with it. I mean, I beat up Bruce. It was self-defense. We were both fighting and I handled him, but Darnell took it too far."

"Why didn't you tell the truth, Devin? Haven't we talked about that in the past? I always told you and your brother if you're ever in trouble, tell the truth no matter what. Remember?"

"I was scared dad. I panicked."

"You know, some of you guys are a trip. You can make songs about being hardcore, but as soon as reality kicks in, and you actually face a situation that you rap about, you cower."

Devin hung his head low.

"How do you plan to fix this, Devin?"

"I'm going to tell the truth from now on. When I go to court I'll tell the judge everything. Man up and see what happens. And from now on, I'll make music that's actually real to me. Music that'll make you guys proud of me too."

"We were always proud of you son. You've been gifted since you were a kid, and you never got into any trouble until now. You and Trey are like brothers, but I hope you learn from this son."

"Oh trust me I am," Devin nodded.

The door to the waiting room opened, and when Connie saw Devin sitting there at the table, she rushed over to hug him. Then Peaches followed suit.

"Oh baby, are you okay?" Connie asked frantically, stroking the top of his head.

"I'm all right, Mom," Devin replied with a slight smile that quickly went away.

"We're going to get you out of here, baby. I promise. We'll get you the best lawyer in California. I already called Mr. Schutz. He used to be my attorney here in L.A. and he's good."

"Thanks, Mom, but I can get my own attorney."

"Baby, no one is as good at Mr. Schutz."

"All right, well, at least let me pay for his fees."

"Okay. I'll have him to come down to your arraignment tomorrow."

"Thanks, Mom, and I'm really sorry I let you down."

"Time's up!" Stevenson barged in. "We need to finish processing Devin and lock him away."

Devin approached his dad, and they hugged. Dean whispered to his son, "Stay strong and come out of this like the man I raised you to be."

Devin looked up into his father's eyes, eyes much like his own, and said, "I won't let you down again. I promise."

"I love you Devin." Connie hugged him.

"Love you too Mom."

"Take care of yourself Devin. Be strong in there," Peaches hugged him.

"Thanks Auntie. Love you."

"I love you too. You'll be all right. You're a Morris and a Wilson. Our families are soldiers."

Dean watched them take his son away in handcuffs, and he felt like someone had ripped his heart out and stomped on it. He understood what every parent went through when it was him arresting their sons and daughters. No parent wanted to see their child in jail. Connie grabbed Dean's hand, and they headed out of the station.

"Take us back to Tracey's house," Dean said to the limo driver. They were staying at Tracey's house for the week. The driver drove off, and Dean leaned his head back against the cushion-leather seat and glared out the tinted windows. As he started to shut his eyes to process everything, he felt Connie touching his hand. She shook him awake.

"Dean, we need to help Devin. We can't just go back to Tracey's house and do nothing."

"There's nothing else we can do, Connie."

"I can't believe you won't help your own flesh and your blood!"

Dean sat up straight in his seat. Enough was enough.

"Look Connie, Devin is a grown man, and you need to pull your tits from his mouth and let him be that man."

"Dean, this is not the time to see how grown up our son is, he's in trouble. We have a responsibility to help *our* son!"

"Can I say something?" Peaches interjected.

"No! Mind your business!" Dean shouted.

"Well damn, if it's like that, tell the driver to take me to a hotel!" Peaches declared.

"Right now, you and Connie sound like two pesky alley cats in my ear. Frankly, y'all are getting on my last nerves!"

"Forget it. You don't understand," Connie rolled her eyes. She started to massage the side of her temples as she felt a headache coming on.

The rest of the ride to Malibu was quiet. Dean was thankful for the peace so he could try to process everything that was going on. He couldn't wait to get to Tracey's house so he could go to sleep in the guest room, wake up, and start the day over again. Right now, he felt a little overwhelmed. Although, he knew he could handle it, he felt that Connie wasn't making it easy for him. He hoped that eventually her reasoning would kick in over her heightened level of emotions.

CHAPTER TWENTY-FOUR
GET IT TOGETHER

Keith overslept on Monday morning. He was still feeling tired from the events that happened with Trey and Devin over the weekend. He dragged his body out of bed and took a shower, but he still felt out of sorts. He knew he didn't have the energy to work today, so he dried himself off and made a call to Jose. He had made Jose the project supervisor, since he'd been doing a great job leading the guys during his absence.

"Hey Jose it's me, Keith."

"Hey boss, is everything okay? We're so sorry to hear about your son and your brother-in-law, homes."

"Me too, but I think they'll be okay. Say listen man, you mind taking over for a few days. I have to deal with this situation."

"I don't mind boss, but I'm headed to Puerto Rico after tomorrow, remember? You gave me the rest of the week off."

Keith sucked his teeth. "Oh yeah that's right. Well ask Robert if he can lead."

"Robert? But he just started."

Keith scratched the side of his temple and tried to think of someone else.

"Are you okay boss? I mean lately you just seem like you don't want to do this anymore, homes."

"That's a good question Jose, and I'm not sure," Keith lay back on his bed and looked up the ceiling.

"Well, if you want to sell the company, my uncle and I have been talking about partnering up. I learned a lot from you about this work and this business. If you sell it to us, we could keep the company name since Smith Landscaping is established with good clients and all."

"Let me think about that, but keeping the company name is a no-go. I can tell you that right now. You guys will have to start from scratch just like I did. Ain't no handouts, homey," Keith told him. "Anyway, later for that conversation, you just put Chris on the project details for me since Robert is not ready yet."

"Will do Boss. Take care of yourself homes."

"Later."

Keith got out of bed and made himself a bowl of cereal then retreated back to his room. He turned on the TV and started watching what seemed like an endless run of talk shows. Bored, he turned to Sports Center. *This is more like it,* he said to himself, as he finished his cereal and began to drift off to sleep just as his cellphone started ringing. He was about to hit the ignore button since he didn't recognize the number, but decided to answer it in case it was the hospital calling about Trey.

"Hello?"

"Hey baby."

"Hey baby? Who is this?"

"You forgot about me already?"

"Tell me who you are or I'm hanging up."

"It's Candy. You forgot about me already?"

Keith thought about it. He tried to remember her, but couldn't.

"Okay I'll give you a hint. We met at the fight in Las Vegas two weeks ago. You were with your friend Tyson and his boys."

"Oh yeah I remember," he lamented, feeling bad just thinking about it.

"I'm in town today and I was wondering if you wanted to go out to dinner later on."

Keith twisted his lips into a frown behind the phone. "I don't think so. What happened in Vegas stays in Vegas."

"Oh really, so it's like that? So you back with Tracey now?"

"Does it matter? Look, lose my number alright."

"You don't have to be nasty about it."

"I can be however I want," Keith started to remember everything about her, and he got upset. "You had no business telling your friends to post pictures of us on the internet like we're a couple. You just wanted to make my wife jealous, didn't you?"

"So what if I did!" She barked. "I never liked Tracey anyway."

"Don't call me anymore. We're not friends. We're not anything. I already told *TMZ* that you were just a random skeezer trying to roll with us that night."

"Skeezer? I don't think so baby. I get much respect in this game."

"Well not from me. How could any man ever respect you for the way you act and how you live? Lose my number! Bye!" Keith hung up the phone. Just then he heard a knock at his front door. "Dag man, I'm supposed to be off today and everybody is bugging me," He said to himself out loud, as he peeped through the peephole and noticed his father-in-law standing on the other side with Dean Jr. next to him. "What is this?" he mumbled under his breath.

"Hey Keith, how's it going bro?" Dean Jr. spoke first, shook his hand, gave him a half hug.

"Can we come in?" Dean Sr. asked.

"Of course," Keith stepped aside. "Have a seat. You guys want something to drink?"

"Nah, we're not going to stay long. We're headed up to the hospital to see Trey," Dean Sr. said, sitting down on the sofa next to Dean Jr.

"So wassup?" Keith cracked opened a beer, and leaned back in the chair across from them, with his long legs stretched out before him.

"Tracey needs you right now bro," Dean Jr. stated. "Whatever is going on with you guys personally, you need to put it aside. She doesn't need to be by herself with the kids right now."

"I know that."

"You know it, but what do you plan to do about it?" Dean Sr. questioned.

"I don't know," He shrugged. "I'll have to figure that out."

"Well, we won't be here that long. I need to get back to business in New York and with my own family, and dad and mom have things in Chicago to attend to, so what we're really trying to say is that you need to get it together, bro. Not tomorrow. Not next week. Not another month from now, but today."

"Look," Keith stood up from the chair. "I'm tired of everybody telling me how to live my life. Where were you guys when Tracey was boning Noah? Did you try to stop her from flying out to Paris to screw him? Has anybody told *her* how wrong *she* was? I mean she put everybody's personal business out there, and now this whole family is screwed up behind it!"

Dean Sr. and Dean Jr. both stood up at the same time and looked Keith in the eyes, and then stared him down.

"What's up?" Keith sat the beer down and stood at a stance.

"It's not like that bro," Dean Jr. tried to assure him.

"I can't tell. Ya'll standing in my face like you want beef or something."

"Keith, what's happened to you son?" Dean Sr. rested his hands on Keith's shoulder. "Where is the spiritually mature Keith that I met years ago? The one who had the voice of reason?"

Keith walked away, went into the kitchen and grabbed another beer.

"Keith," Dean Sr. approached him and took the beer from his hands. "This isn't the answer. Neither is partying. Neither is hanging out with the wrong crowds. Look at what just happened with Trey. Have you thought about how easily that could've been you in that club too? You don't know what's going on out here these days my man. It's too late to be driving backwards. And yes, we've all talked to Tracey about what happened between her and Noah, and her book. It was wrong, she's sorry for it, but you're letting Noah win every day that you're not with her."

"Keith, dad is right. Besides, every man in Hollywood knows you and my sister have been separated for some months now. Don't think they haven't been trying to holler at her. If you don't want to get back with her that's your choice, but if you don't make a decision soon about what you want, some other brother will take your place. It may be sooner than what you think too. Believe that!"

"Yeah whatever, chief!" Keith sneered.

"Well, we've said enough, but you know where we stand," Dean Sr. said, firmly, as he turned to leave out.

"When the real Keith shows back up, tell him to give Dean Jr. a call, okay?" Dean Jr. rolled his eyes at Keith and he and his dad walked out the door.

CHAPTER TWENTY-FIVE
THE PRICE OF FAME
September: One Month Later...

Dean Jr. was surprised that his younger brother Devin couldn't remember how to tie a necktie, so he tied it for him.

"Not bad," Devin examined the tie before the mirror in his bedroom. It looked picture perfect, as far as he was concerned.

"Not bad? That tie is sharp, bro! I'm in corporate America, baby, I make business deals with international business men and women," Dean bragged. "I know how to tie a necktie with my eyes closed," he said, and then he quickly tied his own in what seemed like a one-hand trick to Devin.

"Have you talked to Andrea?" Dean asked.

"I have, but she don't want nothing to do with me, man," Devin replied, recalling the times he phoned her. The last time he called her she finally said to him, "Look, don't call me anymore. You only want me back because you're going to jail. You're just as selfish as you can be! I found somebody who really loves me, and you know what? He may not have the money you got or the fame, but he got plenty of love for me!" The breakup added to Devin's depressed mood these days. As he tucked a picture of his daughter Leah inside his suit pocket, he realized his mother was right. She once told him, "When a woman is fed up, there'll be nothing you can do about it." He missed Andrea, and wished he had done right by her. Despite his brother being in town, he thought of Andrea often. He thought of her when he ate take-out instead of a home cooked meal. He thought of her when he ran out of clean underwear, because she washed his clothes. He thought her when the refrigerator was empty, because she always went to the store. Nothing that he and Dean did together could replace the absence of Andrea. His house in the Baldwin Hills was big, but it felt twice as empty without Andrea around. Devin hadn't been able to sleep good at night since their breakup, Bruce's murder, and Trey getting shot. He felt his world was crumbling down.

"You doing all right?" Dean asked, seeing that Devin was in deep thought.

"I'm as good as I can be."

"Hey man, everything will work out. Just do your time, keep your nose clean and come out stronger all right?" Dean patted his young brother on the back. "I know you scared, man, but one day this will all be a memory. You'll look back and say to yourself, I made it through that situation, and now I'm a better person."

"I hope you're right, Dean." They embraced each other, squeezed tight and then released.

"And hey, if you don't want to go back into the music business when you get out, you can come to New York and work for me. Maybe starting fresh will be a good thing for you."

Devin nodded. "Maybe. We'll see what's up."

The news media and paparazzi were waiting for Devin outside of the court building in downtown L.A. Devin's heart began to race with fear. Not from the news reporters shoving microphones to his mouth the minute he stepped out of the limo, but fear of what awaited him inside the court building. The seriousness of what was about to happen set in, and he could feel his stomach forming knots.

Once inside the court building, Devin rushed down the hall to the men's room, and Dean followed behind him.

"You all right?" Dean asked.

"Yeah, I'm good," Devin splashed cold water on his face.

"Here, keep this just in case," Dean reached inside the pocket of his Tom Ford suit and handed Devin a handkerchief.

"Thanks."

As they walked the long hallway, Devin could see the family sitting outside of the courtroom, and his attorney sat across from the family reading over papers.

"Oh Devin!" Connie quickly stood up and threw her arms around him. "How are you, baby?"

"Hey Ma, I'm okay." He relaxed his shoulders and tried to appear poised so she wouldn't worry about him. She quickly took the handkerchief from his hand and started wiping his sweaty face.

"Ma, I need to see my attorney. We need to talk before we go inside."

"Okay." Connie stepped back and stared him up and down, then reached out to readjust his necktie. She patted out a few wrinkles she thought she saw on his shoulder pads. "You look handsome."

"Thanks Ma, but really I need to—"

"Oh Devin, I love you so much," Connie cut him off with a hug.

"Ma, please don't cry come on now, be strong." Devin could feel her hot tears against the front of his suit jacket. He blinked back a few tears of his own because he hated to see his mother cry. Even when his Grandpa Scott died, he cried harder because he saw how sad his mother was.

"Connie, let Devin handle his business like a man. Come on," Dean Sr. stood up and approached them. He took hold of Connie's hand and sat her down on the bench.

Mr. Schutz pulled Devin aside from the family and briefly rehearsed everything he was going to say, not say, and how his posture and tone should be when he responded to questions.

"By law the judge will inform you of your rights once we're in session," Mr. Schutz explained to Devin. "But remember, the judge doesn't have to agree with our settlement, so don't be surprised, understand?"

"Yes, sir."

"Let's just hope Judge Anderson is in a good mood too. I heard she's been busy with her husband in the hospital these days, so hopefully she's well-rested."

Devin took a seat next to his parents after the pep talk with his lawyer. Connie kept probing and asking if he was okay, and Dean Sr. kept begging her to relax. Finally, Peaches had to escort Connie into the ladies' room to try to get her to calm down.

"Son, I know your head is probably spinning right now, but this will all be over with soon. You remember our conversation, don't you?" Dean Sr. asked him. Devin dropped his head in his lap and tried to fight back his tears, but he was overwhelmed. He couldn't handle his mother's sadness. He couldn't handle losing Andrea, and he felt sorry for Trey. Bruce was dead, and his friends had been injured in the shooting. Now, he was going to jail.

"Come on now. You're my soldier." Dean hugged him. "Don't shed not one more tear. You don't want anyone to mistake your tears for a weakness. Keep your chin up, shoulders back, and take whatever is given like a man."

"I'm sorry I let you down, Dad." Tears dropped from Devin's eyes to the floor.

"I forgive you, son," Dean assured him. "Now it's time for you to forgive yourself."

"Devin."

Devin lifted his head and raised his eyes slowly. Tracey was standing in front of him.

"Can we talk for just one minute before you go inside?" she asked, and Devin followed her far enough so the family couldn't hear their private talk.

"I didn't think you were going to come," Devin alleged.

"I had to pray about it, Devin," she stared into her brother's eyes. She could see that he was hurting.

"What happened to Trey that night wasn't your fault, Devin," she expressed. "And I can't let you carry that with you to jail. I'm sorry it took me so long to come to terms with everything, but I needed time."

Devin sniffed, wiped one last tear. "That's cool. I understand. I would've been mad too if it was my son. I'm his uncle and I should've discouraged the whole beef thing. I *was* wrong, because I produced the diss track."

"Well, it's my fault too that all of this happened because of my book. I'm sorry." She hugged him. "I'm so sorry for all those mean things I said to you at the hospital too. I didn't mean it. I love you, and you'll always be my brother no matter what."

"I love you too."

"Devin, Tracey, it's time," Dean Jr. approached them, as the courtroom doors opened.

"All rise!" the bailiff announced, and Judge Anderson approached the bench wearing a long black robe. Devin's hands shook at his side as he watched Judge Anderson take her seat behind the bench. She was breathing heavy like she was rushing. She adjusted her seat, and then pushed her dark-framed glasses over the bridge of her nose.

"You may now be seated," the bailiff said. "Court is now in session."

Judge Anderson shuffled around papers as if she was looking for something, and then her law clerk handed her Devin's file. Devin watched her lips move as she read through his file silently to herself, and then she moved the microphone close to her mouth and began to speak.

"This case is the State of California versus Devin Sean Wilson, docket number 455CR." She spoke the generalities and Devin watched the court reporter click away on the stenotype machine.

"With that said, will the Defendant please stand," Judge Anderson instructed. "In the matter of the State of California versus Devin Sean Wilson, how do you plead?"

Devin felt like he had swallowed an apple whole. When he opened his mouth, no words came out.

"I'm sorry, but can you repeat that? I see your mouth moving, but I didn't hear anything," Judge Anderson asked.

Mr. Schutz quickly poured Devin a glass of water and handed it to Devin, who took a few sips before he tried to speak again.

"Your honor can you repeat the question to my client, he's a little nervous, as you can imagine."

"Mr. Wilson," Judge Anderson stated more firmly. "You have been charged with second-degree assault against the deceased, Bruce "B-Money" Benjamin, how do you plead?"

"Guilty your honor," Devin felt the words leave his mouth, but not his heart. A part of him still felt like he was trying to defend his nephew.

"Do you know and understand the rights you are waving, Mr. Wilson?" the Judge asked.

"Yes, your honor."

Judge Anderson continued with a long list of questions to make sure Devin fully understood his rights. With each question, Devin tried to keep his knees from buckling.

"Counsel, have you reached a settlement?" Judge Anderson asked Mr. Schutz sharply.

"Yes, your honor. The people have agreed to the minimum sentence of two years in prison. We also agreed that Mr. Wilson shall be placed in a minimum security correctional facility, your honor."

"Mr. Wilson, do you understand that by pleading guilty you waive your rights to a jury and to be cross-examined?"

"Yes, your honor."

"Are you pleading guilty because you did in fact strike Bruce Benjamin?"

"Yes, your honor."

"Did anyone give you money or gifts to persuade your decision, or did you agree to give them money or gifts in return for a lesser charge?"

"No, your honor."

"The court may take a fifteen minute break, and I will return with my decision."

Devin wanted to collapse to his knees and beg the judge to allow the case to be over with. He didn't want to drag things out any more. He wanted this to be quick. *Are you guilty? Yes,* and then off to jail he would go. Instead, he felt things were dragging out. He tried to avoid looking at the prosecution or over his shoulder at B-Money's family, who were giving his family dirty looks.

"Just relax, this will be over with soon," Mr. Schultz whispered to Devin.

When Judge Anderson returned to the courtroom a few minutes later, the court rose and then sat per instruction from the Bailiff.

"After reviewing the facts in this case, including the video evidence of the assault against the deceased, I hereby deny the Defendant's settlement."

"Oh no! Don't deny my baby!" Devin heard his mother cry.

Judge Anderson, stroke the gavel. "Order in the court!"

Devin looked over his shoulder and saw his Aunt Peaches walk his mother out the courtroom. He decided not to turn around anymore to see what was going on. It was making him more nervous and anxious again.

"Per California law," Judge Anderson continued. "The maximum sentence for second-degree assault is five years, and the minimum is two years. It is therefore, my judgment to hereby sentence the defendant, Devin Sean Wilson to the *maximum* of five years in a California State prison with the possibility of parole *after* serving a *minimum* of two years. The court will honor part of the settlement, in which the prosecution has agreed that based on the nature of the crime committed and no prior convictions, that Mr. Wilson shall enter a minimum security facility. Mr. Wilson, do you understand your sentence?"

"Yes, your honor."

"Do you have any questions whatsoever regarding your sentence?"

"No, your honor."

"At this time, the family of the deceased, Bruce "B-Money" Benjamin will share a few words with the defendant. Mr. Wilson, please stand and face Mrs. Benjamin, who has decided to speak on behalf of the family. Go on, Mrs. Benjamin."

Devin watched a short Hispanic woman stand up from the public galley. She was wearing a ponytail, a purple floral dress, and red lipstick. She held up a piece of notebook paper with words written on the front and back. She cried as she started to read the sentences on the paper, and Devin could barely make out what she was saying since her Spanish accent was so heavy.

"…and you should not have taken my Brucey into that alley," Mrs. Benjamin was saying. "I wish the judge had sentenced you to life in prison just like she did Darnell. You'll pay for what you did!" she shouted, and another relative sat her down as she cried uncontrollably.

"Mr. Wilson, do you have anything you wish to say to the Benjamin family at this time?" Judge Anderson asked.

"Yes, your honor."

"You may proceed."

Devin faced the Benjamin family, who sat across from where he was. It was Mrs. Benjamin, and her daughters, and a tall dark-skinned man he assumed was Bruce's father.

"I'm sorry for your loss, and I wish I could take back everything that happened that night. In my anger, I felt I was defending myself and my nephew, Trey because Bruce tried to kill all of us that night. I'm not a violent man. My parents didn't raise me to be that way. I do realize now that I shouldn't have taken the law into my own hands. I should've called the police, and I feel bad that I didn't. All I wanted to do was make music. I never intended for anything like this to happen. I never started a beef with Bruce because music was my focus, but Bruce made trouble for us. I know that saying all of this won't make it any easier for you, but I hope you can see the whole truth in what happened. I'm not a bad person. I'm just a man who made the wrong choices that night. Again, I'm sorry," Devin sat back down after he was finished, and he could hear Bruce's family rambling something in Spanish that didn't sound like sympathy or forgiveness towards him.

"To the Benjamin family, the court would like to extend its condolences for your loss," Judge Anderson spoke. "To Mr. Wilson, I hope you spend your time in prison learning your lesson behind this, and that you'll never again take the law into your own hands, nor obstruct justice by holding back the truth. It is for those reasons your settlement was denied. Case dismissed. Bailiff, please escort Mr. Wilson out of the courtroom."

Devin held out his hands as the bailiff handcuffed his wrists. Devin refused to look over his shoulder. He didn't want to see the look of his family's faces. He was glad it was over with. As the officer led him out of the courtroom and into the backseat of the police car, he felt glad it was over. He laid back and fell asleep from the exhaustion of it all. When Devin woke up, he found himself in unfamiliar territory–California State Prison. As the officers pulled him out of the car, he already missed the good life he once had, and he wondered if he could ever get it back again...

CHAPTER TWENTY-SIX
WHEN IT STILL HURTS

The ride to Dean's parents' house made him feel like he was in the car all by himself. He was talking, but Connie was staring out the window. Since Devin's arrest a few weeks ago, Connie wasn't sure of much of anything. She slept often, and when she wasn't sleeping, she spent a lot of time in her garden planting vegetables. When Devin called collect, it pained her to hear his voice, and to know that her baby and youngest child was behind bars like a caged animal. The Benjamin's filed a civil suit against Devin to try to get money, but they lost. The very fact that they tried to get money off of Bruce's murder made Connie feel more hurt. It didn't help her feel any better when the news media was outside of her house for weeks after the judge's decision. They didn't care that she was a grieving mother. They just wanted a statement from her about the plight of her children, and they wanted to smear her good name and legacy. Dean could see how Connie had cocooned herself away from the world. He was trying to give her time with her own thoughts, but he was getting concerned as to how much longer she would be mentally checked out.

When Dean pulled up in front of his parents' red brick row house on the south side of Chicago, he saw right away that the yard hadn't been attended to. He and Connie paid the neighborhood youth to keep the yard up for their parents. It was a positive way for them to earn money, but Dean could see for himself from the tall grass growing wildly, that while they had been in California, the kids had taken a break.

Dean walked inside the house and immediately turned up his nose at the strong odor and headed towards the kitchen. Connie had rushed ahead of him.

"Why does this house stink like this?" Connie asked the housekeeper, Nellie about the poor condition of the house. Dishes were piled in the sink and the trash needed to be taken out.

"It smells like cat pee and mothballs in here," Dean complained. "Let me go upstairs and check on Pops." Dean put his hand over his mouth and nose and walked up the stairs.

"Is that you, Johnny?" his father called him from his bedroom. Dean hated that he called him by his deceased younger brother's name, but he tried to be sympathetic since he was dealing with Alzheimer's disease.

"It's me, Dean!" He entered his room. The doctors told him and Connie it was helpful not to tell his father he was wrong, but to just say the right answers so he wouldn't get frustrated.

Meanwhile, Connie was glad Dean had left the kitchen. She didn't want Dean hovering over her while she was trying to clean up the things Nellie should have taken care of. She washed the dishes first, cleaned the kitchen counter off, disinfected door handles, cleaned out the refrigerator, and scrubbed all the spills.

"Rest yourself chile'," her mother-in-law said, once her show went off. She was watching the small TV set that was on the kitchen table. Connie and Dean tried to renovate their house, including getting them new appliances and TVs, but Dean's parents didn't want them to change a single thing. Connie always felt like she had stepped back into the sixties every time they visited her in-laws home.

"Can't, Mama, this place needs cleaning. The nurse can't work around all this mess when she comes back on Monday," Connie said, recalling the nurse's schedule. The nurse stayed with their parents during the week, and went home on the weekends. Nellie's job was to clean the house every day, including the weekends. Connie could see that like the kids in the neighborhood, Nellie was slacking on the job since her and Dean's absence.

"I will start fixing your parents' lunch," Nellie uttered.

Connie glanced at the watch on her wrist. "It's noon. It should have been ready. If you can't do your job, then I will hire somebody else to do it. You're just standing around watching me. I mean, have you planned on cleaning up this place? Have you planned to fix their lunch? A good housekeeper is a good organizer. I know, because my mother was a maid for years."

"Yes ma'am," Nellie mumbled under her breath, and staggered a little as she moved out of Connie's way. Her eyes were glossy and she stared at Connie in a haze.

"I pay your company good money and I expect better service than this," Connie complained.

Yes ma'am," Nellie chuckled.

"Did you just laugh?"

"No, I didn't laugh, Mrs. Wilson," Nellie tried to fix her facial expression.

Connie looked away. "Something still stinks in here, after all this cleaning I've done. It must be this trashcan." She opened the trashcan sitting in the corner of the kitchen. "This trashcan is filled with pissy *Depends*!"

"I was going to take that out," Nellie claimed.

"Sure you were."

Connie opened the back door, and stepped outside. She saw a swarm of bees and flies around the trashcans in the yard. The trash had never been set out to be picked up. Just when she thought she had seen it all, she felt something run across her feet, and when she looked to her right, a giant rat was eyeballing her.

"AAAHHHHH!"

Connie ran back in the house and slammed the door.

"YOU!" Connie pointed at Nellie. Nellie's eyes widened as she held the loaf of bread in her hands to make sandwiches for Mr. and Mrs. Wilson.

"You are fired! Get out!"

Dean came running down the stairs when he heard Connie screaming. He rushed into the kitchen.

"What's wrong, baby?"

"Nellie is fired!" Connie shouted.

"I'll get my things." Nellie slowly walked out of the kitchen.

"What is going?" Mrs. Wilson looked up from the TV, adjusted her hearing aid.

"It's okay, Mama, don't worry," Dean said to her.

"But where is Ms. Nellie going?" she put on her bifocals, and watched Nellie gather her things. Her eyes looked big like two fifty-cent pieces behind her glasses.

"Mama, don't worry about Nellie. We'll find you some better help around here. Seems like everybody is off their jobs. We leave town for a short while and the help suddenly stops doing their job!" Connie fussed.

"I'll make you and Daddy lunch. Dean," Connie turned to him. "I need you to sit those trashcans outside of the fence so they can be picked up. I'm not going back out there. A rat ran across my feet."

Dean looked at his mother and then shifted his gaze back to Connie. "What? You scared of rats?"

Dean chuckled. "No, I'm not scared of rats, but you need to watch your tone with me. I'm not the help. I don't work for you."

Connie threw up her hands. "Whatever!"

"Connie don't disrespect me."

"Fine, can you *please* take the trash out. I would appreciate it."

"That's more like it," Dean said, grabbing the trash and taking it out back.

Connie served Mrs. Wilson a sandwich and headed upstairs to take Mr. Wilson his lunch too. She knocked on the bedroom door and then entered. The TV was playing, and Mr. Wilson was nodding off to sleep, but the room felt extremely hot. *Why didn't Dean turn on the air conditioner when he came up here? I have to do everything myself!* Connie thought. She set the tray down and walked over to the A.C. unit and turned it on. As she turned the switch on the AC unit, she spotted Dean out back cleaning the yard. Dean had stripped down to his T-shirt. He was sweeping and bagging more trash that loiterers had tossed in the yard.

"Dad, I have your lunch."

Mr. Wilson opened his eyes, and when he saw Connie his eyes expanded in fear. "No, get away!" he waved her off.

"Shhh, it's okay, it's me, Connie, Dean's wife."

"Who?"

"Con-nee, Dean's wife."

Mr. Wilson squinted his eyes, sized her up and down from head to toe.

"Oh okay," his shoulders relaxed. "You're Connie, right?"

"Yes, Dad, I'm Connie."

"You're Connie, Dean's wife Connie," he repeated. Connie sat the tray in his lap and he began to eat the sandwich on his own. Suddenly Connie heard screaming from out back and rushed over to the window. Dean was screaming like a woman as he jumped over the rats that ran through the yard.

Connie laughed. "I thought he wasn't scared. Oh well, I need to call pest control," Connie said aloud to herself. "This is why I wanted you guys to come live with me and Dean, but unfortunately it didn't work out because you guys were too scared to be out of your own environment. I understand it, but now it's just hard for me and Dean to find you guys good help. We could have taken better care of you at our house." She sighed, as she leaned down to get the Yellow Pages inside the cabinet of the TV stand. When she glanced at the back of the cabinet, she saw a shining bottle. At first, she thought nothing of it as she closed the cabinet back, and set the phonebook at the foot of Mr. Wilson's bed. *What was that bottle?* She wondered curiously, scratching the side of her temple. She opened the cabinet back up, kneeled down and looked inside. She could see the inscription on the half-pint bottle, *Bacardi Gold*. Right away her heart began to race with delight. She put her hand to her mouth and closed her eyes as she remembered its mellow rich flavors of caramel mixed with a little vanilla. It used to go down smooth whenever she drunk it. She looked over her shoulder at Mr. Wilson, who had finished his sandwich and moved on to his cup of fruit cocktail, while watching TV. She looked back inside the cabinet and reached for the bottle.

Don't do it! Part of her conscience spoke.

Just one sip, that's all, she told herself. *One sip won't hurt you. You've been sober for over twenty years now! You can handle it.*

Connie quickly grabbed the bottle, stuffed it in her shirt. She slowly rose to her feet with her back turned to Mr. Wilson. He wasn't paying her any attention. She walked over to the window and saw that Dean was still cleaning the backyard, so she hurried into the bathroom down the hall, and locked the door.

"So, Nellie, you forgot to take your bottle with you, huh?" Connie assumed. "I can finish it for you," she eyed the bottle. "Wait, what am I doing? I can't do this." She sat the bottle on the floor. *Go on. One sip. It won't hurt you and nobody will know!* Connie's green eyes caught sight of the bottle of mouthwash on the sink. *You can cover it up the way you used to do.* Her gaze shifted from the mouthwash back to the Bacardi and then back to the mouthwash. *Take a sip and hurry up!* Connie grabbed the bottle and quickly twisted the top off. Its sweet aroma danced across the bridge of her nose, as her heart pounded heavily with eagerness. Suddenly her mind began to flashback to when she got so drunk that she decided to drive through WHKY radio station. She nearly killed Smokey and his girlfriend. She remembered how badly she was injured with a concussion and had to get stitches through her arms. It took a year to build her good reputation again. *But you're not driving. Dean is doing the driving! It's okay, now go ahead and drink it!*

Connie's unsteady arm tilted the bottle up to her lips.

"CONNIE!"

She looked over her shoulder, and wasn't sure if that was Dean's voice or Mrs. Wilson calling her.

"CONNIE ARE YOU ALL RIGHT UP THERE, GAL!"

Connie quickly sat the bottle down, peeped her head out the bathroom door. "I'm okay. I'm using the restroom. Be down in a minute!"

"OKAY!"

Connie sat back on the toilet with the lid down. She wiped the sweat from her forehead. "I can't do this," she shook her head. *One sip. Come on. Stop making a big deal out of this.* Connie reached for the bottle again. Sat it on her lap. Stared at it, and then held it up to her nose. She imaged how much more relaxed she would feel if she took a sip. She tilted the bottle up again with her arm shaking unsteadily, and parted her lips. Her lips came close to the brim and then she stopped. *Come on! It's just a sip. If you don't hurry up Dean will be back in the house. One quick sip now hurry!*

"God please help me, in Jesus name!" She cried. Suddenly she felt a need to pull out her cellphone, and found herself scrolling through the pictures of her children and grandchildren. She wondered how they would feel if their grandmother became an alcoholic again. Suddenly, her shoulders began to relax; her heart rate began to slow down. She caught her breath and began to breathe very slowly. Reasoning started to kick it, and she began to see the triggers that led her to this place. She stared at the bottle and saw it for what it was—poison to an alcoholic like her. She saw that if she drank the liquor, it wouldn't take away the pain she felt from her children letting her down, but it would bring more harm to her. It would erase all of her years of sobriety, peace of mind, and destroy the legacy she had built. She stood up from the toilet, lifted the lid, and poured the Bacardi down the toilet bowl. She felt so relieved that she cried, "Thank you God! Never again! Never!"

* * *

Dean was singing along to Rene and Angela's 'You Don't Have to Cry' on the radio, as he and Connie headed home from a long day of cleaning at his parents' house. He glanced over at Connie who was staring out the window. She wasn't responding to the small talk he was trying to make with her.

"Connie, we're not going to end another day like this."

"What're you talking about?" she looked out the window at the full moon above, and wished she could travel to a faraway place.

"You need to start talking and stop acting cold like someone killed your best friend. If this is about Devin, you need to just accept reality and move on."

She turned to face him. Crossed her arms. "That's so typical of you, isn't it Dean? To just blow things off, like the offer from Detective Stevenson. You never once mentioned it to me or Devin. You blew it off when we could have accepted the offer. Detective Stevenson called me and said that things could have been different with Devin and I wasn't sure what he meant, but thanks to you our son is in jail when he could be free right now."

"Connie, that's obstruction of justice and then you *both* would be in jail right now if anyone ever found out. I couldn't let something like that happen. Didn't you hear when the judge asked Devin if he ever gave money or gifts for a better deal? You cannot obstruct justice!"

"Why is it that you could get Peaches out of jail but not your own son?"

"I don't believe this." Dean heaved a loud sigh. "Your sister got out of jail because she finally agreed to testify against her drug dealing boyfriend. That's how she got out. I never did anything dirty."

"Cut the bull, Dean!" Connie snapped. "You wanted Devin to go to jail because you know how much I loved him and spoiled him. You were jealous of our relationship. Just admit it."

"Oh come on, Connie, that's not true and you know it!" He gestured sharply with his hand, and then quickly placed it back on the steering wheel. "Now is not the time to throw cheap shots at me when I'm trying to help you. You're acting like all of this is my fault. It makes no sense to send my own son to jail, and you're crazy to think something sick like that!"

"Oh yeah? Well maybe I'm crazy because nobody seems to

understand what I'm going through, especially you," she retorted. "You don't even talk about Devin. You act like his arrest never even happened. Our friends asked how he was doing and you skipped the subject and started talking about Dean Jr. You're embarrassed. Devin embarrassed you, and you're ashamed of him."

"I may have felt embarrassed Connie, but our friends was asking me that question right after it happened."

"It? Listen to you, you can't even say it. Just admit what happened Dean."

"Admit what?"

Connie shook her head feeling frustrated. "You can't say it because you know I'm right."

Dean looked away and heaved a long sigh. "Okay, fine, maybe you're right. I was embarrassed, and I did feel ashamed…then. But I'm not now. I'm at a place where I can talk about it, but you can't. You don't talk at all."

"Because you never listen. You and Peaches both accuse me of being too emotional about everything, so I keep my feelings to myself."

"Is that why you drunk that bottle of Bacardi at my folks' house? Because you *think* we don't understand how you feel? That's a cop out, Connie! I expected better of you."

Connie's head jolted back and her eyes widened. "So what you looking through trashcans now?"

"No, I could smell it when I went in to use the bathroom. It's only natural for me to look to see where it was coming from."

"You think you know all the answers, don't you, Dean?"

"I know you drunk that bottle, and I was trying to give you a chance to admit it. See if you would be honest."

"I didn't drink the bottle, Dean." She looked over at him and held his stare while they sat at a red light.

"Then why did—"

"I poured it down the toilet," she cut him off. "I wanted to drink it. I did. I was two seconds from gulping it down, and hell, I would've driven to the bar afterwards to drink some more until I passed out. Now are you satisfied?!"

Dean was silent for a moment as he thought about what his wife just admitted to him. "But why? How could you even think to do something like that again, Connie?"

"Because you guys drive me to drinking is why!"

Dean rolled his eyes at her and sped off as soon as the light turned green. His Bentley went flying down the street.

When they got home, they didn't take a shower together like they normally would. They used separate showers this time. Connie finished first and headed downstairs to warm up some leftovers for herself. Dean came down minutes later and warmed up his own food, after he saw that Connie didn't heat up everything for them to share like she normally did.

"Is this how it's going to be?" Dean asked, joining her at the dining table with his own plate of food.

"I don't know what you're talking about, Dean." Connie crossed one leg over the other and leaned back in the dining room chair.

"Connie, I don't want to play games, but here is what I want you to know. Our children's issues are their own. We raised them the best we could. The way they want to live their lives is their choice, and they have to live with the consequences, good or bad. Just because I'm a guy who looks at the facts of situations doesn't mean I don't care about our children, and it doesn't mean I don't care about you either."

Connie rolled her eyes to the ceiling.

"You seem to think that some of the things our children have done doesn't affect me, but you're wrong. You don't think I was hurt from what Tracey wrote in her book about me and pretty much downplayed me like I was a token piece to this family? Sure she apologized, but I was hurt, but what could I do about it? The book was published," Dean stated. "You don't think I was hurt when my own son went to jail when I used to be a cop? Hell yes that hurt! We raised him better than that, but he wouldn't listen to me. What could I do about it? Nothing." Dean paused, ate a few forks of food, and then continued.

"And furthermore, if you don't want to talk to me and share what's going on with you, I can't help you the way you need to be helped. I'm not a mind reader."

"You should know me by now, Dean."

"I know you Connie. I know when people tell you the truth and you disagree that you shut down. You went berserk when Devin was arrested. You wouldn't listen to anybody, not me or Peaches. You even tried to take charge when I asked you several times to let me handle everything. I didn't want you to have to carry that load. I know how close you and Devin are, and I was never jealous of your relationship, but I could see that you always held on to him too tight. If he had a fall you were ready to run him to the hospital over a little bruise. If he didn't like his dinner, you cooked him something else.

"It's no wonder that no woman was ever good enough for him. Not even Andrea. You did spoil him, but none of that stopped me from loving him just as much as you do. For you to say I never tried to help my own son really hurts. For you to say that I don't care about you or love you hurts even more. I'm the same man who got on that plane and flew to New York when you needed me, but you've been shutting me out and not listening to me at all during this whole incident and that's unfair."

Connie felt her emotions swelling up inside and she started crying. Dean set his fork down on his plate, walked over to her end of the table and hugged her.

"I know it hurts, baby," Dean stroked her back. "Let it go. Let it all out. We still have our own lives to live. My father used to say 'after you give your best, have no regrets.'"

Connie wiped her eyes. "I'm sorry for what I said to you, Dean."

"That's okay. You said those words out of your pain, but baby please don't shut me out like that anymore. And baby please listen to me sometimes, and know that I have your best interest at heart."

"I know you do."

"I'm here for you. You're never alone," he stroked her cheek.

"I just need time to get through this, Dean."

"We'll get through this together."

"I love you."

"I love you too, and we're a team no matter what."

"I'm glad to have you by my side."

"Always."

Part Four

CHAPTER TWENTY-SEVEN
SECRET'S OUT

Hank pulled into the driveway outside of Peaches' five bedroom home on Thackeray Street. He spotted two squirrels running through the trimmed shrubs that evenly lined the outside of her house. Hank always loved Highland Park and dreamed of living there as a kid. He walked up the steps that looked like they were newly paved. If it weren't for the squirrels wrestling with each other in the bushes, he knew the only sound he would hear was white noise, because the neighborhood was so quiet. He was used to the loud noises from the inner city. Hank rang the doorbell and waited for Peaches to answer. He checked himself out before the glass door. He was wearing his favorite blue linen outfit with the short sleeves and pants, and a pair of black sandals with long white socks. His son, Hank Jr., told him before he left. "Dad, socks and sandals is old school. You look whack."

Hank told him, "The only person in this house who is "whack" is you. You're thirty-five years old with no job, two kids that you don't care for, and you living with me." Hank knew that would shut him up quick.

Peaches opened the door with a smile that stretched across her round brown cheeks. Her natural locks were pulled up into a neat bun.

"Come on, let me in, girl. It's a little warm out here and Sweet Daddy may melt."

As soon as Peaches opened the door, Hank dropped the flowers on the table that he bought for her, picked her up in one easy swoop, and carried her upstairs.

"Big Daddy been missing you, girl." Hank laid her down easy on the bed and took off his clothes.

"Oh yeah? Well, I've been a bad girl, and I can't wait for you to spank me."

BJ kept staring at the yellow Dodge Challenger in his mother's driveway, with tags that read "SUGAR" in the front. He then walked around the car, checking it out, and noticed the back tags said, "DADDY."

"Dad, that's Uncle Hank's car, isn't it?" Junior asked, ringing his grandmother's doorbell again.

"Looks that way," BJ grinded his teeth.

"I know grandma is here. That's her BMW parked in front of it," Junior said. "I wonder what's taking her so long to answer the door."

BJ looked at his watch. "Let's go Junior. We've waited long enough."

"But what about the extra table and chairs we're supposed to take to Aunt Connie and Uncle Dean's house for the cookout?"

"Since your Uncle Hank is here. It doesn't look like your grandmother needs our help anymore."

The door finally slid open, and a set of bubble eyes stared back at them.

"It's us, Grandma!" Junior was glad she opened the door.

"Sorry it took so long, come on in," Peaches opened the door, fully dressed in cropped pants, a blouse, and sandals.

"Where's Uncle Hank?" BJ asked, bluntly.

"Uncle Hank?"

"Yes, I saw his car in the driveway, so I know he's here."

"Oh Uncle Hank, he's um…he's in the basement taking a look at my hot water heater. For some reason, my water has been running cold."

BJ twisted his lips, as he headed straight towards her basement with Junior following behind him.

"Hey, the chairs and tables are not in the basement. They're outback in the shed," Peaches ran behind them.

Hank was sitting down on the sofa, watching TV and channel flipping. He looked up when he heard feet trampling down the stairs.

"BJ, my man, wassup youngblood?" Hank rose from the leather sofa and extended his hand. "You're not gonna shake my hand?"

"I thought you were down here fixing the–"

"Water heater, right Hank?" Peaches answered before Hank could reply.

Hank smirked, slightly tilted his head. "Yeah, something like that, but um…the *heat* is just fine, wouldn't you agree, Peaches?" He winked at her.

BJ could feel his temper rising at the thought of Uncle Hank being skin-to-skin with his mother.

"Funny thing about those water heaters is that sometimes people think they're too old, but all is takes is for the right *touch* to turn it up a notch. Ain't that right, Peaches?" Hank grinned as he chewed on a toothpick.

Peaches swallowed hard, wiped the sweat beads from her forehead and tried to think of what to say.

"Junior, here is the key to the shed out back. Why don't you go load up the table and chairs in your father's truck," Peaches handed her grandson the key.

"Yes ma'am," Junior unlocked the back door and went out to the shed.

BJ's nostrils flared as he gave Peaches and Hank the evil eye.

"I don't think anything was wrong with the water heater. This house is practically brand new," BJ stated.

"So what if it wasn't," Hank challenged, he and BJ stood eye-to-eye. Peaches noticed BJ's hands forming fists. She quickly stepped in front of BJ and pushed him away from Hank.

"BJ, why don't you go on upstairs and get yourself something cold to drink and a snack, okay?"

"No. I don't want a drink. I want to know why Hank is here."

"No you don't, baby. Please, just go on upstairs."

"I said no!"

"Hey, don't yell at your mother like that!" Hank barked.

"I can do whatever I want and there's nothing you can do to stop me. Not unless you want to lose your other eye."

Hank swung at BJ, but BJ ducked just in time.

"Stop it! Both of y'all stop it!" Peaches cried. "Now BJ, look, this is going to end right now. I've had enough of this crap!"

"Peaches, I'm leaving but I'll see you at the cookout," Hank stormed pass BJ who attempted to go after him until Peaches grabbed his arm.

"No BJ! Don't do it!" Peaches pulled him back.

"That's alright," BJ snatched his arm away. "I'll see him at the cookout and handle him then."

"No you won't either!" Peaches argued. "Look BJ, I just turned sixty-two years old. What I do with my life is my business. I'm grown!"

"You're a whore for a mother is what you are!"

SMACK.

BJ held the side of his cheek.

"You will not disrespect me like me that, ever! Now you get out of my house until you can show me some respect!"

"That's the last time you'll ever hit me, woman. I hope it felt good, because next time you do that I will hit you back, and I will punch you like a man."

"Do it! Do it, BJ, I dare you!" Peaches challenged. BJ shoved her out of his way and stormed up the stairs and out the door. As much as he wanted to hit her, a part of him couldn't bring himself to actually do it.

Connie could see that something was bothering BJ as he directed his son where to put the table and chairs when they arrived at her house.

"Dad, is it all right to play the new XBOX in the game room?"

"No, we need to get going."

"BJ, you guys aren't staying for the cookout?" Connie asked, after they set up everything outside on the lawn.

"No, I don't want to be here when my mother comes, and I certainly don't want to be around Hank," BJ cut his eyes at Hank who seemed to be explaining everything that happened to his Uncle Dean who was preparing the meats on the grill.

Connie sighed. "Junior, go on inside to the game room and play," she told him. "And Sandra and Bianca, if you wouldn't mind helping Anna stuff the devil eggs in the kitchen. BJ and I are going to sit out here and talk."

"Sure no problem," Sandra said, and Bianca followed her inside the house.

"BJ, have a seat on this other lawn chair, next to me," Connie gestured for BJ to sit down.

"Now what's bothering you? Are you okay?"

BJ stared at her for a moment then looked away. Connie could see his jaw twitching so she knew he was grinding his teeth, because he was angry. He did it all the time as a kid.

"Do you want to talk about it?"

"No I don't."

"Something happened at your mother's house because I overheard bits and pieces while Hank was talking to Dean. Tell me what's going on."

BJ huffed as he stood up from the chair and clinched his fist. "How could Peaches sleep with Uncle Hank? It doesn't get any worse than that!

He's family, for goodness sake!"

"Not really. By law they could marry each other. They have no blood ties, you know."

"You knew about this Aunt Connie?"

"I suspected something was going on, but she never came out and told me. You just did."

"Aunt Connie, Peaches is always with some guy. Now she's sleeping with Uncle Hank, I mean come on! This is embarrassing."

"There's nothing to be embarrassed about, BJ. Your mother and Hank are both grown."

"He's family though Aunt Connie."

"I can see your point, but you have to respect your mother's choices."

"She's so immature and so promiscuous for an older lady. I would have expected her to be mature by now."

"You have to understand that your mother lost her younger years. She's still playing catch-up, but those are years she'll never get back. Unfortunately, from time-to-time, you and I will just have to deal with some of her ways. The good thing is she's clean. She works hard. She's respected by the community, and most of all she loves you."

"But Aunt Connie—"

"BJ, your mother moved back to Chicago just to be with you, and to get to know her grandchildren better. She didn't want to come back here. She was afraid that she would go back out there and get caught up again, but I admire her courage. She loved you that much to risk her own sobriety. Yet, you won't give her a chance to even prove that she can be a better mother to you, and that's not fair, BJ."

"It is fair. She was the one who abandoned me!"

"And she's sorry for that, BJ. When are you going to let go and forgive her, huh?"

"Never!"

"Now who's being childish and immature?" "Aunt Connie it's not that simple with me. It never has been."

"Because you won't let go. It's quite simple actually."

BJ rubbed his chin in frustration. "No it's not."

"I know you love your mother BJ. Otherwise you wouldn't keep getting upset about who she chooses to date."

BJ sat back down in the chair, clapped his hands together.

"BJ, you have so much anger inside of you. I can tell. If you talk about it, maybe I can help you," Connie reached for his hand, and her gentle way made him relax, and he found himself holding his Aunt's hand.

"Aunt Connie, I don't fit in. I never fit in with this family except with you."

"You believe that's your mother's fault?"

"Yes I do!"

"BJ, it's not your mother's fault. You're the one who isolate yourself from the family. In fact, Tracey told me that you didn't even want to support her when she came here for her book tour. When Dean asked if you wanted to fly to California to support Tracey during her difficult time, you didn't want to do that either. Yet, when Bianca had something as simple as her tonsils removed, Tracey flew her family out here to be by her side.

"When Sandra celebrated her birthday last year, Tracey was the one who came out here to help her plan the party, and she paid for everything. Dean Jr. invited you to New York even paid for the tickets so you could go to the boat show in Long Island because he knows you love boats and fishing. You turned him down cold at the last minute. Your cousins are always reaching out to you. Everyone in this family has reached out to you, but you continue to turn a cold shoulder."

"I send you gifts on your birthday."

"BJ," Connie looked him in the eyes. "I'm not the only family you have. When you were young, I was the only family you had and I took care of you, but now it's time for you to see the whole Morris and Wilson families."

BJ didn't know what to say. He just looked off in deep thought.

"You have to stop being afraid to love, BJ. If you don't let go of your fears and your anger, you'll end up a lonely, miserable man."

BJ chuckled. "Have I really been that mean?"

"Yes you have. You're very bitter, and you treat people like you're still in the military."

He laughed harder, mostly in disbelief that he had been so cold.

"It's good to laugh at ourselves like this. You're way too serious sometimes BJ."

"I don't know how to stop being angry Aunt Connie."

"Well, just start with the little things. Engage with people. Let them in. Let them see that you like to have fun. Be approachable. Maybe you can image them as me, and then you'll treat them nice. And start with your wife, Sandra. She deserves it," Connie said as Sandra and Bianca approached them.

"I'll try," BJ replied, and he stood up, took hold of Sandra's hand and kissed the back of it.

"Wow," she blushed. "What were you and your Aunt talking about?" she asked, as Connie walked off to greet Dean Jr. and his family, and a few of her good friends who had just arrived.

"Sandra, I'm not good at this," BJ said, still holding Sandra's hand, as he tried to be affectionate.

"I know. Just let me help you."

BJ nodded his head in agreement, and then gave his son Junior a hug. "You're the best boy! Don't forget it!"

"Thanks Dad."

"You too Bianca. You guys go on and mingle with the family. I need to have a word with Peaches," BJ said, noticing her as soon as she walked out onto the lawn. He watched as she approached Hank, and turned his head when they kissed. He saw Hank pointing towards him, and Peaches rolled her eyes and went back inside the house. BJ could see that she was still upset.

"Go to your mother, BJ. It's time," Sandra kissed his lips, and joined the rest of the family for the gathering.

BJ walked inside the house. He saw Peaches in the kitchen grabbing a big bowl of potato salad out the frig.

"I can help you with that," BJ offered.

"Nope. I got it myself. I don't need your help."

"I got it," BJ insisted, taking the bowl from her. He took it outside and set it in a big cooler where the cold foods were.

"We need to talk," BJ said, feeling nervous although it didn't sound that way to Peaches.

"Oh yeah? Well what's up?" Peaches twisted her lips, folded her arms.

"Inside the house," BJ pointed, and Peaches reluctantly followed him inside and into the den to talk privately.

"I should not have called you a whore."

"Tell me something I don't know, BJ!"

BJ was tempted to argue back. He could already hear the countering words in his head, but he took a deep breath before he spoke again.

"I'm sorry," he uttered.

"Okay." Peaches started to walk off. To her it didn't sound sincere.

"Wait," BJ grabbed her by the arm. "Mom, I'm really sorry."

Tears formed in Peaches eyes.

"I have not made things easy for you, but from now on. I will try."

"You called me Mom," Peaches choked, wiped her tears. "I've been waiting so long, so many years to hear you say that," she threw her arms around him. BJ hesitated at first, but slowly he found himself lifting his arms and hugging her back. This time, he didn't let go until she released first.

"BJ, I know I wasn't the type of mother you wanted me to be when you were growing up. Your Aunt Connie took good care of you and so did the Smith's. All I ever wanted was a chance to take care of you myself, and be the mother I was supposed to be to you back then, know what I'm saying? I'm not perfect, but I just think you owe me a fair shot at trying."

"I'll give you that."

"Thanks baby!" Peaches threw her arms around his neck, kissed his cheek.

"So," BJ stepped back, not wanting to feel too mushy. "That guy Andre is out the picture, then?"

"He was never in it. He was just an old friend who happened to give me a ride that day," she admitted. "I never bedded him. Not that I needed to tell you all of that, but I'm not a hoe! I've been with Hank for almost a year now."

"Really? You kept that a secret for a long time."

"Well, it's out now. No need to hide anymore, especially since things are serious between us now."

"I know one thing, Hank had better treat you right."

"He will. He's good people, you'll see."

"I'm finished talking to you now," BJ stated, stoically.

"No, no, no, see, you're supposed to say, 'mother, if *you* are finished perhaps we can go back outside to be with the family.'"

BJ laughed shook his head. "Man, I have a lot to work on."

"Don't worry. We're all here to help you, son."

"We better head back out and grab some grub before all the food is gone," BJ suggested.

"You got that right!"

CHAPTER TWENTY-EIGHT
PRAYER WORKS

Trey clapped his hands after Sonny gave his sermon. He was a guest speaker at a new church that he and his family were attending in Malibu. All eyes were on Trey as he made his way to the front of the church on his crutches. Jazmine wrapped her arm around his waist and guided him.

"Good morning everybody, I'm Trey Smith," he spoke proudly into the microphone. The church stood up and gave him a standing ovation. He glanced at his mother who was crying tears of joy as she sat in the front row with his little brother and sister. He wished his father was there.

"I'm proof that prayer works."

"Amen!" the church applauded.

"I just want to thank God for saving my life and the church for your prayers and coming by to visit me in the hospital. It meant a lot to me and my family. The nerve-endings in my back will make me walk with a slight limp after this, but I'm blessed be alive."

"Amen!" the church clapped.

"Now that I'm better, I ask that you please pray for my Uncle Devin and that he remains strong. I also ask that you pray for the family of Bruce Benjamin, who was my biological father. We went to his funeral because as Christians we don't hold grudges."

"That's right!" a woman with a big hat shouted.

"Pray for my father too, know what I'm saying? He just needs to be reminded that he's loved. Go by and visit him the way y'all came to visit me, and maybe it will help him to get back here," Trey said. "Before I take my seat and give back the mike, I thank this young lady right here, Jazmine. Out of all the fans I had, she was never one of them. She was my real friend. She was the person who was never scared of losing my friendship because she always told me the truth about myself. This is the kind of the woman I need in my life."

The audience laughed, seeing that he and Jazmine were so young and already talking about marriage.

"I also thank my mother because she never left my side. Despite how the media bashes her at times, and what some people may think about her, I see differently. I was with my mother during the come up, know what I'm saying? I was with her during her struggles to make it in this business, and I was with her through the domestic violence she suffered, and the battles she went through when we didn't have a penny to our names. We had to go back and live with my grandparents. We went through all of that, just me and her. While the world may see her one way, I see her as a mother who struggled to survive and raise her son. Thank you Mom. Thank you for everything," Trey watched Tracey wipe her tears of joy.

"Thank you all again, and we will meet this afternoon at my house for the church brunch."

"Thanks for embarrassing me at the church," Jazmine said to Trey as they sat on the grassy lawn overlooking the ocean.

"Why were you embarrassed? You should be proud to be my girl," Trey blushed.

"Pah-lease!" She sucked her teeth. Trey loved that she didn't sweat him.

"I'm going to make one more album before I announce my retirement from the rap game."

"Why?"

"One reason is I'm still under contract. Second, I'm ready to put out some songs about what happened to me."

"Maybe you shouldn't talk about it anymore and just move on."

"Don't worry I won't bring up any dirt. I'll just rap about surviving it, know what I'm saying? I also plan to mention how I had a beautiful girl like you by my side to support me."

"No, please don't do that!"

"Why not? It'll be all over the internet soon that you're my girl anyway, especially when I join you in Atlanta."

Jazmine's mouth dropped in shock. "Do you mean that—"

"Yep, I'm transferring from USC to Morehouse in January. They already accepted my application. So I'll come visit you at Spelman."

"Get outta here!" She hit him playfully.

"I'm serious. It's time for a change, and I'm ready for it."

"I'm so happy for you, Trey. I can't wait for you to come to A-Town!"

"Well you know Hot-lanta ain't hot until they have Trey Mikes living there," He stroked the fuzz on his chin.

"Whatever. You better make sure you tell your mom your plans."

"She already knows. She wanted me to get away from here. She was like, 'maybe you should go back to school, and go away someplace. Get away from California until the smoke clears.' I was like all right."

"Well don't come to the "A" causing no drama neither."

Trey looked over his shoulder, and saw that everyone looked preoccupied with what they were doing—talking, eating, and the kids were running around playing.

"Only drama I plan to make is with you." He quickly planted a kiss on Jazmine's full lips.

"You are so sneaky."

"I know. Give me one more," Trey puckered his lips.

'Muah' Jazmine kissed him again. "You better make sure you keep it real with me, Trey."

He blushed. "You know you're the only girl for me. Always."

CHAPTER TWENTY-NINE
BFF

After everyone left the church brunch, me and Kay-Kay hung out on my patio and watched the waves crashing into the shoreline. We sipped on glasses of wine, and listened to Rihanna croon *Diamonds* from my iPod stereo.

"It's beautiful out here, isn't it?" Kay-Kay asked, gazing out at the moonlight bouncing off the water.

"Gorgeous! That's why I love it out here so much. It's my own little piece of paradise. It's far away from the City of Angels, Hollywood, and the busy world of entertainment."

"Could you ever imagine us being where we are now, Tracey?"

"Girl, no! We were so ratchet!"

We burst out laughing.

"Hey, remember when you crashed your Ferrari after we partied hard at that club down in Miami?"

"Yes and my dad bought me another one with no problem. My mother was pissed!" I laughed. "Speaking of my father, we reconciled, you know?"

"Did you? Get outta here!"

"He came by not long ago, and promised to keep in touch."

"Well has he?"

"Sure did," I sat my glass to the side. "I was there for his kidney replacement. He's doing better now. He called me yesterday and said as soon as he heals he wants to take Trey and KJ fishing."

"That's wonderful!"

"Yeah, it's still hard to believe he wants to be in our lives."

"Girl, just embrace it, don't even question it. Life is too short to dwell on the past."

"I know that's right."

"So what's next for you girl? You're rich and famous like you've always wanted to be."

"Well you're sitting on a nice fortune yourself, girl."

Kay-Kay blushed. "Yeah well, you're like one of the Kardashians, with your two companies. You don't have to work another day in your life if you don't want to."

"I didn't think I could make it on my own without Kyle. In fact, I didn't think I could make it on my own without a man, period," I admitted. "All my life I've depended on a man in some way shape or form, but God has shown me with his help if I lean on him, he would take care of me."

"That's true. Sometimes it's about trusting yourself too," Kay-Kay added

"You're right," I swallowed the rest of my wine and then poured another.

"No more movies for you I take it?"

"I don't know if I would say *never*, but I did just turn down a fifteen-million-dollar deal."

"Girl get out of here!"

"It was the same old crap girl. They wanted me to get nude and bed some dude. I'm done with all of that. I'm a mother. I can't have my kids seeing me in bed with a man who's not their father. It's not about the money anymore or the fame. I just want to leave behind a legacy that will focus on me being a good person, mother, and a wife. That is, if I'm still married within the next year."

"Still no word from Keith, huh?"

"We talk, but it's always about the kids. I mean, he was there to show support for Trey and Devin, but we haven't talked about *us* in months."

"I'll keep praying for you guys."

I leaned over the railing, and stared out at the ocean. Kay got up from the patio chair and stood next to me. I was singing *Diamonds* under my breath and just thinking about my future.

"Are you going to be okay?" Kay asked me.

I shrugged. "I have been so far, but it's not the same without Keith here. The only reason I haven't filed for a divorce is because I still love him, Kay."

She rubbed my shoulder, "I know you do. It's not like you to wait for any man to decide what he wants."

I glanced at her, and suddenly there was a distressing look on her face like she wanted to say something else.

"Are *you* okay?" I asked, curiously.

Kay sighed. "Not really."

"You know something about Keith that I don't?"

"Nah, it's nothing like that. I've been trying to figure out a way to tell you."

"Tell me what?"

"We're moving to Atlanta."

I coughed and nearly choked on my wine in disbelief. "Are you serious?"

"Yes. Damien and I bought a house. We just closed on it last week. Damien's boxing center is finally finished too. He's retired now, but he wants to start training other guys to box professionally. You already know I had bought a salon and spa down there too. Jazmine is already going to Spelman, so everything has come together the way we planned. Don't worry, I'll keep an eye on Trey," she grinned. "We're moving next month."

"You're leaving me, Kay-Kay? Seriously?" I ran my fingers through my hair and blew hot air from my lips. I thought, *this totally sucks!*

"I've been meaning to find a good time to tell you, but there was so much going on with you and Keith, then Trey got shot, and there was Devin's trial. I didn't know of a good time."

"What about your family? You've been living in California most of your life, just like me. Are you going to leave your parents behind and your brothers?"

"Girl, pah-lease! You know I've never been that close to them. Besides, I'm grown. I have my own family."

"But I'm your family too, Kay. What about me?"

She huffed out loud. "Now the old Tracey is talking. The selfish one."

I thought about it for a moment, said, "I'm sorry, but this is hard, Kay. You're leaving me."

"I can never leave you, Tracey. We'll talk every day, text, email, Skype, and the whole nine!"

"It won't be the same." I walked away and sat down on the patio chair. Kay sat next to me and said nothing. I kept thinking about all my years of friendship with Kay-Kay, and how we had always been together. It was a miracle that she ended up in California with me. We did everything together, even had our children around the same time. She was my sister from another mother. I glanced at her, and I could see it wasn't easy for her to tell me. We've been connected at the hips for nearly thirty years. First Keith leaves me, my son is going away to college, and now Kay-Kay is leaving me. It will be me and my little ones, forever. I felt lonely just thinking about it, but by the same token, I realized at some point I had to be my own person. I reflected on the fact that I was doing all right so far. I proved I could hold my own. I told myself not to be scared, but to trust God.

"You know what," I broke the silence between us. "You have my love and my blessings. I wish you all the best in Atlanta, girl."

Kay raised her brow in shock. She was surprised by my sudden change of heart. "You really mean that or is that the wine talking?"

"Girl, stand up and give me a hug before I think about it too hard and start crying."

"I'm already there," Kay sniffed, and when I saw her tears. I couldn't hold back my own.

"I love you, Keyshia King."

"Wow, I haven't heard you say my government name since we first met."

We both laughed.

"I love you too, Tracey Gina Michaels-Smith."

"Best friends forever girl!"

We *clicked* glasses.

"You know it! We're BFFs and divas for life!"

Part Five

CHAPTER THIRTY
A BROKEN HEART CAN MEND

It was a Saturday, and Keith told Tyson he would hang out with him, but at the last minute he called and told him he couldn't make it. Instead, he grabbed a six pack of beer out of the fridge and flopped his six-four body on the cheap, flimsy couch. As he flipped the channels, he thought about watching *First 48*, but decided he'd seen enough shootings courtroom drama, and jail since Trey was shot, and Devin ending up in jail. Through it all, he tried to support Tracey, but he couldn't stop feeling all the familiar magnetic attractions to her whenever he was near her.

As he gulped down the last beer, feelings of guilt came over him about the way he had been living his life the past few months. He gazed across the room and wondered to himself, *How did I end up in this place? Without my wife? Without my kids?* When he turned to the next channel, it was a commercial about lawn care, and he thought about his job. His employees complained about his lack of focus and direction in his work, and two of them had quit, including Jose who once offered to buy his company from him. When the commercial went off, the channel showed season two of Divas of LA. The intro showed Tracey at the press conference in London. Keith turned the volume up and watched the whole show, and when it went off he started processing everything in his head. *Kyle was behind all of this drama! Wow, that doesn't surprise me. I always felt there was something fishy about that dude,* he thought to himself. *Tracey never listened to me when I told her to check him out. Find out more about him from his other clients. All she saw was dollar signs at the time. I'm just glad she finally saw the truth and got rid of him!*

Keith picked up his phone and ordered a pizza for delivery. Eating out had become such a routine that the food delivery people started giving him discounts and would call his name by heart. He propped the pillow behind his head and threw his feet up on the table before him. He continued to channel flip and stopped at *VH1-Soul*. They were showing an old classic video of Alexander O'Neal, singing *A Broken Heart Can Mend*. His thoughts wandered on Tracey again. He felt the lyrics rung true for him from Alexander's song. In the back of his mind, he always feared that Tracey would one day break his heart. He knew about her celebrity and the way she had been with guys in the past, but he was willing to take the chance on loving her anyway. *Now look at where we are,* he thought, as he got up to answer the door.

"Thanks, man." Keith reached in his wallet to hand the pizza guy a twenty, and a wallet-size picture of his family fell to the ground. Keith stared at the picture and noticed the family portrait had been taken together just a year ago. They were all wearing blue jeans and white T's. "Um, that will be fifteen dollars, Keith," the pizza boy repeated.

Keith snapped out of his daze. "Oh, thanks Jerry, sorry about that, man." Keith handed him a twenty dollar bill and bent down to pick up the picture.

"Do you need change?"

"Nah man. You keep it."

"Thanks Keith. Have a good night and enjoy your pizza."

Keith went back inside, set the pizza on the table before him, and took the video off pause. He started eating his pizza while simultaneously singing along with Alexander O'Neal. It was baffling to him how quickly things could change. One bad mistake could ruin a whole family, Keith was thinking as he set the picture down on the table and stared at it. He started to wish he could return to the good ole' days. He thought about the day his daughter Alexis was born and how he cried when the doctor placed her in his arms. It was a dream come true for him to finally have a family of his own. He had lost a child once- a son whom he thought was his. He viewed Alexis as a blessing. When Tracey announced that she was pregnant again, the same feelings of joy overcame him when his son was born. He realized there were many good times that he shared with Tracey, and their children were their greatest blessing. When things really got hard, like when his mother got really sick, Tracey was right there to support him. His mother loved Tracey and the kids. Keith thought about when his mother called him when she heard he had left Tracey. "Boy, if you don't hurry up and lick your wounds you better. Tracey and the kids need you. Now don't make me call Sonny again." Keith also began to think about all their vacations together, and holiday trips to Chicago and New York. Even their anniversaries were fun. He realized that Tracey went out of her way to make him happy and she tried to be a good mother and wife. Sure she had her career, and he had to play a house husband, but when she was home, she was very good to all of them. A part of him felt guilty for being hard on her. He always knew she was bourgeois and materialistic, but that never stopped him from falling in love with her. He could see that deep down she was sweet and kind, and that she had a good heart. Keith turned the volume down on the TV and reached for his phone to call Tracey, hear her voice—see how things were going and how she was holding up after all the drama with Trey and Devin.

BANG, BANG, BANG, BANG.

Keith looked at the door, set the phone down and slowly rose to his feet. He peeped through the hole and it was Tyson.

"What in the world does this dude want?" he squinted.

"I know you're in there, Keith, open up, man!'

Keith slowly opened the door.

"What's up, man? I told you I couldn't hang out," Keith reminded him.

"Man, look, you need to get out the house. We haven't hung out in two weeks. Look at you, you growing a homely beard, hair all over your head like a gorilla. Funky chest out looking like a Chia pet! Wassup, homey? You ain't smoking that stuff, are you?"

"Are you through running your mouth? Because frankly, I don't want to hear all of this." Keith walked away from him and flopped down on the sofa.

"Have you had a bath? It smells like corn chips and butt up in here."

"Nope. If you don't like it, get out."

"Keith, come on man get cleaned up. We found this new spot, and the honeys are banging man!"

"Nah man. I'm done with that stuff. That's your life."

"Choir boy is getting his conscious back I see," Tyson picked up Keith's bible off the table and then a book that looked like an exam. "Next you'll be calling your wife begging her to take you back huh?"

"If I did, what's wrong with that?"

"She dogged you out, man that's what's wrong with that!"

"You know what Tyson," Keith stood up from the sofa, and he

towered over the shorter Tyson. "Tracey and I would still be together if it wasn't for you."

Tyson laughed. "Whatcha trying to say, dawg? I broke y'all up? She's the one who cheated on you."

"Yeah I know all of that, but maybe if people like you didn't stick your noses in our relationship we could have worked things out."

"So now you're feeling sorry for yourself? Come on man, get cleaned up and let's go grab some drinks and hit the strip clubs."

"Tyson, I can't do that anymore, man. I been sitting here thinking about how I wasted the past five months hanging out like I'm some kid."

"Aw man, you were just having fun. Don't beat yourself up."

"Tyson, you're young, man. You have no obligations to anyone, but I'm a father and I'm…I'm still a husband too."

"This is how it is?"

Keith shook his head. "Yep, I got some repenting to do, and I need to make some strides to get myself together. I can't do that running the streets with you."

"All right man," Tyson slapped him a five. "I respect you, dawg. Hit me up for the next charity event."

"Now *that* I can do."

CHAPTER THIRTY-ONE
LOVE IS A CHOICE

When I got home, the kids were playing in the pool, and Clara the nanny was watching them. I picked the mail off the shelf in the corridor, and flipped through the bills and at least twenty different pieces of fan mail that sometimes manages to escape my business P.O. address. Some fans still prefer to write, despite the fact that I have a Facebook community page, Twitter, Instagram, and all the rest of those social media websites that you can think of. I only check one of them on the regular basis. Anyway, I came across an eight by ten envelope from Pepperdine addressed to Keith. It was marked as confidential and I saw that Clara had signed for it, so I called him, but got his voicemail. Usually I just waited until it was time for his visit with the kids, and I would have Clara to give him his mail or phone messages. However, the envelope looked important so I left him a message. I went outside to watch my kids play for a little while in the pool. Minutes later, I rushed back in when I heard the phone rang. It wasn't Keith; it was Mom.

After a few words of small talk, she started probing. It was typical of her to be nosy, but I wasn't mad. I realized my mother asked questions because she cared.

"Anyway, what about you, Mom? How are you holding up now?" I asked. My Dad had told me about her mental meltdown after Devin's arrest. That explained why she hadn't returned my phone calls.

"I'm much better, baby," she said. "We had a good cookout last week, and honey, let me tell you," she said, perkily. "Peaches and Hank moved in together!"

"It's about time!"

"You knew?"

"Aunt Peaches told me about it a few weeks ago. I figured something was up when she was out here when Trey was in the hospital. Uncle Hank kept calling her phone. I promised that I wouldn't say anything, but I'm glad everybody knows now."

"The nerve of her! I hang out with my sister almost every day and she didn't say a thing!"

"Mom, Seriously?" I laughed behind the phone. "You know good and well that you can't hold water. We love you, but we know you have the gift to gab. No offense."

I could picture my mother's mouth dropping in surprise behind the phone.

"Forget y'all!"

I cracked up laughing.

"Anyway, I was just calling to check in to make sure you and my grandkids were doing okay. I know you guys couldn't make it out because you had an important business meeting."

"I did. I turned down a fifteen million dollar movie deal."

"Really? Why?"

"I'm a mother now. I have to be careful of the roles I choose to play."

"I'm so proud of you."

"Thanks Mom."

"Well, I won't hold you, but I do miss you guys."

"We miss you too Mom. We'll see you in a couple of months for the holidays."

"Speaking of which, Thanksgiving won't be at my house this year."

"Then whose house will it be?"

"BJ's house, and Christmas will be in New York with Dean and his family."

"Get out of here! BJ is opening his home?"

"He finally agreed to let Sandra have the family over."

"Wow! What brought that on?"

"It's a long story. I'll share it with you some other time. Your father is calling me for dinner."

"Dad is cooking?"

"He thinks he's Bobby Flay since he beat Dean Jr. this year by making the best ribs at the cookout. I'm having a ball letting him think he's top chef."

"I bet you are. That's probably some good eating."

"It's been delicious!"

"Well you guys enjoy it."

"We most certainly will!"

"I love you, Mom. Talk to you soon."

"I love you too honey. Kiss my grandbabies for me."

After hanging up with Mom, I felt glad that everything seemed to be coming together in my sweet home Chicago. I went to help the children with their homework, gave them their baths, read them a bedtime story, then put them in bed. This was the life I really loved, being a mother. It was hard work but well worth it. Who knows how my babies will turn out? I'm not sure if they'll ever have any interests in Hollywood, but I'm going to do my best to show them that the world has so much more to offer. I'm glad that Trey finally sees that too. Sometimes I wish my life had a reset button, but then again, that would make me a perfect person because I would be able to change all of my mistakes. It was because of my experiences–good and bad that I've become the person I am today. Now I'm determined that no matter what happens, I know I can handle it. If I end up being a single mom again, I know I can handle it. If I never work in Hollywood again, I know I can handle that too. In both of those situations, I've proved I could survive. I can do anything by the power and strength that God empowers upon me.

KEITH

When Tracey called and left Keith a message about having mail at the house, he was busy getting a haircut and a clean shave. When he left the barbershop, he treated himself to a new outfit and a pair of sneakers. It had been months since he treated himself to anything personally, besides a cold beer. When he left the mall, he went back to his apartment took a long shower and got dressed. When he got dressed, he grabbed the full trash bag that was filled with cases of beer. He decided not to drink anymore, and tossed the beers into an outside recycling bin. He also changed his cellphone number today, so he didn't have to worry about Candy calling him again or some random woman he met while running the streets with Tyson. It was a good thing he caught Tracey's message in time. He made a mental note to give her the new number. Meanwhile, he was going to call his staff first and let them know the new number.

"Yo Chris, I heard you haven't showed up to work in a few days," Keith dialed one of his employees from his Bluetooth, as he headed down the highway to Malibu.

Chris blew what sounded like a fake cough. "Oh yeah man, I was sick."

"Well, if you plan to come back you'll need a doctor's note."

"My man Keith, so you're back to being a boss huh?"

"You better believe it. Bring the note on Monday if you want to keep your job. And remember this number from now on, Chief."

"I gotchu homey."

"Later," Keith hung up, feeling good about himself. He couldn't wait to get back to work and straighten things out.

Keith still felt awkward about ringing the doorbell to his own house. When Clara answered the door, she invited him in like he was a guest. While Clara went down the hall to get Tracey from her office, Keith could hear Raheem Devaughn's *Ridiculous* in the background. It was coming from Tracey's office. He mumbled the lyrics under his breath while he waited for her at the front door. When Tracey started walking down the hall towards him, Keith couldn't stop blushing. He thought she looked amazing. He stared at her lip gloss, hair, and thought her makeup was flawless. Every time he saw her she looked more beautiful to him, even when he wanted to be mad at her, it never stopped him from being attracted to her.

"Did you have a nice day today?" he asked. He could tell Tracey was surprised by him asking, because she stuttered when she answered.

"Uhm, it was, it was pretty good, and yours?"

"It was great."

"Good for you," she smiled, feeding off of his energy.

"I read that you uh–passed up a fifteen-million-dollar movie offer because you didn't want to do a sex scene. Was that true?"

"It's true. Some things in life are just not worth it."

Keith couldn't believe what he was hearing, but he was glad what he read was finally true in a good way.

"Well, here is your mail. Don't let me keep you," She handed him a few small envelopes, along with the bigger one from Pepperdine.

"If you don't mind, I can just open it right here," he said, standing in the corridor. Tracey nodded, giving him the go ahead.

"Yes! It's my Divinity Degree!" Keith smiled proudly.

"Really? That's awesome! Congratulations, Keith!"

"Thanks, uhm, yeah, I guess it is," his smile quickly faded away. He knew he was supposed to feel excited, but his emotions felt mixed.

"What's wrong?" Tracey asked.

"I don't deserve this."

"Oh course you do. It's all you ever talked about since the day we met."

Keith felt himself tearing up. "Tracey, I–I haven't been living right you know? I've never been a hypocrite like that."

"We all fall down sometimes, but as long as we keep getting back up is what counts, right?"

"I guess so. I take it you heard about me."

He watched Tracey's eyes shift away from his. They looked hurt, and she blinked back a few tears.

"I'm sorry Tracey. I really am. She never meant anything to me."

"I know you slept with Candy to hurt me Keith, and if it makes you happy, it worked."

"It doesn't make me happy at all. It really hurts me to my heart that I went that far. I should have kicked her out my hotel room. I let my flesh get the best of me."

"I don't want to hear about it, Keith. Please spare me the details."

Keith shamefully dropped his head, mumbled. "I understand."

"Well look, it's getting late, and I have to get up early and take the kids to school in the morning so–"

"Can I see them? I mean, can I just tell them goodnight? I know they're probably sleep, but I just need to take a look at them before I go."

"Okay," Tracey answered, and Keith could tell she was still feeling hurt from him confirming the rumors about him and Candy. Keith followed her upstairs, and admired her curvy figure moving from side-to-side. Her legs still looked smooth and sexy underneath her skirt. Together, they walked into the children's room. They had their own rooms, but tonight they decided to sleep in one room together. "They look like little angels." Keith admired them sleeping. He kissed each one of them on the forehead. "And they're beautiful, just like their mother," Keith turned to Tracey, and they gazed into each other's eyes for a moment, but then Tracey looked away. Keith stepped forward, erasing the distance between them.

"I missed you, Tracey," He gently stroked her cheeks. "And I'm very sorry for staying away from you and the kids for so long. I was hurting, but I'm over it now. I realize it was stupid to let anyone keep me away from you. I acted immature when we could've worked things out. I wish I could take it all back."

Tears streamed down Tracey's cheeks, and Keith wiped away each one with the tips of his thumbs.

"Don't cry, please don't cry. I'm a jerk. I don't deserve your tears," he planted a soft feathery kiss on her lips, whispered, "I still love you. I love you so much. Please forgive me, Tracey. Baby take me back, I need you."

"It hurts Keith," Tracey sniffed.

"I know. I'm sorry," Keith kneeled down on his knees. "Will you have me as your husband again? In sickness and in health until death do us part, and in good times and in bad? Will you stay by my side the way I promise to stay by yours, no matter what happens again? I promise to love you forever, Tracey."

Tracey choked in tears. "Yes."

"I love you."

"I love you too," she cupped his cheeks and kissed his lips.

"We'll get back to where we used to be with God's help. We'll take it one day at a time. Hopefully, our marriage will be stronger than what it was before."

"I can't wait to start over with you. It's been lonely without you. I felt like someone snatched a piece of my soul," Tracey's eyes danced with his.

"I'm here now baby and I don't plan to leave you ever again. So let's start over, and let's start right now." Keith easily scooped her up into his arms. He carried her off to their bedroom where he made beautiful love to her. There were tears of joy, pain, and ecstasy. They wiped away each other's tears, kissed away the tears, and loved all the hurt away until they fell into a deep sleep.

In the morning Keith was awakened from the sun sneezing its rays through the window. At first he thought he was still in his apartment, but when he rolled over and saw Tracey sleeping next to him, like an innocent baby, his lips curved a big smile. He was happy to be home, and he felt even happier knowing that he was back with the woman he truly loved. He felt thankful that she never gave up on him, and waited for him to find his back to her. Slowly, he eased his way out of bed and tried not to wake her, as he got down on his knees and put his hands together. He raised his eyes heavenward and said, "Thank you God! For without my wife and children I felt empty and lost, but with them, I am now complete."

A Message from Calidream Publishing:

Dear Reader, we hope you enjoyed reading, *Riding the Waves*. Please take just a few minutes to share your review on Goodreads, Amazon or Barnes and Noble. Reviews are very important. Your feedback will not only help other readers, but the author of this book.

Thank you very much for your support!

ABOUT THE AUTHOR

Selena Haskins enjoys writing stories about family, love and relationships. Selena also addresses issues of poverty, race, substance abuse, and the family dynamics in her stories. By the same token, Selena infuses messages of hope, love, and forgiveness, which she believes are attributes for humanity.

Riding the Waves is Selena's second novel– a sequel to her debut novel, *A River Moves Forward*. Selena has also written a non-fiction novel, with five other authors titled, *Just Between Us-Inspiring Stories by Women*, which has been a bestseller, and ranked in the top five on Amazon for inspirational stories.

For more information about Selena, and to connect with her through social media, please visit her website: www.booksbyselena.com.

www.ingramcontent.com/pod-product-compliance
Lightning Source LLC
Chambersburg PA
CBHW060537180626
46817CB00002B/614